THE
TRAITOR'S
SON

PRAISE FOR DAVE DUNCAN

"Dave Duncan writes rollicking adventure novels filled with subtle characterization and made bitter-sweet by an underlying darkness. Without striving for grand effects or momentous meetings between genres, he has produced one excellent book after another."

LOCUS MAGAZINE

"Duncan is an exceedingly finished stylist and a master of world building and characterization."

BOOKLIST

"Dave Duncan has long been one of the great unsung figures of Canadian fantasy and science fiction, graced with a fertile imagination, a prolific output, and keen writerly skills."

QUILL AND QUIRE

"When you're looking for a good adventure, Dave Duncan is a sure thing . . . [with] his sly and fast-paced plotting, his ability to construct intriguingly different worlds, and his knack for quick and entertaining characterization and dialogue."

ECLECTIC RUCKUS

THE
TRAITOR'S
SON

DAVE DUNCAN

THE TRAITOR'S SON
By Dave Duncan

Shadowpaw Press
Regina, Saskatchewan, Canada
www.shadowpawpress.com

Trade Paperback ISBN: 978-1-989398-91-3
Ebook ISBN: 978-1-989398-92-0

Edited by Robert Runté
Cover design by Jeff Minkevics

Shadowpaw Press is grateful for
the financial support of Creative Saskatchewan.

CONTENTS

1: FIVE-OH-FIVE   1
2: FIVE-TEN   76
3: FIVE-ELEVEN   177
4: FIVE-TWELVE   299

Appendix   325
Dave Duncan's Legacy   327
By Robert Runté, PhD

About Dave Duncan   333
About Shadowpaw Press   335
More Science Fiction and Fantasy   336

Be not afraid of greatness. Some are born great, some achieve greatness, and others have greatness thrust upon them.

—William Shakespeare, *Twelfth Night.*

They know the world is dying, but they hope not in their lifetimes. Meanwhile they're top dogs and will do anything to stay that way.

—Saul Vandam

1: FIVE-OH-FIVE

THERE WAS A BUMP. Crockery rattled on the shelves, and some sand sprinkled down from the ceiling.

It was the forty-fifth of January, so winter was almost over. In just four days, people could emerge from the bunkers and see the sun again. Tomorrow would be Doig's birthday. He happened to know that his gift was going to be a new pair of socks because two-year-old Camilla had told him so—"in secret." Camilla was down on the floor, being amused by Helen while Mom made supper. Doig was doing his homework, plugged into the voicebox to listen to an ancient crackly voice telling him how planets moved around stars in stretched-out circles called ellipses. He'd known that for years and found it hard to concentrate when nice smells kept drifting across from the stove to make his tummy grumble.

Then came the bump. That's what miners called a rockfall. Camilla yelped.

"It's all right," Doig said, removing the headphones. "Nothing to worry about, Cammy. Right, Mom?"

But Mom had turned pale and had her hands to her mouth.

Doig remembered her looking like that once when the vermin inspectors came around unexpectedly. He jumped up and went to her. He put his arms around her, which is what Dad had done that other time. Then the girls took fright and rushed to join in the family hug.

"It's all right," he repeated. "Helen, unplug the headphones so we can all listen. There'll be a Hear-This, won't there, Mom?"

"Yes," she said. "It just took me by surprise. Nothing to worry about. Do let go of me, Camilla or the stew will burn." But she was trembling.

The voicebox cut off the lecture about stars and planets and spoke in a new voice. "Hear-This. There has been a small bump in Cross Cut Twelve. The damage is being assessed, and we will report the results as soon as they become available."

"All right!" Doig said, much relieved. "Dad works in Cross Cut Seventeen. Maybe he'll come home a bit early, right, Mom?"

"Maybe." She was still white. "Or he could be late if there's some problems. Helen, lay the table, please."

The bunkers of Copper Island were abandoned mine tunnels, still showing rough rock with twinkles of native copper in them. The Grays' was cramped for five people, just one room with two bunk beds, a table with four stools, a chest for clothes, and some shelves. The voicebox stood on a corner shelf, table-height, that Doig used as a desk. It was cluttered with other stuff that had no special home, like the chess set, which closed up like a box. If Dad was really late tonight, he and Doig wouldn't be able to finish the game they had been forced to shut down last night just before lights out.

Dishes clattered. Food was spooned out, stools pulled into place. Dad wasn't due yet. Normally, they never ate until he got home. Doig watched to see that Dad's share was left in the pan and was relieved to see that it was. He glanced uneasily at Mom, but she was all smiles now.

"January is almost over already!" she said. "We'll be up-top playing snowballs next week."

The temperature up-top had been reported as minus-forty that morning. Doig didn't say so. Forty was a lot warmer than midwinter, but it was still a long way from snowball weather. "My friend Jim says he'll let me have some rides on his sled." That got the girls excited, asking if they could go too.

Mom caught his eye and nodded approval.

Then she rose and brought the stewpan to the table. "Your Dad's going to be late. I'll cook something hot for him when he gets here." There was a lot left because she'd hardly eaten anything herself. Helen and Camilla tucked into the unexpected extra.

Horrified, Doig shook his head. When Mom insisted, he reluctantly let her heap his plate with what was left. Dad worked in Cross Cut Seventeen, not Twelve. Why did she think he wasn't coming back?

He decided he would not believe that until he had to. He washed the dishes as usual and went back to his homework as usual, expecting at any moment that his lecture would be interrupted by another Hear-This or—much better—Dad walking in as usual, just apologizing for being late.

But what came was a tap on the door while Mom was tucking Camilla into the lowest of the children's three-level bunks. Doig threw off the headphones and reached the door before she did. He opened it a crack and peered out.

The man in the passage wore an office jacket, and the tag on it said ROBINS. Doig didn't know him and, for a moment, was speechless. The man, too, seemed nonplused. Then he frowned down at a list he held.

Doig slid outside and pulled the door shut. He held onto

the handle, and when he felt Mom tug on the other side, braced his shoulder against the jamb to keep her from opening it.

"I'm Doig Gray, sir."

Robins folded the list away. "You're over sixteen?"

"Yes, sir." That was a lie. He'd be fifteen tomorrow, but he looked older.

Robins believed him. "Son of Pablo Gray?"

"Yes, sir." Robins was a crew name. Always be polite to crew.

"Then I deeply regret to inform you that your father died in that bump in the mine today. It would have been instantaneous—he would have felt no pain."

Unable to speak, Doig nodded.

"There will be a remembrance for him tomorrow or the next day. We'll tell you exactly when."

This time, he managed to croak, "Thank you, sir."

Robins murmured, "Sorry," and walked away.

Doig went back in. He didn't have to say anything to Mom because he could see that she knew. She hugged him, and he hugged her back. He whispered, "Instantaneous. No p-pain." Then the tears came, and he couldn't say anything more. Helen was brushing her teeth and didn't notice.

Doig went back to his desk, but he couldn't concentrate. He opened up the chess set and studied the game that now would never be finished. As usual, Dad had been playing one rook short. Doig could sometimes beat him if given rook odds like that and almost always if Dad played without his queen. They wouldn't be playing anymore. Never.

More games are lost than won. That had been one of Dad's favourite sayings. Doig could remember when he had become old enough to realize that every game should have both a winner and a loser, so the proverb made no sense. It had annoyed him horribly until Dad explained: "In chess, especially, most games are stalemates, which means nobody wins. But when a game isn't a draw, it's almost always because the loser made a mistake, not because the winner was especially clever. The winner didn't win; the loser lost."

So what it really meant was, *Don't make mistakes and watch until the other guy does.*

Well, Dad had lost the game today, galactic-scale.

As Doig closed the chess set box, the Hear-This came. Three men had died in the bump.

There had been more names than that on Robins' list.

IN THE MIDDLE of the night, he heard Mom sobbing, so he climbed down from his bunk. It squeaked and creaked, but he knew it would not wake the girls. He felt his way across the room—two steps to the table, three beyond it. He found Mom sitting on the edge of her bunk by then, waiting for him. They touched, and she pulled him down beside her. Each put an arm around the other.

He whispered, "What happens at a remembrance?"

"Not much. One of us two says good things about him, that's all. Fond memories. Friends can add little speeches. Doig . . . don't expect many people to come."

"Why not? Dad had lots of friends."

She put her mouth very close to his ear as if someone might be right there in the bunker, in the darkness, listening. "At least one too many." Then she said in a louder whisper. "Because it'll be held in working hours, and no one can afford to miss a day's wages."

Now, he leaned closer for the intimate breathing of words. "You think he was murdered." Not a question.

"Uh-huh," meaning yes.

Even quieter. "Why?"

"Talked too much."

About what, for planet's sake? "I'll speak for him at the remembrance, okay?"

"No. You're in danger. I'm not."

That didn't make much sense because Mom must know the reason why Dad had been murdered, and Doig certainly didn't. But by that same argument, he shouldn't argue with her. So he agreed, and after a few minutes, she told him to go back to bed and be very careful who he talked to from now on.

He lay awake for a long time, wondering what Dad could have said to get himself murdered, who could have been listening in the dark, and what would happen if he disconnected the voicebox for a little while so nobody could eavesdrop.

THE FOLLOWING MORNING, he left at the usual time but did not go to school. The passageways of Copper Island were a poorly lit maze, abandoned mine tunnels that wound up and down and twisted like snarled yarn, following wherever the seams of metal had led them. He was heading to a part he had rarely visited and got lost a couple of times. Eventually, he reached the mine head and joined the lineup of men filing in. Although it was still below ground, it was high enough that the air was bitterly cold, and winter icicles clung to the rocky walls.

He shivered and stuffed his hands in his sleeves. Nobody questioned him or

looked him in the face until he reached the gate.

The man there wore a body suit of black spider fur that must have cost a fortune. He was checking off the arrivals' names on a slate. His name tag read FINN. That was another crew name. There were only twelve crew names, so they weren't hard to remember.

"Gray? Who're you?" Finn's face, the only visible part of him, was horribly ugly, with a loose, slobbery mouth and big moles on his lip.

"Doig Gray. My father, Pablo Gray, died yesterday. I need a job. Sir."

"Stand back there and wait."

So Doig moved aside. He shivered and shivered. And shivered, until the last late arrival had been grossly insulted and told that he would be docked half a day's pay. Then Finn said, "Come with me," and let Doig in. A lot of men were still waiting for the cage to come back up, but after Finn had locked the gate, he led Doig to a side door.

They went along a narrow, dim tunnel, past several doors. Finn opened one to a small office furnished with a small desk and one chair. He sat down and switched on what Doig thought must be a voicebox until he saw that it had a small screen, and so was a tiny viewbox. Finn tapped the keyboard until he found what he wanted.

"How old are you, Gray?"

Spiders eat me! Today was his birthday, and he'd forgotten. "Sixteen today, sir."

It didn't work. Finn looked up at him with narrowed eyes. "You're a few weeks out, aren't you?" There was something queer about his eyes, as if one was bigger than the other.

"Sir?"

"Like fifty-four of them. You're cargo and still young enough that I could have you beaten just for lying to me, right?"

"Yes, sir."

"Son of . . . mm. Do you know you're illegitimate?"

"Am not!" Doig snapped and quickly added, "sir."

"You were born less than thirty-three weeks after your

parents' wedding. That makes you, legally, a bastard. Your family name should be Doig, not Gray, even if he was willing to admit to being your father."

Doig clenched his fists, but out of sight, behind his back. Mustn't lose his temper with a crewman! Nor punch him on the nose. "Sir, I was born just two days before that limit, and the midwife certified that I was a premature baby."

Finn tapped again. "They always do." He sounded disappointed. "Anyway, you're too young for the mine. Go to the Island Employment Office, and they'll find you a job doing something interesting, like cleaning toilets."

"Sir, I have two sisters, and my mother doesn't earn enough to feed all four of us."

Finn frowned at the viewbox. "That doesn't bother me. I can't hire . . . mm?" he tapped again. "You're a marked student!"

"I am?" What did that mean?

"Yes, you are. So get your shitty little ass back up to the schoolroom. They'll probably warm it for being late. The remembrance for your father is at two o'clock. You'll get time off for that."

He led Doig back to the gate and unlocked it. He didn't kick his butt out but looked as if he wanted to.

THE SENIORS' schoolroom was an irregularly shaped cavern, bright in some places and dim in others. The expected seven other boys were all seated at their desks, wearing headphones and staring at viewboxes. Three of them noticed Doig's arrival and looked up in surprise. They all quickly looked down again as if he must not be seen.

Mrs. Wills, the schoolmarm, was at her own desk near the

door. She saw him and gestured for him to sit on the chair beside her. She spoke in a whisper, but she always did that when other students were working.

"I was very sorry to hear such terrible news, Doig. Your father was such a likeable man, always friendly, always smiling, eager to help your education in any way he could."

The voicebox had not announced the names of the dead, so how did she know? She was cargo, not crew. Doig nodded his thanks, not trusting his voice to react properly to sympathy.

"You can have the day off, you know. Several days, if you need them. I have to report your absences, but I can justify them in such cases."

He managed, "Thank you." Then, "What does it mean that I'm a marked student?"

"Just that you're clever, and you work hard. You'll probably be granted a scholarship to Wong Memorial University next year."

He wondered why he'd never been warned about that. He'd been born in the Pale, but he'd lived on Copper Island as long as he could remember.

"And you don't cause trouble," Mrs. Wills added even more quietly. Quiet meant warnings now.

"Trouble isn't a good idea, I guess."

"No," she said. "It certainly isn't."

"I wondered if being a marked student meant that I might be dangerous. Or something."

"Oh, no," she said, with a hint of a shrug that might mean anything. "You'll only be dangerous if you cause trouble."

THE HOME VOICEBOX had a message on it to say that the remembrance for Pablo Gray would be held at two o'clock. Doig went to the junior school to tell Mom, who worked there.

Then he went out and wandered the tunnels for a couple of hours because he couldn't sit still. He couldn't go to the gym because the lights were not turned on during working hours. He wasn't hungry and had no credit to buy anything at the deli anyway. Thinking of Dad and the things he might say if Mom hadn't warned him not to, he realized how very little he knew about his father. He hadn't been very old—four years more than twice Doig's age, in fact, which raised interesting questions about the near future. Mom had been a couple of years younger than Dad.

When it was nearly two, he went back to the school to collect Mom. Her friend Mrs. Molinski looked after Camilla during the day. Helen would not be attending the remembrance. She hadn't been told about Dad yet and wouldn't be until Mom could arrange a day off work.

When they arrived at Memory Hall, the door was closed. It was being guarded by a teenage girl whose shapeless dress and rough-cut hair screamed, "Cargo!" Her name tag confirmed it: FAURÉ was not a crew name. Doig knew her from school, but they had rarely spoken.

Bored and uncaring, she told Mom, "A few minutes yet," and ignored Doig as if he did not exist.

So he waited with Mom, nobody speaking. Then the door opened, and about a dozen people filed out, men and women both, some of them weeping.

"Okay, you can go in now."

So they went in. The "hall" was a much smaller cave than Doig had expected, and poorly finished, the walls left rough. Soft music warbled from some invisible voicebox. The benches would hold maybe twenty people, all facing toward a coffin supported on two trestles. There was another door behind the coffin, but there could not have been time to take one out and bring in another, so the coffin was only a symbol. He felt better, knowing that Dad wasn't inside that box. It looked so small, and Dad had always seemed much larger than life. Maybe nobody was in there—no body. Maybe when the bump brought down the roof of Cross Cut Number Whatever, they just left the dead under the rubble. Couldn't dig a grave up-top at this time of year anyway.

Mom went to the closest bench, the one nearest the door. Doig had expected her to go the front as chief mourner, but he settled beside her without a word. A young man in office clothes strolled in and went to sit on the front bench. On Copper Island, those sorts of clothes meant crew, so perhaps a mine official had come to apologize?

Another, older man in cargo-style clothes came wandering in, nodded to Doig and Mom, and chose to sit two rows ahead of them. Doig knew him—Masaru Desjardins, one of Dad's chess friends. He worked in Administration, running communications. It was good to know that somebody else cared.

After a while, Crewman Robins entered by the far door and looked over the four mourners. He wore pale green office clothes. The music faded away.

"That would appear to be all," he said. "Would someone please close the other door?"

Being nearest, Doig rose and did so, then returned to his place beside Mom.

Robins cleared his throat harshly. "We are gathered here to honour the memory of Pablo Gray, who died in yesterday's tragic roof collapse. Mining may not be the grandest of occupations, but it is vital to all of us. Everyone knows that Copper Island is the only source of metal for the colony, and without it, we would not be progressing toward our great and prosperous future. He gave his life for us all. It is especially tragic that this should happen so close to his release date." Pause. "I expect some of you have memories of, um, Pablo that you would like to share with us."

Mom rose. Her voice came out calm and firm, more angry than sorrowful. "I can say nothing better or truer than this: Pablo was always loyal to the colony and dedicated to its future prosperity. In almost sixteen years of marriage, he never raised his hand or voice to me or any of our children. He never once lost his temper, and he always had time to listen. Can you say as much about anyone else you know?"

She sat down. Doig's hand found hers. He squeezed to indicate that she had done well. But was that to be all? A man's life snuffed out, and in seconds, his memory gone too?

The young man who had gone to the front had twisted around to watch Mom as she spoke. He was the ugly man named Finn that Doig had met earlier. Then, he had been muffled in fur. Now, he was dressed in formal office wear, clothes that only crew could ever afford. He continued to stare at her, ignoring Doig. And he looked uglier than ever. His ears stuck out like mug handles.

Mr. Desjardins heaved himself to his feet, a burly, untidy sack of a man.

"Just want to say . . . Pablo founded the island chess club many years ago and taught the rest of us to play. He was an incredible player. Nobody could beat him when he was serious. He used to play without a rook or even his queen, just to make it interesting."

He stood for a moment, gathering his thoughts. "He was a foreman in the mine, and everyone wanted to be on his shift, but I was never so lucky. And before that, before he came to the island, he'd been a surgeon, and he was always ready to come and help if someone got sick and the medic was too busy."

Stunned, Doig looked to Mom. Her hand squeezed his tight, like a warning. She didn't look at him, but for a moment, her lips parted to show her teeth. He had never known that Dad had been a surgeon! Why hadn't she said so when she spoke, and why didn't she want Desjardins mentioning it?

And why had a surgeon left the Pale to come to a nowhere place like Copper Island to work in a mine? Release date? Why had Robins mentioned a release date?

"He's a great loss." The fat man sat down. Then he bobbed halfway upright and almost shouted, "Pablo never hurt anyone!"

Crewman Robins said, "If there's no one else . . ."

Doig stood up, ignoring a downward tug from Mom. "No one ever had a better Dad than I did. All my life, I'll mourn yesterday, remembering what I lost."

He sat down because if he had tried to continue, his voice would have cracked. Mom smiled in approval—and probably in relief that he had said no more.

"Farewell, Pablo, er, Gray." Robins turned around and left.

Suddenly feeling as if invisible hands were throttling him, Doig dragged Mom to the door and went out. At least a score of people were waiting out there for the next remembrance. Why had so few come for Dad?

"Mrs. Gray?" It was Mr. Desjardins. "Really, really sorry about what they . . . about what happened." He thrust a hand forward to Doig. "Doig, isn't it?"

"Yes, sir." As Doig accepted the shake, the older man palmed something to him. Just from the feel of it, he could tell that it was a mem stud. Without looking at it, he slipped it into his pocket.

"Really liked what you said about your Dad, Doig. He's a great loss to all of us. Mustn't say too much, right? But you're old enough to have known him and to, um, make him your example in life, right?"

Wary now, Doig said, "I will try, sir."

Then it was over. Desjardins melted away like a blob of grease in a hot pan. The Finn man had disappeared. The new mourners were disappearing into Memory Hall.

The passages were deserted with everyone at work. Doig walked home with Mom, both of them silent with their thoughts until suddenly, she stopped and said. "Here's as safe as any—no one can see us, and we're not close to any lights."

Huh? Yes, that was true. It was a dark twist in the corridor, and he had heard whispers that some of the lights had microphone bugs in them like the home voiceboxes were said to.

Mom said, "What did he give you?"

"How'd you know—"

"I saw your reaction. What was it?"

"A mem stud."

"Give it to me."

He passed it over, seeing it for the first time. It was an unusual green colour. Mom put it in her mouth and bit on it, crunched it, and swallowed—gagging a little, then getting it down.

"Mom!" he said angrily. Had she gone crazy? He wondered if Dad's death had rattled her brains. But the way he'd been given the stud was weird. The time and place were screwy, too.

"They dissolve in stomach acid. It was those that killed your father. I mean, what was recorded on them did. Doig, never forget this: you must never trust a crewman and only very few cargo. If you'd put that stud in a viewbox or even our voicebox, they'd know, and there might be another accident. Understand?"

"You think Mr. Desjardins betrayed Dad?"

"Somebody did, and somebody told Desjardins to give you

the stud as a trap for you. If you try to follow in your father's footsteps, you'll fall over the same cliff he did before you can cause any trouble. Understand?"

"'Fall' as in 'pushed'?" How many men had died in that fake bump? More than three.

"Of course, but it's not safe to talk about it."

"Then I'll just say this. I swear by my ancestors—"

She tried to put a hand over his mouth, but he pushed it away and continued more quietly. "I swear that one day I will find out who killed my father and be . . . *mmph* . . ."

She hugged him tight, her other hand firmly over his mouth. "You're a very brave boy and a very clever one. But your father was a very clever man, and look where it got him—he's dead, I'm a widow with no supporter, and his children are growing up on this island hell among rabble and scum. What you should do is try to get sent back to the Pale next year, to university, and there grow up to find a safe, honest job and a nice wife, to raise worthy grandchildren to your father's memory. Now promise me you'll stay out of trouble—until you're grown up."

More games are lost than won.

"I promise."

She smiled for the first time since the bump. "I'd say not ever, but I think you're too like your father not to."

"I hope so," he said. "He always said he liked to right wrongs."

"Yes, he did. That was the problem. Wrongs don't like to be righted."

"What did that Robins man mean about Dad's 'release'?"

Mom lowered her voice even more. "Copper Island is a penal colony, Doig. A prison. Now, keep your head down, and don't worry about me or the girls. We'll be all right."

She walked on before he could ask what that meant. But

until he was ready to win whatever the game was, he must be sure not to lose it.

He followed her into the bunker. She was looking around as if she'd never seen it before. Then she smiled again, but this time, without a trace of humour. She put a finger to her lips to remind him that she thought there were microphones.

He could see what she was looking at—a mess. Clothes and bedclothes were all over the place. The rug and the voicebox had been moved. Someone had searched the bunker while they were out and deliberately rummaged it so that they would know—so that they would be scared. And if Mom and the girls were to be all right, then the person they wanted to scare must be him, Doig.

They had succeeded. He wished he could tell them, whoever they were, that it was all right to stop now. He wasn't going to cause any trouble, whatever that meant. His time was not yet, but it *would* come. Revenge would be his life's work—when he was grown up.

MOM HAD BEEN GRANTED two days off work, so that night, she tried to explain to Helen about Dad. Camilla didn't seem to notice his absence and would forget him altogether in a few months, Mom said. Helen made no fuss, but when she was being tucked into bed, she said, "Will Daddy come back from 'Dead' tomorrow?"

Doig went to school the next morning. At least he would have something to keep his mind busy there, so he wouldn't be sitting around the bunker, going crazy as Mom struggled to stay cheerful in front of Helen.

Mrs. Wills strode in with her usual disgusting sparkle. "Good morning, all!"

Which required a choral response of, "Good morning, Mrs. Wills."

"Good news. I haven't finished preparing the next lesson, so I'm going to give you a quick test." She laughed at the groans. Mrs. Wills allowed groans and quiet "Yeahs!" as appropriate. Doig had known other teachers who didn't.

"It's an observation test. I'm going to show you a brief video and then ask you some questions to see how much you noticed. I'm sure you've all seen it many times before because it's quite famous. But don't assume you know everything in it. Head-phones on. Watch and listen very carefully."

She glanced at Doig as she said that. He wondered if this could be another trap. Or a warning? They were coming so fast he couldn't tell which were which.

THE SUPPLY of videos on Copper Island was limited. Whether they were instruction manuals or wild romances or historical dramas, everyone had seen all of them far too many times. The moment his viewbox screen flickered into life, he knew that he was looking at a video made inside *Moctezuma* before it landed. He'd watched it dozens of times. It was replayed every Founders' Day. This copy was clearer than he remembered, remarkably so, considering that the original must be five hundred years old.

Four women and two men sat in a semicircle of chairs. They all wore hospital gowns, and each of them was hooked up to an IV. A woman in a mask and scrubs was tending them, reading dials, murmuring encouragement. They all looked haggard and deathly sick.

Then, a tall, angular man strode into the scene. He had the pale colouring of Northern Europe, which had mostly disappeared from the colony now, overwhelmed by darker pigmentations. He carried himself like a victorious warrior in one of the ancient Earth fictional dramas that were shown every Sunday, helped by the fact that his tunic and pants had a knife-edge perfection never seen in real life, even on crew. He was Captain Ira Vandam, whose godlike face gazed upward and onward on every credit note.

Doig could have repeated the speech that was about to follow word for word.

"Greetings, friends!" Vandam moved around the group, patting the men on the shoulder and kissing the women on the cheek, except for his wife, whom he kissed on the lips.

"Welcome back to life, all of you, especially my dear Wilma. I've missed you, darling, this last millennium. I won't ask how you all are feeling because I know only too well myself, having been through it three times—and without Marlene, here, to help me. I won't tell you yet how many centuries you've been frozen because it won't make you feel any better.

"But I will give you the good news. *Moctezuma* is now in orbit around Neweden, which you will recall was our third and final target. Third time lucky! Our first objective world, Fortuna, turned out to have lower-than-expected oxygen partial pressure, equivalent to about a 3,500-metre elevation on Earth. Our species is barely fertile at that altitude.

"The ship's systems worked perfectly, though. As soon as the telemetry came in, the members of the steering committee were awakened, and after extensive study, we voted four-nothing to bypass Fortuna and continue the voyage. So we slingshotted around Fortuna's star and carried on to Krasivyy as planned.

"Krasivyy turned out to be even worse! Had we approached its system ten years or so earlier, *Moctezuma* would likely have been destroyed before it even achieved orbit. We had narrowly missed a flare from the star, which stripped the ozone layer off of the planet and undoubtedly caused major damage to the biota. Such flares must be rare, because they had never been noticed from Earth, but rare isn't good enough! Once again, the steering committee voted to continue the voyage.

"And so, we have come to Neweden. I'll show you some views in a moment, but it looks very much like Old Earth from orbit: blue and white and green. Its days are only twenty minutes longer than Earth's, and you all know how critical it is to stay close to our genetically determined diurnal cycle. We can certainly handle these days! Neweden has almost no orbital tilt, so days and nights are the same length year-round. That means that we won't have seasons in the way Old Earth has, but we will have seasons because the planet's orbit is more eccentric than the solar observatories predicted. Both summer and winter are likely to be extreme.

"So, the news is good. The steering committee is working hard to pick some possible landing sites. We do have some concerns about life support since the voyage has lasted so much longer than we hoped. We shall have to make our landing as soon as we have thawed out the third bank of cold coffins. Our air-recycling plant, especially, will be hard-pressed to sustain all thirty of us."

"SO," Mrs. Wills said as the headphones came off, "now I'll ask you some questions to see how well you observed. Ready?"

Doig's screen lit up with:

How many men and how many women had just been revived from the cold coffins?

He tapped:

2 men & 4 women.

**From left to right, your left, in what order
did they sit?**

M W W M W W.

Who was the person looking after them?

Dr. Marlene Robins.

She had been the only woman on the steering committee.
So on and so on, all child's play. The sting came in the tail:

**Did you see or hear anything that surprised
you?**

Yes, Doig had. The last sentence of the captain's speech
had been new to him. It was not included in the standard
version shown on Founders' Day. It did not conform to the
standard history of the colony.

He lied. He tapped:

No.

He wanted to add, *My dad never told me whatever it was
that I'm not supposed to know, so stop hassling me.*

But he didn't.

USUALLY, Mom left some lunch for him in the larder, but today, she would likely be there with the girls and they could share a meal. The corridors were so dimly lit that light always showed under the door if there was anyone home. Dad used to push it open and call "It's me!" as if he were entering a building of many rooms—even their real home up-top had only two. Doig and now Helen had taken to doing the same sometimes, but not anymore. It would be too cruel even to think about.

He opened the door and found himself looking over the top of a man's head. Having grown at least ten centimetres in the past year, Doig was still adjusting to an adult's view of the world, and he could see Mom right over this visitor. More surprising than that, though, was what the man was wearing. His pants were quite standard, but above that, he wore only a T-shirt. Nowhere in the bunkers was warm enough for that in winter, so either he wanted to show how tough he was (or how stupid) or how tightly it clung. Doig might be taller, but this newcomer was twice as wide. Not many of the old-timer miners who had worked with picks, shovels, and wheelbarrows all their lives had arms and shoulders like those.

Facing him, Mom was as rigid and tense as if a tiger were about to spring on her. Helen was curled up tiny on her bunk, staring in fright at the stranger.

He spun around, and Doig recognized him even before he read his name tag. Yesterday, he had overestimated the man's height due to the effect of the furs. Crewman Finn was much shorter than he had thought. But his muscles could not make up for his face, with its moles and mismatched eyes. Now, he displayed a set of bad teeth in a much-too-friendly smile.

"Ah, Doig! Good timing. I just came to give your mother some good news."

If the news was good, why did Mom look as if she had just been handed her death warrant?

"Good morning, sir." This was all Doig's own fault. Yesterday, he'd alerted Finn to his mother's troubles, but also to his mother herself. Finn had no doubt seen her image in his viewbox and realized that she was a young and still attractive widow. Available. And vulnerable! Horribly vulnerable.

Mom said, "Doig!" sharply. He realized that his fists were clenched and he was hyperventilating. With a great effort, he relaxed and said, "Yes, Mom. So, what's the good news?" As if he couldn't guess from the brute's smirk.

"Mr. Finn has found me new employment! I'll earn enough to raise the girls without your dad's pay coming in. And we'll have better accommodation, too, both here in the bunkers and up-top."

The bed would certainly be softer. How old was this slaver bastard? Not much over twenty. How many crewmen lived on Copper Island? Doig had no idea. He caught a glimpse of a crew name tag once in a while, but they changed often, so there were probably only three or four at a time. Finn must be just a junior serving his turn in the barrel. Had he won the bidding for Mom or simply claimed her on an I-saw-her-first basis? And when his time here was up, would he take her back to the Pale or leave her behind for his replacement, like office furniture?

"You haven't told him the rest of the news, Mary," Finn said, and that easy familiarity set Doig's blood pressure soaring again.

Mom took a deep breath. "Mr. Finn says he has been able—"

"Hassan, Mary, please!" Finn said.

She took another breath and began again. "Your marks are so good that, er, Hassan, has been able to arrange a scholarship for you to attend the university right away!"

His good marks or his mother's pretty boobs? It could be a

death sentence. Doig might have failed the tests or just been classified as a natural-born troublemaker regardless.

"Starting when, sir?"

"Right away. Classes begin on February second."

Four days! Doig gasped. His world rocked.

Mom said, "I was just trying to explain to Mr., er, to Hassan, that you're still very young and unaccustomed to the ways of living in the Pale. We do have some family there, but we haven't heard from them in years, so we can't be sure they will be willing to offer any support, or help, or . . ." Her voice trailed off, and she gnawed her lip.

Tests or not, someone had decided that it would be safer to get Junior out of the way to guarantee he wouldn't grow up to cause whatever sort of trouble his father had caused or was suspected of causing. Crosscuts weren't the only dangerous places. Accidents could happen on the sled trip over to the mainland, too.

"Even if his relatives don't come through, Mary," the crewman said, "it won't matter. Scholarship students get food and board and a living allowance for things like clothes."

And what was the alternative? If a sentence of death had been passed, it could be carried out anywhere, and Mom and the girls could be allowed to starve—wipe out the whole troublesome brood!

To his own astonishment, Doig heard himself say, "But that's marvellous news! It's very, very, very kind of you, sir. I realize I was rude to you yesterday, and I do hope you'll forgive me and attribute my bad manners to the shock of my father's death. How can I possibly get to Wong Memorial by Monday?" Alive, by preference.

Oh, Vandam! Now he'd done it! Had he gone insane?

Finn suspected mockery, and his eyes narrowed, the left one more than the right. "The ore carrier's crossing tomorrow. We can squeeze you in there. Come to the mine at the same time you did yesterday, and I'll see you safely embarked."

"Oh, thank you, sir. I'll always be very grateful to you for this." Doig offered a hand, wondering if those massive forearm muscles would crush it to pulp, but they didn't. Finn's grip was firm, no more.

"Oh, Doig!" Mom quavered. "I do think we should talk this over first."

Lose husband on Wednesday, son on Friday? "No, Mom. Mr. Finn and I have shaken hands on it. Remember what Dad always said about a man's word being his bond!"

"Mary, I'll be honest with you," Finn said. Had he not been honest so far? "I had no idea this part of the slum was kept so cold, and I'm freezing. Why don't I come back after lunch and take you to see where I . . . I mean, where you and your daughters will be staying?"

Mom nodded faintly. She sank down on a stool. "That would be nice."

Finn thumped a hand on Doig's shoulder and squeezed like an ore crusher to show what he could have done in the handshake. "I've found some useful babble about mainland living that I'll let you bone up on, lad. Come with me. It'll only take a moment. He'll be right back, Mary."

He propelled Doig out into the passage. About ten metres along the corridor, he stopped, let go, and smiled at him. Smiled up at him, that was.

"That was a very quick decision you made, lad. I admire a man who can think on his feet like that."

"It was an easy one, sir."

"It took courage, though. Your mother's quite upset."

"I'll explain it to her when I get back, sir." Feeling pressured, Doig backed up a step.

Finn followed. "Doig, I'm not a monster. Your father was sentenced to death a dozen years ago. Did you know that?"

"No, sir."

"Well, he was! He was preaching revolution, promoting policies that would have wrecked the colony and led to the extinction of the entire human presence on Neweden. But he was a fine surgeon. He'd saved many people's lives, so the chairman of the day commuted his sentence to exile on Copper Island."

Doig just nodded. There had to be some reason for Dad's working in the mine, whether this tale was true or not.

"And a couple of months ago, evidence turned up that he was still at it! He'd found a way to continue spreading his lies about Chairman Ruckles and the Board. Yes, from this island."

"You're telling me that Chairman Ruckles himself ordered my dad killed?"

"No, I'm not!" Finn snapped quickly. "I certainly did not say that. But that accident might have saved your father from something worse. That's all I'm saying."

But it wasn't all he had meant.

"I didn't know all this, sir."

"I'm sure you didn't. But you're not made of miner stuff. That's why I called my uncle, who's chancellor of Wong Memorial University, and told him we had a brainy kid being wasted out here on this lump of rock. The colony doesn't have enough clever folk that we can afford to waste any. Here, take these." Finn reached into a pocket and held out three mem studs. "I downloaded some stuff that will give you some background on mainland life. Watch them in school this afternoon."

Finn shivered as a sign that he was about to leave.

"Sir? I know Mom will worry about the crossing. Will I be able to call her from the mainland to say I've arrived safely?"

There were several implications in that question. Finn's

oddball eyes slitted again, but then he nodded. "I'll see that you can. And I'll have someone meet you."

"She'll be very happy to hear that, sir."

"I hope so." Doig's continued thanks were spoken to a retreating back.

He turned and headed homeward. *More games are lost than won.* Dad's game had ended. Doig's was just beginning, and he must hope that the other side, whoever they were, had just made a really bad mistake by letting him live.

MOM'S EYES WERE RED, but she had dried her cheeks. She pointed to his plate, waiting for him. "You're a stupid, impetuous boy. I've always loved and treasured you, but now I admire you."

He nodded and touched his finger to his lips to warn her that the listeners would still be listening. "It was an easy decision, Mom. How else could I ever get off this stinking island? You raising me to be a miner?"

She shook her head. "But to dare that crossing in January!"

"Well, I shan't drown, anyway. Finn must spend half his days lifting weights. Do his muscles speed your heartbeat?"

He got a glare for that. "All they tell me is that he'll be a sucker for flattery. Oh, Doig—" A single gesture at the girls implied that she had no choice, that she hated what was being forced upon her.

Doig nodded to show that he knew that and he didn't blame her. "Dad would understand. Mr. Finn says he'll arrange for me to call you when I arrive at the mainland."

"I'll pace the floor until I hear from you, love." She winked.

He almost choked on that wink, half-laughing, half-gasping with pride. She was treating him as an adult! She meant that she would make Finn wait to start collecting his payoff.

"What's your new job to be?" he asked, telling his eyes to twinkle. Helen was listening but missing all the tints and shadows. Camilla was vigorously spreading custard everywhere.

"Keeping house, cooking," Mom said airily. "Laying tables."

Laying Finn, of course. The thought made Doig's stomach curl up in knots. *Oh, Dad, Dad!* But Finn was a strong young hunk if the lights were off, and women were scarce on Copper Island. If Mom must whore to support the girls, she would be much better off as one crewman's mistress than a communal slut for all the cargo miners. Finn was doing himself well. And one day in the future, Doig would cut his throat for it.

"And he'll find you a better place to live," Doig told Helen with a smile.

"One of the crew bunkers for the next few days," Mom said. "About five times this size, he says, with proper furniture. And when we move up-top, one of those lovely cottages on the ridge. Those are even bigger, he says! His posting here is for a year, and he promises that he'll take us back to the mainland with him when it ends in November."

Vandam! Doig had forgotten to ask about that. But Finn could break a promise to him just as easily as he could break one to Mom. Or almost as easily. Some men drew the line at lying to men but saw nothing wrong in lying to women. They made jokes about lying to, to lie with.

The light flickered to warn everyone that lunchtime was over. Doig jumped up and ran out the door, still chewing.

MRS. WILLS GAVE him a broad smile to show that she knew. She didn't say anything, but he had barely settled in his place when his viewbox lit up with: *Congratulations on the scholarship! I won't tell the others in case they swarm you later.*

Doig glanced around. Only Kam Petrovich was bigger than he was, but they were all sons of miners and destined to become miners themselves, and if they decided to set upon him, he wouldn't be going anywhere on Friday. He nodded his thanks across the room to her.

Then he put on his headphones and inspected the studs that Finn had given him. Taking one at random, he plugged it in.

A glamorous young woman appeared on the screen, the sort of doxy seen on videos in the communal hall on Sundays but never in the flesh on Copper Island. She was standing in front of a wooded landscape equally unknown on the island. She wore an eye-catching, low-cut red dress, and her hair was sculpted into an elaborate castle on top of her head. Her teeth negated all her efforts, though, being unpleasantly protruding.

"Spiders," she drawled. All mainland people had that funny, drawly way of speaking. "Almost everything that moves on land is a spider of one sort or another. The name comes from an order of eight-legged animals on Old Earth, but our spiders are completely different. Old Earth spiders breathe by oxygen diffusion and can never grow much larger than a man's hand. Our spiders have evolved a much more efficient breathing system. It's more efficient than earthly mammals or even birds have, so spiders can grow to enormous size and move incredibly swiftly. Some spiders in Southmain were visible from Moctezuma while it was in orbit.

"Let us start with the most dangerous. Here is the tiger, the one with stripes. As you can see, its shoulders are almost as high as a man's. Those mandibles can bite a man in half. Tigers hunt alone and are deadly, but fortunately rare.

"Less dangerous individually are the wolf spiders, like this.

As you can see, wolves are much smaller, but they are very fast and even one of them can kill a human. You never see just one, though, because the males run in packs. Nor do you ever see a female because they stay home in the den, and the males feed them."

Doig had seen wolves before, on another historical record, the death of Ivan Wong, the first human being to set foot on Neweden. As a child, he'd had nightmares about the death of Ivan Wong.

The slinky miss went on to talk about birds, small spiders whose ancestors had converted one or two pairs of legs into wings. Doig found this absurd. If an animal could grow wings at will, why couldn't he? Then he could fly over to the Pale. Was this all just an elaborate joke? Was Finn spoofing him?

The glamour girl went on to display and describe herbivorous spiders, both large and small, most of which were edible. After that came bug spiders and verminous spiders, which did occur on the island, and suddenly, Doig's worldview flipped again. The spider inspectors went around the bunkers looking for vermin sometimes, but was that all they were looking for? They always seemed to trouble Mom, and perhaps she was concerned about more than her reputation as a housewife. What else might they be looking for? Mem studs, for instance?

This, he realized, wasn't the first sudden double-take he'd experienced in the last three days. He was viewing the world and the people in it in whole new ways. Revelations were coming much too fast and unlikely to stop anytime soon. How many mainland girls dressed like that one?

She disappeared, and a confident young man took her place and announced that he was going to talk about blazers, how to use them, where it was necessary to carry them, and even where it was illegal not to. That was more interesting. Having grown up on a bare rock, Doig had a lot to learn.

"The human settlement on Northmain is called the Pale. It is bounded by the ocean and a fence, which keeps the really dangerous spiders out—mostly. Once in a while, they do break in. The Pale is divided into the Town and the agricultural area, usually called the Purlieu. Now, in the Town, everyone is advised to carry one of these, called a house blazer. Out in the Purlieu, the law insists that you carry a heavier-grade weapon, called a field blazer . . ."

A mem stud could hold a lot of information, but the blazer talk ended that one. The next one contained maps. It began with one of the Gut, the channel joining the eastern and western oceans, separating Northmain and Southmain. The Pale seemed dangerously tiny compared to them, and the map covered only a small part of Neweden.

Touchdown, where *Moctezuma* had landed, was another island, bigger than Copper. He found Ivan Wong University in the Town, where he would be going. A plan of the campus just confused him because he didn't know what most of the words meant. He needed Dad!

Then, he realized that everyone else had gone home except Mrs. Wills, who was standing beside him. He stood up, cramped after sitting still too long.

"Again, congratulations, Doig. I'm truly sorry about your dad. I hope you do well in the Pale."

He thanked her and put Finn's studs in his pocket for future reference.

BACK HOME, he found Helen very excited about their new home, which she had visited with Mom and Camilla and Mr. Finn. Doig looked to Mom for her reaction.

THE TRAITOR'S SON   31

She nodded and added, "But you were born in a better one. I bought a pack for you."

"What for?"

"Your clothes. And anything else you want to take. I washed your spare socks. They're not dry yet."

He hadn't thought of packing, like they did four times a year, moving between bunkers and up-top, but of course, he would need a bag of his own for this move. He didn't own much because he'd been growing too fast to collect many clothes. But as he looked around, he spotted something he would really like to keep.

"Mom? Can I have Dad's chess set?"

She looked around from where she was heating supper on the hotplate. She shrugged. "Of course. I don't suppose Hassan knows the difference between a pawn and a king."

"Yes, he does. He's king, and anyone else is a pawn."

Doig opened the box and studied the game that Dad hadn't lived to finish. Dad would have won, of course, if he wanted to. It would have been mate in four, which Doig hadn't seen at the time, just before lights out on Tuesday. The boards and pieces used in the chess club were much larger, but this set was tiny, designed for travelling, with a lid, a slot in the middle of each square, and a little key under the base of each piece to lock it in place. You didn't bother twisting them like that during a game, of course, except that Doig liked to do it with the knights to keep them facing the right way.

There was no use immortalizing that unfinished game. He tipped out the pieces on Helen's bed and began putting them back in their home places, locking each one with a quarter turn. The pieces were small and simple in design, carved out of spider bone. Even the king wasn't as long as his little finger, and the pawns were as small as mem studs.

Were any of them mem studs?

He peered at the tongue under the black one he was holding, and no, it wasn't. Nevertheless, he started over, checking the underside of every piece. He struck ore with a white bishop. Its key would fit in a viewbox. Mom clearly didn't know because she wasn't watching him. When he finished, he had found that all the pawns of both colours were just what they seemed, and so were all the black pieces. The white pieces were mem studs—king, queen, rooks, knights, and bishops. These eight must have been Dad's secret store of records. *Oh, Dad!* The sense of loss hit Doig then harder than ever. Dad was gone. Doig soon would be gone, but he would take the chess set with him and one day when it was safe, he would find out what the deadly secrets were that had led to that murderous bump in Cross Cut Twelve.

He ate supper without noticing. He answered direct questions from Mom or Helen, but his mind was far away. It wasn't anywhere, really. His future ended tomorrow morning, and he had nothing to replace it, no conception of the mainland, how it would differ from the island, or who his friends would be. He would be stepping into a void.

"Are you listening?"

"Sorry. What?"

"I said my brother is Thatcher Doig, and his wife is called Sarah."

"Thatcher Doig and Sarah. Okay."

"I'll write it down for you and what I think used to be their address, but don't expect much."

"I don't expect anything," Doig said. "Nothing at all."

Oh, how true that was! Life ended just ahead, at a great big blank.

IN THE MORNING, they went to the mine door while the men were filing in and being checked off by Hassan Finn. They all looked with suspicion at the family group watching them. The air was as cold as yesterday. Doig was wearing every warm thing he possessed, including a rather ratty thick sweater that Mom had bought for him yesterday, and he was still shivering. He hoped that came from a combination of cold and excitement, not cold and sheer terror. In the night, he'd dreamed he was aboard a starship about to crash into a planet.

He would have to get rid of the others soon, or he would start to weep like Helen.

"Mom, you're all going to freeze here," he said. "I'll be all right, and I'll call you when we reach the mainland, I promise. Now, take Camilla away before she freezes solid. You don't want to be an icicle, do you, Cammy?"

He hugged and kissed all three of them in turn and shooed them away. When the last dozen or so miners had been admitted, he went forward and said, "Good morning, sir," to the bundle of fur that contained Hassan Finn, recognizable by his moles and his sneer. Why had Doig not noticed on Wednesday how short he was?

Finn just grunted. He locked the gate and walked away. Doig followed. This time, they went to a different door, opening directly into a large, smelly room where furs hung on hooks around the walls. Two men were dressing.

"This is Doig," Finn said. "Mike Murugan and Jiang Forester. Dress him up so he won't freeze, but make Vandam sure you bring the furs back here. They belong to the mine."

They both said, "Yes, sir." Murugan and Forester were cargo names.

Finn started to turn away and then reversed back to Doig and said, "Good luck, kid. But you keep out of trouble, or it'll count against me, and I'll take it out on your mother, understand?"

Doig just said, "Yes, sir, I understand. I'm very grateful for your help, sir."

Finn departed, slamming the door.

"That one," Mike said, "is one of the stinkiest dollops of puke I ever did meet."

Jiang pointed to the far wall. "Try one of those, kiddo. What's the story?"

"My dad died in the bump on Tuesday. Finn's sending me to the mainland so I won't get in the way while he's humping my mom."

Mike spat on the floor. "Typical crew shit."

"They're just as bad in the Pale," Jiang said.

Was that how they really felt about crew, or were they trying to lead Doig into saying something dangerous that could be held against him? Remembering that more games are lost than won, he didn't comment.

He heaved a brownish fur suit off its hook and was appalled by both its stink and its weight. He carried it over to a bench. Obviously, one had to start at the bottom and work up, so he slid a foot in. Not surprisingly, his shoe was too big, so he pulled his foot out, but the shoe stayed in.

"Let me help," Mike said, lumbering over and taking the furs from him. "Listen, kiddo. Is your trip really urgent? I mean, it can't wait until March?"

"Yes, it's urgent. Classes start on Monday."

Mike put the fur suit back on its hook and brought another. "Just asking because this ice-ferry service of ours is getting dangerous. Most years, we don't run past the fifth week of January. If the tides start to move while we're on the ice, then we'll go straight down among the octopussies."

"Why're you still running now, then?" Doig got both feet and shoes in.

"Stand up. Because the colony is desperate for copper. We're getting double pay on this one."

"But this is definitely the last sled run," Jiang said, coming to help. "The rest of the ore can wait until March and go by boat, see?"

With a twin heave, they loaded the rest of a ton of fur onto Doig, who staggered under the weight. Even the hood on his head felt heavy. Were the sledmen just chaffing the newbie about the danger, or had the Board decided to wipe out the last of the Grays and ordered Finn to arrange it?

Well, they weren't lying about the shortage of copper. Doig had heard Dad and other men talking about the poor quality of the veins they were mining now and the increasing demand as the colony grew. It seemed unlikely that the Board would throw away two men, the sled, and its cargo just to dispose of the Gray brat.

"If you can risk it, I can," he said. "You may have to winch me up-top, though."

They chuckled encouragingly. "Now this mask, see," Jiang said, producing a contraption of dark plastic, "keeps your face from freezing, and when we get aboard, we plug an air pipe in here, see, and it gives you warmed air to breathe. It's minus thirty-seven out there this morning, and a good nor'easter is blowing up. Don't put it on yet because you won't be able to see."

Carrying his mask, Doig plodded after Mike as he led the way. Jiang brought up the rear. The tunnel was long, and its gradient steep. They went through four or five doors, and each time the temperature dropped, until Doig felt his eyelashes and the inside of his nostrils prickle. Yet the rest of him was sweating inside the furs.

Mike stopped at an especially imposing door. "Mask on now. You won't be able to see a thing until we get outside. The sun's still small, but your eyes have been cooped up in the bunkers for about fifteen weeks; they've forgotten what sunlight is."

"And they keep cutting back on bunker lighting to save power," Jiang added.

Any unidentified "they" always meant the crewmen who ran the island, whoever they happened to be at the time.

The sledmen made sure Doig's mask was firmly in place, then donned their own, and Mike opened the door to admit wind and snow and a white blaze of daylight. The snow was local, although wreaths of it swirled across the ground under a bright blue sky.

Doig had never been up-top when the sea ice was still unbroken. The world was a white sheet spread out before him. He could recognize the crewmen's quarters on the ridge, every cottage half-buried in drifts. The cargoes' shacks nearer the sea were even less visible, but the solar power towers and wind turbines looked much as usual. The blades were whirling busily. Now that aphelion was past, the atmosphere was starting to move again.

Jiang and Mike stared southward. Doig could guess that they were looking for the signs of the tide. At aphelion, Neweden was so far from the sun that both winds and ocean tides were slight. In December, the sea between Copper Island and Northmain froze over like a puddle. Now, at the end of January, the sun was coming closer, and with almost no warning, the winds and tides would return and bring breakup. The half-gale already blowing must be an advance warning.

Doig could recall seeing a video of an especially violent breakup, a great turbulent wave crashing through the ice sheet, a thundering wall of foam tipping slabs of ice up like walls so they broke and crashed down, even throwing the pieces high in the air. If breakup began in the next couple of hours, then he would be feeding the octopussies, as Mike had said.

"I'm game," Jiang said, his voice muffled by his mask.

"Me, too," Mike said. "You, kiddo?"

"If I don't freeze to death right here, count me in."

"With this breeze cooling our asses, we'll be there in no time. Climb aboard."

The sled was right in front of them, a copper box with two open holds, each one heaped with shiny nuggets of metallic copper, the gaps filled with snow. The newly mined metal shone orange-red, brighter than the blackening metal of the sled itself. Amidships, between the two loads of cargo, stood a girder structure shaped roughly like an A, supporting a very large fan. Below it, within the girders, was a bench just wide enough for three.

"You go in the middle, kiddo," Mike said and reached past him to grab a microphone. "Sled to Control. Cut off power."

"Control to sled. Power off," said a metallic voice. The sledmen unplugged some cables, hanging them on high supports where they would be visible for next time, no matter how much the snow drifted. Then both scrambled aboard, and Doig found himself sandwiched between two enormous furry spiders. He thought Mike was on his left and Jiang on his right, but he couldn't tell voices or faces behind their masks. Through a shield of thick glass—ominously cracked in two places—he was looking down a long, gentle ramp to the frozen sea.

Probably-Jiang strapped him in, saying, "Can be a bit bumpy at the shore."

"Worse every day, likely," Probably-Mike added. "Now, let's thaw your lungs out." He plugged a tube into Doig's mask, flipped a switch, and created a draft of air that soon became warm. It felt blissful, although, for some reason, it made him pop out in goosebumps all over.

There came a jumble of three distorted voices: "Batteries ninety-one percent starboard, eighty-nine port . . . Sled to Control, crew and passenger embarked, departing. . . Control to Sled, copy departure, safe voyage . . . Cable cast off starboard . . . Cable cast off port . . . Fan starting . . ."

The sled trembled, and the great overhead fan began to turn, casting long shadows on the ramp ahead, for the day was still young. Faster and louder it spun, the shadows becoming a blur. Then Doig felt movement. The snowdrifts started to crawl past, going uphill. The whine of the motors rose higher yet, and he realized that the fan was being used to dampen their acceleration, to reduce the impact when they hit the crumpled ice at the junction of land and sea.

"Hang on!" one of the sledmen bellowed. Doig grabbed the rail and bounced hard against his straps. The sled creaked and rocked, then made it out onto the icy plain of the sea in one piece. Mike or Jiang threw a switch to reverse the fan, and gradually, their speed increased. After a while, the two of them hauled on cables to turn the fan at an angle and veer their course a bit to the south.

The sea wasn't quite flat. The ice rolled in gentle folds, which Doig suspected were caused by the rising tides and should not be thought about. The rush of air buffeted his mask, and he could feel the cold through it.

"Why don't they close this in like a cabin to keep you guys warm?"

"'Cos the windows mist up at minus-seventy or so," said the man on his right. "Let us know if you start getting queasy. Vandam's holy balls, it's getting worse, Mike," he added, confirming Doig's guess as to which one was which. "Never seen it this humpy."

"Yup. Last trip for me until March, credits or no credits."

"Easy for you to say. I don't have a spare girl in the Pale."

"Then you've got a whole month to find one."

Far from feeling queasy, Doig found that he was enjoying the experience. The speed as they rushed over the frozen sea was exhilarating. Overnight, he had stopped being a schoolboy. Fate had thrown him headlong into an adult role, a terrifying but undeniable fact. Life was now his game to win or lose.

"Real sorry about your old man, Doig," Jiang growled. "He was pure metal, he was, and what they did to him this week was a Vandam crime!"

"That it was," said Mike. "He should never have been on Copper Island in the first place, gentleman like him. You going to take up where he left off? It's time somebody gave those turds what they deserve."

"How well did you know him?" Doig asked.

"Pretty well," Mike said.

Jiang added, "Better than most, you could say."

Did that mean that they had served Dad as couriers between island and Northmain? Or were they Board spies trying to trap Doig into saying something stupid?

"It's real solid of you both to say these things. I do 'preciate it. As for me, I first have to take a few years to grow up. Then I'll see what can be done about the turds you mentioned."

"Good man!" Jiang thumped Doig's knee. "You ever heard of the Accident Squad, son?"

"Just rumours." *Scary rumours.*

"That's all anyone ever hears. But last Friday, after we'd delivered our load of copper in the Pale, three men came aboard. They didn't give their names, and they wore no tags. They carried a heavy box."

Suddenly, Doig felt sick to his stomach, and it wasn't the ups and downs of the ice doing it. "And?"

"They went back to the mainland with us on Tuesday morning. Without the box."

And on Tuesday afternoon, Dad had died in a rock fall.

Doig coughed away the foul taste in his throat. "Thanks. Would you know any of them again?"

Mike said, "No, we wouldn't. We wouldn't even if we did, understand? It's not just us, lad; we have families to think of."

"Yes, I understand." Just as Mom had children to think of.

Not long after that, Mike pointed out the faint cone of Mount Moctezuma, emerging from the ice mist along the horizon, white on white. It was ahead and a few degrees to the right, like a beacon.

Doig sat for what seemed like a very long time, wishing he had on warmer socks and thinking about the Accident Squad. The Board must have sent them, or perhaps just Chairman Ruckles himself. What had they brought in the box—dynamite? And how could a man ever track them down to make them pay for what they had done?

His brooding was interrupted when Jiang unbuckled his straps and stood up, hanging onto the rail. He stared southward for a while and then resumed his seat.

Mike said, "Well?"

"Could be. Can you squeeze a little bit more oomph out of this bucket?"

"Not without having it fall apart. Why don't we lighten up a bit?" Then he laughed. "I don't mean you, Doig lad! You don't weigh enough to matter."

That was a relief, but the worry was obviously that breakup was on the way. The wind would be building a swell, and the swell would be flexing the ice up and down, and even thick ice could be brittle. Jiang clambered out of his seat, over the back of the bench, and began kicking and heaving lumps of copper overboard. He could have done better with a big shovel or a lever, but he didn't have either.

"Can I help?" Doig reached for his buckles.

Mike said, "No! You might fall off, and then we'd have to go back and fetch you, which could take an hour against this wind. In fact, that would Vandam near screw us." After a few moments he muttered, "Think the wind's getting stronger."

Which was both good and bad news, Doig decided. He kept staring south, wondering what Jiang had seen, but he didn't stand up, so he saw nothing. He wondered how Mike could stay so calm, how he dared make his living in such a dangerous way. The sled couldn't jump; one crack in the ice across their path would wreck it, and they would drown. Or perhaps the crash would kill them outright. That would be better.

Jiang uttered one brief cry. . . Doig whipped his head around, and Jiang wasn't there.

"He's fallen off! Turn around, Mike! Turn around!"

"Can't." Mike was staring straight ahead, his expression hidden by his mask. "The fall probably killed him anyway. What's the sea doing?"

Doig hastily unbuckled and stood up, clinging grimly to the hand bar. "I can see a sort of glittery line on the horizon. South and east of us."

"Then it's still possible that you and me will come out of this alive. We won't if I go back to look for Jiang."

Doig sat down again and buckled in. He wondered if Jiang had jumped to lighten the load. Or if Finn had insisted on one more run just to get Doig out of the way permanently.

THE CLIFFS of Northmain stood high above the ice, which was heaped against their bases in a crumpled nightmare of white and black. Mike kept the sled well away from that, running parallel to the shore, heading into the Gut that separated the two continents.

"We're probably safe now," he said. "Breakup usually comes a tide or two later in the harbour."

All Doig could think of to say was, "I'm sorry about Jiang."

"He was straight metal. I'll need your help to turn the fan in a minute."

The harbour was a long, V-shaped notch in the cliffs. A road ran down one side of it—hacked out of the rock in places, masonry in others. At the base, it became a pier, and a long box that must be a ship had been hauled up onto it, clear of the ice. The sled's arrival had been seen, and men were waiting there to secure it as Mike drove it ashore and the slope brought it to a halt alongside the ship.

They had arrived. The danger was over. Doig wanted to melt.

Dockhands came running with cables to secure the sled as Mike turned off the fan and its great blades slowed. When Doig unplugged his breathing tube, the January air hit his throat as if he'd swallowed an icicle. He clambered down, clutching his pack, clumsy in his furs, awkward after the long inaction. It must be close to noon already because his shadow on the ice was about a metre long, which was as short as it ever got.

A dockhand straightened up from winding a rope on a bollard and said, "You cut it fine this time, Jiang, old . . . Jiang?"

"Jiang didn't make it." Doig shouldered his pack and trudged off after Mike. Walking uphill in the fur suit wasn't easy; the ice was slippery, and his feet had pins and needles.

Before they reached the top of the road, they came to a doorway set in the rock and Doig followed Mike through into a corridor leading upward. Beyond three more doors intended to keep the cold out, they arrived at a dressing room with furs hung on hooks. Doig began shedding his with relief.

"How old are you, lad?" Mike asked.

"Fifteen, sir." They were both cargo, but Mike was much older, and Doig was in awe of the way he'd kept his cool, driving the sled with breakup chasing it like a pack of wolves.

"No shit? Then I'll tell you something, Doig Gray. If your father were here now and knew how you'd behaved on the sled, he'd be weeping with pride. You're a real chip off the old block, you are. You've got the nerves of a warrior."

To which there was nothing to say except, "Thank you, sir. I'm real sorry about Jiang."

"And don't feel any blame over that, son. It was nothing to do with you. He wasn't lightening the load because of you. He was lightening the load because those shitheads on Copper Island insisted on one more load delivered before breakup."

Doig just said "Thank you" again.

Another door led into a workroom cluttered with sacks and boxes, likely intended for delivery to Copper Island or somewhere else. Two desks were both presently deserted, but Mike went straight to one of them, clicked a switch, and said, "Mike Murugan. Put me through to the island."

So that was a radio. Doig stayed to watch and listen.

A speaker crackled, and Hassan Finn's voice said, "Copper Island."

"Mike Murugan, sir."

"Ah, about time. You made it?"

"Only just, sir. The tide was right behind us when we docked. We had to lighten the load at that, and . . ."

"What d'you mean, 'lighten the load?' That copper is needed urgently."

"Yes, sir. But we lost more than that. Jiang Forester was doing it, and he slipped. We lost him overboard."

Finn said, "Fuck! Give the harbourmaster a full report. The brat made it, though?"

"Yes. He's here."

"Put him on."

Mike moved aside and gestured for Doig to come to the microphone. The speaker said, "Doig?" in Mom's voice.

"Yes, Mom. I'm here."

"You're all right? What's this about a man falling off?"

"'Fraid so, Mom, but I'm fine. It was an exciting journey, and I'm very excited to be here . . ."

Mike sighed. "He's cut you off. Remember what I said about puke?"

"I won't forget him when I'm grown up, Mike."

"Let me know if I can help." Mike thumped him on the shoulder in approval and led the way to another door. It led to a small waiting room, bright and warm. The walls were smooth and white, and the benches looked comfortable. Two people were sitting there, well apart, being entertained by the same communal viewbox, currently showing a male juggler.

The first one to jump up was a woman in a brightly striped dress that looked like summer wear. Her hair was pinned up, her fingernails were painted bright red, and she had jewels attached to her earlobes. She pranced across to greet Mike with a tight embrace and the sort of kiss that Doig had never seen attempted in public before, only on videos. Mike's reaction alarmed her, and she broke loose, asking what was wrong.

The other greeter was a boy of around twelve. His hair, too, was carefully coifed, although it was less ostentatious than the woman's. His clothes were as fancy as Hassan Finn's, and he wore the same name tag: FINN. His eyes were normal, but he had similar widespread ears, and his jaw looked too large for the rest of his face. The Finns could not be known for their looks.

"About fucking time," he said. "I've been waiting here for a fucking hour."

Doig said, "I'm sorry to hear that."

The punk scowled. "Mind your manners, Gray. You're not on the island now, but you're still cargo trash."

"Sir. I'm sorry to hear that, sir."

"Better. How old is your mother?"

What business of his was that? "Early thirties—sir."

The kid leered. "Great balls of fire! I see what Hassan meant when he told me he was so horny he was ready to screw anything on two legs. But don't worry. He's got a pecker like a pickaxe. He'll keep her happy."

What a contemptible pair! One day . . .

Doig had never met a juvenile crewman before and hoped he would never do so again. If the university was full of such vermin, it would be a worse place to live than Copper Island.

DOIG WOULD HAVE PREFERRED to saunter and take in all the sights, but his guide raced along. Doig had no difficulty matching Finn Junior's pace, being about twenty centimetres taller. His pack was not heavy.

This part of the Town was underground, but it was not an abandoned mine like the island. Its streets were wider and higher, better lit, and much warmer. The walls and arched ceilings were smooth and mostly brightly coloured. Store windows showed flashy goods on offer. People, even those wearing cargo name tags, were well-dressed and groomed. The air seemed fresher and sometimes brought delicious food smells, not the stinks of the island. Signs at crossings bore road signs with names Doig had seen on the map, most of them names of the *Moctezuma* crew: Wilma Vandam, Engineer Heiser, and so on. He had arrived in a brand-new world. He was seeing what he had missed all his life.

Finn Junior arrived at last at a wide staircase and proceeded to run up it. Doig followed close behind. The higher tunnel was still underground, yet no colder. A few more minutes brought them to an imposing arch below a sign that proclaimed they had arrived at Ivan M. Wong Memorial University. The warren beyond differed only in that the people were mostly young. Doig noted grins and nudges directed at him. His haircut? Probably mostly his tattered clothing.

Finn consulted a wall directory, and then another, and at last made a successful landing at a door marked CHANCEL-LOR. He marched in, forgetting to wait for Doig to open it for him. It led to a large and fussily decorated office with padded couches around the walls, flashy tiles on the floor, and a shapely young woman in a low-cut dress seated behind a massive desk of black stone in the centre. There was no one else there. She was obviously guardian of the most important item in sight, the other door, the one behind her.

Finn marched right over to her desk. "I'm here to see the chancellor."

She ignored him, continuing to type at her viewbox, frowning at the screen.

Doig, joining his guide, saw that her name tag read SULEYMAN. That was a crew name, which explained Finn's frustrated silence.

He tried again. "All I had to do was to deliver this cargo, so I'll leave him with you and be on my way."

Crewman Suleyman stopped typing and smiled beautifully at him. "Onassis, isn't it? Your uncle had to go to lunch. He told me to tell you to wait until he got back."

"But I need lunch, too!"

She shrugged. "I'm just passing on his orders." With that, she turned off the viewbox, rose as gracefully as a sunrise, and headed for the door.

Hoping for one of those smiles, Doig was there first to open it for her. He failed to get as much as a nod, let alone a smile— who did he think he was? He wasn't a who; he was a what. But even a what could be alarmed at hearing the lock click behind her. Onassis heard it, too, and flushed even redder.

Doig chose a couch and sat down. Lunch? He had almost forgotten what teeth were for. He was too warm, a rare sensation in January. He shed a couple of layers, including the ratty sweater his mother had bought yesterday, and managed to stuff them all into his pack.

Onassis dared to go to the inner door and try that. It was indeed locked, so he chose a couch where he did not have to look at Doig. He glared at the tiled floor instead.

After about ten minutes, he quietly exploded. "I'm going to fix her. I'll report her rudeness to Uncle Gunter!" When Doig did not comment, he added, "She shouldn't treat me like that. We Finns are the first family of Neweden!"

That sounded like an interesting scrap of planetary politics, so Doig said, "I didn't know that, sir."

"Then I'll show you. Come here." With that, Onassis brazenly went to sit at Suleyman's desk and turned on her viewbox.

Doig wandered across to watch over the brat's shoulder. The viewbox was the finest he had ever seen, with the largest screen, and he could recall Dad telling him that the Pale could access hundreds of thousands of videos.

Finn, an awkward, picky typist, demanded *Show First Birth Finn*. Doig expected to see him blocked by a passport demand, but either the Finn name or the chancellor's line was enough to gain entry. After a brief moment, the overly familiar face of the long-dead Captain Ira Vandam appeared, beaming. He was posed in front of a hospital bed, curtained to conceal the occupant, if any.

"Fellow colonists! I am overjoyed to tell you that we have reached a truly historic moment in the history of Neweden. The first member of our crew to give birth is now delivered of a healthy, and very loud, son."

The captain vanished and was replaced by a picture of a man and a somewhat pregnant woman, arms around each other. The background showed the enormous silvery mass of the *Moctezuma*, more than a kilometre long, sprawled like some vast beached sea creature, seeming to overshadow the volcano named after it, distantly visible, off to the left. Obviously, that was a file shot, not the birth scene.

Then Vandam was back—he must have been the greatest lens hog in the history of the galaxy. This time, he held a small bundle of towelling, the only part of the contents visible being the tiny, grumpy face of a newborn baby, fast asleep.

"Yes, the happy parents are our good friends Jean-Luc and Dolores Finn! And they have chosen to name their son—Snorri! The happy mother is now resting, but all the rest of us can now celebrate the arrival of the first human to be born on this planet."

The end.

"See?" Onassis announced cheerfully.

"No."

"What'cha mean—no?"

"Try that again with *First Birth Robins*," Doig said, throwing out the first crew name that came to mind.

Onassis gave him a searing glance and did as suggested. Captain Vandam appeared again and repeated his previous performance exactly, except that the proud parents were a different couple, and the baby's name was different, too.

Another end.

Onassis was understandably furious. "How'd you know that, cargo scum?"

"I used my eyes and ears, sir. The captain seemed to hesitate each time he had to speak a name. His tunic was creased in his first appearance and not in the second, so the whole clip was a patch-up. I'm sure he wasn't responsible. Some joker, perhaps centuries later, must have made eleven copies of the original, cutting and pasting in the rest of the crew."

As a joke, it was on the level of the fairy tales told by parents to small children. It might lead to a few fights in primary schools, but how could an eleven- or twelve-year-old like Onassis Finn still believe in the fraud?

"See if there's one for Dendrologist Wong," Doig suggested. There wasn't. "Try Gray, sir."

"Who cares? All you cargo came out of a bottle," Onassis snapped, but he did try *Show First Birth Gray*. The inevitable Ira Vandam appeared again, already clutching a well-wrapped newborn.

This time, the background showed a row of sterile-looking metal machines. There ought to be about twenty of them, including spares, because although each incubator could nurture a fertilized ovum into a newborn baby, no machinery could raise that baby for the fifteen or so years needed to turn it into an operational adult. Only loving, fully human parents could do that, so every woman on the *Moctezuma* received a foster child to be reared with her own. The starship's cargo had been ten thousand frozen ova. In the past, Doig had wondered how many of those had ever been successfully cultivated, but the viewbox he had asked had declined to tell him. Not all ten thousand, certainly.

"Fellow colonists," the captain proclaimed, "we have reached another major milestone in our long trek from starship to inhabited world! Here is our first incubator baby, decanted less than an hour ago, fully healthy. Indeed, Dr. Robins tells me he outweighs any of the naturally gestated babies born so far. And my dear wife, Wilma, has agreed to be the one to foster him. Wilma?"

Unlike her husband, Mrs. Vandam did not have a speaking role in every stud of the old records, but her serene smile was easily recognized. She walked into the picture to accept the baby. From the look of her, she was still nursing her own child, which might be only a week or two old.

The captain did not invite her to speak. Only he was allowed to be the historical voice of Neweden. "The boy's parents are recorded as Scott and Maureen Gray, of Edinburgh, Scotland, and they specified the name Peter for their child if it turned out to be a boy. So tonight, let's all drink a toast to Peter Gray . . ."

Onassis smacked the off switch on the viewbox and jumped to his feet, furious. "You knew that!"

"No, sir. My mom used to tell me that the Doigs were the senior cargo family, but my dad always laughed at that story, so I never believed her."

Onassis stomped back to his sulking couch. Doig wandered around the room, studying the pictures. They were all terrestrial scenes, old and blurry now and irrelevant to Neweden. He was amused by a pastoral scene of a herd of hour-legged domestic animals—probably sheep—being guarded by a half-naked shepherd boy armed with a long hook. On Neweden, the spiders would eat the lot of them before lunchtime.

Which reminded him: he was starving.

AFTER ANOTHER HOUR OR SO, when Doig had become more worried about the inflation of his bladder than the deflation of his stomach, the click of a lock brought both him and Onassis to their feet. The outer door swung open. In wandered a portly, grey-haired man in a rumpled grey office suit. His face was puffy and rubicund, and his eyes were both protuberant and watery, unpleasantly like freshly shucked shellfish.

"Uncle Guntur!" Onassis said.

The chancellor cleared phlegm noisily. "Ah, you've arrived. And this must be the, um, youth that your brother mentioned. Well done! We'll look after him now. Run along, then."

Doig failed to see his former escort's reaction, being intent on studying the chancellor's companion, who could not be much older than himself. She was so gorgeous that she could have just walked out of a fiction video. The hair hanging to her shoulders was gold (a colour he had never seen on a real person before), her skin was a divine bronze, and her dark blue dress was the sort of costume he associated with the scorching heat of summer, exposing arms and legs and shoulders—and cleavage. He dragged his eyes away from her as Onassis left, slamming the door behind him.

"Gray?" Guntur Finn said. "First name?"

"Doig, sir."

"Mm. Any relation to Doig Hogg, the optometrist?"

"None that I'm aware of, sir." Why should he be?

"Mm. You do look on the young side. Carina?"

"Yes, sir?"

"Why don't you take, um, him, off and give him the admission test? If he passes, tell Aliyah to enrol him."

"And if he doesn't?"

"Show him where to apply for a job. Lock the door on your way out."

After a brief struggle with a key, Chancellor Finn let himself into the inner office and was gone.

Carina turned her attention to Doig. Her name tag read BRUKNAR, which was cargo, not crew. She smiled.

Vandam! He smiled back, hoping he did not look as overwhelmed as he felt. He could smell flowers. It was a good job he wasn't a couple of years older, or he'd be overwhelmed. No, it was a real *shame* that he wasn't a couple of years older.

"When was the last time you ate, Doig?"

"December, I think. Early December."

"Then let's attend to that first, shall we?"

He sprang to open the door, then had to shoot across the room like an idiot to fetch his pack. Once they were both out in the corridor, Carina locked the door and led the way. There were fewer people around than before. *Talk! Converse!* What should he try to talk about?

"Can you tell me, ma'am, why—"

"Call me Carina, Doig. I'm cargo, too."

"Um, yeah. I understand why I had to wait until the chancellor had finished eating his lunch, but why did he order his secretary to lock Onassis in, too?"

"Guntur Finn doesn't eat lunch, Doig; he drinks it. Because he resents his brother's side of the family—Hassan, Onassis, or any of the rest of them. His brother has fathered three or four ugly little Finns. All Guntur has managed is a couple of deformed freaks that fortunately died young."

Doig said, "Oh." His education had begun.

"The Finns are hopelessly inbred. Mind you, they're not as bad as the Lee lot. I never met a Lee who could find his ass in broad daylight."

Vandam's holy balls! Planetologist Vladimir Lee had been one of the four members of Moctezuma's steering Board. And if

Guntur disliked his nephew Hassan, would he spite him by rejecting the student he had recommended?

"You're telling me that the chancellor of Wong University is a drunken congenital idiot?"

"Concisely and precisely stated. He hands out diplomas and interviews applicants, especially female applicants. It keeps him out of the way. Aliyah Suleyman does the work. You met her."

So why had Carina Bruknar been drinking lunch with Guntur Finn? Was she an applicant for something? Or what else was she?

"Onassis is a stupid little prick," Doig said. "Hassan looks like something that grows in a dark, damp place, but he didn't seem specially gorked."

"His father managed to marry a Robins. Guntur had to settle for yet another cousin. Something smells good."

She led the way into a large, bright, chatter-filled area full of mouth-watering odours. The ceiling was supported by pillars, each one encircled by an eating shelf and a ring of stools, mostly unoccupied now that lunchtime was over. A few people were lined up at the serving counter.

Carina laid a hand on his arm to stop him. "Doig," she said quietly, "before we get into that crowd, I want to say that I'm sickened by what was done to your father. I can't remember him myself, but I know my parents were both outraged when the news was being passed around yesterday."

"You don't believe the bump in the mine was an accident?"

"Of course, it wasn't! He said things that ought to be said. Maybe he went a bit far, and many times, he had been ordered to stop, but he should never have been sent to the mine. The Board never answered any of your father's accusations."

Five new people Doig had met already that day, and three

of them had supported Dad. If more than half the colonists thought that way, why hadn't they spoken up long ago?

"Come," Carina said, releasing his arm. "You must be starving."

"Um. Is that door over there with the M on it what I think it is?"

"Yes, but that's a gold M. That means it's for crew. Cargo guys go to the one over there with the black M."

THEY MET AGAIN at the food line. Doig stared in agony at the selection. "I don't have much credit, Carina."

"Mine is infinite—I use Guntur's. Help yourself to all you can eat."

Taking her at her word, he filled a tray. She took a single fruit of a type that he didn't recognize, explaining that she had eaten while watching Guntur Finn drink lunch. They found a place. Doig ate as fast as he could, which was very.

"What's this admission test?" he asked between mouthfuls.

Carina honoured him with another smile. "A list of questions to weed out the worst of the Finns and Lees. Silly stuff, like, 'What's seven times ninety-one?'"

"Six hundred thirty-seven."

"That was quick. Can you do seventeen times ninety-one?"

"Fifteen hundred forty-seven."

Lustrous dark eyes blinked, and perfectly curved eyebrows rose in surprise. "I'll have to take your word for that."

"Well, it's easy after the first question. Just add nine hundred ten to six hundred thirty-seven."

"Mm," she said. "I think you may have to skip a grade or two. Who was chief engineer on *Moctezuma*?"

"Dhaval Heiser."

"Second engineer?"

"Alison Guldberg."

This time, Carina gave him a very odd look. "Doig, you don't need to worry about the test at all."

THE LIBRARY WAS A PILLARED hall much like the cafeteria, except that the tables carried viewboxes, four around each pillar, although at least half of them seemed to be labelled OUT OF ORDER. There were only four students working there, and Carina chose a pillar well away from them. She turned on a box, typed a few words, then turned to look up at Doig. "Are you happy using your real name? Would you rather be Doig White or something like that?"

"Would that fool the Board?"

"No. It might stop endless people commiserating with you, though."

"Then I'm proud to remain my father's son."

She typed again briefly, stood up, and let him have the stool. "Don't rush it; you have plenty of time. I'll sit around here and catch up on a slushy romance I'm reading."

Refusing to believe Carina Bruknar would ever waste her time reading slushy romances and wishing he hadn't eaten so much, Doig sat down and studied the screen.

As she had warned him, some of the questions tested his knowledge of colonial history and others his mental agility. A few posed ethical questions:

> ***You are out in the Purlieu with a woman and a three-year-old boy. A tiger spider comes racing toward you. Do you:***

1. *Run away alone.*
2. *Grab up the boy and run with him because even carrying him, you will still be faster than the woman.*
3. *Take the woman's hand and pull her along with you because she is young enough to bear more children.*
4. *Run toward the tiger in the hope that it will be satisfied to eat you so both of the others can escape.*

Recalling the mem stud that Hassan Finn had given him, Doig typed, "I burn the tiger with the blazer that I am legally required to carry when out in the Purlieu."

Besides, tigers attacked from ambush, so you never saw them coming.

Thoroughly enjoying himself, he found most of the questions childishly simple.

If an apple and a half cost a credit and a half, what do twelve cost?

Surely even Finns and Lees ought to manage that one?

But not all were toddler-grade. Shown a maze with letters scattered over it, he was asked what the letters he would find spelled out along the shortest route to the centre. Since the first letter from the entrance was M and the next had to be either O or T, he glanced at the centre to confirm it was labelled A, but then he confirmed this too-obvious answer by using the intervening letters to trace out the path to the centre. The real answer wasn't *Moctezuma.* It was *more azalea.*

How often do we cut Saturday, February 42, out of the calendar, and why?

Every seven years, to keep the calendar in step with the seasons, the year being 378.143 days long.

Give four reasons why Moctezuma's steering Board chose the landing site it did.

Easy.

1. It is about halfway between the north pole and the equator, and they thought it would have the most moderate climate.
2. For the same reason, they wanted a site on the coast.
3. There were ample forests to log.
4. The bedrock around Mount Moctezuma is pumice, a rock that is soft to cut and a good insulator. Some of it can also be used to make cement.

Then came something different.

You are about to see a video clip of a well-known scene. What is happening, and when?

Flip to five women and three men sitting on chairs, a larger number of each standing behind them, and all of them watching Guess-Who himself, Captain Ira Vandam, standing before them. He holds a bowl above his own eye level. He is making a speech, of course. Then he reaches up and takes a piece of paper out of the bowl. Cut.

Answer:

This was recorded soon after the landing, when the atmosphere was known to be breathable, and the heat of the landing rockets had dissipated. Captain Vandam is randomly selecting a crewman to have the honour of being the first human to walk on the planet.

Whose name was picked?

Dendrologist Ivan M. Wong.

End of test. Elapsed time, sixteen minutes. *Ping!*
He had no idea it had taken so long. Real fun, though.

"That was quick," Carina said. "Let me see how you scored." She typed briefly on her own viewbox. Then she looked at Doig as if he were a new species of spider caught playing a flute.

"You just turned fifteen. Normal matriculation age is sixteen, but we can certainly accept you on the basis of this test. In fact, Aliyah can promote you to second year easily."

"I think I'd prefer to start at the bottom, Carina. I have a lot of social learning to do."

She smiled. "And you don't want to attract too much attention from on high?"

He nodded. *More games are lost . . .*

She nodded back as if that was another right answer. "Let's go and report to Aliyah." But she typed a sentence or two before turning off the viewbox.

AS THEY LEFT THE LIBRARY, Carina said, "Doig, you're right to keep your head down for a while, but don't get paranoid. If the Board were truly worried about you, they would swat you as easily as they swatted your dad. Being known as Pablo Gray's son is actually a sort of protection against casual murder because your death would be noticed. But you can't live in fear of everyone. You will have to trust some people, and university is a great place for making friends. Also, students are notoriously wordy. Hotheads preach revolution in the Mudhole every week, but nobody ever does anything about it; they just talk. Keep your mouth shut and your ears open."

"Always good advice," he said.

"Can you trust me?"

"I trust you so far."

"That's the right answer, I suppose. All students have to share a room, usually with someone in their own year, but there are very few guys of your age around. My brother Buster is a couple of quarters ahead of you, and he feels, as I do, that Chairman Ruckles and his gang are tyrants, and incompetent tyrants, at that. He'd like to meet you. If the two of you hit it off, he'll help you find your feet here."

What she said made sense—Doig mustn't let Dad's murder drive him paranoid. He had everything to learn, and if he behaved himself, the enemy would probably allow him a few years to do so. When he was older and had studied all of Dad's secret chess-piece files, he could decide what he was going to do about them.

"That's a very generous offer. Thank you."

"Thank him."

When they arrived at the chancellor's office, Aliyah Suleyman was back at her black stone desk. She looked up with an enquiring smile.

"Boy genius," Carina said. "Not one mistake. Talking of mistakes, is Guntur still breathing?"

"He's awake and asking for you."

Carina glanced at Doig and rolled her eyes. "Time to get

back to work. I told Buster to get his ass over here pronto. Good luck, Doig."

He thanked her and watched in disbelief as she went over to the inner door, went inside, and locked it behind her. He hadn't believed what he'd been suspecting.

Aliyah saw his shock. "It's a shitty job, but it pays well," she said.

"Does she have any choice?"

"No. It happens to lots of pretty cargo girls. Doig, I've never seen a flawless test result in the five years I've worked here. I'll pare it down a bit, if you don't mind, just to be on the safe side. I can put you in first year or second. I could almost put you in third, but you'd get mercilessly hassled."

"First will be fine, thank you. I need time, lots of time."

"First it is, then, but you'll have to play Lee. That means—" She saw his grin. "Okay. Now, have you decided what you'll major in?"

"Sorry . . . I don't—"

"What subjects interest you most? You have to name something now, but you can always change it later."

"Earth history." He saw her surprise, perhaps a trace of disappointment. "We're doing things wrong here," he said. "We need to start over somehow."

Understanding, she nodded. "Fine. Sounds innocent. Don't worry about credit. Students get enough for food and basic accommodation and a minimal clothing allowance. If that pack is all you've got, you'll need more. I'll keep your credit topped up for your first year or so."

"This is wonderfully kind of you."

She gave him a soulful gaze and held it for a moment to indicate sincerity. "Not all crewmen support Chairman Waldo Ruckles and his gang. But nobody says things like that in front of strangers, understand?"

"Yes, ma'am." But Doig also understood that not all statements were true. Paranoia strikes again.

"And some women don't have any choice. Now, we'll be migrating up-top in a week or so. I'll bunk you in 223 for now . . ."

At that moment, the door flew open. The youth who avalanched in was shorter than Doig but wider and thicker. He had untidy pale brown hair, a broad jaw, a snub nose, a big grin, and a hand the size of a dinner plate, which he extended as he charged at Doig.

"I'm Buster Bruknar," he announced unnecessarily, wrapping Doig's hand in his. "I'm really honoured to meet you, and if you ever need any help trashing the brutes that did for your dad, I'll be really hurt if you don't invite me to the party." Without letting go, he glanced at the inner door, then at Aliyah, and finally at the ceiling, rolling his eyes.

"I'll save a seat for you," Doig said, feeling somewhat overwhelmed.

"And I promise to hit them with it." Buster let go of Doig's hands and turned to Aliyah. "What's needed, ma'am?"

"Just show him around. He's going into first grade, bunker 223."

Buster ran his gaze over Doig, undoubtedly noting the haircut and clothes.

"Where'ja wanna start, boss?"

"Let's dump my pack first," Doig suggested.

"Right." Buster spun around.

Doig ran after him.

THEY TROTTED downstairs and along a tunnel narrower than those above.

"We use these in Winter and Wummer quarters. Spring and Harvest, we're in the sheds up-top; classrooms are all down here and used year-round. Winter quarter means December and January. Spring is February through April, Summer May through August, and Harvest September through November. Fourteen weeks, fifteen, ten, fifteen, and winter again, right?" Buster moved as fast as he spoke.

"Right." Copper Island did much the same.

"But you're not allowed to attend more than three quarters in a row—it's not healthy. I plan to take Harvest off and work in the Purlieu."

Bunker 223 was roomier than the Gray house on Copper Island, well-lit, better ventilated, and furnished with two beds, two chests, one table, and one voicebox. Doig dropped his pack on the floor, not claiming either bed.

"They're all like this," Buster said. "I'm in 365 with a guy called Spurt. That's not his real name, but . . . never mind. We'll be moving up-top so soon I might as well stay there until then."

Doig jumped into the momentary silence. "Viewbox?"

"Plenty in the library, twenty-four hours. Movies, lectures, files. Spurt spends a lot of time there. Let's go. What's next, boss? Blazer, certainly! Can't go up-top without a blazer. Haircut? Clothes? Library? Cafeteria? The Mudhole? That's the beer garden. Lecture rooms, labs? Swimming pool? I do twenty laps there every morning—you gotta work hard to stay fit in the bunkers. Or the gym? I work out there a lot."

Doig was not surprised to hear that. He wondered if his new friend ever sat down.

LATER, they returned to 223 with more clothes than Doig had ever owned in his life, most of them stuffed into another pack, which he would need for his move up-top, and a blazer that would kill a wolf spider—but not the fifty brothers coming behind it. The inside of his head was awash with academic geography.

"Swim now?" Buster asked plaintively.

"Let me find my trunks."

DOIG SKIPPED an evening meal and went to bed early, long before the lights began to fade. He had survived Friday! He wondered how Mom was managing in her new servitude, but he barely had time to remember his sisters before he was asleep.

HE WAS AWAKENED VERY EARLY by aching muscles, the penalty for trying to keep up with Buster. The room lamps were still dark, but the corridor's nightlights gleamed under his door.

He lay there for a while, wondering if this had been the first time in his life that he had slept alone, but also fighting a mighty urge to investigate the secret messages in Dad's chess set. Within a week, likely, he would be moving up-top, which would put him much farther from the viewboxes in the library. A brief peek wouldn't hurt, would it? Eventually, the temptation won, and he slipped out of bed, rescued his clothes from the floor, and dressed.

He had hidden the box in the chest, under his new underwear. He laid it down beside the door, where there was enough light to distinguish white pieces from black. Logically, the eight "stud" pieces should be read from left to right, which meant starting with a rook, but which rook? He put both of them in his pocket and tucked the box away in its obvious hiding place.

The corridor was dim and deserted, as was the library when he reached it. He stalked through a petrified forest of pillars to the far side, and there chose a viewbox from which he could keep an eye on the entrance. The two hand-carved rooks were not exact duplicates; one was slightly taller than the other. He wondered if the same would be true of the bishops and knights. Heart in mouth, he plugged in the taller one.

The screen lit up with Dad's face against a background of the sort of rock found in the Copper Island mine. Doig gasped and hastily put on the headphones.

"Greetings," the image said with a heartbreakingly familiar smile. "This is the beginning of my course of lectures on freedom, disparaged by certain persons as my treasonous incitement to revolution. You may decide which term you prefer when you have heard what I have to say and seen what I have to show you. I have spent many years compiling this manual. You will need about fifty hours to view it all.

"I cannot know to whom I have the honour of speaking. I suspect and hope that you are my son, Doig, who is quite smart enough to work out where I have hidden these notes. I am very proud of him and am confident that he will continue my life's work if he gets even half a chance to do so. If, on the other hand, you are a Waldo Ruckles supporter, then I urge you to view the evidence with an open mind. If you do, it will certainly convince you of the need for drastic change in the way this colony is being run.

"While this is the true beginning of my harangue, it is my most recent, and almost certainly the last, of my postings. I have changed this introduction numerous times, but I am certain that this will be the final version.

"As you must know, Copper Island is not just a vital resource for the colony; it is also a prison camp. It is run by four or five crewmen, who usually serve one-year tours. Their terms are staggered throughout the year, but it is extremely rare for crewmen to make the crossing during the winter months. Last Friday, a party of three came over on the sled. Newly arrived prisoners are set to work at once, but these men are being treated as honoured guests by the staff. They are scheduled to go back to the Pale tomorrow, Tuesday, January 45, 505."

That was the day Dad died. So after dictating this message, he went home for supper as usual and began the chess game he would never finish.

"One of those men, I am told, has a cast in his right eye. In that case, he is certainly Dhaval Guldberg, also known as the Cargomaster. He heads up the Accident Squad. So, the Board has decided to silence me permanently. I have been wondering for a long time when they would get around to it. I accept it as a tribute to my campaign and proof that they begin to feel the ground moving under their feet."

Dhaval Guldberg! So Doig had a name to remember. One day, he would find this "Cargomaster" killer and make him pay.

Dad paused for a moment.

"What evidence will I show you? Many things! Almost all of them are taken from the Board's own files, mainly the *Moctezuma* records. But these will not be the records you know. Over the centuries, the originals have been repeatedly edited to suit the current Board's purposes. Let me start by showing you what I mean. Here is a great moment of triumph, which is also exactly the moment when the colony's death knell began to toll. Watch very carefully, and you will see—or hear— the changes that have been made."

His face vanished, and Doig found himself watching one of the scenes he had been shown during the entry test: the crew of

Moctezuma assembled in the mess and Captain Ira Vandam drawing a name out of a bowl. This time, it came with the usual soundtrack. Anxious to find the cheat that Dad had just promised, Doig carefully scanned the spectators, especially the front row, but there was no change there. He had seen it so many times that he always ran a mental commentary just ahead of the action:

The eight persons seated there are the survivors of the third tranche of cold coffins, very recently revived, and one of them is about to die. The nineteen standing behind them have all come from the first and second tranches. Total, with the captain, twenty-eight. All correct so far.

"And the winner is . . . Ivan." Pause for cheers and applause. "How fitting that our tree expert should be the first to touch a Neweden tree! You sure you feel up to this, Ivan?"

From the way the doomed man struggles to his feet, he is far from recovered from his many centuries of hibernation, but he isn't about to admit it. "What, and give up my chance of immortality? Not flaming likely!"

Now, of course, the view switches abruptly to the exterior of the starship. Its fiery descent has blasted out a shallow crater, throwing back the forest and the soil beneath, in some places exposing bedrock. The first explorer isn't going to see much of the planet other than the misty cone of the mountain that will later be named after the ship. A door has opened near the middle of the grounded monster, and a ramp is descending.

Ivan Wong appears in the doorway. He carries a projectile gun, and he wears an earpiece and a mike, but otherwise, his clothes are standard crew dress of shirt and shorts. He takes a deep breath and says, "Heavenly! The air smells of trees and flowers."

As he descends the ramp, moving with care and unsteady on his feet, another crewman appears in the doorway. He remains there, covering Wong with a much heavier weapon. His name is never given, but from other accounts, Doig knows he is microbiologist Aberash Whitehead.

Then comes the dramatic moment when Wong steps off the end of the ramp and places a first sandal on the soil of Neweden. He says, "I claim this world in the name of the crew of Moctezuma and their descendants forever!"

The spectators in the mess can be heard cheering.

Still moving slowly, Wong plods up the slope to the rim of the hollow. Time for the warning . . .

Captain Vandam's voiceover: "Ivan, be careful! You shouldn't go any farther until we know it's safe."

Wong halts as he reaches the great tangle of shattered trees and other vegetation. He turns, raising his arms in triumph. "We have a world, friends! Come forth and multiply!"

Then, of course, comes the disaster. Out from what seemed like an absolutely impassable barrier emerges a long jointed leg, more than a metre long, covered with brownish fur and ending in two claws. It waves in the air, and the adjacent debris shifts. The first leg is joined by another, then a head armed with deadly mandibles. Wong cries out in alarm and tries to flee, staggering unsteadily down the uneven slope.

More legs are followed by the torso of a wolf spider. It hurtles after him on eight long, furred legs. Whitehead fires—a daring shot over Wong's head that kills the monster instantly—but the entire tangled jumble of crushed forest has come alive as a dozen more spiders emerge and wriggle free. Possibly dazed by the sideslip of the blaze, Wong trips and falls headlong. Whitehead runs down the ramp to aid him, which is heroic but foolhardy. As Wong struggles to his feet, the spiders are on them. Whitehead pours bullets everywhere in a continuous roar, but the spiders keep coming. Both men are chopped in pieces. Blood spurts in all directions.

The starship door slams shut. The spiders run off, each one carrying a trophy.

Only once had Doig witnessed that gruesome finale; after that, he had always shut his eyes in time. Now, he kept them open, but he was looking at Dad's face again.

Dad sighs. "I always used to wonder why Ivan Wong is hailed as a hero, and Aberash Whitehead is almost never mentioned. Why do you suppose Wong was so honoured while the man who tried to save him is forgotten? Perhaps because Whitehead left no descendants, and history is written by the winners, as they say. It is also rewritten by the winners. Now, look at what really happened."

Back to the silvery dead-fish shape of *Moctezuma*, this time seen from another camera, on the other side of the ramp. Doig has never seen this version. Ivan Wong steps out and takes his deep breath. He says, "Jesus! It sure is hot out here!"

Says *what?*

The words are wrong, but the action is right. It continues as expected, with Wong planting a sandal on the exposed rock. Again, though, he does not follow the script. "I claim this world in the name of all humankind."

There is no off-stage cheering in this version and no warning from Captain Vandam.

Wong reaches the top and turns, spreading his arms to indicate the vast barrier of debris, two or three metres high, extending the whole length of the ship, more than a kilometre. A few curls of smoke show in places, but that is all. "Why is this crap not all burning?"

The spider starts to emerge and—*cut!*

Dad shakes his head. "Those were the most ironic words spoken that day. Wong was a dendrologist, a tree expert, and he was staring at the remains of an almost incombustible forest. That, of course, was the worst difficulty the colony was to face.

Because of the incendiary heat of a Neweden summer, the trees hereabout have evolved trunks of lignin, which burns very poorly, and silica, which won't burn at all. It was weeks before the rest of the crew understood what he had seen at a glance.

"So which version is genuine? The second one. I found it tucked away in the colonial archives. The official version has been doctored for general consumption. Scores or perhaps hundreds of the records you have been spoonfed all your lives have been doctored like that. As far as I know, there is always a true version in the archives if you know the password to access them.

"Now I have proved to you that the Board has been lying to you and your ancestors for five centuries. What can you do about it? Legally nothing. You are their slaves. How did we get into this mess? I'll tell you."

The voice and the face were hypnotic. Doig could not shake the sense that Dad was speaking directly to him alone.

"The seeds of evil were planted long before *Moctezuma* was launched. Who named it *Moctezuma*, and why? That's an interesting question, too. Was it called that before it was launched?

"No matter how clever its computers or how comprehensive its libraries, a colony ship must carry a human crew to make the difficult decisions when unforeseen problems arise, as they will. Thirty was accepted as the viable minimum—fifteen couples, locked away in cold coffins for the ages-long voyage. They were chosen from the world's best. They had to be young, fit, clever, and so on. They had to share a common language, and English was the most widespread on Old Earth. Furthermore, morality was in vogue again, so it was decreed that they must all be legally married. The godly of the world would not support a program to build a flying brothel. As always, the righteous felt they must regulate sex. As always, regulation made the trouble worse.

"Of course, thirty people are not enough to found a population. Within a century, they would be inbred. In two, they would be incapable of reproduction. Thus, the cargo of ten thousand frozen ova.

"Consider the sort of people who would consent to make this journey. No matter how highly educated they were, the men knew they would be pioneers—clearing forests, plowing, planting, and harvesting. If they survived the voyage, they would be facing a life of danger and physical toil. Give them their due: not one of them lived past the age of sixty, and half died before their eldest child reached eighteen.

"And the women knew they would have to be baby factories. While their husbands laboured in the hills and fields, they would reward their husbands with children. They would also have to foster the babies hatched in incubators. And they did! Despite a gruesome death toll, that crew of thirty grew in seventeen years to a population of almost three hundred.

"So, what went wrong? In these files—it's in the taller bishop stud, I think—you will find that well-known recording of the garrulous Captain Vandam greeting the eight survivors of the third tranche of thawed-out corpsicles, the eight we saw sitting in the Wong clip. He laments the fact that two of the cold coffins malfunctioned; Garbhán Rustad and Wendelin Leonhardt have died en route. So he says.

"The first tranche of ten included the four members of the Steering Board. The other six were next to be thawed out—understandably so because they included the Board members' own spouses. There is a recording of Vandam welcoming them, and there, he speaks of the thirty crew members."

That was the fragment that Mrs. Wills had shown to Doig on his last day in her schoolroom. He had noticed that discrepancy and been careful not to say so. How had she obtained that forgotten video? Whose side had she been on—Dad's or the Board's?

"Fair enough," Dad continued. "So, the captain didn't know of the fatalities then? He learned of them later when the third-tranche corpsicles were about to be brought out? That's the official version, but I don't believe it. Consider the members of the steering committee. They have a new world below them and no choice but to land their spaceship and try to survive there. Four of them! Wouldn't one of their first actions be to check on their twenty-six fellow travellers? Of course, it would! And at that time, they were all alive.

"It was only later that two of the machines flatlined. Someone pulled the plug on them. Garbhán Rustad and Wendelin Leonhardt were murdered. By whom? I don't know and never will. It could have been whoever chose the ship's name. And perhaps they had to die if the life support system had decayed so much that it could not support thirty people.

"When Ivan Wong's name was pulled out of the bowl, how many names were in the bowl? Again, we can never know. No women's names, of course—brood mares were too precious to risk. I suspect that all the names were those of the shaky, still not completely recuperated third-tranche males. Would a fitter man have survived the first encounter with Neweden fauna? Probably not. Anyone other than a dendrologist might not have gone to examine the heap of timber. Nobody knew of the spiders, but I cannot help wondering if Wong was sent into whatever danger might lurk out there because he was male and physically vulnerable.

"An hour after *Moctezuma* landed, the thirty were down to twenty-six. Leonhardt, Rustad, Wong, and Whitehead had all gone, leaving fifteen women and eleven men. Four of the women were widows, but they did their duty. The four of them were ultimately to foster forty cargo babies and produce twenty-nine babies of their own.

"Who were the fathers? We can never know that, can we? Because the steering committee decreed that only legally married fathers could pass on their family names. Out-of-wedlock babies were named after their mothers. Perhaps some of the men had two wives, or perhaps the excess women were shared around, but Leonhardt, Rustad, and Whitehead left no descendants. Wong's case was exceptional, which is why we have twelve crew names, not eleven.

"The women on Neweden lost their freedom right there! I do not demean them if I say that they were predisposed to serve as breeders—they made that decision when they enlisted. By the terms of the charter, the four members of the steering committee were to decide which planet would be settled. Rightly or wrongly, they rejected the first two and then had to accept the third. Then they were to thaw out the other twenty-six and take a vote on where in this world the ship would land. Within six months of landing, the committee was to call elections to form a governing council.

"But somewhere in the tumult of fighting off spiders, growing crops, and gestating babies, the charter was forgotten. Descendants of the original steering committee govern us still, only now, they call themselves the Board of Directors. In five centuries, only descendants of those twelve men have ever sat on the Board."

A hand came into view, holding a cup. Dad accepted it gratefully and drank.

"Now that I've proved how the Board lies to you, I want to give you an idea of how deadly their policies are and how the colony is doomed to extinction. The spiders will win!"

With a jolt, Doig realized that the ceiling lights were glowing brighter, indicating that morning had arrived. He pulled out the stud, turned off the viewbox, and ran. Out in the corridor, he slowed to a more normal pace. When he reached 223, he replaced the two rooks in the box, hid the box under his clothes again, and dived into bed.

He was just in time. A few moments later, there was a perfunctory tap on his door, and in walked Buster, wearing sandals and swimming trunks.

"Lazy, lazy!"

"Let me guess," Doig said. "Either you are determined to drag me off to the pool with you at this inhuman hour, or you are seeking congratulations on a new chest hair. What will that make? Three?"

"Even one would be good at my age," Buster retorted reasonably. "But if you don't get out of that sweaty heap pronto, I shall drag you to the pool naked. That'll give the girls a real laugh."

Doig sighed and threw back the covers, revealing that he was fully dressed. Buster opened his mouth to demand an explanation. Doig put a finger to his lips to warn that eavesdroppers might be listening.

Paranoia!

AFTER BUSTER HAD swum twenty laps and Doig ten, they dressed and met again at the cafeteria, where Doig ate a hearty breakfast and Buster two. "What now, boss? I've got no classes I can't skip. Workout at the gym? You know how to play squash?"

"I've got family I'd like to look up, Thatcher and Sarah Doig. My mom thinks they may live at 1567 Lee Avenue."

Buster pulled a face. "That's not a good part of town. Year-round bunker dwellers. And it's a long walk."

"I wouldn't want to tire you."

"Very thoughtful of you. Why don't we run it?"

THEY COULDN'T RUN much of it because there were too many people in the corridors. It was a very long way by Copper Island standards, probably ten kilometres, all of it underground. It made Doig wonder how many of the last five hundred years the colony had spent just digging.

Lee Avenue, when they reached it, was narrow and dim, almost as dismal as a tunnel on the island. The air was as bad, too. All of which told Doig how his attitude had changed already. He had never realized that he had been raised in a prison camp.

The door of 1567 was warped and splitting, but light showed through the cracks. Not wanting to damage his knuckles, he thumped on it with the side of his fist and got a splinter.

It was opened almost at once by a man of about twenty wearing a towel around his waist and shaving soap on one side of his face. He did not look pleased at having his toilet interrupted. "Who're you?"

"Hi. We're looking for Mr. and Mrs. Thatcher Doig."

"They're at work. I'm Boris. Whatcha want?"

"I guess I'm your cousin, Doig Gray."

Boris curled his freshly shaven upper lip. "The traitor's son? We heard the news 'bout him, thank you, and we all agreed it's long overdue."

"Are there many more of you in there, Boris?"

"That is none of your business."

Buster laid a weighty hand on Doig's shoulder. "He's a smidgen out of your weight class, boss. You want me to fix him for you?"

"No," Doig said. "Well, Cousin, I'm enrolled in Wong

University now, in case you want to invite me to any birthday parties or something. Or if you need a letter written, maybe. Glad to help."

"Why should we? You didn't invite us to the funeral, although we'd have really enjoyed that after all these years of living with the shame of having a traitor in the family."

Boris closed the door.

"Let's jog back," Buster said, "and I'll show you how to play squash."

TWO DAYS later came the Hear-This that rain was falling up-top, the snow was melting, and students could start moving into the cabins up there. To Buster, that meant immediately, of course.

Doig had made no more efforts to study Dad's files, so only when he was packing did he learn that the chess set had gone. He had no doubt that the Board had taken it. The Accident Squad was watching him, and he had blundered by trying to hide it. If he had left it in clear sight—as Dad always had—the searchers might have ignored it.

More games are lost than won.

2: FIVE-TEN

MAYDAY WAS the official start of summer and a traditional holiday. As it was also Graduation Day for Ivan M. Wong Memorial ("the Only") University, a crowd of several hundred had gathered in Vandam Square to watch Chancellor Finn hand out diplomas.

Vandam Square marked the centre of the Town. The Town was a downright ugly settlement, bearing no comparison to the great, wondrous cities of Earth seen in the ancient videos. Much of it lay completely underground. All the surface buildings were basically pits cut into the pumice, which was brought out in blocks to build an igloo-like dome over the hole. A poor family would be crammed into a single dome, but a wealthy crewman's house might comprise half a dozen, so the city as a whole looked like stone froth. Roofs were adorned with solar panels. The Pale could boast no high, admirable buildings at all unless you liked wind-turbine towers, which howled for days on end in the summer storms.

Judging by the humidity and the ominous calm, there might be a storm on the way already. Trees and other vegeta-

tion were discouraged in the Town because they attracted
spider vermin, so there was no shade to be had in the square
except under a temporary awning at the south end, where the
chancellor and other dignitaries were gathered. Everyone else—
meaning mostly students and their families—just stood around
and watched, males sometimes whooping for an especially
pretty girl.

An hour before sunset, the temperature was still in the high
thirties. The ground was too hot to sit on, and only the dignitaries had chairs, so everyone else just stood. Few people wore
more than the minimum the law allowed, namely shorts,
sandals, blazer, and name tag on a neckband. Women could
skip the neckband and pin the tag on their bras.

The year's graduates were gathered to one side of the
awning, waiting until Aliyah Suleyman spoke their name into a
microphone, which boomed it out of loudspeakers. Then they
would come forward, and Aliyah would give the diploma to
Gunter Finn, who handed over the sacred piece of paper. If the
graduate had a crew surname, the chancellor would shake their
hand. If not, not. Then they were free to go. For three years,
Doig had watched the ceremony as a spectator and considered
it a meagre way to honour several years' labour.

When it was his turn, he left the group and strolled toward
old Guntur, more often known as Grunter. His walk took only
a few moments, but as he progressed, he became aware of a
curious low noise, growing louder. He thought for a moment
that it was thunder, but it wasn't. It was cheering.

Oh, crud! They were cheering him! The whole square was
full of noisy maniacs waving their arms and howling his name.
Whose idea had this been?

Idiots! Idiots! Why couldn't they see that shouting Doig's
name was practically inviting the Accident Squad to come and
get him? Like father, like son—the Board never tolerated

dissent. Its policy had always been to chop off any head that rose above the crowd. He wondered if the ovation had been started by Board moles, *agents provocateurs*.

Grunter Finn was peering around in bewilderment, forgetting to hand over the diploma. Predictably, he turned to the trusty Aliyah for guidance.

Disgusted, Doig took the paper from the chancellor's hand and stalked off. The cheering redoubled and then faded away.

Idiots! Idiots!

FOR FOUR YEARS, Doig had studied and learned. He had begun by learning that he already knew more than most of his contemporaries did, thanks more to his parents than to the teachers on Copper Island. He had also realized that very few students were as smart as he was. He had tried hard not to let that show, fudging his exams to stay within the pack. Most of the time, when supposed to be studying, he had been prying into the old colonial records. In three years, he had learned a great deal more than he had been taught, but he still could not see how to use that information against the cabal that ruled the planet.

On his sabbatical quarters, he had always chosen to take Harvest Quarter off to help in the fields of the Purlieu—roasting in September, freezing in November. He had learned how to drive a spider-mule cart. More importantly, he had learned a lot about life and work and people. Now, he was fit, fully grown, and could no longer pose as a student, so he should be ready to join the family business of advocating revolution.

Five years ago, an orphaned boy had sworn revenge. As a young man, he had not forgotten that oath, but he had discovered more important goals that must take priority. Yet, he had no clear idea of how to begin. If there was any opposition movement at all, it was so far underground that he had never heard a whisper of it. No one had ever tried to enlist him.

He had no job lined up because prospective employers shied away from hiring the son of the infamous traitor. They might sympathize in secret, but either they would not risk drawing the Board's attention to their business, or they were warned off as soon as he applied. He must eat, so he must find a job, and the last resort would be working for the government— teaching, sweeping streets, basic nursing care. There, he was sure, he would be readily accepted because there, the Board could watch him better.

He even lacked a place to call home. This last quarter, he had lived in one of the student sheds, officially called cabins, but in practice, merely flimsy wicker shacks. He was supposed to have moved out of there yesterday, April 28, but no one would care if he stayed on as long as he could stand the steadily increasing heat and wild weather that foretold the coming of perihelion. Life there was better now, as the increasing temperatures suppressed the spider vermin. It was an old joke that you could tell students by the bite marks.

He went in and tossed his diploma on the clothes hamper. Then he stretched out on the bed to stare at the fading sunlight visible through the chinks in the walls. Now what? Tonight, there would be the traditional communal carouse at the Trog's Rest. Tomorrow—reality!

Where exactly did one begin a revolution? He wondered if he was secretly waiting for the Board to make the first move. After today's obscene cheering in Vandam Square, they couldn't claim to have forgotten about him. They might appoint him headmaster of Copper Island High, for example: a lifetime career, acceptance mandatory.

As always, thoughts of the island awoke his longing to know

where his mother and sisters were and how they fared. Communication with the island was limited to radio, to which cargo had no access, so Doig had heard nothing of his family since he came to the Pale. While he had won access to most of the Board's technical files, he still could not retrieve crewmen's personal data, so he had no idea where Hassan Finn was.

The voicebox clicked and said, "Doig? You in?"

Doig sprang from bed to stool in one easy movement and hit the switch. "Buster? You back in town?"

"I am, and heading for the Trog. I'll buy you a beer."

"I'll buy you two. Five minutes!" Traditionally, beer was free at the Trog's Rest on Mayday because it was about to close down for the summer.

He strode out into the breathlessly hot night. Streetlights were posted no higher than shoulder height in the Town, so on a clear night, you could always see the sky bedecked with stars. The glorious Summer Cluster was just starting to rise in the east.

Soon, he heard ahead of him a steady roar of speech and laughter from the Trog's Rest—the above-ground equivalent of the underground's Mudhole—the students' watering place during up-top quarters, mostly shunned by town residents. He could even see the glow of the Trog's Rest's lights on adjacent buildings. There was no shortage of power in summer, when the weather alternated between sunlight almost melting solar panels and storms spinning wind turbines in a manic frenzy.

Unlike most buildings, the saloon was open to the weather, with just a roof of solar panels supported on posts. In winter and summer, it was deserted. Closer yet, Doig began to detect the odours of sweat and vomit. Several younger celebrants were sitting on the street outside, leaning against the wall, out cold, if anything could be cold on such a night. A couple of senior men were keeping an eye on them to make sure nobody choked.

The crowd was solid. He elbowed his way in, looking for Buster, who was always either late or early, never on time.

A youth he knew looked twice at him and then said, "Mr. Gray! I'm with you, sir."

Only crewmen were ever addressed as "sir."

Before Doig could comment, two more joined in with "Me, too!" and the acclaim began to spread as heads turned to welcome the newcomer. Seeing an empty stool against the wall, Doig sprang up on it and raised his arms for silence. He got a cheer instead. *Vandam's hairy ass!* Again, his supporters were practically shouting for the Accident Squad to come and get him.

When the drunken tumult faded, and the whole big room was silent except for the whir of the fans, he bellowed, "My name is Doig Gray." He received more hoots of approval. "You are cheering my father, not me. Pablo Gray is dead! I am a loyal colonist, not a traitor, understand? I do not lead revolutions! I do not support revolutions! So shut up, you fatheads, and go on with the party."

He jumped down and sat on the stool. Half a dozen mugs of beer were at once thumped down on the table beside him, most of them almost empty. As Buster's sister had told him on his first day, students talked of revolution a lot but never did anything about it. Their parents talked less but did no more.

He chose a full mug and drank deeply. He took salt tablets from the dish provided and swallowed them to replace what he had lost in sweat.

When he set the mug down, he saw another stool approaching over the packed heads and recognized the brawny arm supporting it. In a moment, Buster squeezed out of the throng, clutching a beer in his free hand. He set that down, and they clasped hands in greeting.

Buster had graduated at the end of January and—typically

—volunteered to work on the Frontier Squad, which paid well but was by far the most dangerous occupation on the planet. Assessing him, Doig noted a deep tan, even more muscle than before, and eyes that seemed to have aged five years, not just fifteen weeks. Had life stopped being all fun?

"Must be nice to be popular," Buster said and refilled his mug from the collection on the table.

"Farting idiots. Think they're trying to get me killed?"

"Not trying to, but likely to."

"Why, for ancestors' sake? I've done nothing."

"You've become a legend," Buster said with a smirk.

"I'm not a legend; I'm a myth." Doig drank more beer to see if that would help. It didn't.

"You're a born leader, that's why," Buster said with unusual solemnity. "You're mega-smart, but you try not to show it. You treat everyone the same, no matter who they are. You never make enemies. You almost never make mistakes. People appreciate these things, even if they don't understand what they're sensing."

"I sense that you've had far too much beer."

"Not yet, I haven't. But congratulations on achieving adulthood, Doctor Gray. What're you going to do now?"

Doig sighed and leaned back against the wall. "I know what I'd like to do, Professor Bruknar. I just don't know how to go about it. The Board has its eye on me, I'm certain. One bad move, and it's back to Copper Island for me. Or worse."

Buster nodded. "You once mentioned an ambition to hang a certain crewman's vital organs on your wall."

"I haven't forgotten him, but I have never seen the man with a cast in his eye around Town. He may be dead already, for all I know. If not, he stays out of sight on Touchdown Island. Besides, if I go after Dhaval Guldberg, Dhaval Guldberg will be certain to come after me." Revenge would need patience and careful planning. "I must put duty before pleasure."

"Duty being?"

"Saving the colony from the Board."

"Good luck with that. Still no news of your mom?"

"None. How was the frontier?"

"Grim," Buster admitted. "I should have listened to you. Things are not what they say they are out there, Doig. We're told that the Purlieu itself is enclosed by two fences, fifty metres apart, with the space between them cleared to make a killing ground for any spiders that get through or over the outer fence, right? Maybe it was once, but it's not now. In most places, it's a single fence of copper mesh.

"We're also told that the Purlieu Squad is building another fence outside the outer fence to enlarge our farmland, right? Wrong again. I doubt we extended our purlieu by one hectare all the time I was out there. The outside is dense jungle, with a spider behind every tree. The wolves won't touch the wire itself, but they can bite through trees. A wolf can do in half a minute what takes me half a day with a saw, plus the rest of the day sharpening the saw again. So now, they've learned how to drop whole trees on the fence and come swarming through the gap. We spent far more time repairing the damage than we did expanding the Pale. We were hunters and hunted, not builders."

"Many men lost?"

"Three on my gang. Overall, at least a dozen."

That explained Buster's sombre look, but Doig was not surprised. Anonymous hands had laid more mugs on the table with enough beer to float a ferry. He selected one. "Do you know why the starship was named *Moctezuma*?"

Buster blinked at the apparent change of subject. "No, but I have a feeling that I'm about to."

"Moctezuma was a stone-age emperor in southern North America. A handful of brigands under a man called Hernando Cortes killed him and stole his empire."

Buster stuck out his jaw. "Why name a colony ship after the loser? Wouldn't *Cortes* have sounded better?"

"Moctezuma was reputed to keep thousands of concubines."

Concubines such as, to pick one example, Buster's sister, Carina. Buster's face darkened, and his knuckles whitened. "You telling me that the Board deliberately murders cargo boys to leave more girls for the crewmen?"

"Yes! Yes! And yes! Not deliberately murders, but puts them in harm's way as much as possible. Moctezuma did that, except he had the losers sacrificed in public, on pyramids, and then eaten. Same principle. Here, they usually feed us to the wolves, which leave no bodies to be counted. And it started before the starship even landed."

"Whitehead and . . .?"

"Leonhardt. They were murdered. The cold coffins were all working when the steering Board was awakened, but two 'malfunctioned' later. I wonder how many pretty girls Chairman Ruckles has to play with?"

"As many as he can keep bearing, I expect," Buster growled. "That's how Carina escaped from old Guntur Finn. She filed a complaint that he'd been screwing her for years but had given her nothing to show for it, so she was being wasted."

"But then they assigned her to someone else, didn't they? She wasn't free to choose a husband?"

Buster grinned as he raised another mug. "She'd made previous arrangements. She had an understanding with a younger, up-and-coming crewman. He's the one who filed the complaint, and he's already got her working on a nephew for me."

"Congratulations!" If motherhood was what Carina wanted, then that was the way to go about it. *If you can't fight them, join them.* "Would there be any chance that she could arrange for me to make a pitch to her up-and-coming crewman?"

"I can ask her. What have you got in mind?"

"Saving the human race from extinction on Neweden."

Before Buster could comment, a stool scraped on the floor, and another man joined them.

Doig immediately recognized him. His name was Saul Lama, and he had been Doig's contemporary as a student. He had not been present at the graduation that morning, likely because he had been erratic in his choice of classes, skipping some quarters, so he would not have collected the required minimum credits. He was gaunt, a human skeleton, his bare chest narrow and hairless. His manner was, as always, furtive. He seemed to have few friends, and Doig distrusted him, although he did not know why.

Buster, who was unhappy with mediums and never occupied the middle ground on anything, actively disliked him. "This is a private discussion."

Saul said, "So you had better leave."

Doig felt tingles of apprehension flavoured with a curious flicker of excitement. "No. Buster will stay and listen to your proposal."

"What makes you think I have a proposal?" Saul said softly. Perhaps because of his lack of flesh, he never seemed to sweat. Even there in the Trog Sauna, his face wasn't shiny. Buster's was wetter than the beer-soaked table, and Doig had dribbles running down his ribs. Saul must belong to a cold-blooded species.

"Intuition," Doig said. While he didn't think Saul was a member of the Accident Squad, he might be one of their helpers. "Your smile is wonderfully sinister. Do you practice it in a mirror?"

Saul had zero sense of humour. "Six or seven years ago, somebody broke into some very private files and has been rummaging through them ever since." His voice was barely audible over the racket.

"You think that was me? Six years ago, I was only a child."

"The rightful owners can still detect when the records are being accessed, though. The intrusions stopped for a couple of months in early 505; then they resumed and have continued intermittently ever since."

Buster made a chortling noise and hunted through the mug forest to find more beer.

"And you are accusing me?" Doig asked.

"Oh, we couldn't expect you to admit to a major crime like that."

"My father never told me any passwords."

"I never said he did."

"And who are 'we'?"

Saul removed his LAMA nametag, slid it into the pocket of his shorts, and brought out another, which read VANDAM.

"It's a major crime for cargo to wear crew nametags," Buster said.

"But the reverse isn't."

"Ha! I wondered why you always made me want to puke. Five years spying for the Board? How often did you file your reports—weekly? Daily? Hourly?"

"Where is this leading, sir?" Doig asked.

Saul produced a small roll of paper tied with a ribbon. He offered it to Doig. "An invitation from my Uncle Waldo to spend perihelion with him and Aunt Mabel on Touchdown."

Buster thumped his beer mug down on the table so hard that it splashed. "You must think he's absolutely shrieking crazy! You think he knows a password you want, and you expect him to go to Touchdown so you can torture it out of him?"

Lowering his voice even further, Saul whispered, "Go away, you stupid musclebound lout."

"Would you please put that cargo name tag back on again for a couple of minutes so I can beat all the fucking crap out of you?"

Doig was still staring at an invitation that was at once incredible and yet somehow not unexpected. The Board had made a martyr out of his father and would not want to make the same mistake with him. He had often wondered if they might just try to buy him, but the idea had always seemed too absurd to believe.

> *Chairman and Mrs. Ruckles cordially request the*
> *pleasure and honour of the company of Mr. Doig Gray*
> *as their guest on Touchdown over the coming perihelion*
> *vacation. Other members of the Board will attend and*
> *look forward to discussing with Mr. Gray any and all*
> *problems of mutual interest. In the names of his*
> *ancestors, the chairman extends to Mr. Gray his*
> *personal guarantee of safety.*
>
> *(Signed) W. Ruckles, Chairman*

Personal guarantee be damned! These were the scum who had murdered his father and turned his mother into a whore. Trusting them would be a huge risk.

On the other hand, here was the answer to his problem, handed to him.

More games are lost than won. Had the other side just made a mistake here, or was he about to?

He handed the paper to Buster. "When and how do I go?" he asked Saul.

"Shit!" The outraged Buster hurled his mug down on the floor. It shattered, provoking shouts of protest from owners of nearby bare legs.

"Start of perihelion," Saul said, as calmly as if Doig's acceptance had never been in doubt. "We must catch the tide, so it'll be either at sunrise or sunset."

The perihelion break officially covered the two weeks from June 8 through July 7, when direct sunlight delivered third-degree burns.

"I am happy to accept the invitation. Will you pass that on, or must I write a formal acceptance?"

"You would be insane to refuse. I'll tell Aunt Mabel. Where can I get in touch with you?"

"Down under," Doig said. "I've decided to enrol in one postgrad class." That decision was less than two seconds old, and a flicker of surprise in Saul's cold eyes suggested that he had expected otherwise. Aliyah Suleyman would arrange it, though, and backdate it. She would even fake a scholarship if Doig asked.

Saul stood up. "I'll wire you as soon as I know exactly. And you, Loudmouth Bruknar, will be going back for another tour on the Frontier Squad. Let's hope the spiders have better luck this time." He oozed off into the crowd.

"Slime!" Buster said.

"Just ambitious," Doig said, his mind wrestling with more important problems than Saul Lama-Vandam. "If he's nasty enough, he may get appointed to the Board one day. Bb5 a6? Hard to see Saul as a bishop, though."

"What the Vandam—"

"Chess. Defence against the Ruy Lopez opening."

"You are crazy."

"Or Ruckles is. They made my dad a martyr, so they're going to try to buy me—a crew bride and a plushy job, maybe?'

"Congratulations. I'll be thinking of you as the spiders cut me up."

"I didn't say I was going to accept. And they won't dare try any rough stuff while I'm Ruckles's guest."

"You're betting your life on that?"

Doig eyed all the sweaty backs around them and decided that nobody could possibly be eavesdropping in such a din. "Listen," he whispered. "You know those Hear-Thises that flash up on every viewbox and voicebox whenever there's an emergency? Like a spider intrusion? I'm almost certain that I can hack into that system."

"'Almost' is a weighty word. Almost dead or almost alive?"

"So, the day I step on the Touchdown ferry, it will be officially announced—*my* officially—that Chairman Ruckles and the Board have invited Doig Gray to Touchdown for consultations."

Buster's eyes widened. "That'll make them go apoplectic!"

"But if I don't come back, everyone will know who did it and where." Ever since leaving Copper Island, Doig had cherished a secret dream of picking up the banner that Dad had dropped, and the enemy had just handed him a way to establish himself as leader of the opposition. *More games are lost than won.* True, but not always helpful.

"You are criminally insane, but it's been fun knowing you."

Doig said, "I'm more worried about you, buddy. Saul was serious about conscripting you to a lifetime job on the Frontier Squad."

"Me?" Buster exclaimed. "You're the one who's walking into the spiders' den. Let's get some more beer and drink each other's health."

BEING AN ADULT NOW, Doig drank much less of the Trog's watery beer than he had on previous Maydays, and his gait was steady as he plodded homeward. Tomorrow, he would see Aliyah about enrolling in some course or other—Advanced Machiavellianism, perhaps? That might help him work out what the chairman was up to with his sweetie-pie house party invitation. Ruckles must have been watching too many third-millennium videos.

Doig took his bucket from just inside the door and went to fill it at the communal well. When he returned, he did not turn on his lamp because the wicker walls let in enough of the outside illumination but provided little privacy. He stripped and washed himself to remove the sweat, knowing that he would replace it all during the night. Days were bad enough, nights were worse, and that weird invitation was not going to help him sleep. He could also look forward to the drunks from Trog's Rest trouping back here, raucous and randy.

He had just begun brushing his teeth when there came a tap on the door—a gentle tap, certainly not Buster's, probably not even male. He had, alas, no intimate girlfriend who might come calling at this time of night.

"Just a moment!" he said—quietly because sound went right through the wicker. He dropped his brush and wiped his mouth. "Enter."

The door opened, and a girl peered in. Not a young woman —a girl of around nine or ten. In the dim light, she looked vaguely familiar, but child molestation was punishable by death and certainly not one of his vices. He couldn't afford vices. Was this some effort to entrap him?

"I don't know you," he said, "so would you please—"

She put her finger to her lips and beckoned.

He shook his head. "Go away."

She came in and followed as he backed away. "You used to know me, Doig." She grinned.

"Helen!" At the last moment, he managed to turn a shout into a whisper. They collided and hugged. He lifted her up and swung her around. "Oh, Helen! You've grown."

"Not as much as you have. Follow me and keep quiet."

She led him outside. Every summer, the storms blew some of the shacks to pieces, and the replacements were never quite the same, so over the years, the student settlement had become a maniacal maze. After several twists and turns, Helen stopped outside a door. "Remember to keep quiet," she whispered.

By then, Doig had guessed. He went in. There was only one person present, a shadowy shape in the near-darkness, but he knew who she was, and she held out her arms.

"Mom!" Another embrace. How small she was! They had been the same height when they parted, and now she barely came up to his chin. They hugged for a moment without speaking. Four years!

The door clicked shut. Helen had gone.

"She's going to keep watch," his mother said and sat down on the edge of the bed—the shack had been stripped of everything else, even the mattress. And even the voicebox, which was always assumed to include a bug.

Doig settled beside her.

"She may find lots of things she shouldn't watch. Oh, Mom! How are you? How's Camilla?" Other questions boiled in his mind: why had she waited so long? Where was she living? *How* was she living, which in a woman's case almost invariably meant with whom?

"Cammy's fine. I'm not supposed to be here, but Helen went to watch your graduation. Doig, Doig, why in the world did you have them cheer you like that, Son? That was crazy. What—"

"I had nothing to do with it, Mom. It happened again tonight at the beer wallow."

"If not you, then who's doing it?" she said in an angry-parent tone.

"It could be the Board, trying to make me seem like a rabble-rouser, but I think it's just . . . hard to explain. People see me as Dad's heir, his successor. They've made me into a legend."

"Well, tell them to stop! You know what happened to your father. Find yourself a good job and a nice wife and settle down."

It was strange to be mothered again after so long. Perhaps in daylight, she would realize that he wasn't a child anymore. He certainly wasn't going to tell her about the chairman's invitation to visit Touchdown; she'd go supernova.

"When did you come back from the island, Mom? Why didn't you get in touch with me?"

"I came back with Hassan when his tour finished. And I didn't look you up because he told me not—"

Doig leaped to his feet. "You're not still with that muscle-bound troll, are you?"

"Sit down and don't shout."

He was not shouting. He did not sit down. He was shaking. "I swore I'd kill that ugly, slobbering—"

"Don't be childish, Doig. You'll get yourself thrown to the spiders."

"He made you a whore!"

"He saved me from being a whore. You know what happens to single women on Copper Island. You were fifteen when you lost your father. Your brother isn't three yet."

"B-b-brother?"

"Jean-Luc Doig."

A sudden urge to vomit stopped Doig from saying anything for a moment. His mother caught his hand and pulled him down beside her.

"Hassan was true to his word. He brought us back with him to the Pale as he promised. He's been a good father to your sisters, and so far, he hasn't brought any other women into the household."

Doig could believe that. What man would marry his daughter to a Finn or a Lee? What woman would choose such a husband? Not that a cargo woman would have any say in the matter if a crewman fancied her.

And what was wrong with his mother's voice? She sounded as if she had lost a lot of teeth. Why did she keep her head turned so that he could only see the right side of her face? In case he might see bruises, visible even in this light? Was that Finn swine beating her?

"He isn't too swift," she said, "but he tries to be a good man. He treats me well. Tonight, he's gone to the gym as usual, but then, he's going to watch the wrestling. I promised him I wouldn't go out, but then Helen came home and told me about that cheering this afternoon. Doig, Doig, don't make the mistakes your father made! Stay away from the Board. Don't make them angry."

"Tell me what Dad was up to on the island. Why did they set the Accident Squad on him after so long?"

"You don't need to know. Just—"

"I *do* need to know! If I'm not going to make the same mistakes Dad made, I have to know where he went wrong. Now tell me!"

Silence. He waited until finally she whispered, "They built a radio so he could contact his friends back here in the Pale. It was hidden in Cross Cut Twelve."

"What friends?"

"I'm not going to tell you. Besides, I expect they're all dead, too, by now."

Not according to what Saul Lama-Vandam had said an hour ago.

Doig tried another track. "Then listen! I know enough to know that Dad was right; the colony is dying. I am not going to start preaching revolution because it's too late for that, and I know what would happen to me if I did. What I don't know is what he thought ought to be done. He must have had a plan—didn't he?"

His mother sniffed a couple of times, and he realized that she was close to tears.

"What's the matter?"

"You sound so like him now. Your voice—"

"Good. Now tell me what Dad thought needed to be done."

She sniffed again. "I don't know! He always refused to tell me anything because he said I had to live and look after you and the girls."

"But he did have a plan?"

Silence.

"Mom! Tell me or say goodbye and go away."

Her whisper dropped to the very limit of audibility. "I don't know. He talked in his sleep sometimes. I often heard him refer to someone or something called Sabine. That was a code word, I think. And a person called Halapeno Guzman. They both seemed to excite him. Oh, Doig, please do be careful!"

"Mom, that cheering shocked me, too. But it probably frightened the Board more. They want a revolution even less than I do. Listen. Chairman Ruckles wants to meet me. Shush! He probably hopes to bribe me with some very plush job, so I won't make waves."

That was one theory, the one most likely to appeal to her. There were others.

Helen opened the door. "They're coming!"

True. Doig registered raucous voices and knew that drunken students looking for a place to shack up in would not be fussy about which shack they chose.

His mother stood up. He followed, they shared a farewell hug and exchanged mumbled farewells, and then she was gone.

THE NEXT DAY he went down to Only U and enrolled in a postgrad course in remote sensing. He spent the rest of the day in the library, researching the two clues his mother had given him.

Sabine or Sabina had been a woman's name on Old Earth, but he could find no evidence that it had ever been used on Neweden. A river in southern North America had been called Sabine. There were hills in Southern Europe by that name, which came with a legend that had been more than three millennia old even before *Moctezuma* was launched. How or why would anyone in a colony umpteen light years away have ever heard the name?

"Halapeno Guzman" was tougher. Guzman was a fairly common cargo name, with several thousand entries spread over the colony's five centuries, but he could find no usage of "Halapeno" as a given name, ever, in any family. He was about to give up when he remembered Jacinta Ruckles, archivist on the *Moctezuma*. In one of the ancient video records, her name was mentioned, and the J was not sounded. The language had changed in several ways. Sure enough, he found one incidence of a man whose name was written as Jalapeno—the eldest son of Gabriel and Wanda Guzman, born 132, sentenced to death for attempted kidnapping, executed in the spider pens, October 154.

That was a lot more helpful. Now Doig knew what to tell the Board.

JUNE 8: The eastern sky was just starting to brighten as Doig arrived at the dock gate with his pack on his back. He was about fifteen minutes early and not surprised when Saul Vandam arrived about fifteen minutes late. He, too, had a blazer hung on his belt, but his looked more effective than Doig's standard house issue. They exchanged nods, no words. Both men were well covered, with hats on and goggles handy. May's semi-nudity would be fatal this close to perihelion; the sun could char skin in seconds.

The ferry office window was closed, although chinks of light showed under the shutter. Saul beat on it several times before it flew open, displaying a black beard on a surly face. The tag below it was shadowed and illegible.

"We're closed," the beard said. "Can't you read? Next sailing July 8."

"I'm expected—Saul Vandam."

The face grew even surlier. "One of them, huh? And who's he?"

"A friend of mine."

"One hundred credits, one way."

"I said he's a friend of mine."

"And I said one hundred credits."

"One more word out of you, and you'll be issued a one-way ticket to Copper Island."

The face snarled and slammed the shutter. The gate beside it clicked, and they went through.

"It's not what you know that counts," Doig remarked, "it's who knew your mother."

"No. It's who married your mother. That's quite different."

Doig should have remembered that Saul had no sense of humour.

The sea cliffs seemed much higher, and the road down to the water much longer, than Doig remembered from that far-off day when he had arrived on the sled with Mike Murugan. That was because the tide was out, and the slippery weeds coating the last third or so of the long road showed the huge range of perihelion tides. Once, Saul slipped, and Doig caught his arm before he fell. Saul shook his hand off without a word.

The long barge-like boat that he had seen pulled up above the high-water mark back in January five years ago was now afloat, with a gang of stevedores taking bales and sacks from a cart and heaving them in through a hatch, where other men aboard received them. Two more men were tending the hawsers. As Doig watched, he saw that they were moving the boat to match the slowly rising tide, untying it from one pair of bollards and hauling it along to the next pair. Predictably, they were very large men.

By the time the passengers reached the work gang, the sky was growing lighter, much lighter. The sun had not risen yet, but its higher rays had found both Mount Moctezuma to the north and a huge cloud to the south and were painting them yellow and orange.

A slim man not much older than Doig emerged from the hatch, jumped ashore, and paused to stare at the menace in the sky. Then he turned and advanced to meet the passengers. He saluted Saul, seeming to know him of old. His tag read MELCHIOR.

"'Morning, sir."

Saul just nodded.

"I'm afraid we'll have to put this off, sir," the ferryman said, gesturing at the storm. "Don't want to get caught by that horror."

Saul shook his head. "That won't be here for hours yet."

"But the waves outrun the wind, sir, always. That's going to give us a nasty storm surge. We can see what it's like for the evening tide if that's all right with you—sir."

"It isn't. Proceed as planned." Saul had been sly and shifty when masquerading as cargo in Only U, so now he was catching up by throwing his weight around.

Melchior drew a calming breath. "Sir, the solar panels lose power in a rainstorm, sir. There's less light then, and some of them short-circuit."

"You have batteries."

"But they barely hold a charge anymore, sir. We can't get replacements, sir. The shop has run out of aluminum, sir."

"You will do as I say, boy, or I'll have your hide."

Melchior saluted again, but his jaw was clenched.

"Hi. I'm Doig."

The ferryman glanced at the GRAY name tag, clasped the hand Doig was offering in both of his own and pumped it vigorously. "I'm honoured to meet you, Mr. Gray."

"Just Doig. Can't think why you feel honoured, Captain. I haven't done anything. Yet."

"Call me Conrad. And when you're ready to start, Doig, I'll be with you all the way."

Saul Vandam was scowling. He spun on his heel and stalked over to the hatch. The stevedores stopped work to let him pass, and he climbed aboard, saluted with vulgar gestures behind his back. The ferry was not much to look at, just a long box shape with the cabin roof and most of the sides enclosed in solar panels. It had no sails or visible fans to provide drive. It was already pitching as ripples whispered of the monster swell that had sent them.

"Were you just hassling my sulky friend, or are you seriously worried?" Doig asked.

Conrad shrugged. "Bit of both. But I'll die happy if I take that asshole with me. The young ones are always the worst. And if you . . ." He stopped, puzzled—undoubtedly wondering why the son of Pablo Gray was heading to the crew's lair.

"I have been invited to spend perihelion on Touchdown so I can advise the Board on necessary improvements in planetary governance."

Any moment now, the voiceboxes and viewboxes of the Pale were going to rouse the inhabitants with the Hear-This announcing Mr. Doig Gray's visit to Touchdown to advise the Board.

"Hot pusspuss!" Conrad said. "Knock some sense into those shitheads, you mean? But keep your back to the wall while you're there, sir. You lot all done? Thanks, guys."

The stevedores inside were climbing out, the cart was empty, and dazzling flames on the eastern horizon were the edge of the sun's corona. It was time to go indoors or muffle up with gloves and goggles. The two men handling the hawsers were looking expectantly at Melchior.

"All aboard, sir," he told Doig. "Amidships is the calmest, but you're welcome to sit up front with me, sir, if you're sure your stomach will behave."

"I'll be happy to sit up front with you, Captain, although if I have to upchuck, I'd rather do it on the other guy. And I wish you'd stop calling me 'sir.' I'm a smartass kid fresh out of school, nothing more."

"Balls. You're a symbol of hope, sir!" Grinning, he gestured for Doig to go first, then clambered in behind him and closed the hatch.

A symbol of vain hope?

The interior was dim, the headroom low. Doig found himself amidships, facing four rows of three chairs apiece, all high-backed, thickly padded, and equipped with straps to keep the occupant in place when the ship pitched or rolled. Only one was close to a window slit, and Saul Vandam had already claimed it. Cargo areas forward and aft of the seating, separated from it by low walls, were currently cluttered with the bales and boxes that the stevedores had loaded.

Melchior led the way to the pilot's bench at the front, where there was at least a good view and ample room for two. Already, the ferry was rolling, pitching, and drifting away from the dock. He handed Doig a bag. "Just in case. You can empty it over that other guy after we dock."

A hum from the motors, a thrill of vibration felt in the bones, and the ferry was on its way. Despite his concerns about the weather and the reception that might be awaiting him on Touchdown, Doig was excited. This was the closest he had ever been to the sort of high technology that had brought mankind to Neweden.

When the ferry left the calm of the harbour and passed out into the Gut, it found the swell flexing its muscles and was soon moving in all directions at once.

"It's reflecting off the cliffs," Melchior said. "It'll steady when the tide really starts to run."

"How long will that be?"

"'Bout an hour."

It took less time than that before the motion simplified into a steady rocking, which was much easier to take. When the brown-mottled coast had shrunk to a landscape, Melchior cut the motors back to a whisper, explaining that he needed them only to keep the ferry from turning broadside to the swell. The sun went behind a cloud, whose shadow swept westward along the cliffs like a great drape being drawn.

"Nasty weather," Doig remarked and silently cursed himself as a nervous babbler.

"It's going to get worse," Melchior assured him. "Shouldn't be a problem as long as I can see where we're going. I'll try not to hit Touchdown straight on."

"I find that remark comforting, to some extent."

The wind began to whip the swell into foam, and rain struck like a hammer. Water streamed down the windshield. Doig did not like the way the pilot was gnawing his lip.

"Explain the bore to me. I grew up on Copper Island, and we never had tides like that."

"The Gut does it. It narrows and shallows, so the tide gets squeezed up and breaks into a wave. We need to stay just behind that, and then it'll sweep us along at thirty, forty klicks. You never moved so fast in your life!"

On the ice sled from Copper Island, Jiang and Mike had bragged of doing sixty klicks.

Doig was watching rain streaming down the windshield. "How can you tell where we are?"

"I have a compass. And I can still see the shore." But a moment later, Melchior said, "Damn! Listen."

"I can't hear . . . You mean the crackling?"

"No. That's the solar panels shorting."

"The low, deep rumble?"

"Right. That's the bore. The storm surge is driving it. It's breaking too soon, behind us." Melchior turned his head and shouted back to Vandam, "Hang on, sir! This is going to be wild." His hands ran over switches as if they were viewbox keys. Motors hummed to life, and the ferry swung around to face seaward and began to pick up speed, charging toward the approaching threat. Doig could see the white line of it steadily coming, and was reminded of the breakup he had seen from the sled years ago, practically chasing him into the harbour. The sea had almost claimed him then.

The all-points Hear-This he had pirated onto the voicebox circuit would have gone out by now. If the ferry went down with all hands, the cargo would assume that the Board had murdered him as it had murdered his father. That would be a tough way to start a revolution.

The ferry throbbed and sprayed up water in a bow wave. The roar of the bore grew louder. The white wall of death kept growing higher.

"You going to take us over that or under it?"

"Over it, I hope. If I don't take it straight on, it will roll us. Damn, it's so big already!" Again, Melchior turned the boat in an arc and called for more power. Now he was running from the bore, and inevitably, it was gaining on them. Then the whole ferry began to shake in a palsy. The bow sank, and the stern rose. Cargo slid or rolled. A sudden howl from the motors warned that the screws were out of the water. Melchior slammed a switch that turned them off. The bow was buried in foam.

"Is this normal?" Doig asked, just to see if he could speak at all.

"No. If it turns us sideways, we'll roll."

And that would be that. For a few moments, the stern swung from side to side, but then the ferry settled back to an even keel and rode the calmer surge behind the frontal surf. Melchior was able to start the motors again and gain some control. It was soon clear that they were riding the tide, but the bore itself was outrunning them.

He gave Doig a reassuring nod. "That was our white-knuckle special, reserved for our most honoured passengers."

"I do hope my buddy enjoyed it."

"I hope he crapped his pants."

But he probably hadn't. Saul was too cold-blooded to be human.

Yet the trouble was not over. The downpour grew heavier, the wind stronger and gustier. Visibility dropped to a few metres of grey sea. The ferry was rolling harder, either because Melchior was steering to the left or because the swell had changed direction. The ferryman was biting his lip again. All he had to go by was a compass and his own instincts. Even a sense of time could not be of much use when the bore had been stronger than normal.

"How do you find Touchdown?"

"Just lucky." Melchior glanced resignedly at his companion. "You're taking this very well, sir."

Flattered, Doig jerked a thumb to indicate the crewman amidships. "So's he."

"But he's done it dozens of times."

"This bad?"

"No. I never done it this bad, either."

As if satisfied by its results, the squall abruptly eased to reveal foamy breakers leaping at massive cliffs less than a hundred metres away.

Melchior sighed in relief. "That's Touchdown. Stand by for a sharp turn." He had landmarks to guide him now, and swung the boat to the left just as it cleared the island. The tide itself shot them around into the calmer water in the lee, although Doig's stomach thought he had slid over a cliff.

"What would have happened if we'd gone by here?"

"We'd have had to come back. Would have been a smoother ride 'cause there's no bore on the ebb. That's if we survived the storm."

Doig thought he had found yet another argument to put to

the Board. "How long is this antique tub of yours going to hold together?"

"Long enough, I expect. The crew need it, so they'll sacrifice other things to patch it and keep it running."

"But what's it made of?" It lacked the red, black, and green tones of copper, and the local timber was useless.

"Don't know. Some metal they salvaged from the starship. Parts of the hull, maybe."

"Is there anything of *Moctezuma* left?" Doig asked.

"I never seen it," the ferryman said, "but from what I been told, no. Not a rivet."

And there was the heart of the colony's problems.

TOUCHDOWN'S HARBOUR, named Freshwater Cove, was a cliff-wrapped bay at the west end of the island. Tufts of jungle along the skyline were a warning that spiders might lurk up there, and the only sign of five centuries of human habitation was a pier on the north shore. With the tide nearing the full, much of it must be underwater, but the visible portion was still long, continuing as a trail up the side of the cliff. It was also deserted. Doig waited with interest to see how Melchior would manage without help. He couldn't just moor the ferry because the tide was still running.

He could start by enlisting a passenger. "Doig . . . sir.. . . would you mind . . .?"

"Of course not, but you'd better use small words and lots of them."

"There's a boat hook clipped above the hatch. I'm going to pull in to that dinghy, see? If you could hook it, pull in the cable, and loop that over the cleat? Then I'll come back and make it fast."

"I think I can manage that," Doig said and freed himself from the safety straps he had worn for half the morning.

Walking aft, of course, brought him close to Saul Vandam, who gave him a cold stare, as if whatever had happened or hadn't happened was all Doig's fault. Although crew families made up a small fraction of the population, at least a quarter of the students in Only U had been crew. They had tended to keep to themselves, and, of course, they had excluded the cargo imposter, Saul Lama. His sour disposition had made him no friends amongst cargo either.

Being free to flaunt his noble ancestry now, he ought to have been more amicable, but on the night he had accosted Doig and Buster in the Trog's Rest, he had been worse than ever, and today's berating of Conrad Melchior had carried arrogance to insane extremes. He was an interesting psychological puzzle.

He had also been a spy and, very likely, a stealer of chess sets. By admitting to Doig that he was not cargo, as he had pretended to be for years, he was not behaving in the way the Accident Squad's assassins were reputed to. But what law said they had to follow any rules at all?

The bobbing dinghy was moored to a buoy, which must be on a very long tether, able to swing with the tide. Melchior edged the ferry up against it, and Doig had no trouble pulling it in with the hook. If he couldn't lead a revolution, he might make a dockhand. Melchior came back and made the ferry secure to the buoy, as he had promised. Then he removed the dinghy's rain cover and held the boat as steady as he could for the passengers to board before scrambling in himself and closing the ferry hatch. Every move showed that he was an expert at his job.

The dinghy was barely big enough for three. Melchior took up the oars. "Can I help with that?" Doig asked.

The ferryman smiled. "I think we'd go in circles. It's no great sorrow." He thereupon made rowing seem easy with long, powerful strokes. Even through goggles, the glare off the water was painful. The muggy heat was a torment, but the clouds were moving in on the sun again as the main storm approached.

Doig was intrigued by the boat itself. It was made of wood, but the finest wood he had ever seen, smooth and apparently very strong, for the planks were thin. As well as being fireproof, local timber was coarse, fibrous, and weak. It was also one of the main topics he wanted to bring before the Board—always assuming that the Board had been sincere in its offer to discuss the colony's problems with him. In this case, though, Conrad Melchior might know the answer.

Doig tapped the wood with a knuckle. "Where does this timber come from?"

"Nobody knows."

"Driftwood, then?"

Nod. "Wish we had more of it."

The dinghy grounded on the pier and bumped a couple of times in the ripples. Melchior scrambled out. Doig, not to be outdone, jumped out the other side and helped heave the little craft up beyond the current limits of the waves. The water was warm already. By the end of perihelion, it would be too hot to bear.

Saul was still sitting in the dinghy.

"Sir?" Melchior spoke softly, but there was a hint of impatience in his voice. "We must move this skiff above the high tide mark—well beyond. Will you please get out? Now? Sir?"

Saul did clamber out but continued to stare up the trail as if looking for something. "I don't think you should do that, boy."

With a sudden premonition of trouble, Doig moved around the boat, closer to the other two.

"Why not, sir?" Melchior asked, barely moving his lips.

"Because I don't see anyone coming to meet us. There's always a spare buggy left in the parking area up there, but it will only hold two, and my task is to deliver this other cargo to the house. If you stay here, you have the choice of being eaten by spiders or of going back out to the ferry and waiting there until I can send men to help you unload it after sunset. You could wait in the parking enclosure, of course. The wolves can't get in there, but scorpions can. The wolf death is quicker."

The ferryman stared at him for a long moment. Heavy drops of rain began to fall. Then he said, "And do you know why there's nobody here to meet us?"

"Tell me," Saul taunted, and Doig braced himself for trouble.

"Because, boy, they could see the storm coming and knew that nobody but a fucking inbred Lee degenerate would ever attempt the crossing in such—"

Saul struck Melchior across the face with a crack as loud as pottery hitting a flagstone floor. The ferryman's fist clenched, and he had begun to throw a punch before Doig grabbed his arm with both hands. It lifted Doig clean off the ground, which showed why the rowing had seemed so easy, but even Melchior could not connect with that weight hanging on.

"Stop it!" Doig bellowed in his ear. "He wants you to do that!"

Melchior glared at him, eye to eye and teeth bared. Then he relaxed and set Doig down. A lifetime of training took hold again.

"I think you had better do as the crewman suggests," Doig said. "Go back out to the ferry and stand watch in case the buoy drags its anchor. We'll send someone down to relieve you. Come on." The two of them pushed the dinghy back into the rising waves.

Melchior scrambled aboard. He said, "Thanks, lad," and picked up the oars.

"Our day will come," Doig said quietly. "I promise."

SAUL VANDAM WAS ALREADY PLODDING up the long trail to the top of the cliffs. Catching up with him was an ordeal, with the wind howling and spraying hot rain. At least the sun was hidden by clouds, although once in a while, its ghostly shape would glimmer through, warning of a lurking monster, huge and malevolent.

When Doig drew alongside, Saul snapped, "Prime your blazer, fool. You expect wolves to shout warnings?" He was carrying his with the safety catch off.

Doig obeyed. Eyeing his companion's skinny build, he said, "If Melchior had hit you, he would have broken your jaw."

"And I would have watched him die for it."

There was no sane reply to that. The man was mad.

If the wind grew much stronger, they would have to finish their trek on hands and knees, down among the bug and scorpion spiders. Twice, it caught Saul and sent him staggering toward the edge. Doig made no move to catch him.

At last, they reached their destination, an area of bare rock enclosed by a high wire fence. The metal, Doig noticed, was badly weathered copper but of a much higher grade than the fences he had seen on the Purlieu when he was helping with the harvest.

Most of the enclosure was empty. It contained only two vehicles, each four-wheeled and barely large enough to hold two people. Beyond it, and close on either side, was jungle. Nowhere showed a trace of green. The forest canopy had turned silvery white, re-budding its leaves to shelter them from the ferocious perihelion glare. Everything else, from the ground up to well over man-height, was a maze of repulsive fungi in every shape and size imaginable—red, brown, and white, speckled and blotched. There might be wolf spiders standing in full view there, and the eye would not make them out.

"You said there would only be one cart here . . . sir."

"They often won't start if they've been sitting here a long time. The boy's better off on the barge than walking back down the hill alone." Saul was at least five, maybe ten, years younger than the man he was calling a boy.

And if both carts wouldn't start, what then? A question not to be asked.

The rain was coming down in torrents. After a struggle with a complicated latch, Saul managed to open the gate, and Doig followed him in. "I hope you saw how this works because you'll have to open the other gate when we leave."

Who would have guessed? "Yes, sir."

"They shut with a simple push, but the wolves know our habits and lie in wait at the exit."

"You'll cover me, sir?"

"As much as I can," Saul agreed unwillingly.

"They're really smart enough to justify that complicated lock?"

"They are now. They weren't once." Saul opened the first car, climbed in, and tried the motor. It hummed into life at once.

Doig threw his pack in, then walked over to the exit gate and peered out. Even without the blinding rain, the situation could not have been more perfect for an ambush. The trail wound off into hillocky jungle, disappearing from view less than fifty metres away. Wolves could cover that distance in two seconds. The fungi lining the road provided much closer cover but were as insubstantial as foam. Any wolves hiding behind them could leap out right through them. He couldn't see any, and standing there dithering while that motor was humming could only increase his danger.

He unlatched the gate, nodded to Saul in the car, and pushed the gate wide, wishing it weren't so heavy. The car swashed through, spraying him with mud. He thrust the gate back as hard as he could, grabbed the car door handle, and leaped in on top of Saul.

The car door closed itself behind him, not slammed by anything hitting the outside, and yet his heart was clattering like a chain on a windlass back in the mines.

"The gate isn't shut," Saul said.

"Back up and push it. Sir." Nothing was going to get Doig Gray out there again now. The spiders would be rallying to the sound of the motor.

Grumbling under his breath, the crewman did as Doig suggested.

Emergency presumably over, Saul drove slowly along the trail, the car constantly rolling and bumping. Noticing how fiercely he was gripping the wheel, Doig realized that the danger couldn't be over after all. In many places, water covered the track, sometimes flowing swiftly across it. Saul forded those hazards very cautiously at a crawl.

"How deep does it have to be to short out the motor?" Doig asked.

"Shut up."

Wouldn't it have made more sense to bring both cars?

When they came to a clearing, Saul stopped the car and pointed to open water on their right. It was more of a swamp than a lake, though, with many patches of vegetation growing in it. Rippled by the wind, about two hundred metres wide, it ran off into the mist, too straight to be natural.

Doig could guess what it must be. "That's the crater *Moctezuma* made?" *And where Ivan Wong died.*

"Right."

"So there's nothing left of the ship at all?"

Saul shook his head and sent the car forward again.

"But the pioneers set up farms here on Touchdown," Doig said.

"The colony outgrew them, and the Board moved everyone to the Pale."

Doig had known about the move but not that the jungle had reclaimed the island. How long before it took over the Pale as well once humanity was extinct?

Moreover, while prying into the colony's ancient records, he had found a recording of Captain Vandam proudly announcing that Touchdown had been cleared of spiders. When had they returned? And how? Wolves couldn't swim.

THE RAIN DROPPED to a downpour and then a drizzle. The gale paused to catch its breath, and the sunlight grew dangerously bright. Both men put on goggles. Then Doig said, "What in the world is that?"

"That" was a building with vertical walls and a gable roof higher than the trees. It was like nothing he had seen or heard of on Neweden, especially since it was shiny, silvery bright, all metal but not copper.

"That's Government House," Saul said coldly. "Better known as Vandam Palace. It wasn't named after me."

No, but it *was* a palace, the sort of grandiose royal house that megalomaniacal kings and emperors of old Earth had built to overawe their subjects. None of them had claimed to rule an entire planet, of course. How much of the cannibalized *Moctezuma* had gone into building this monstrosity?

The car hummed across a swath of open ground and through an open gate into a wired enclosure much like the one at the harbour, except that it abutted Vandam Palace. Two men in goggles and sun gear emerged from the building and came to close the gate. Only then did a vehicle-sized door open to receive the visitors, and Doig had arrived at his destination.

THE GARAGE WAS PREDICTABLY large and contained more vehicles than he had ever seen all together in his life. Making no effort to park the car, Saul just stepped out, and a flunky replaced him in the driver's seat.

Doig had disembarked by that time, complete with pack, and was gaping around him. "How do they keep this place so cool?"

"It's called air conditioning," Saul said. "Originally part of the starship's life-support system, I expect. This way."

As they headed for a door, two youths in identical brown shirts and pants came forward to meet them—and bowed. *Bowed?* Doig had never seen that done in real life, only in Earth videos. The one whose shirt was embroidered with the name LOUIS had chosen him. Louis was a cargo name, of course.

Showing no surprise at Doig's cargo nametag, he said, "Welcome to Vandam Palace, sir. You would like to freshen up after your journey?"

"Yes, indeed. And a cool drink, please."

What he was offered was a spacious room with tiled walls and floor, a shower in one corner, glass-fronted closets with racks of clothes, and a bar. Louis went to the bar. "Wine, beer, fruit juice, iced water, sir?"

Doig realized that he was expected to strip and shower. After the cramped communal facilities in Only U, nudity was no problem for him, and the roominess was an extreme luxury. He proceeded to indulge in simultaneous warm water external and cool water internal.

"Ferryman Melchior is still out at the harbour. Can you see that someone goes to rescue him, please?"

"Um . . . I can mention it to someone, sir." Louis gathered up what looked like a pile of towels but turned out to be only one huge one. "Fresh clothing, sir?"

"My name is Doig, so call me that, please."

Avoiding eye contact, Louis said, "My permanent orders are to address all visitors as 'sir' or 'ma'am,' sir."

"In that case, I do prefer 'sir.' What's your first name?"

"Louis, sir."

Swathed in the elephantine towel, Doig managed to uncover his face long enough to check his helper for signs of humour. He saw none. "Louis Louis?"

"Yes, sir."

"Who was the humourist—your father or your mother?"

"My mother's family name is Louis, sir. My father's could not be established." Now, he failed to hide his understandable embarrassment, which made Doig feel like the worst sort of heel.

"I apologize for prying into your private affairs, and I admire your mother's courage. Bear your name with pride, Louis Louis. What colour shorts do you recommend to match my knees?"

But it turned out that guests in Vandam Palace wore long pants, even in summer, and shirts with puffy sleeves and lace cuffs. Louis held out a matching set in grey, which seemed an appropriate choice. Doig took them, and Louis picked up Doig's pack.

"What about the clothes I was wearing?" Doig asked.

"The laundry will deliver them to your room, sir."

He then led Doig out to a hallway, where an older man in the same plain brown livery asked his name and peered at a list before telling Louis, "East twenty-nine."

Several corridors and two staircases later, Doig asked, "How big is Vandam Palace?"

"I don't know the numbers, sir, but I am available to give you a tour anytime you find convenient. It takes about an hour. There are four wings, each with four stories aboveground."

Don't ask about belowground and who lives there. The total floor area probably exceeded the Wong University campus, but the grandeur was even more impressive than the size: high ceilings, multicoloured tiles on the floors, art on the walls. Doig could not decide whether it made him more disgusted or fearful. Why had he been brought here to see all these trappings of power? He had always assumed that crew lived better than cargo, but he had never imagined that a building like this existed on Neweden. Was he being bribed or threatened? *Probably both.*

East twenty-nine, when they reached it, was the sort of room that old videos depicted in ancient royal palaces, with thick spider-fur carpet from wall to wall and tall windows looking out on the tropical storm that raged impotently outside. The viewbox was a hundred times larger than any he had ever seen. There was even a life-sized statue of a naked woman opposite the great bed, which was about the size of a squash court, but the most welcome sight was Carina Bruknar, seated at ease in one of the thickly padded chairs.

As soon as Louis had been thanked and dismissed with a reminder about Conrad Melchior, trapped in the hell of a moored boat, Doig advanced with delight to greet his visitor.

She looked as lovely as ever, clad in a slinky, silky blue robe that suited her colouring.

"Carina! Wonderful to see you."

She offered a hand on which blue jewels glinted. "Excuse me if I don't bounce up to embrace you." She was visibly pregnant but not yet near to term.

Doig pulled another chair close. "Congratulations are in order? Buster told me you were about to make him an uncle."

"Ah, that explains why my back hurts so much! I thought I was just making a baby, but now you mention it, I am also making two uncles, one aunt, two grandmothers, and a grandfather."

"Busy lady. And who helped you organize this happy event?" An up-and-coming crewman, Buster had said.

Carina had not lost her secretive little smile. "You remember Chi Brigham? He would have been a senior when you matriculated."

"Vaguely." Crew, of course, with that name. "Big? Husky?"

"And very energetic." Meaning: a big improvement over Guntur Finn. He could not be very much over twenty even yet.

"Congratulations again. Buster's back in town, by the way." Meaning: he survived his tour on the Frontier Squad.

"Thanks, but Chi checked on him for me. Give him my regards. I may even name my little handiwork after him. Or would two Buster Bruknars be one too many, do you think?" Meaning: of course, I'm not married.

"I don't think the world could possibly have too many Buster Bruknars."

"What was that you were telling the boy about the ferryman?"

Doig told her about his journey, and she flushed with anger. "Chi has the ferries file. Press that bell push three times."

Doig looked where she pointed and obeyed. "What happens now?"

"Your servant will answer. Three means emergency, so he'd better be out of breath when he arrives."

As Doig resumed his seat, Carina said, "I know Saul Vandam. If the ferryboat is damaged, he will have cooked his own goose this time."

"He's a prick of the first water."

She smiled briefly. "His problem is that he's only legally crew."

"What's 'legally crew'?"

"His mother was a Lee, ugly and half-witted, but crew. She got it on with a junior cook—cargo, of course. That's a scandal. So the cook was adopted by an obliging Vandam to give his posthumous brat a crew name."

Posthumous? "What happened to the father?"

"A messy accident. But Saul is only legally crew. He knows it, and everyone who matters knows it."

Even if that explained everything, Doig decided, it excused nothing. He switched to his own troubles. "Carina, since you knew I was coming, you must know why I'm here. Are they trying to bribe me, threaten me, or disappear me?"

"That will be a Board decision." She hesitated as if wondering where to start. "The Board members and their womenfolk live here year-round. They invite guests to visit, especially at perihelion. It's a tradition that each of the twelve crew clans is represented here just now so that problems and disputes can be talked out. The Board members can meet at any time, of course, all year round, but their annual formal meeting with clan representatives is on July 1. That's when they assign files and so on. Last year, Chi was given the ferry file, for instance, and he's hoping for something more challenging this time. But this year, I think you will head the agenda."

"Why? I haven't done anything."

"That could be what's worrying them. You haven't done anything, and yet, somehow, you've become your father's heir. Everyone—and I do mean everyone, the whole colony—is waiting to see what you're going to do."

It was bizarre. But if anyone could work it out, it would be Carina. She was cunning, and she had a foot in both camps, crew and cargo. Doig tried again. "Buster says I've become a legend. He's right, but I don't know why."

"I'm only guessing," she said, "but I think it was your father's death that made everyone start thinking. It reminded them of his warnings; made them realize that nothing had improved in ten years and many things were getting worse. The food ration's been cut three times in that time and I know they'll have to cut it again soon. The Board isn't doing anything. Anyone who complains has an 'accident.' You are the only hope they've got."

"'They' being the cargo?"

"And some crew also. You're here, aren't you?"

A loud knock was followed immediately by the door swinging open and young Louis entering. He was panting quite convincingly. "Sir?"

"I rang," Carina said. "Who did you tell about the ferryman?"

"My supervisor, ma'am."

She groaned. "Then find Crewman Chi Brigham and tell him his secretary needs him to come here instantly. He's probably playing squash. If he isn't, put out a general Hear-This."

Without so much as a glance at Doig, Louis vanished like a soap bubble, forgetting to shut the door. Doig did so and returned.

"You will get a hearing," Carina said, as if there had been no interruption, "but probably not a public one." Then, she smiled. "Bribery is a definite possibility because two martyrs in one family would not be popular. You may even be offered adoption, so the preliminary testing will start right away, I'm sure."

"What sort of testing?"

"Fluttering eyelashes and heaving bosoms. To see if you're susceptible. Heavens, lad, you can't suppose the crew have survived all these centuries without some infusions of cargo blood? They'd all be gibbering Finns and troglodytic Lees. So, once in a while, they adopt a promising young cargo, boy or girl. Gatecrashers, like Saul Vandam's daddy, are not allowed, so don't enjoy your vacation too much, Mr. Gray, or you may make yourself even more vulnerable than you are already. But you will probably get offers. That's all right."

"That's disgusting."

"It's the way the colony is run; the way it has always been run. For it to grow, we must have babies, and there are a lot more women around than men. I was wasted on Guntur Finn. Chi and I are very happy. He already has a child by his masseuse. She and I get along well. One day, he will take a wife, which may be trickier." She frowned at his expression. "Doig, be careful! I told you that Saul Vandam's father was a junior cook? Late one evening, he was carving a roast in the kitchen and accidentally castrated himself. He must also have hamstrung himself so he couldn't walk. He just lay there and bled to death. The Accident Squad is not a legend, Doig."

Doig wanted to ask her if she knew a crewman named Dhaval Guldberg, who had a cast in one eye. He didn't because he was certain that his room would be bugged.

CHI BRIGHAM, arriving soon after that, turned out to be built on the same broad lines as Buster, only one size larger. Chi wasn't panting as hard as Louis had, but then, he had twice the lung capacity. He looked somewhat askance at finding one of his concubines in a young man's bedroom.

"This is Doig Gray, love," Carina said.

Chi said, "Ah! The heir apparent." He stepped close and offered a hand to shake, which was a considerable surprise. "So, what's the emergency?"

Carina said, "Tell him."

Doig told the story again. Brigham listened without a word, arms folded.

At the end, he said, "I appreciate your efforts, Gray. When I looked out my window this morning and saw that storm about to break, I at once called the Pale dock and told them not to let the ferry leave. Unfortunately, I was a few minutes too late. Conrad Melchior is the best we've got, the only one who could have had a hope of bringing you through that, and I'm happy to tell you that he's safe. He waited until you and Vandam had left and then followed in the second car. But Vandam's nonsense put him at considerable risk because wolves home in on moving cars. The noise from the wind may have saved him."

Encouraged, Doig said, "When we disembarked, Vandam struck him. I managed to . . . managed to get between them before anything more happened."

The big man seemed to grow bigger. "Saul Vandam? Don't know him."

"At Only U, he called himself Saul Lama."

"Mm. I think I remember him."

"I do," Carina said, "and he's a nasty piece of carrion. Legal crew, half Lee, half cargo."

"And he ordered Conrad to sail against his better judgment?"

"Yes, sir. He insisted."

"You're very green, lad," Chi said. "Melchior didn't tell me that outright because I'd have had to report Saul to the Board, and they would almost certainly support Saul against Melchior. And against you if you backed him up. I'd lose my best ferry- man, and you'd be in even greater danger than you are already. Crew always overrides cargo, understand? But the way Conrad excused 'his' mistake when he reported it to me let me guess what had happened, and now you've just come out and said it. Don't repeat it to anyone else, and deny it if you're asked."

Doig strongly wanted to ask, "Why?" but he didn't. "Thank you, sir."

Chi smiled. "However, I think I'll go and have a talk with Saul myself."

"Be careful, darling," Carina said.

"Careful not to kill him, you mean?" Chuckling, Chi started to turn and then stopped to look at Doig again. "I was told about your little voicebox Hear-This this morning. That will raise a lot of hackles when it gets around. What are you going to tell the Board?"

"Depends what they ask me, sir."

The big man shook his head in disbelief. "I hope you know what you're doing, Gray."

"I'd very much like to have a short talk with you before that meeting, sir, if that would be possible."

The crewman studied him for a moment more and then nodded. "Tell your boy to keep dressing you in grey. That will make you easier to find." He bent to give Carina a kiss and then strode off.

When they had gone, Doig wandered across the room to study the statue. It was beautifully carved, but he especially admired the way its oiled finish brought out the fine grain of the wood. Then, he investigated the inconspicuous door in the corner and discovered a luxurious private bathroom. All the pipes were made of copper, and his mind reeled when he thought of all the copper that must have gone into outfitting the palace. Then he thought of his father, grubbing his life away in those hot, cramped, badly ventilated tunnels on the island. The wonder was that he had not died sooner, which had no doubt been the intention.

LATER, Doig let Louis take him on the promised tour of Vandam Palace, which took about two hours and left Doig more furious than ever. Everywhere was adorned with pictures, sculptures, or other works of art. There were game courts, swimming pools, air conditioning, and grandiose windows (most of which were currently shuttered against the storm and the bloated sun), and there were other areas that Louis ignored and walked past. *Those must be for crew only*, Doig thought, but didn't want to embarrass Louis by asking.

He wondered if his father had ever been shown the true extent of the crew's rapacity. The starship had been designed to make a soft landing so that it could be cannibalized to provide the first colonists with both raw materials and high-tech salvage to build their settlement. Obviously, the lion's share of it all had gone into building this Valhalla, home of the gods.

He did wheedle an unwilling Louis into confirming that the reason nametags were not worn was that there was a clan dress code for men. A red shirt and blue slacks meant one crew clan, and a green shirt and white slacks another. Monochrome meant cargo, but Doig was the only cargo in sight, other than staff, who all wore brown. Women wore anything they wanted because they didn't matter; also, because most of them were married and thus had dual clan loyalty.

The tour ended back at Doig's room. "So where now?" he asked.

Louis looked puzzled. "Nowhere, sir. You've seen it all, except for residents' private quarters, of course."

"You haven't shown me where the staff live and work."

Puzzled became alarmed. "Cargo quarters are not included in the standard tour, sir."

"And I'm cargo, so this tour is not standard. Why don't you go and fetch me some brown clothes like yours, then no one will notice me?"

Louis's first reaction was horror, but after a moment, he grinned, nodded, and hurried off as if to obey, although Doig suspected that he might be going to check with higher authority. If he did, permission must have been granted very quickly because he returned in no time with the required garments. Doig changed, and the tour resumed.

The work areas were mainly underground, which was only to be expected on Neweden, where *homo sapiens* had almost become *homo troglodytes*. The kitchens and laundry were enormous. The staff's living areas were far inferior to the crew's but still well above Copper Island standards, or even the poorer parts of the Town, like the Thatcher Doigs'. What Doig noted most carefully, both upstairs and downstairs, were the exits. He had a suspicion that there might come a point where the spiders outside would seem less dangerous than the bipeds inside.

LOUIS ALSO CONDUCTED him to dinner that evening, guiding him to his assigned place, marked with his room number, E29. A hasty glance suggested that there were about thirty tables, each set for a dozen people. There was space in the great room for about twice that many, but these must be the upper crust, the *crème de la crème* of the ruling class. With white tablecloths and elaborate table settings, they were mimicking the video records of the Earth their ancestors had known, but their cutlery wasn't silver or gold, it was 3D-printed recycled spider bone.

In his years of illicit prying into the crew's secret archives, Doig had tried to estimate the colony's population. All but a few hundred of the ten thousand fertilized ova that *Moctezuma* had carried on its age-long voyage had perished unused. His best guess was that at least fifty thousand cargo and one thousand crew lived on Neweden. Even if the correct numbers were twice that, far too many of the colonists had died too young, especially young men. The original plans for the colony had predicted that the population would be well into the millions by now.

Having been one of the first to arrive, he could sit and study the others as they trooped in, each person or group guided by a brown-clad servant like Louis. Most of the men were mature, even elderly, but many of the women were young, many of them visibly pregnant. There were some young men among them, the up-and-coming types like Chi Brigham, who was escorting both Carina and another girl of about the same age. Chi wore a blue shirt and green pants, so those must mean the Brigham clan, which seemed to be fairly rare. Red above white was the most numerous.

The women wore all sorts of flashy dresses, frequently low cut or lacy. Two trophy mates per man seemed to be the limit, but no doubt others had been left at home to look after all the children.

These people were the enemy, and yet Doig knew almost nothing about them. King Evil, Chairman Waldo Ruckles himself, must be present somewhere, but Doig could not see him and had no idea what the other members of the Board looked like. Was the big man an absolute monarch, or could the lesser directors overrule him? Most critically of all, perhaps, what was the power of public opinion—not the views of the cargo plebs in the Pale, which counted for nothing—but the overall beliefs of the rest of the crew parasites he was watching as they gathered to feast? Did the Board have to take those into account? Had Doig himself been summoned here for a mock trial before this milling crowd?

Then the chair to his left was lifted back to make way for a shimmering white gown, which sat down as the chair was replaced.

An elderly, silver-haired lady with carefully starched wrinkles regarded him with deep disfavour—he was not wearing crew colours. "Are you in the correct seat, boy?"

"That is my room number, ma'am. I am Doig Gray, son of the late Pablo Gray."

Her parched face flushed under her makeup. Without a word, she rose and left the hall. Doig made a note of her room number so he could ask Louis to find out who she was and perhaps even why she had been deliberately insulted by being seated next to a baseborn slob like him.

He could not believe that she had been chosen as one of the bosom heavers that Carina had predicted. Mustn't give up hope —the chair on his right was still empty. The couple beyond it had sat down in the wrong order if the correct protocol was to alternate men and women. She was worthy of a bronze medal at least, with her un-heaved bosom enhanced by about seven months' pregnancy.

Then, his right-hand neighbour slid into place. He turned to offer her a smile of welcome, and it died stillborn. He knew her. Her face froze with shock and then blushed deep scarlet.

She was petite, curly-haired, and a never-ending fizz of fun.

Her dress was a wisp of lace, more blatant than any he had seen yet, but she had the figure and panache to justify anything. She had been a year behind him at Wong Memorial U. She was the only girl he had ever kissed.

He swallowed a gulp and said, "Babette Abraham! How wonderful to meet you here!"

"Doig Gray, you are looking well."

"And you are lovelier than ever. Don't your nipples get cold in that dress?"

"Technically, they aren't in the dress, just near it. What effect does it have on you?"

"Don't ask. You can guess." And then they both grinned. Dinner with Babette would certainly be fun, not the ordeal he had been expecting. "So, what's your real name?"

She had very long lashes but did not bat even one of them. "Babette Dattu."

"Descendant of Guy Dattu, a junior electronic engineer on *Moctezuma*."

She sighed. "And you guessed months ago that I was crew, didn't you?"

He nodded. "Much to my regret, I decided that you were off limits. What did you have in mind then, other than the carnal pleasure of abusing my body?"

"Just spying on what you were doing or planning to do. Bonus points if I could get you into bed."

"You came very close."

An anonymous arm reached in to fill her glass and then his. She raised hers in a toast. "To your success in whatever it is!"

"To the most beautiful girl in the room." He took a sip. Wine, probably. He'd always wondered how it tasted. "What are you doing here?" Then he guessed the answer and almost dropped the glass.

"Not what I thought I was doing, evidently."

No, she could never have faked that blush, so she had not been expecting him. "Which was?"

Plates had appeared in front of all eleven people now seated at the table. Doig took up a fork and poked at whatever was on the plate without noticing.

Babette did the same. "Husband hunting. Look around you. Notice lots of young men and even more young women? Look at what the women are wearing, what there is of it. Perihelion on Touchdown is the crewmen's hunting season."

"Then you are what was called a debutante back on Old Earth. Eighteen, nineteenth century or so." Doig had majored in Earth history. He hoped his expertise would find more practical applications than that.

She wrinkled her nose. "Does that make it right?"

"Not unless the wares on show have a reasonable say in the consequences." Crew girls presumably always got married. Cargo girls did so unless some crewman appropriated them first.

"In my case, I don't," Babette said, pulling a face at what she had just eaten. "My father is an incurable gambler; he is hugely in debt. If he cannot find a million credits or so by August 1, he will be degraded to cargo, and all the rest of us as well. He was even told to bring my brother, Ewan, who is very good-looking."

Doig winced. "To hunt or be hunted?"

"Whichever comes first."

"How does Ewan feel about this?"

"Terrified, like me."

Their plates were removed, others substituted.

"You weren't placed next to me because I have a million credits," he said, "because I don't. But you are expected to wield the same sort of wiles. I was invited here to meet with the

Board. They want to know what I'm up to, and I assume that you are expected to help them find out."

Babette was never slow on the uptake. She nodded. "You mean they want me to do what I failed to do last March?"

"Which was what?"

"Fuck you."

"Your delicacy of phrase is excused only by the awe-inspiring aspirations it inspires. If that was all that's involved, I would hoist you on my shoulder and carry you up to my room at a gallop. But it's not."

Plates were removed and replaced. Doig poked at whatever the new stuff was. He had been hungry when he sat down, but now he felt quite sick. He liked Babette a lot. She was fun, she was smart, and she was extremely persistent. She gave the impression that she would do anything on a dare, and he had broken off their friendship when the temptation to find out became perilously close to irresistible. That same urge was going to be very hard to refuse for the next two weeks. Even leaving sex off the agenda, he was desperately lonely and in need of a friend.

Babette said, "Hoist away. If I don't like it, I'll scream."

He swallowed a mouthful without tasting it. "Do you know Saul Vandam? He used to call himself Saul Lama."

"No. This puree is delicious, isn't it?"

"No. His father was cargo, a junior cook, here in the palace . . ."

When he finished the gruesome story, Babette had laid down her fork and was staring at him in pale horror.

He said, "I'm afraid there's more than just a million credits at stake for me, dear Babette. Much as I would love to take you up on your offer, my answer must still be no. It would give them a monstrous hold over me."

"You mean I'm the bait in a trap?"

"Why else have you been seated next to me?"

She nodded. She was being forced to choose between Doig and her family. After a moment, she rose and walked away. Doig finished the meal with an empty chair on either side of him and without having another word addressed to him.

HE KNEW her room number from the table marker, of course, and he had to pass by it on his way to his own, just four doors along from it. No one could ever accuse the Board of being overly subtle. He tapped. After a moment, the door opened a tiny crack, and then wider. He beckoned, and she stepped out into the corridor. Her eyes were red, her cheeks still damp.

"You want to come to my room and talk?" he whispered.

"Just talk?" She nodded vigorously.

"Remember that my room is certainly bugged."

Again, she nodded. "Virginal as shit."

They went along to his room. Hoping that there were no hidden cameras, only microphones, he stayed well away from her as he spoke for the benefit of the hidden audience. "Oh, darling Mavis!"

Babette loved pranks. Showing her perfect set of teeth in a huge grin, she rolled her eyes and panted loudly. "Darling! At last. Kiss me. Kiss me all over."

"Have you eaten?" he asked.

"Yes. I had a tray brought to my room."

Doig pressed the bell push. "Then you hide in the bathroom, and I'll tell Louis to fetch us a bottle of wine."

"Make it the fizzy kind, darling. And a large-size bottle. You will need lots of refreshment because I shan't ever let you stop."

He wagged a reproving finger at her. He had forbidden touching, but pornophonic conversation was well within

Babette's sense of humour. She showed her teeth again and then began kissing the back of her hand noisily.

He wouldn't dare take one sip of that wine.

Louis arrived, received his orders, and soon returned with a large bottle and two glasses. No doubt, he then went off to inform his supervisor that success was at hand.

DOIG OPENED the wine and poured out two glasses of it. He left one for Babette, then went into the bathroom and tipped all the rest into the toilet. When he returned, Babette was posed on a chair in her scandal of a dress, sipping wine and swinging one dream of a leg. No doubt she was grateful for his concession, and no doubt she would play by the letter of their agreement, but Babette would not be Babette if she didn't torment him a bit, just on principle. If his resistance did snap and he grabbed her up in his arms and . . . he tried not to think about it.

He couldn't *not* think about it.

"So when did you get here?" he asked.

They talked for a while, but afterward, he could not recall a single thing they discussed. He did remember her eyes and her smile and his longing.

She eventually broke the spell. "Tell me again why you're here?"

"Because Chairman Ruckles invited me. I haven't met him or his wife yet, but I only got here today." He yawned. "Excuse me."

"But why did he invite you?"

"Probably to ask me if I'm a traitor like my father was." *Ancestors, forgive me!*

"And are you?"

"Certainly not." He yawned again.

"You are not going to sleep yet!" Babette said loudly. "Not after so long. If you don't screw me at least twice, I will tear your eyes out."

"Then take off that ridiculous garment before I rip it to shreds."

To his alarm, she did exactly that and, in another two seconds, was stark naked. She marched over to the bed, and he admired the view in breathless silence as she staked out a central barrier with a row of pillows before climbing in. She was still playing by the agreed rules, if only marginally. "What happened to the virginal thing?" he asked.

"I am one and can prove it. Your decision."

"You think I can't resist such an offer, miss?"

"I'm very confident that you can, sir."

He should have guessed Babette would find a solution. If the Board was indeed spying on them, it could never claim that she had not done her best to seduce the designated prey. And as long as Doig behaved himself, he could not be accused of raping a crewwoman, as Saul Vandam's father had.

He stripped off his outer garments and climbed into bed on the other side. He foresaw a difficult night ahead, but it had been a very hard day. They held hands under the barrier for only a little while before he drifted off to sleep.

"OH, it's a beautiful morning for a quick screw! Is there a good hard-on anywhere close?"

Doig opened an eye. A still-naked Babette was standing by the window, peering out at the dawn.

"Of course there is, you foul-mouthed little floozy. But you're not going to get it." He slid out of bed and headed to the bathroom to relieve the pressure in his bladder. By the time he returned, she had gone. He treated himself to another twenty minutes' bed rest, then put on a robe, removed the pillows that partitioned the bed, and rang for Louis. Louis arrived promptly with a large breakfast tray. No doubt, he noted that both sides of the bed had been slept on.

"I can't possibly eat that much!" Doig said. He had been taught that no scrap of food should ever be wasted.

Louis actually smiled. "I'll see that what's left gets a good home, sir."

"You mean you have to eat my leftovers?"

"If you saw the alternative, sir, you would understand that I will adore eating your leftovers. Please ring when you're ready for your shave."

THE DAY WENT OFF VERY WELL. GOING outside in the sunshine would be both stupid and dangerous, but Vandam Palace was an infinitely more pleasant shelter than the bunkers in the Town, even Only U's bunkers. He dared to hold Babette's hand as they wandered around, exploring and enjoying. They played table tennis, exercised in the gym, and twice went swimming. He could swim faster, but she was the better diver.

Although most of the windows were shuttered against the sunlight, there were peepholes to let residents enjoy the scenery. Eastward, the Gut that had been so violent yesterday was mirror-calm; to the north, Mount Moctezuma flaunted its perfect cone, dominating the more distant and hazy Mount Ramesses; while to the west, the Gut trailed off toward the Western Ocean; and south lay the unexplored Faraway Hills.

No flunky tracked down Doig to tell him that Crewman Chi Brigham would see him now. He did catch a glimpse of

Chi playing table tennis with his masseuse. Why and when had he acquired a bandage on his left hand?

DOIG WAS LOOKING FORWARD to dinner with Babette, but their servants—Louis and Doris, respectively—led them to opposite sides of the dining room. Doig was shown to a table for twelve at which only two seats were yet occupied, but the couple had left a space between them, and that was the place that bore his room number and the chair Louis drew back for him.

Doig obediently sat where he was supposed to and nodded politely to the lady on his right, who at once greeted him with a startlingly ugly smile. She had a long nose, a very wide mouth, and a protruding rack of the largest teeth he had ever seen. She was certainly in her forties but dressed like a twenty-year-old, flaunting much mother-of-pearl jewellery. He had seen her before somewhere.

"I'm Doig Gray, ma'am."

"Oh yes, I know! Are you having fun here, Doig?"

Kindergarten? "Yes, thank you, ma'am." He turned to the man on his left, who wore a brown shirt and yellow pants, meaning that he was crew but of no clan that Doig had yet identified. He was offering a hand to shake, which Doig, of course, accepted.

"Blago Wong," the man mumbled. "My wife, Lizzie."

Doig said he was honoured. Blago's hand was softer than Chi Brigham's, but that made two crewmen who had treated him as a member of the same species. While Blago was not truly obese, he sagged. He looked soft all over as if he were a balloon with a leak in need of a gaseous infusion to reinflate. He was older than his wife, the scraps of hair he had left being white, and his scalp blotched with age spots.

Since nothing more followed, Doig decided it must be up to him to kick the conversational ball. "Do you and Mrs. Wong live here on the Island, sir?"

"Mm? Oh yes. She's the arachnologist, you know."

Doig turned to face the teeth and recalled where he had seen them before. "Of course! I should have recognized you at once, ma'am. You narrated a video on spiders." Hassan Finn had given Doig a copy, years ago. He still had it somewhere.

"Oh, that!" she simpered. "Just an introductory course. Several years ago now." About a quarter of a century ago, more likely. "Are you interested in spiders, Doig?"

"I'd be a lot happier if there weren't any."

That remark turned out to be a mistake.

"Oh, but that would wipe out practically all the fauna of Neweden! The entire biosphere would collapse. Earth had so many different phyla—*arthropoda*, *vertebrata*, *insecta*, and so on —each with its own body plan . . ."

Doig thought he detected amused glances in his direction from the rest of the chairs, as if he had been seated beside the resident Chief Bore. Even the arrival of the first course failed to slow her tirade. She could even eat with those teeth.

"Have you ever seen a queen wolf, Doig? No, of course, you haven't. We have the only one in captivity right here on Touch-down, although she isn't actually in captivity, of course . . . 'on display' would be a better description. We're going to take young Ernie out to see her after dinner. I'm sure you'd like to come, wouldn't you?"

"Of course," Doig said weakly. Was this a practical joke, a test of courage, or a quick assassination?

"He's got very good genes," her husband mumbled.

"Sir?"

"The Venugopalan boy. We're thinking of getting him adopted so that he can marry our granddaughter. Excellent genes. Strong as a tiger. Quite smart, too. He's five-eighths crew anyway."

Meaning that his mother, grandmother, and great-grandmother had all been cargo women serving as unmarried bed partners to his male crew ancestors. How did that extra one-eighth man get involved, though? Doig tried to work it out while doing justice to superb food and wasting half an ear letting Lizzie drone on about spiders and Blago blather about genealogy. He could prove, Blago said, that every cargo colonist had some crew blood in him if you just traced his ancestry far enough back. That was inevitable after five hundred years of cargo servitude and occasional crew adoption, but Doig didn't say so. The Lees' and Finns' problem was that they didn't have enough.

At one point, he managed to slide a question into a millisecond gap in Lizzie's endless lecture. "Sir, I've always been curious about your honoured ancestor, Ivan Wong. The starship set out with fifteen couples. Rustad and Leonhardt died on the journey, and Ivan Wong was slain by the spiders, as was Aberash Whitehead, while trying to rescue him. That left eleven couples and four widows, yet we have twelve crew clans."

"Oh, quite simple, lad," Wong huffed. "Madeline Wong, my esteemed ancestress, was one of the first of the women to give birth. She insisted that she had been impregnated before the voyage began, and none of the surviving men claimed credit, so she was allowed to name her son after his father as a posthumous birth. He grew up to be a lusty lad, fathering six sons of his own. Madeline went on to be very prolific, but all of her later offspring had to take her maiden name, um . . . which escapes me at the moment."

"Are you aware," Lizzie said, "that the largest tiger spider ever recorded was estimated to weigh over a tonne, and . . ."

And so it went as course after course was laid before Doig, and he played the role of meat in a conversational sandwich.

HE HAD ARRANGED with Babette that they would watch videos on the giant viewbox in her room after dinner, but Lizzie Wong pre-empted that without a thought. She would have been astonished to hear that anyone would value anything ahead of seeing a real, live queen wolf. Thus, Doig found himself accompanying the lady to the garage in the company of her granddaughter, Klara Wong, and the prospective adoptee, Ernie Venugopalan. Grandfather Blago had excused himself on the grounds that he had seen the monster before, and there was only room for four in the bus.

Klara was a meek and demure damsel who had no eyes or ears for anyone except her Ernie. Blago might have exaggerated when comparing Venugopalan's strength to that of a tiger spider, but he was tall and built on the same generous body plan as Buster Bruknar and Chi Brigham. Blago had described him as smart, but Doig would have to withhold judgment on that. On first impression, he seemed an amiable enough guy— and who would not accept promotion from cargo to crew, even if it meant having to accept such grandparents-in-law?

Doig, for one. Mouldering in a palace was not his idea of life and would be an unthinkable betrayal of his father and everything he had fought for.

The bus was waiting for them. It could carry seven people plus the driver, but the empty places were swiftly taken by armed guards. Doig managed to acquire a window seat as far as possible from Loquacious Lizzie, where he was pinned by a taciturn man named Carlo, who was forty-ish, compact, and armed with the most fearsome blazer Doig had ever seen.

He would really rather be watching videos with Babette.

The bus hummed out into the night. The sun had gone away to roast the other side of the planet, but it had left the sky ablaze with auroras, waves and walls of green and red dancing everywhere, their light bright enough to read by and yet strangely lifeless, casting no shadows. The leafless trees seemed dead, mere silvery corpses reaching upward in silent appeal. The air was as hot as a steam bath and thick with stenches of damp fungi. Much of the fungoid undergrowth was equally monochromatic, but some aberrant species amongst them fluoresced in lurid flickers of green and yellow.

At first, the road was recognizable as the way he had come from Freshwater Cove, but then the bus turned off on a trail that did not deserve even that name, being no more than a cut through the forest, largely overgrown by fast-growing fungi. The bus proceeded in a painful, lurching crawl, crushing puffballs as it went.

"What happens," Doig asked his companion, "if the bus breaks down?"

"The House will send out other vehicles."

"You can radio for help?"

Carlo snorted. "That would really bring the buggers swarming! No, we'd just sit and stew until we were missed." His manner suggested that he disapproved of the whole idea of the expedition. Doig would applaud that motion heartily.

"The reason the ground is so irregular—" Lizzie Wong was on her feet, hanging onto a strap and speaking to everyone whether they liked it or not, "—is that we are currently driving over the remains of Vandam City, the first human settlement. It was built in the first century with blocks of pumice, which proved unsuitable as a building material. Many of the houses collapsed during heavy rainstorms. After Ira Vandam died, the main colony was moved to the Pale, where the pumice is of better quality and thickness. I do hope nobody is susceptible to seasickness?"

She should have asked that sooner.

"Now, the wolf queen you are about to view was captured as a cub twenty-five years ago. She continues to grow and produce young, one every few days. The males scour the countryside for food and bring it back to feed their dam. If they fail to find enough to satisfy her, she will eat them instead. That is their destined fate—to return their substance to their mother. Dead males are scavenged and brought back as more fodder."

Klara made a gagging noise, which Lizzie ignored.

"What do the females do?" The deep rumble came from Venugopalan.

"A female is immune to her brothers while she's still immature. Later, she wanders away and gets caught by some other pack. If she's lucky, she'll land up in the territory of a queen that has just died, in which case, the surviving males switch their loyalty and adopt her. Females can live a long time. Our wolf queen's predecessor lived to the ripe old age of sixty-three."

If the first colonists had cleared Touchdown Island of all predatory fauna, had the wolf spiders found their own way back, or had they been re-established as guardians of the crew's Olympus? Trespassers will be eaten?

The bus lumbered to a halt, eased back and forth a few centimetres, and then fell silent.

"We have arrived," Lizzie announced. "Our armed friends will just check that everything is quite safe, and then we can go and call on 'Tina'—that's our nickname for her. Tina is resting during perihelion, which we all like to do, although the biological term is 'estivating.' All her sons are asleep around her. I would ask you all not to make any unnecessary noise."

Doig thought, *Hear, hear!* with little hope that the woman would apply that caution to herself.

The driver had aligned the bus so that its door was open against a gate. Now, the gate was opened, and one of the guards went to explore. Another stood at the entrance with blazer ready in case something else came back in his stead, but after a few minutes, the man returned safely, and the tour of inspection could begin.

"Come then! Let us go and call on Tina. Gray, would you like to lead the way?"

No! No! No! Hard as it was to see Lizzie Wong as the senior assassin of the Accident Squad, Doig's imagination could come close, and he emphatically did not want to be first into this spider trap. Why him? He was farther back in the bus than the others and would have to squeeze past them. Before he could frame a polite refusal, he was saved by big Ernie Venugopalan.

"Let me go first, ma'am," he growled. "It looks kinda narrow in there, and if I got stuck behind you all, I'd feel like a cork in a bottle."

So, he led the tourists out of the bus and into the tunnel of wire mesh, barely wide enough for his great shoulders and so low that he had to crouch while he walked. Klara followed him, and Doig went next while Lizzie and some guards brought up the rear. The path curved away into the fungoid undergrowth of the jungle. If this was a zoo, then it was the humans who were in the cage.

Venugopalan stopped and fingered the wire. "Is this supposed to be spider-proof?"

"Oh, yes. They never touch metal if they can help it. But do watch your step!"

The warning was necessary, for the footing varied from

tricky to treacherous. Originally, there had been a wooden subfloor under the wire, but in most places, the fibrous local timber had crumbled to shreds, so the wire now conformed to the uneven rocky surface below. Protruding loops and broken ends offered countless opportunities to trip in the dim lighting. Doig was forced to steady himself by holding onto the sides of the passage, half expecting razor-sharp mandibles to snip his fingers off at any minute.

The stench of the fungi was an appalling combination of feces and rotting meat punctuated by worse odours at frequent intervals. Where the cage crossed patches of soil, the spongy growths grew up through the floor to be trampled by the people in front. Despite the relentless heat, everywhere was dripping wet. The air was steam. Doig's clothes clung to him like paint. Why had he ever consented to attend this nightmare?

"Listen!" Lizzie called, so everyone stopped to listen.

What Doig could hear sounded like a storm wind finding an ill-fitting door. It wailed, but without a wind's changes in pitch—just a steady, never-ending note, somewhere around high C.

"As you all know," the schoolmarm continued, "spiders don't have lungs as we do. They constantly inhale through a nostril just below the upper pair of eyes and steadily exhale through their posterior orifice. Normally, it's too quiet for our ears to notice, but what you are hearing is the sound of about a hundred male wolves breathing."

"A sort of communal fart, you mean?" Venugopalan asked, rising at once in Doig's estimation.

Lizzie ignored the vulgarity. "When we get closer, you young folk may be able to hear Tina's own breathing, although it's almost above normal human range. Go on, then. It's not far now."

But it was uphill in that steam bath and even more treacherous than before. If Tina was twenty-five years old and her predecessor had lived to be sixty-three, then the corridor must be close to a century old, possibly much older. Originally, the rock had been cut to form stairs, and the wire mesh fitted over them—presumably so that the wolves couldn't burrow in under the sides—but the soft pumice had long since crumbled under the tread of human feet. The wire mesh, likewise, was in bad shape, and sharp ends kept scraping Doig's legs. He tried not to wonder what sort of infection he might contract. He doubted he would live to die of it because he was about to succumb to hyperthermia.

Eventually, the path levelled out and edged along a rocky slope almost steep enough to be called a cliff. On the right, it overlooked a crater about twenty metres across, the entire floor of which was covered with estivating wolf spiders, snoring away in perfect harmony. Their fur looked pale grey in the auroral light that gleamed brightly here through the gap in the forest canopy. They seemed to be packed several deep, but torsos were hard to distinguish under the tangle of legs.

"They won't waken as long as we're quiet," Lizzie said stridently. "Keep going, and in a moment, you'll see Tina herself."

The wire tunnel ended another three or four metres along, and the tourists obediently shuffled forward until they could see the queen wolf lying under an overhang at the far side of the hollow. She was about half the size of the bus, a vast, shapeless blob. Her head was a much smaller blob, undersized for her overall mass, although the great curved blades of her mandibles had to be well over a metre long. Doig always thought of spiders as being suspended under the M shape formed by their many-jointed legs, but Tina was lying on the ground with her eight furred legs all over the place, some bent, some straight. She probably couldn't move from her present location.

"Incredible, isn't she? If you come back in, say, August,

you'll see that this whole hollow is paved with her castings. As you know, spiders have no anuses. They regurgitate whatever they can't digest, which certainly isn't much, and that material is known as casting, or pellets. Most of what she eats goes into making—"

At some point during that harangue, Klara Wong shrilled, "You mean they're wallowing in vomit?" so loudly that Doig turned to look at her.

Thus, he was facing forward when, beyond her, Ernie Venugopalan fell. He might just have fainted, for his size must make him more susceptible to heatstroke than most. Or, he could have lost his balance on the ramshackle footing, but whatever the cause, he toppled against the fragile wire fence and tore the structure loose from the hillside.

Doig felt it go, saw the wolf queen react, and grabbed at the fence with his left hand. With his right, he gave Lizzie a massive shove on her scrawny chest, throwing her backward; then, he more or less fell on top of her.

The wire tunnel reacted like a giant sock as Venugopalan's weight hit it. It not only ripped free of its moorings, it stretched until corroded wires snapped. The big man tore clean out through the end of the assembly and went bouncing and rolling down the rocky, tree-stump-strewn hillside to land with a horrible splat on the piled wolf bodies. He was probably dead by then. Doig hoped he was because all the wolves wakened, and those within reach were all over him instantly, mandibles slashing. He made no sound as he was cut to pieces.

Klara followed him down, but more slowly, scrabbling and screaming, until she caught on a tree stump. Oh, how she screamed! Every one of the hundreds of spider legs in the hollow was waving as its owner struggled to break free of the heap and join in the butchery. As the first wolves clambered up toward her, blazers blazed, flames of sunlight in the night sending spiders' burning corpses rolling back down onto their brothers, who promptly butchered them and then tried to carry the pieces over to the queen.

Lizzie was yelling at the top of her voice. "Don' shoot the mother! Don' shoot the mother! Don' shoot . . ."

She was laying on her back at about a forty-five-degree angle, with Doig pinned on top of her by the wire netting that had tightened around them as it stretched. He managed to free his bleeding fingers from the mesh but found that he was helpless to do more. He was trapped in a cage of thorns.

One of the guards had managed to cut himself out of the cage and at once picked his way down to them. He began hacking at the fencing with a knife—certainly more interested in freeing Lizzie than Doig, for cargo were always expendable, but the death of a crewman would set off an inquiry. Whatever his intentions, he had to free Doig first because he was on top.

Klara was still halfway down the slope, still screaming and apparently unable to move. More and more wolves were trying to reach her, and the guards' blazers were certain to run out of charge soon. The moment he was freed, Doig slithered carefully down the slope, setting off showers of dirt and pebbles. When he was almost level with her, she stopped screaming.

"My leg! I've broken my leg."

He held out a hand, and she reached for it. He gripped her wrist. "Help me as much as you can. Push with the other foot."

He heaved. She howled in pain. "My leg . . ."

"Help me!" he bellowed. "I can't lift you. I have to drag you. The wolves will cut you in pieces." For a moment, he had a nightmare vision of himself arriving back at the cage holding only a severed arm.

He heaved her higher, scrambled up half a metre, and heaved again. She fell silent and went limp, which made her seem twice as heavy. The spiders were approaching on a wider front now simply because the direct approach was blocked by other spiders fighting over the loot of dead brethren. Doig was faced with the choice of abandoning Klara or dying with her.

Help came just in time. Carlo, Doig's companion on the bus, the guard who had freed Lizzie, came slithering down and took hold of Klara's other arm. Between them, the two men dragged her up to the path and into the remains of the wire tunnel. The other three guards emptied their blazers in holding back the pursuit. Doig was barely able to rise from his knees, gasping for breath and dizzy from the heat. Someone tipped a water bottle over his head, but that helped very little in the overpowering humidity.

"We're safe in here," someone said. "It's too narrow for them to follow us."

Possibly, the spiders did try to follow, but Doig noticed very little of what was happening on the way back to the bus and even less of the drive back to the palace.

THE DRIVER MUST HAVE RADIOED AHEAD because medics were waiting in the garage with a couple of gurneys for the wounded ladies. Klara was conscious but still close to hysterical, with many nasty scrapes and bruises in addition to her broken leg. She was whisked away.

Doig tottered to a bench to wait until the air conditioning could revive him. He was overheated and dehydrated. He had received at least a dozen scratches and about as many punctures from corroded wire in a fungoid jungle. Very likely, he was destined to die of blood poisoning within a day or two.

Lizzie was badly scratched but quite mobile. Her husband had been summoned. Sobbing dramatically, she threw herself into his flabby arms to be comforted. All Doig caught of their conversation was a remark of Blago's: "We'll find a nice young crewman to marry her."

Had it been an accident or a murder conspiracy aimed at either Doig or Ernie Venugopalan? Or both? Lizzie had wanted Doig to go first along the corridor. Had he accepted, would she have sent Venugopalan after him in the hope that their combined weight would do the trick and kill two cargo birds with one stone? It seemed unlikely, for surely she would have not allowed her own granddaughter to go between the two men, and she had been very close to Doig when it happened. No, Lizzie had to be innocent of anything more than an insane obsession with spiders.

That did not mean that the Accident Squad had not arranged the evening's entertainment for Doig's benefit. With the spiders estivating, it might have been safe enough for a couple of men to go into the hollow and undermine the tunnel supports. The Accident Squad never worried about collateral damage and might even favour it for adding realism.

"Doig, Doig! Why are you not in the hospital?" Babette had arrived.

"Don' know where 'tis."

"Can you stand?" She dragged him to his feet and more or less held him up as his knees buckled. Displaying much more strength than he would have expected, she began staggering across the floor with him, supporting him by holding one of his arms over her shoulder.

Then suddenly, "Let me help, ma'am!" Louis slid under Doig's other arm so he didn't have to worry anymore about falling down. The two of them could drag him wherever they were going, wherever they wanted.

A man's voice: "You can't bring him in here. This is the crew clinic."

"Well, I'm crew," Babette yelled, "and he's the chairman's personal guest, so get your fat ass out of our way."

A bed. Bliss to lie down! He was vaguely aware of drapes being pulled around the bed to give him privacy. The never-ending screech of complaint from the next cubicle sounded like Lizzie Wong.

He was comforted to hear that Babette was still with him, snapping our orders: "Louis, find an IV for him; he's dried out like a raisin. These cuts need treatment before they fester. I'm going to wash him." She proceeded to strip Doig, rolling him around like dough, totally shameless.

"So romantic," he murmured.

"I've wanted to do this for months. Be quiet while I enjoy the view."

"Take your hands off of my penis!" he yelled, although Babette's hands were nowhere near it, and she had not removed his underwear.

Lizzie's voice stopped in mid-gripe.

Babette caught on right away. "But it's so beautiful!"

The next-door silence remained pregnant.

"Well, be gentle with it!"

But then two men in scrubs appeared and, in outrage, ordered Babette and Louis to leave.

"You," the older one told Doig, "are cargo and ought to be in your own ward, but I have orders to treat you here." Clearly, that was shameful, unprecedented, and medically unethical.

"Does it matter? I'm sure to die of sepsis, aren't I?"

"You would over there. Here, you have a reasonable chance."

They washed, stitched, bandaged, and infused the patient. They fretted over his damaged hand for a long time, finally waking him to tell him to get some sleep.

He awoke a few times to drink more water, although never

to dispose of any—it stayed in there. He was disturbed once by someone in a nearby bed shouting for more painkillers. The voice was vaguely familiar, but he couldn't place it.

AT LAST, he knew that it was morning and that he ached all over. Louis was there with a pile of clean clothes and an air of great urgency.

"Sir, sir! The Board wants to see you, sir. In twenty minutes, sir."

Doig hauled himself awake as if from a great depth. His head felt like a rock on the end of his neck. He was hot, too hot; his pulse, too fast. "Mustn't keep the Board waiting." Louis helped him sit up.

Another man in a white coat swirled in through the drapes. "Where do you think you're going?" He laid an ice-cold hand on Doig's forehead. "You're running a fever." He checked Doig's pulse and pulled a face.

"The Board wants him, sir," Louis bleated.

"Gotta go," Doig said. "I'll leave my fever here and come back for it later."

He tried to get out of bed, and the world swayed. "One of the signs of sepsis is delirium, isn't it?"

The medic nodded.

"Then I'll need a wheelchair." If the Board was going to play dirty by calling the meeting while he was on a sickbed, then Doig could play the invalid card. Anything stupid he said, he could later blame on his infection.

He refused the clothes Louis had brought. With no further argument, they wrapped him in a robe and steadied him as he transferred to the wheelchair. He didn't feel like him at all. His head throbbed, and his tongue was bigger than his mouth.

Most of the other beds were curtained off, but as Louis was wheeling him out of the ward, he caught a glimpse of the man in the next bed, the one who had been calling for painkillers in the night. It was Saul Vandam, sitting up with his rib cage heavily bandaged and his left arm in a sling. His face was a pudding of black and blue bruises, and his snarl of anger when he saw Doig displayed a wide gap where his front teeth used to be. That explained why his voice had been so slurred. Recalling how he had seen Chi Brigham with a bandaged hand yesterday, Doig sent the patient a get-well wave as he went by.

LOUIS WHEELED HIM TO AN ELEVATOR, the first one Doig had ever seen except in videos. He hadn't known there were such things on the planet, although, of course, there would have been some on *Moctezuma*. When they reached his room, he refused Louis's offers of proper clothes, breakfast, or even a shave. He lingered there only long enough to see himself in a mirror and make sure he looked as sick as he felt. He looked vandam ghastly. *Good.*

"Lead on," he said. "Give me the Board or give me death." *Or both.*

There was a microscopic possibility, he reflected as he was trundled back to the elevator, that the Board just wanted to thank him for going to Klara's assistance in the spiders' lair. Much more likely, they were demonstrating their ability to make him dance to their tune. Chairman Ruckles was at last going to enjoy "the pleasure and honour of the company of Mr. Doig Gray" by showing him how insignificant he was. Pulling legs off a spider bug.

He still thought that they were more likely to try to bribe him than kill him. They had mishandled the Pablo Doig case.

They had sentenced the troublemaker to death for treason, then commuted that sentence to exile on Copper Island. But when he failed to die there as expected, and they arranged a fatal accident, the crime had backfired. The colony had forgotten Pablo after so many years and had been outraged to learn that he had been kept alive for so long in the notorious hellhole, only to be murdered—no one doubted that the Accident Squad had arranged his death. That had resurrected his cause. Recalling his warnings and complaints, people realized that nothing had been done. The tyrants still ruled, and the colony was still sliding toward extinction. But Pablo had a son . . .

That was how he saw it, but did they?

Could they bend their proud necks enough to try to buy him off? Marry him off to some cuddly and loyal crew girl, someone like Babette Dattu, say? Let him live in the palace, give him a managerial post of some sort? Then he would no longer be Doig Gray but Doig Legal Crew, and everyone could peacefully doze off to sleep again.

Or maybe not. He was about to find out.

THE ELEVATOR TOOK him to the very top of the palace, to a small hallway with a single door marked PRIVATE.

"You are quite sure you are well enough for this, sir?" Louis whispered.

"I'm quite sure I am not. Keep going."

Louis tapped on the door, and it swung wide.

The man who opened it was an armed guard in blue livery, and another just like him was visible inside. *Interesting!* Doig still had to learn the layers of power in the palace—whether the chairman ruled the Board or the Board could outvote the chairman. Could the crewmen attending this annual perihelion assembly overrule them all? That the Board needed armed protection for its meetings suggested that it wasn't quite divine.

"Doig Gray?" the sentry barked.

"Who else were you expecting?"

Louis fled. Scowling, the guard wheeled Doig across the little anteroom. The other man rapped on the door to the inner sanctum, the holy of holies. He opened it and stood aside so that Doig and his pusher could enter.

The council chamber was at the apex of the palace, a giant triangle whose walls paralleled the roof, sloping upward to meet at least ten metres overhead. The shutters on the great gable window were open, revealing a superb view northward over the island jungle, the whiteness of the morning bore frothing up the Gut, the distant cone of Mount Moctezuma, and the very distant one of Mount Ramesses. It all took Doig's breath away, so he needed a moment to notice the rest of the room. A great horseshoe table could have seated a dozen people easily but for this occasion, held only four. Directly facing him with his back to the light was a large, middle-aged man wearing a red shirt and white trousers: Chairman Ruckles himself, bigger than he seemed in his pictures. His hair was grey and thinning, his torso bulky, and his face as rugged as a boulder. Boulders did not smile.

There was a conspicuous lack of a fifth chair set between the ends of the horseshoe for the convenience of the witness, so it was fortunate that the witness had come with his own. The guard pushed Doig's wheelchair into position and then presumably departed because the door clicked shut.

Here beginneth the confrontation. It might not have any historical significance for the human colony on Neweden, but it certainly would for Doig Gray. He had been dragged from his sickbed, given no advance warning of the meeting, and denied his requested talk with Chi Brigham. Fortunately, he felt so deathly ill that he didn't care. Nothing was going to scare him in his present mood.

"Good morning, Mr. Gray. I am Chairman Ruckles."

Free of any obligation to bow, Doig inclined his head respectfully. "Honoured to meet you, sir."

"Are you well enough to hold this discussion?"

"I'm undoubtedly better than I'm going to be. It's probably now or never. Fire when ready."

Ruckles gestured to the man on his right, Doig's left. "Director Leo Heiser."

Heiser was a small man, older than Ruckles, with a thin, sharp face like a fragment of agate. He had few teeth left, so his voice was slurred and wet. Before Doig could speak, he sprayed, "What happened to you?"

Unless this little band of brothers was a gaggle of imbeciles, they knew perfectly well what had happened last night in the wolves' lair—knew better than Doig did, for they must know whether they had ordered it to happen.

"I was repeatedly scratched and punctured by wire mesh when the cage collapsed. I was very lucky not to lose my left hand. I may be dead in a week."

"You struck lady crewman Wong."

"I pushed her down. Otherwise, the falling roof would have broken her neck."

"You must have superhuman reflexes to act so fast."

"Her good fortune."

The chairman indicated the closer of the two men to his left, who was lardy fat and had mean little eyes like a spider, although only two of them. "Director Quang Zelenitsky."

Again, Doig nodded, which made the room sway and did not help his headache. "Honoured."

"Two days ago, you hacked into the Pale's communication system to broadcast illegal propaganda."

They had rehearsed this inquisition.

"I borrowed the network to announce this meeting, sir. I did no damage to the system, and what I said was perfectly true."

"You broke the law! You trying to start a revolution like your father did?"

The law was whatever the Board said it was, so the statement could not be challenged. But the question could be answered. "No, sir. I was merely bragging. It is a great honour for cargo as young as I to be invited to attend a meeting of the Board."

Zelenitsky scowled, making his mouth pucker in plump waves, and his eyes shrink even smaller.

But the fourth man was smiling. Ruckles said, "And Director Virgilio Vandam."

Finding a Vandam on the Board was no surprise. Very likely, there had always been one down through the centuries. This Virgilio was the youngest member of the Board. He was spare and intense, like an athlete. If Doig were to find a friend at the table, it would be this Virgilio, although that might be a trap, too.

"Honoured, sir."

"I would very much like to hear how you broke the password on the archive files, Doig."

"I didn't break any password, sir."

"Then your father told you his."

"No, sir. My father told me almost nothing. I didn't even know he'd been a surgeon or why he worked in the mines, sir."

"But you've been rummaging through the files for years."

"I guessed my father's password. There are a lot of passwords listed, although only two others seem to be in general use nowadays."

Heiser broke in. "You, us, and who else? Who are the rest of your gang?"

Only then did Doig realize that the interrogators were spaced so widely that he could not see them all at the same time. *More trickery!* It was meant to disconcert him, but he just felt annoyed by their pettiness. He turned his throbbing head to look at the old man.

"I have no gang, sir."

Heiser thumped the table. "Don't lie to us! Your father and his gang started breaking into the files years ago and are still doing so. You started up soon after you were shipped back to the mainland."

"Nothing to do with me, sir. I thought the other users were all related to the Board."

"You're lying, Gray, and we want the truth."

"Mr. Gray has answered the question." All eyes turned to the chairman. "Mr. Gray, your father was exiled for treason, for advocating rebellion. Do you plan to follow in his footsteps?"

"I was only fifteen when he . . . er, died, sir. I barely remember him. But—"

"Answer the questions!" old Heiser said in a shower of spit.

"I am answering the question. The brief answer is no. I do not believe in violence. I will never advocate rebellion because the present situation is much too dire for that."

"Then why do they cheer you?" demanded fat Zelenitsky. "When you were handed your diploma on Mayday, everyone clapped. When you went to the end-of-term drunk in the Trog's Rest, everybody cheered you. Why, huh? They didn't cheer anyone else. Why should they cheer you?"

Doig shrugged. "I wish I knew, sir. Did your spies tell you what I replied?"

"What did you reply?"

"I said that I was a loyal colonist, not a traitor. I called them fatheads and told them to get on with the party."

Ruckles had an orator's resonant voice. He said, "You also told them that they were cheering your father."

"I did, and I reminded them that he was dead—sir. I would prefer to remain alive." The way Doig's head was throbbing at the moment, he wasn't completely certain of that. "I have done absolutely nothing to encourage anyone to cheer me." He tried to look earnest because he was telling the truth. "I seem to have become a myth."

Myths didn't contract septicemia. If he died of it, he would become a legend of what might have been.

Ruckles said, "You say the situation is dire. What situation?"

Studying the big man silhouetted against the light, Doig was reminded of the queen spider. He decided that all the others were decoration; Ruckles was the danger. He was clever, confident, experienced, and ruthless. The others might yawl and yawp, but in the end, *he* would decide.

"I agree with my father on one thing, sir. The colony is dying. Unless this Board does new things and provides strong leadership, there will not be one human being alive on Neweden in fifty years. Maybe twenty years."

"That is a very serious and irresponsible charge, Gray. Justify it."

"Last night, sir, I received multiple scratches from corroded wire in a fungoid jungle. I am very likely to die of blood poisoning within a few days. It will only take one infected wound to kill me, but I don't know which one of my collection. That makes me a good metaphor for the human colony as a whole. I can list the colony's problems for you, but I can't say which of them will bring the roof down. I am sure the members of the Board are all aware of most of these troubles and can dismiss all of them individually. It is when I look at them together that they terrify me."

Ruckles stared at him for a long moment as if deciding whether he was worth bothering with. Then he said, "And have you any solutions to propose?"

"I have one suggestion to make, yes."

"You have the floor. Proceed."

Doig drew a deep breath. Luckily, he had been planning this speech ever since May Day and could roll it off without thinking. He didn't feel capable of thinking, certainly not thinking on his feet while slumped in a wheelchair.

"First, sirs, this planet is not truly habitable. Fortuna was ideal, the first choice according to Earth's telemetry, but it did not measure up when *Moctezuma* came close. Krasivyy also failed. Of all the millions of other promising planets in the galaxy, the only one that *Moctezuma* had a hope of reaching from there before the ship itself died of old age was this one. It was the third choice and is third-rate. The original settlers did very well just to survive the first perihelion. Human beings cannot live here without technology. Back to the stone age is not an option.

"Secondly, the steering committee, your revered predecessors, lacked enough time to find the optimum landing site. They had to revive the corpsicles because the cold coffins were breaking down, and the ship's life support system was no longer able to sustain thirty activated people for more than a few days. The steering Board chose this place for several reasons, which are recorded in the archives. One of the main ones was that the remote sensors had detected a large deposit of native copper, a raw metal that needed no complex extraction. Copper would be more useful if we had tin or zinc to alloy with it, but even so, that copper has served their descendants well—it has supplied us with many kilometres of water pipes and electrical wires to knit the settlement together. It also makes fences that the spiders won't touch. That was a fortunate bonus.

"I spent my childhood on Copper Island, sirs, and I assure you that the remaining veins are thinner and deeper, and the newest tunnels are too hot and too airless to be worked properly. The deposit is very nearly worked out."

Of course, the huge amounts of copper that had gone into building the palace could be salvaged by tearing it down, but he must not suggest that.

"Thirdly, they thought that a location near the sea would have a more moderate climate than one inland, which may not be true—we don't know. They reasonably assumed that we could eat seafood, for the virgin oceans of Old Earth teemed with edible fish. Sadly, our octopussies are both dangerous and poisonous. They also expected to build ships and explore the shores of the world. The Gut connects two oceans. If this were a human world, the nation that controlled it would be a great maritime—"

"Must we listen to all this crap?" old Heiser grumbled, wiping drool off his chin. "Kindergarten lessons!"

"I would like to hear more of it," said Virgilio, the young one. "Never hurts to listen to contrary opinions."

Ruckles's nod signalled Doig to continue.

"Fourthly, it was a tragedy that Ivan Wong was not revived sooner. Had he had even a couple more days in orbit to recover his strength and start assessing the telemetry, he would have vetoed this site, I am certain." Doig sensed a bristle of anger from his audience—their crew ancestors were sacred and must not be criticized. "He was the ship's dendrologist! Almost his first words when he went ashore to claim the world for humankind were to question why *Moctezuma*'s landing had not set the forest ablaze. This was perhaps the greatest blow of all, gentlemen. The wood hereabouts does not burn well and is too fibrous and siliceous to make decent timber."

"You think Wong could have detected that from orbit?" Ruckles sounded skeptical, but he was leaning forward, paying attention.

"Yes, sir. I inspected some of the old records myself, and *I* could. Of course, I knew the answer, but I could see no burn marks in these forests. Other Neweden forests do burn. There were even a few fires visible from *Moctezuma* in orbit. Wood could have provided us with fuel and building material for both houses and ships. Its lack has been one of our great impediments."

"Fuel?" Heiser spluttered. "What need for wood to burn? We have solar panels and wind turbines."

"We do now, but the old solar panels were made of material salvaged from the starship, and those ran out generations ago. The newer ones are greatly inferior. As for wind turbines, they have moving parts and wear out with use. They cannot be built of copper because it isn't strong enough, and again, the metals scavenged from *Moctezuma* are all gone. You have about half a year's supply of ball bearings left, but after that, the lights start to go out. The ferry that brought me here is a floating wreck. Its motors are failing and cannot be repaired, the batteries are no longer reliable, and the solar panels short out when it rains. How many more ferries do you have?"

That was the main question he had wanted to put to Chi Brigham. The fact that Chi had not granted his request for a talk, plus the silence that greeted his question now, told him that the answer could not be much larger than "none."

It would be wonderful to take a break so he could enjoy a few hours' sleep.

"Where was I? Fifthly? Fifthly, then, the fields of the Pale are fading. We have found so few edible local plants that we are almost completely dependent on terrestrial crops, which impoverish the local soil very quickly. They need phosphorus and fixed nitrogen, and those, we cannot supply."

"So, we clear more forest," said the fat Zelenitsky.

Virgilio, next to him, was shaking his head. With an inquiring look, Doig tossed him the verbal ball.

"We're out of wire," he agreed.

"The spiders can eat through anything else," Doig added. "The Frontier Squad lost a dozen men this spring."

Which meant a dozen excess women to be shared out among the crewmen. He wondered how many women these four odious specimens owned in total.

"That's about it, Mr. Chairman. The mission forecast was that the human population of Neweden would reach five million people after five hundred years. It's nowhere near that." The Board's own estimate was around fifty thousand, but Doig wasn't supposed to know that and didn't believe it. "Our supplies of raw materials are running out, and our existing technology is failing, day by day. Unless you do something, we are doomed. You will have to cut the food ration again."

"Who told you that?" fat Quang asked.

"The numbers, sir. You used ten percent fewer carts to bring in the spring crops this year."

"Bah!" Old Heiser was still in attack mode. "What a waste of time! We knew all this. Throw him outside and let the sun boil his brain."

Eyes turned to Waldo Ruckles, who nodded his big head graciously. "Thank you, Mr. Gray. A very succinct presentation. I could add a few more problems to your list—the spiders seem to be getting smarter, for example, and the water table under the Pale is dropping. But you have amply made your point. The Board understands all these dangers. We don't talk about them because we don't want to create a panic. Talk is cheap, as they say. What do you propose we do about it?"

Right from the moment he had received the invitation to visit Touchdown, Doig had foreseen that question, so he had an answer ready, but even after five years of studying the problem, it wasn't much of an answer.

"Explore. Since we have exhausted the materials *Moctezuma* brought to Neweden, we must exploit more of the planet's own resources. We must start again, back where our ancestors on Old Earth began, with iron and charcoal. We also must find usable timber. I believe, although I cannot prove, that this location was a bad compromise, climate-wise. Instead of avoiding the worst of two extremes, it suffers from both. Closer to the poles, we could escape the worst of perihelion. Nearer the equator, we would suffer less cold at aphelion. One enemy would be better than two."

Virgilio said, "Easy to say. 'Go find usable timber.' Where do you propose to start, and how do you exploit it when you've found it?"

He must know the answer to that! Doig turned to him. "Upstream, sir. This building is full of wood carvings. This table is made of timber—beautiful, isn't it? It's all driftwood, washed up on the shores. West of here, two great rivers empty into the Gut—the Mississippi from Northmain and the Nile from Southmain. Our ancient orbital photographs show that they both drain enormous areas, and the old records show that the north river is the source of most of that timber. We go find the forest, cut it, and float it downstream to the sea."

Ruckles said, "Leo, you looked into this for us."

The old man nodded. "Yes, I did, Mr. Chairman. And I learned that the early colonists did exactly what Gray is proposing. As he monotonously kept reminding us, they had resources then that we no longer have. Starting in Year 35, they sent a total of seven missions to explore both those rivers and only two ever returned. At least fifty brave young men died doing just what Gray suggests."

Doig said, "I found reference to nine missions, sir, starting in Year 25 and the last one in 152. A total of twenty-two boats were sent out, carrying approximately one hundred eighty men. Only two boats ever returned, and some fragments of others were washed up. The death toll was one hundred seventy, more than ninety percent." Making one hundred seventy women available to share among the crewmen.

Virgilio said, "Oh, shit! And you seriously suggest that we should try that again?"

"I have studied those records very carefully, sir. We have one resource that they did not have. The colony was still very small back then, but now we have a surplus of people, almost more than we can feed."

Virgilio tried to speak; Ruckles's sonorous voice overruled him. "Why did you choose to major in Earth history, Gray?"

"Because it covers thousands of years and billions of people, sir. I zeroed in eventually on the Europeans' settlement of North America—the sixteenth to early nineteenth centuries by their count. They explored an entire continent on water, salt or fresh. That included rivers with rapids and shallows. They went everywhere inland by canoe."

In the silence, Virgilio Vandam said, "Aha! Did any of our nine missions use canoes?"

"Yes, sir. A few used dories built of driftwood, like the one kept here in Freshwater Cove, but most used lightweight canoes. Both of the two that returned did. Spiders accounted for most of their casualties, and the survivors managed to get back because they were going downstream. There were not enough of them left to paddle against a current. We must assume that spiders killed the great majority of the rest."

"It would certainly be worth looking into," Ruckles said. "How would you build these canoes of yours?"

"Ribs and fabric, sir. Wood for the ribs, I think would be best. Sacrifice a few of your statues or a piece of this table, perhaps. The best fabric would be spider skin. It is tough and waterproof. It can be stitched and glued."

"How soon could you draw up a specific proposal for us?"

"One day after I recover my health, sir." If he ever did. His heartbeat was now astronomical.

Virgilio said, "I think Doig has given us plenty to think about. It would be a mercy to summon a medic and return him to the crew hospital. He is too valuable to risk."

"Objections?" Ruckles said. "Motion carried. Thank you, Mr. Gray."

Doig mumbled something and closed his eyes. His chair began to move.

THE NEXT FEW days came and went. Medics stuck things in his arms and kept him relatively clean, heavily sedated, and as comfortable as possible. The only good part was that it seemed every time he opened his eyes, Babette was there. What she said and what he said didn't matter and weren't remembered, but he was always very glad to see her and feel her hand, cool on his.

One morning, he awoke thinking that they must have stopped the sedation, that his fever had gone, and he was hungry. The headache had gone, too. His eyelids were still a bit crusty, but he forced them open—and saw Babette's smile. It grew bigger, full of hope.

"Feeling better?" she asked.

"Have you found a husband yet?"

"I'm still looking for volunteers." Meaning: just ask me.

"Then I do feel better." Meaning: then let's do it.

"How's Ewan?"

"Crazy happy. He's going to be a birthday present."

"For an ugly old man or a gorgeous girl?"

"A bit of both. Female, but not as pretty as me. Her father is very rich."

"Could he afford a double wedding?"

"Hold the violin music," said a familiar voice, and the curtains were pulled partly open. The intruder wasn't a medic —he was Waldo Ruckles himself, armed with a notepad.

Babette jumped up. Ruckles opened the curtains the rest of the way, revealing the six-bed ward with no one else in sight.

"Sit down, please, Miss Dattu." Ruckles was in his Loving Father role, the caring leader seen on viewboxes everywhere. He wore his red and white clan colours in fancy ruffles, and his mane of grey hair was freshly coifed. He remained on his feet at the end of the bed. "Feeling better, Doig?"

"Yes, thank you, sir." *Yes, Waldo* would have felt better.

"From what I overheard just now and from what I've been told about your visiting schedule, Babette, you are seriously interested in him?"

"Yes, sir." Babette did not smile. Knowing her temper, Doig hoped she wouldn't explode.

"Well, let's see what we can arrange. Doig, you proposed verbally that the colony should resume sending out exploratory expeditions, specifically, sending canoes up the two big rivers. Am I right?"

"Yes, sir."

"The full crew Board agreed. Will you take on the job of organizing such an expedition and lead it next year?"

"If I have full authority, yes."

Ruckles considered that for a moment and then made a

note on his pad. He was a proficient actor. "I can't give you *carte blanche*. To put it frankly, most members of the Board consider that you're still just a dreamy-eyed kid, and while what you propose may be feasible, it won't produce any useful results. We are planning to put Chi Brigham in charge. You'll have to report to him. I expect him to keep you on a loose leash, but he will have veto power."

Brigham was only three, or possibly four, years older than Doig, but he was crew. That made all the difference.

Recalling Saul Vandam's bandages and gap-toothed scowl, Doig said, "I admire Crewman Brigham's style, sir. I think I'd get along fine with him."

"Then it's agreed?"

Doig looked at Babette for a moment and said, "Sir?"

"You want your friend included in the package?" Ruckles asked.

Doig really wanted to punch him, but that was neither politically advisable nor physically possible at the moment. "Miss Dattu is not part of any package that I know of."

Ruckles gave him a don't-fuck-with-me-boy look. "You're cargo; she's crew. You can't marry without Board approval. Is that what you're asking?"

"If we could marry, I would ask her to do so. If she consented—and I haven't asked her yet—and you could arrange it for us, then I would be very happy and most grateful, but I will not change my name. No adoption. I am cargo and Pablo Gray's son until the day I die."

Ruckles shrugged as if that were too trivial to worry about. He looked to Babette.

"I can't," she said. "My father has to sell me to pay off his vandam debts."

"I dislike your vulgar turn of phrase, Dattu. Would you

renounce crew status to marry this man if the debts were not a problem?"

"Yes."

"Then it's decided. I'll inform the Board. We'll order you downgraded for unseemly behaviour and announce next year's expedition. I suggest you get to work as soon as possible, Gray." He turned on his smile, being the loving father again. "And congratulations, both of you. Now, I'll get out of your way."

He swung around and marched out of the room. Doig held up his arms, and Babette fell into them.

HE HAD BARELY RETURNED to his room, attended to his toilet, and dressed—fighting off Louis's insistent assistance— when he was summoned to a conference with Chi Brigham, held in the latter's sumptuous quarters: three bedrooms, north view, sculptures everywhere, paintings on every wall. The only other person present was Carina Brucknar, Chi's "secretary," who held a notepad and was evidently going to take notes during the meeting. As it progressed, Doig was both surprised and pleased that Chi frequently asked her opinion and listened to what she said. That would be one more reason why she preferred him over Gunter Finn.

Myrtle, Chi's "masseuse," did not appear.

Doig was still as weak as air after days of fever, but excitement was a wonderful tonic. He was going to marry Babette and lead an expedition into the unknown. What more could a man ask of life? He accepted a glass of wine but sipped it sparingly.

Chi sat down opposite him in one of the amazingly comfortable chairs with his legs crossed in the manner of a man settling in for a long session. "This discussion is being videocorded. It is the first meeting of the Interior Exploration Squad, July 2, 510. Present are designated leader Doig Gray, recording secretary Carina Bruknar, and myself, Chi Brigham, as Board liaison."

Doig was shocked to realize that he'd lost a week in the hospital.

"Gray, will you outline the objectives?"

"Um, yes . . . Firstly, to acquire means to explore the interior. Secondly, to start doing so. I have a list of seventeen anomalies that should be investigated—things like remote sensor indications of bog iron near the surface. It will take years to examine all of them."

Chi nodded as if that were a major understatement. "How will you begin?"

"Build a couple of small canoes to train canoeists, then two larger versions for Mission One, due to leave next February, as soon as the Gut is free of ice."

"Spiders? Wolves, tigers, and Vandam knows what other horrors you'll find out there?"

Doig shrugged. Obviously, he would lead some men to their deaths, possibly including himself. "Blazers by day and a portable wire fence to enclose our camps at night."

"Is that all?" Carina demanded suddenly. She was looking at Chi, not Doig.

"All for now. Note that defence will be a priority item. Describe these canoes, Gray."

"There are records of terrestrial canoes made of tree bark. We don't have any of that, but de-furred spider skin is waterproof and reasonably light. We can sew it and waterproof the seams with glue made from boiled spider bones. The leather will have to be stretched over a frame, and for that, we shall need to find timber."

"Why not spider bones?" Chi asked. "They're hollow and

light. When steamed, they can be bent to any shape you want, and they can be glued."

Doig said, "Thank you, sir. I should have thought of that."

Carina gave him an odd look as if his humble tone were seriously out of character. Doig had thought of using bone, of course; he was just practising his politics, sacrificing a pawn to win a game. But he was already impressed by Chi Brigham.

And so it went. How big was a canoe? Seven or eight metres long. How many men would it carry? Five or six, with baggage.

How far could a canoe travel in a day? The ancient records implied—assuming the old units were what they seemed to be—up to a hundred kilometres a day, but half that would be very good going.

"So, ideally, sir, if an expedition could use the whole of the travel season, February through May, making eighteen weeks, it could explore everything within a radius of three thousand kilometres. That's unlikely ever to be reached in practice, of course, but it means that most of the two river basins should be accessible, and together, they make up roughly fifteen percent of the accessible land area of Neweden."

"Our ancestors tried this, many times. They stopped because very few of the explorers ever returned. The death toll was unacceptable."

Chi sounded as if he were questioning the Board's decision. He must be out of bounds there because he didn't have the power to kill the project. At least, Doig didn't think he did. Was Ruckles playing foul?

"The death toll was more than ninety percent, but we have an incentive that our ancestors did not."

"Namely?"

"That all our families and friends, the entire colony, will die unless we succeed in finding new resources."

Chi pouted but went back to practicalities. "Where are you going to build these canoes? We do have a shipyard, but it is presently fully committed to building ferries. As I'm sure you noticed, the ferry you came over on is a floating wreck. We are constructing two smaller ones, but they are taking up all our resources."

"A canoe must be portable, sir, so anywhere within reasonable reach of the dock will do. To bypass rapids, the canoeists lay down their paddles, strap on shoulder pads, and carry it."

Chi nodded. "And how many men are you going to need to build these vessels?"

"A dozen, at least. The explorers themselves must make the canoes. That way, they will know how to repair them if they are damaged, and they will build them as if their own lives depend on it because they will."

"Think you can find a dozen able-bodied young men willing to face a survival rate of eight or nine percent?"

"With the tribe's survival at stake? Yes, sir. Biologically speaking, that's what young men are for."

"They have other uses, too," Carina said with a smile at Chi.

Doig thought he was doing very well. His illness had saved him from having to prepare a written proposal for the Board, and so far, he had found answers to all of Chi's questions. But then, he found himself thrown into a financial swamp when Chi asked what he expected to be paid. He had no experience of money. He would need a house big enough for two, but he had absolutely no idea what that would cost and little more what anything else cost, either. And his crew-reared bride-to-be would know even less.

Chi did because he had been building two new ferries. And his secretary did. Soon, the two of them were volleying numbers back and forth like squash balls while Doig just listened and added totals in his head. And wondered why, if Carina was so helpful to Chi in his sinecure employment, Babette couldn't do as much for him. After all, canoe building wouldn't be all grunt beef work, and with that exception, women could do anything men could. Paddle, even? Why not? Why must the Interior Exploration Project be unisex?

And then he realized the Board would never let him enlist married couples because it would suspect him of planning to set up a daughter colony somewhere.

"What does that come to?" Chi asked Carina, who had been keeping score.

"Nine hundred sixty-two thousand credits," Doig said, "roughly. That's for four canoes and living costs for ten people for a year."

"Call it a million," Chi said. "Which is well over the Board's projection, but I'll put in for the increase. We want this to be a voyage of discovery, not a funeral. Have you any helpers picked out yet, Doig?"

"Only Buster."

Chi raised his eyebrows. "You think you can control Buster?" He looked to Carina.

"I wouldn't give much for Doig's life if he tries to keep my brother out of it," she said.

Chi laughed. "There is that, and you're right. He's quite a guy. I'm almost tempted to volunteer myself until I remember the odds. Doig, my address in the Pale is 72 Brigham Plaza. My voicebox number is 135-72. Anything else we need to talk about right now?"

"Yes, sir. My mother and sisters are living somewhere in Town with Crewman Hassan Finn. I'd like to get in touch with them."

Chi's expression changed as if he had dropped a shutter over his face. "Crewmen's addresses are confidential. If your mother wants to contact you, Finn could get word to you very easily. I won't interfere in his business."

AT LAST, Doig was free to go in search of Babette. He found her in her own room, wearing one of her barely visible gowns and folded into one of the palace's froth-soft chairs. She looked up at him with an expression that somehow combined homicidal fury and molten desire. A bottle of bubbly wine waited in a dew-beaded ice bucket.

"And just where have you been?"

"I was summoned to a meeting with Chi Brigham. It's on—it all looks workable."

She smiled. "Then you're forgiven. Open the wine, and let's celebrate."

He sat down on a straight-backed chair safely out of reach. "I take it that you wish to begin the unseemly behaviour?"

"I consider it a matter of absolute priority."

His own desires were moving rapidly in that direction. "Are your motives hormonal or political?"

"Both. If my mother gets an inkling of our intentions, the entire Dattu family will descend on us in a lynch squad, with you as the intended pendulum. Including in-laws, they can probably muster a posse of a dozen."

"Then we need to have a serious discussion."

Babette purred. "What is there to discuss? I want action!"

"Plenty to discuss. Babette, I love you madly, and I can imagine nothing I want more than having you at my side for the rest of my life. But you are crew, and I am cargo, and we must talk this out. Do you truly realize the change this will make in your existence? Can we be happy if I am burdened with guilt for having dragged you down and you are soured by resentment?"

She frowned and shook off the rainbow mist. "My father ordered me to enrol in Only U because he was horribly in debt as usual and had been bribed by someone to have me spy on you and report what you were doing. Undoubtedly, the Board was behind it. My real status would have frightened you away, so I adopted a cargo name. I learned what it's like to be a dreg. I didn't like it, but I put up with it for two whole years, and to be your wife, I am perfectly willing to put up with it for all the rest of my days. So, throw off your guilt and your clothes and let's unite."

"I can't cook. Can you? How much can you earn? Cargo wives work to keep food on the table. Can you be happy in a one-room pit with a stone roof? That's all we'll be able to afford. The plan is that I will spend the rest of this year and January organizing an expedition into the interior, and then I shall be gone until June, with a very low chance of ever returning. Your friends won't have anything to do with you after you marry a cargo bum, remember? Crew women will laugh at you behind your back. Or maybe in front of your back, and oh shit, why am I saying this? I love you!" He wanted to ram his head into a wall.

"I survived two years in the student bunkers. If you're going to die, I want to bear your child. I'll tell him what a wonderful man his father was . . . no, listen to me, Doig. You are telling everyone that there isn't going to be a future, that the colony is doomed. If you sincerely believe that, then why are you arguing? Without a future, there is only now."

He should have known that he'd never win an argument with Babette. He stood up and went to join her in the big, soft chair. It was a squash, but a very intimate one. They kissed.

"I forgot to bring the wine," he said.

"Vandam the wine. I'm sure I can do it sober if you can."

THANKS TO SAUL VANDAM'S insanity, the ferry had been forced to sit out perihelion at anchor in Freshwater Cove instead of in dock in the Pale, but it had survived the storms with no worse damage than a few broken solar panels. It would take several days to shuttle all the visitors home, and Doig was not at all surprised to find that he was booked on the first sailing on July 8. Order of departure was a measure of status, for no one wanted to leave the palace any sooner than necessary, and the outdoor temperature still hovered in the forties. Babette and her family would be following four days later. Either her parents were still unaware of her unseemly behaviour, or Chairman Ruckles had bought them off.

Around mid-morning, Doig collected his few possessions, pinned on his nametag once again, and said farewell to Louis Louis. "I expect it is the custom for guests to give you a gratuity when they leave," he said, "but I am not crew, and I simply cannot spare a single credit. All I can give you are my heartfelt thanks for your wonderful care."

Louis broke out of his servant role enough to grin. "Your expectations would be disappointed. Most of those crew bastards are as cheap as dirt. But you could give me more than any of them could."

"I could?"

Suddenly, Louis stepped close, much too close for a servant to approach his master, and his hand prodded Doig's belly. Understanding came instantly. Doig accepted the grip—a firm, hard, man-to-man grip, accompanied on both sides with a steady stare. It was a pledge of allegiance. It meant I am your man, and I accept you.

"You could let me come with you when you go upcountry."

The Board's Hear-This of Doig's project had been made the previous evening. He had been in bed with Babette at the time but not too distracted to listen. He assumed it had also been announced in the Pale, and if Louis's reaction was typical, he was going to be mobbed the moment he set foot ashore.

Louis was young enough, certainly, and looked fit, but he did not display the brawn needed to paddle for hours at a stretch or carry almost his own weight on a portage. Nor did Doig himself, for that matter, but he fully intended to add many kilos of muscle before February.

He made excuses, but the promise had been made.

When he arrived at the garage, he was annoyed to be directed to a two-man buggy like the one he had arrived in, not the bus that everyone else was boarding, which would be a lot more comfortable. So, he was being reminded that he was just cargo crap, was he?

He was more than just annoyed when he saw that the driver's seat was empty and the person waiting in the other was Saul Vandam. The awful bruises on his face had faded, but he still had one arm in a sling, and his voice was slurred by a shortage of teeth.

"Why you?" Doig said.

"Because I need to talk with you."

"I don't know how to drive this thing."

"I'll show you. I'm sure it's easier than paddling a canoe."

Doig threw his bundle in the rack and eased into the driver's seat. Saul explained the system, and it did seem easy.

Waiting for the bus to lead the way, since it would certainly contain guards to ward off any hungry spiders, Doig said, "What do you want to talk about?"

"Wait until we're outside. Even in here, they have directional microphones."

So the "legal" crewman thought that way, too, did he?

When the great door opened, and Doig drove the cart outside to join it in the spider-blocking enclosure, the sunlight was a furnace, broiling his eyeballs. He said, "Vandam! This'll cook us before we reach the Cove."

"Never seen a canoe with a roof."

"We won't be paddling in heat like this."

Yet, when the outer gate opened, and they crawled and bounced off through the jungle, there were signs of renewal. The fungi had collapsed into dust, and trees and bushes were unfolding their leaves again, nourished by the torrential rain of the cyclonic storms.

For the first kilometre or so, Doig needed to concentrate on his driving, but when he could spare a few neurons, he said, "Speak, then."

"I know what killed all those earlier expeditions."

"Other than spiders? Spiders tiny, big, or enormous?"

"But I know how to keep the spiders away!" Saul said triumphantly.

"And what do you want in exchange for that information?"

"I want to come with you."

A vandam 'nother one! "Why?"

They bounced over some bumps. Saul said, "Slow down. If you try to keep up with the bus, you'll break an axle."

Doig slowed down and repeated his question. "Why?"

"Because they murdered my father, too."

That Saul shared the same grudge as he did had never occurred to Doig. He drove on past the *Moctezuma* grave site while he thought it out. "Then you deliberately tried to sink the ferry on the way here?"

"As soon as I saw that storm coming, I couldn't resist it. Touchdown depends on that ferry for everything, and its twin was cannibalized for parts three years ago. Three years, and they still don't have a backup! They deserve to starve to death in their island heaven." Saul showed his remaining teeth in a fiendish grin.

Saul Vandam was as mad as a three-legged spider. Despite the oven temperature, Doig shivered. "I'll keep you in mind. I think I'm going to have far more volunteers than I can accept." *Why would I want you after you tried to murder me, asshole?*

"But I can tell you how to keep the spiders at bay!"

"I think I already know that, thank you. I've been picking up hints, anyway."

Saul glared in frustration and said nothing more until they arrived at the pier, where the other travellers were still embarking under the watchful eyes of blue-clad armed guards. No spiders were in evidence.

STAYING RESPECTFULLY behind the crew folk, Doig was the last to board and was pleased to discover that all the passenger seats were filled, and he would again be sitting up front beside Conrad Melchior. The ferry interior was even hotter than the air outside. Half the front windows were gone, though, so there should be a breeze once they started moving.

"Don't count on that," Conrad said when Doig mentioned it. "We won't be going as fast this time. There's no bore on the ebb tide. But the trip may get more exciting if the batteries give out—we lost six solar panels over perihelion." He didn't sound too worried, but he wasn't an excitable man.

As the ferry moved out of Freshwater Cove, Doig glanced behind him. The first cargo area was full of passengers' baggage, and the front-row passengers were busily chattering among themselves. Talk should not be heard over the hum of the motors. "You know that Saul Vandam was deliberately trying to sink us when he insisted you sail that day?"

Melchior shot him a sideways look. "I suspected. There was no sane reason that I could see."

"He's lost a lot of teeth, fractured some ribs, and broken an arm. Fell in the shower, I expect."

"I saw him around and wondered. Useful things, slippery showers. But that doesn't help me. You want a volunteer for your expedition?"

"You've got a good job. Why give it up for a dream?"

"Did have."

"They fired you? They must be crazy."

"Crewman Brigham was very apologetic, but the Board makes the decisions, and I did nearly lose their precious ferry."

Dad hadn't been fooling when he accused the Board of gross incompetence. But, *wow!* Melchior probably knew more about boating than anyone else in the colony. There was no doubt that he had the necessary muscle, too. On that first day, when Melchior had been about to punch Saul, Doig had put all his weight on the ferryman's arm and been lifted off his feet.

"You married? Children?" Doig asked. He'd been too entranced by Babette for the last few days to work out what sort of men he needed for the expedition.

"Yes to both," Melchior said. "Three kids. And I want them to live. I agree with everything your dad said about the colony dying and the Board being too incompetent to save it."

"Then, you are most welcome aboard. We aim to depart right after the ice goes out. Until then, we build canoes and practice paddling them, pack our supplies, and generally shape ourselves into a team."

"Don't start too soon after breakup. There could still be floes coming down the rivers for weeks."

"Thanks," Doig said. The news was unwelcome, except

that it proved Melchior was going to be a big help. "First thing I've gotta find is a place big enough to build the canoes, with access wide enough to carry them out."

"Try the Metal Room at the docks. In the past, they used it to store copper because, at some times of the year, more came in than they could use. Not anymore. It's been shut up for ages. It's unheated, and you'll need to run power lines in for lighting."

"You, Friend Conrad, are going to be a pillar of strength! Next miracle: how about somewhere to stay, me and my wife?"

Doig had never called Babette that before. Even if technically premature, it sounded strange and sweet.

"I know of a rental place on Suleyman Road that's close to the docks. The old man went to join his ancestors about three weeks ago. Expect it's still vacant."

IT WAS A VERY SMALL WEDDING. Buster was happy to be best man, and he brought along a few mutual friends from student days. The registrar looked quite nauseated when Babette handed him the Board letter stating that she had been degraded and, hence, was forbidden to marry any crewman.

The only member of her family who attended was her brother, Ewan Dattu, who played father of the bride, unpinning her Dattu name tag and then stepping aside so that Doig could relabel her as a Gray. But later, when Doig thanked him for being so broad-minded, Ewan spoiled the effect of his gallant gesture: he said he'd come because he wouldn't be able to invite his sister to his own wedding next month.

The Doigs of Lee Avenue had not been invited, but Conrad Melchior came with his wife and youngsters. So, too, did Mike Murugan, the ferryman from Copper Island, who was another confirmed recruit.

The reception afterward was beer at the Trog's Rest, which was all anyone could afford. Trog's also happened to be handy for 147 Suleyman Road. But the word had got around, and an enormous crowd assembled to cheer the happy couple and thrust beer upon them. Most of the males volunteered to go on what was already known as the Doig Gray Expedition.

As darkness fell, Doig—with some assistance from Buster and his gymnast friends—extracted his bride from the lascivious condensation of bachelors around her and conducted her back to their home at 147 Suleyman Road.

"Imagine the trumpets," he said as he unlocked the door. "Visualize the red carpet, the nymphs scattering flower petals, the guard of honour with their shining sabres. Flunkies bowing, dancers swirling . . ."

"Right," she said. "What's that?" she added, pointing to a box on the table. "Did you put that there? Is it a gift for me?"

"No, it isn't," Doig said grimly. "It's a chess set that belonged to my father." He had no doubt that any information stored in the white pieces had long since been removed. The only message it conveyed now was that the Accident Squad was still watching him.

And also, of course, a reminder that more games are lost than won.

3: FIVE-ELEVEN

IT WAS JANUARY 45 AGAIN, the sixth anniversary of his father's murder.

The Metal Room was very cold, a roughly excavated chamber with a door opening to the pier just above the perihelion high-water mark. It had been cool, even back in July when Doig had first seen it, but it was far enough below ground level that even the deadly chill of aphelion had not rendered it uninhabitable. Indeed, Doig was streaming sweat and his breath came out in clouds. *Heave . . . heave . . . heave. . .* Apart from his breathing, the only sound in the big space was the steady creak of the torture machine.

The first day he had seen the Metal Room and commandeered it for the Exploration Squad, he had given Buster his first orders, which were to construct some device that would simulate the work of paddling. It had taken Buster about half a day to collect the parts he needed and build what had at once become known as the torture machine. Doig used it every day, and most of the squad spent some hours on it each week. He was sitting in a low box, clutching a wooden rod whose base was attached to a rope that ran over a couple of pulleys and lifted a pan that contained a selection of weights. He worked half the time with the paddle on his right side and the other half on his left. His arms and shoulders would never match Buster's or Melchior's, but they were a lot more impressive than they had been. Babette teased him about them, and he hoped that no one else knew how stupidly proud of them he was.

The Metal Room was never bright, and now, when the other men had all gone home, a single lamp kept it barely even dim. The canoes didn't help, for Doig's seat was very close to the floor, set between the rock wall to his right and *Lewis*, whose leather skin reached higher than his head.

They had built four canoes, starting with two small ones, *Simon Fraser* and *Alexander Mackenzie*, followed by two full-size, *Lewis* and *Clark*. The first two had been used for training, but the *Mackenzie* had been badly gashed by a floating log and later scrapped for parts.

"Don't you ever stop?" asked a familiar voice.

Buster emerged from the darkness. He reached into the torture machine to grip a rope. Doig's task suddenly became impossible.

"Only when you make me." Doig grabbed his towel and stood up to wipe himself off. "Why aren't you at home with Shadiya, fulfilling your biological destiny?"

"Been there, done that."

At first, Doig had argued that every man of the Exploration Squad must be married and a father because those should have more incentive to come back alive than bachelors would. Chi Brigham had pointed out that family men might give up too easily when going on looked tougher. In the end, they had decided just to take the best, married or not. Buster had recently changed status by meeting a dark-eyed beauty, sweeping her off her feet and marrying her in less than a week.

"Seriously?" Doig said. "Nah, even she can't know yet."

"I've been her husband for more than thirty nights, so she must be." Suddenly, Buster changed his tone. "Listen, boss, I've found a problem. I wanted to tell you when there's no one else around."

Only one more problem? Doig was tempted to tell him to add it to the list and then burn the list. Life was all problems and had been for months. As soon as he solved one, two more appeared. He reached for his shirt. "Fire when ready."

"Remember we tested the leather for cold and the glue, also?

"They withstood much lower temperatures than we could."

"Yes, but what about heat? I just tested the glue, and it melts again at around forty-five degrees."

Glue sealed the seams in the leather skin and held the bone frame together. Doig tried to imagine loaded canoes falling apart in midstream and didn't like what he saw. "How hot does the sea get at perihelion?" Rivers, being shallower, must surely become even hotter.

"Dunno," Buster said. "The oceans never boil at this latitude, I know that, but they're too hot to swim in until mid-August."

Doig pulled on his fur smock. "Human body temperature is thirty-seven degrees. So by the time the water reaches forty-five, we're long dead of hyperthermia."

"Ah!" Buster said. "That's all right then. Must remember to get home before perihelion. Let's go and swill beer."

SEEN BY DAYLIGHT, 147 Suleyman Road was not a prestige address, just an igloo in a row of igloos. In January, approached from below, it was one of two doors at the top of four steps in an alcove. The tunnel was even colder than the Metal Room because it was better ventilated, and Doig's breath smoked in the dim light.

The house was an improvement on his parents' old bunker on Copper Island, but he now knew that almost anywhere was. It had two rooms, so he could brush his teeth and undress in the front room before turning off the light and slipping through into the bedroom, which was a little larger than the bed.

As he slid in under the covers, Babette said, "Which was it tonight? Blonde or brunette?"

He closed his arms around her. "Two redheads and one I couldn't tell in the dark." Alas, her pregnancy was sufficiently advanced now that sex was off the agenda, and life was a lot less bright without it. "How's the bump?"

"They're both doing fine, thank you. Trying to see which can kick harder."

The medics said they could hear only one heartbeat in her grotesquely expanded belly, but Babette refused to believe them. It had to be twins, she insisted, or else he had a pony in there with him.

They snuggled, but after a while, Babette heaved herself into a more comfortable position. "The voicebox said that breakup was going to come early this year. How do they know that?"

"Ten percent air temperature, and ninety percent guess-work. Don't worry; we won't leave until it's safe."

"Safe? What are you calling safe?"

"I meant safe from floating ice. No, the expedition's not safe, but it is necessary, darling. You know that."

She had always known it, of course, but now reality was intruding on dreams like an iceberg emerging from fog. Departure was coming closer and closer. In a week, Doig might be gone, leaving her alone with their unborn child. Her family had officially disowned her, as Doig had warned her they would, although Ewan did drop in once in a while.

"What did you do today?" she asked.

What had he not done today? He'd barely been off his feet since he hauled himself out of bed in the morning. He listed as many of the meetings and decisions and arguments as he could remember but left out the problems. Problems always implied dangers. Sometimes, the whole project felt like jumping off a cliff because the water looked deep.

"What're you going to do about the spiders?"

"Gotta meeting with Brigham tomorrow."

"But how do you know for sure that the crew has some way of controlling them?"

He tried to tell her yet again. He was so tired he could barely keep his mouth moving, but she was lonely and frightened, and he owed her this.

CHI BRIGHAM'S HOUSE, 72 Brigham Plaza, was many times larger than 147 Suleyman Road, having umpteen rooms on at least three levels, not counting servant quarters. It was brighter, warmer, and filled with beautiful, interesting things—paintings, porcelain, sculptures, Carina Bruknar. Carina was now the proud owner of the planet's most beautiful baby ever, Douglas Bruknar. According to his Uncle Buster, little Doug had been named after Doig Gray, the name being as close as could be sneaked past his unwitting crewman daddy. Doig was quite certain that Chi was smart enough to have worked that out.

Right at the start, Doig had appointed Conrad Melchior to be his deputy, and always took him along to his meetings with Chi. That morning, they were shown into the library and kept waiting no more than the five minutes that protocol required. Chi strode in cheerfully, informally dressed as always on Wednesdays because that was the day his friends came to play squash in his courts. He was followed by a servant pushing a trolley of refreshments.

Doig accepted coffee, which was made from the ground-up roots of a local plant genetically modified to produce caffeine. Melchior chose fruit juice, which Doig happened to know was made from sugar, water, and artificial flavouring. When the servant had retired, and the three men were seated in a triangle, Chi announced for the benefit of the cameras that this was the sixty-third meeting of the Interior Exploration Squad executive.

"Item One, as always: scheduled departure date?"

"No change, sir," Melchior said. "Four days after breakup, as long as the weather doesn't turn nasty. That's allowing a day off for family partings."

Item Two was always clothing, one of Doig's responsibilities.

"Close enough, sir. A couple needed refits, but they'll be ready in time." The refits were needed because Elijah Krantz had put on eight kilos since being measured back in August, and Tengiz Silva had lied about his age and was still growing.

Chi said, "Have you given any thought to storage? You won't need furs after the first month, so you could cache them somewhere on the river in case we ever send out an expedition at harvest time. They would need furs for the return journey."

"We did think of that, sir, but we'd need to carry some sort of protective covering for them so that scavengers wouldn't eat them, and that would mean more weight, more baggage. I did ask Idriss to look into it, and he pointed out that the harvest-time expedition couldn't be certain of finding the cache, especially of finding its contents still in wearable condition, and their lives would depend on that."

Taking no offence at having his suggestion stepped on, the crewman nodded. "Good points. Just wondered. Item Three: rations?"

"Worrisome," Doig said. "Some of the dried meat they sent over is vandam rancid. There are rat-spider droppings in the pasta. I think a thunderbolt from the Board itself might be in order, sir."

"I shall speak to the Thunder God," Chi promised. "List the offending suppliers."

But that was not going to be enough. This next bit would be very tricky.

"I mentioned last time that Dell Firmin had stomach trouble. I'm happy to report that he has recovered."

"Good."

Doig made the gesture that meant to cut off the recording. Chi frowned and pressed the mute button—so it was said.

"Not good, sir. We had decided to run tests on the rations, and he was the first volunteer. He was diagnosed with food poisoning. Fortunately, he had tasted only a very small amount. We found a tiny hole in the can, soldered shut. I'd call that attempted murder . . . sir."

Chi bared his teeth in fury and mouthed a word he did not pronounce. "I swear to you that I knew nothing of this! The Board is not behind it!"

He could not know that, of course. The Board might be behind it, or Waldo Ruckles and Dhaval Goldberg might be playing games on their own.

"We have voted, sir, and all the rations so far provided must be withdrawn. They should be destroyed under Board supervision. Crew members will choose rations at random from the main storage warehouses. Sir." Doig waited to see if he had just killed the expedition and perhaps himself. But Chi, at least, was honest. He nodded and released the mute button.

"Glad to hear it. Give Dell my regards. Next item?"

After that, the meeting went smoothly until they came to new business. Doig had been putting off the matter of wolves in the hope that Chi would bring it up first. Now, time was running out.

"New business?"

"Yes, sir. Spider repellant."

For a crewman, Chi was surprisingly likeable. He kept both his women happy, which was no small accomplishment, and he guided the Interior Exploration Squad's preparations with skill and tact. He almost never issued orders. Whenever he disagreed with any of Doig's proposals, he started asking questions and kept on doing so until the correct answer was obvious to both of them. The only exception was when something arose that concerned Chairman Ruckles or the Board. Then, Chi's face would freeze into an expressionless mask, and he would either forbid further discussion or start lying. As Doig had expected, this was one of those times. He hit the mute button again.

"Explain what you mean."

So, here came the challenge. Doig might be about to make a complete fool of himself or sign his own death warrant, but the expedition would probably stand or fall on the answer to his question. "Isn't it true that the Board has some way to control the spiders?"

This time, the silence was longer. Menace filled the air. Melchior, not having been warned in advance, looked both alarmed and totally mystified.

Chi said, "What makes you think that?"

"Because of what I saw and heard that night on Touch-down when I was taken to see the wolf queen. I asked one of

the guards what would happen if the bus broke down. Specifically, I asked if the driver could radio to Vandam Palace for
help in an emergency. He answered, 'That would really bring
the buggers swarming.'

"Then, when the cage collapsed, the queen wolf reacted
first. She moved her legs, and all the males woke up—all of
them at the same instant. Then, I recalled things that Saul
Vandam said on our first trip together in the car. He didn't
mention radio, but there was a pattern. Spiders won't touch a
conductor like copper, and they seem to be sensitive to moving
metal—the cars, the gates, the falling cage that night."

"You think they talk by radio? 'Attention Platoon One,
edible bipeds to your north!'?"

"Not talk. Old Earth had many species that communicated
with calls or songs. I can imagine the queen spider sending
signals: Wake up! Go north! Attack! Return! There are some
aspects of wolf spider anatomy that have never been explained,
or at least are not explained in the archives. Both their
antennae and the long bones in their legs are electrically
conductive—why? Even if those are not used for communication, they should be susceptible to chaotic radio waves of the
right frequency. In short, a jamming device."

But the men working on the Frontier Squad were not
provided with jamming devices, and they died in droves.
Aware that he was very close to accusing the Board of mass
murder, Doig added, "I do ask that you investigate that possibility, sir. It could make the difference between life and death for
the expedition."

"An interesting idea, and one that ought to be investigated,
I agree. Is there any other new business?"

No, there wasn't. As usual, Chi personally showed his visitors to the door. As they crossed the threshold, he pulled them

close and whispered, "Keep your vandam mouths shut about jamming devices, both of you."

BREAKUP CAME on February 1 that year. The air that had lain as still as a corpse for weeks began to stir at first light. At sunrise, the Gut was a white sheet from the chaotic jumble of ice along the shore to the far horizon, but by noon's high tide, it was a stream of dark blue water juggling ice floes.

On February 2, the Interior Expedition Personnel staged a dress rehearsal. Twelve men carried *Lewis* and *Clark* outside and down the pier in a gentle dance of snowflakes. They went back for their supplies and equipment and then pretended to pack the canoes—to do so in reality, on land would have broken their frames. The operation was watched from a distance by Chi Brigham and a couple of heavily muffled men who stayed out of the way and were not introduced.

Two days later, the ice in the harbour had crumbled into harmless slush, so the canoes were launched and manned for the first time, then paddled around the harbour. They performed well once their trim was adjusted and showed far fewer leaks than Doig had feared after his experience with *Mackenzie* and *Fraser*. All the holes were minor and could be patched before Departure Day. The facility with which the teams unloaded the canoes and carried everything back into the Metal Room showed that they had already learned the skills they would need when portaging.

Chi and his two companions were there to watch again, and this time, they stayed until the work was done. Only Chi followed the explorers into the Metal Room, out of the chilly wind, but when everyone was inside, he made a speech, most of which was so predictable that Doig could have written it for him—thanks for hard work, praise for results so far, compliments to Doig and Melchior, and so on.

"Now, leaders, when is Departure Day to be?"

Doig referred all operational questions to his deputy, so he looked to Melchior to answer this one. Since Chi knew that they planned to give everyone a day off, Melchior knew the right answer to give.

"We can launch tomorrow, sir."

"Oh, come now! You're too hard on them. Why don't you give everyone a day off to say goodbye to their families?"

Melchior looked to Doig, Doig looked to Melchior, and they both nodded. That brought cheers, of course. What Chi didn't know was that everyone had already been promised that day off, so the entire company was playing by the same script, being good little cargo boys toadying to their crew masters.

Chi beckoned the two leaders to go back outside with him. As he paused so that Doig could open the door for him, he said, "You remember that you requested some additional electronic equipment?"

Aha! "For camp security, you mean, sir?"

"Right. Well, the equipment is complicated and requires a trained operator, so you will have to carry one more man. That will not be a problem, will it?"

"It certainly would be," Doig said bluntly. "We have six thwarts in each boat. To sit anywhere else risks tearing the skin off the frame, or even splitting the skin wide open. We have sleeping gear, tents, and rations for twelve men. We need an even number of paddlers in each boat, and if the newcomer doesn't pull his weight, there's bound to be resentment. Every other man will be working his butt off."

But Chi could be even blunter. "The Board has ruled that the expedition must be led by a crewman, and that is that. If you have to throw someone off to balance numbers, then do so. The decision is not debatable."

Wasn't it? Of course, no one would expect a crewman to do anything as sweaty as swing a paddle or help carry a canoe around a waterfall. He would expect to give all the orders, so it wouldn't be the Doig Gray Expedition anymore; it would become the Brigham Expedition, or the Ruckles Expedition, or the Vandam-Knows-Who Expedition . . .

The sky was bright enough to dazzle, but breath still smoked in the chill wind. Chi's mysterious two companions were still there, waiting for him in their all-enveloping furs. But now they were close enough to recognize.

One of them was Saul Vandam.

"Him?" Doig yelled. "You expect us to take that crazy shit along with us?"

"Watch your language, Gray!"

"Sir, I will not watch my language for that 'legally crew' maniac. He tried to murder me and Conrad. He ordered the ferry to sail that day because he wanted it to sink. You know that. You beat the hell out of him for it! If you put that—"

His hot anger went suddenly ice cold as he noticed that the other man's nametag read GULDBERG. He was notably walleyed.

For a moment, Doig couldn't breathe. He would have reached for his blazer had he been wearing one. "And you, dear Saul? What are you doing consorting with the human spider beside you? Don't you know that Dhaval Guldberg is head of the Accident Squad? He killed my father. I expect he's the one who castrated your father and laughed while watching him bleed to death."

Clearly, Saul Vandam had not known that. He turned to stare at Guldberg with . . . Horror? Hate? Rage? Fear?

Guldberg was a burly shape in his furs and would probably

look even more so without them. He showed bad teeth in a mocking sneer. "Oh, can't we let bygones be bygones? Junior Cook Vandam wasn't murdered; he committed suicide. We gave him the choice of bleeding to death or having his head pushed into the bread oven to bake. He dropped his pants voluntarily, so it was suicide."

Even Chi pulled a face at that, but he did not speak. Crewmen might not have as much cause to fear the Accident Squad as cargo did, but fear it, they did. Saul looked ready to vomit.

"And my dad just happened to sneeze hard enough to make the tunnel roof fall on him?" Doig asked quietly. He could barely speak at all. He was trembling with the effort needed to restrain himself.

Suddenly, a grip like spider mandibles closed around his arm, tight enough to hurt. Seven months ago, he had restrained Conrad Melchior from striking Saul Vandam. Now, the former ferryman was returning the favour. To say more would be to invite disaster.

Guldberg laughed when he saw that warning. "I wouldn't know, Doig," he said. "I wasn't there."

True, he had left Copper Island in the morning, and Pablo Gray had died in the afternoon. The man who actually lit the fuse must have been one of the crewmen then running the island—Hassan Finn, the one called Robins, and probably a couple more.

"The Board," Chi said, "appointed you to organize this expedition, which you have done splendidly. But it must be led by a crewman, and Saul Vandam has been given that responsibility. He has also been trained to operate the radio equipment. You will see that he is treated with the respect due his rank. Have you any problems with this?"

Doig took several deep breaths. He had plenty of problems.

It wasn't just his own resentment he must control; it was also eleven other men's. Out in the wilderness, any one of them would be capable of beating a crewman to death on principle and blaming a spider bite.

"One Forty-Seven Suleyman Road?" Guldberg said. "And 26 Robins Street?"

Doig's house and Melchior's. The threat was blatant— Babette and her unborn child, Melchior's family. Even resigning from the expedition would be regarded as treason, punishable by disappearance and becoming spider fodder.

Doig took several deep breaths and then got the words out. "No, sir, I have no problems with Crewman Vandam joining us."

"The day after tomorrow, then," Chi said, and the three noble visitors departed.

The two cargo watched them go. After a few minutes, Melchior said, "I don't know if I can keep my hands off that bastard's scrawny throat from now until June."

"You heard the terms—our families are hostage. I have a horrible suspicion that the Board is just putting out the trash, me and him both, with the rest of you just collateral garbage. Even if there really is a spider jammer, the equipment Saul Vandam brings may be utterly useless."

The older man sighed. "And he *certainly* will be. Come on, let's go tell the lads the good news."

"Don't mention spider jamming yet. Once we're on our way will be time enough."

They went back into the dim Metal Room, where the teams were busily patching the leaky seams they had discovered that morning.

Doig stepped onto an upturned bucket that he used as a speaker's platform. "Hear-This!" he shouted, and everyone gathered around. "The Board has decreed that the expedition must be led by a crewman." He waited for the booing to end. "Conrad and I feel as you do, but this is not debatable. We were given clear threats that our families are hostage for our good behaviour."

That remark was met by dead silence. The crew's reign of terror was well known but never mentioned.

"There is a bright side to this, though. He will be bringing some extra weaponry that may be very valuable to us. Now, how do we refit for an extra man? I think that means putting an extra thwart into *Lewis*. To make room and cut weight, I am inclined to throw out two sleeping bags and one tent and then hot bunk the night watch. Has anyone any better ideas?"

"Nothing I dare speak aloud," said Mike Murugan, raising a few chuckles.

"Please!" Doig shouted. "Don't joke about this. My wife is expecting a child. So is Buster's, and others are, too."

That ended the humour, but it would not make Saul Vandam any more popular on the journey.

DOIG ALWAYS WENT HOME for the midday meal; it was the brightest part of the day. That day, when he reached the steps up to 147 and 149, there was someone sitting in the dark at the top. Startled, he stopped, heart pounding.

"I need to speak with you, Mr. Gray." The toothless mumble of the voice was recognizable as Saul Vandam's, but the words were not.

"Since when have I been a mister to you?"

"Since I was told two days ago that I was supposed to lead your fucking mass suicide." He spat to show disgust.

Doig said, "You want to come inside?"

"You don't want your wife to hear what I want to say."

"Say it, then."

"They don't want you to succeed. They don't want us to come back, ever."

Which was what Doig had long suspected, but he didn't think the Board would have told Saul as much. "Why do you think so?"

"I know so. Because if you do find anything worthwhile, it will show up five hundred years of gross incompetence. Also, it will require a satellite settlement to exploit it, and that will reduce their power over us. Yes, they know the world is dying, but they hope not in their lifetimes. Meanwhile, they're top dogs and will do anything to stay that way."

"Have they booby-trapped the canoes?"

"I expect they've planted an Accident Squad specialist among you."

Doig doubted that. "He'll want to come back alive, so he can't kill all of us unless he means to paddle home alone."

"But you and I will be among the dead. You, you crazy idiot, played right into their hands. They had to find some way to silence you, and you volunteered to die. People will see you paddle off into the Gut. End of Doig Gray. You're disposable. I'm dispensable. I'm only 'legal' crew, as you so gently pointed out this morning. They killed my father, too."

His whining was obnoxious. "So, why are you here, on my doorstep?" Doig said. "What do you want me to do?"

"Leave me behind. I won't do any good on the expedition. No one's going to obey any orders I try to give."

"You have been trained in how to work the spider repellant."

"It's just a box with an on-off switch. Keep it charged up with your solar panels and it should work all night. So they told me."

"I'd love to believe you," Doig said. "Past experience makes that somewhat difficult. Does it really work?"

"It worked two nights ago. They showed me on Touchdown Island. But who knows if they gave me the same machine as the one they demonstrated?"

Suddenly, Doig saw the humour of it—black, black humour, but still funny. "Once again, you and I are going to be in the same boat. I will not leave you behind, Saul Legally-Vandam, because my wife would suffer for it. I give you my word that I will do my best to keep the others from killing you as soon as we are out of sight of the colony—unless we run out of food sometime, of course. Try not to look edible. But be there at first light on Friday."

Saul would come, but he would certainly cause trouble somewhere, sometime.

THE PLANNED DEPARTURE date had been announced on a general Hear-This, but Friday's dawn brought an icy wind and blowing snow, which did have the advantage of keeping away the crowds of onlookers that might otherwise have turned up to watch. The expedition team gathered on the white-coated pier to stare mournfully at the metre-high waves and scattered whitecaps. They had not tested their canoe-building skills against water as rough as that. Chi and Saul were there, too, but keeping very quiet.

"You're the seaman," Doig told Melchior. "It's your call."

"My right hand tells me that if we're going to be swamped, the best place to do it is very close to home. My left says that no man can live more than a couple of minutes in water that cold or swim in these furs. My head tells me to put it to a vote."

But that would be an evasion of duty. Despite what Doig

had just told Melchior, and despite whatever the Board might say about Saul Vandam, in the squad's eyes, young Doig Gray was the leader. If he called for a vote, none of them would admit to being scared, so they would all vote to proceed. Without consulting Chi Brigham or Saul Vandam, he walked around to the windward side of the group so his voice would carry.

"Let's give it an hour, guys. If it doesn't calm down by then, we can all go home to momma and try again tomorrow."

In fact, their womenfolk were all present, farther up the pier, huddled outside the door to the Metal Room. A couple of them clutched heavily bundled infants, and some had brought older children, all tearful at the prospect of Father disappearing into the unknown. The delay could be put to good use, though. Doig took the families indoors to see the canoes and the intimidating heap of baggage. He presented all the women to Chi, who responded graciously, even acknowledging the degraded Babette and, in turn, introducing Saul. The formality helped to dry tears and raise morale.

When Doig and Melchior went out to take a weather reading, the sun was up, the snow had stopped, and there were no more whitecaps. It was obviously a go, and they could still catch the tide. Now, they had to repeat their rehearsed launching and loading, although the higher waves made the work harder.

Doig noticed that Chi was staying close to Saul as if worried he might bolt. The nominal leader's thwart was right at the stern of *Lewis*. With the canoes tapering at both ends, he would have very little elbow room, not much space to stretch his legs either, and almost no view because he had Buster Bruknar directly in front of him. Saul said nothing, and no one spoke to him except Doig, who politely welcomed him aboard.

The moment the last man boarded each canoe, paddles dipped, and it was off, clawing away from the dangerous stonework. There were no fancy speeches and no cheers. Nor were there any nametags. Even Saul Vandam noticed and removed his without being told. All men were to be equal on the Interior Expedition.

LIKE OLD EARTH, Neweden had more ocean than continent, and Northmain was the only major land mass in the northern hemisphere. Southmain, which almost touched it at the Gut, was classed as another continent, although a much smaller one. Thus, the great world tide that chased the sun around the planet had a clear run at the Gut, but February's tides were infant brothers of the great floods of perihelion. Even though there was no bore, the flow could still help the canoes along, and they did have a following wind.

As for the cold, a mere fifteen minutes' paddling made Doig feel that he was being boiled inside his furs. Less time than that was enough to produce unmistakable sounds of seasickness from behind him. As bow man, he did not have to watch, although he could see problems aboard *Clark,* which was in the lead.

Around noon, Melchior led them to a cove where they could disembark and stretch their legs. They had made up their lost time, he said, thanks to the wind. Those that could ate some lunch; those that couldn't didn't watch. It was only then, sitting on the shingle and studying the waves, that Doig truly appreciated that the great dream was now reality. Odds were that the future held only an early death for him, but at last, he was doing something to carry his father's banner forward.

He tried not to think about Babette and the child he might never see.

SOON AFTER NOON, the tide turned, but the ebb was always gentler than the flow in the Gut because of its funnel shape, and the wind was still favourable, so the expedition set off again. Melchior, who knew the geography better than anyone, had picked out a first night's campground, a wide sandbank conspicuously void of spiders. He knew it well because high tides around perihelion submerged it and made it a shipping hazard. The expedition came to it at mid-afternoon, which made a long enough first day for aching muscles and hands starting to blister.

Knowing that their island lacked fresh water, they had brought some, but it also lacked the driftwood they had hoped for, so they ate their supper cold. As evening approached, the temperature dropped, and men began unpacking their bedrolls.

"Even here, we need a night watch," Doig announced. "I know we have no spiders, but small octopussies have been known to crawl out of the water and bite people. Also, we must keep an eye on the canoes when the midnight tide arrives. I'll take the first shift with Saul. If we shout the alarm, everyone jump up to help." He appointed two more shifts to follow.

Soon after that, the camp grew very quiet, the silence broken only by the sound of waves and occasional snores. Saul rummaged in his pack and produced a box large enough to hold a man's shoe, plus some wires.

Doug knelt beside him. "Spider repellant?"

"Radio. I have to report home every night as long as we are in range."

"You have forgotten the accident."

"What sort of accident?"

"We shipped some water, and the radio got wet."

Saul said nothing, did nothing, just watched as Doig took

up the box and hurled it as far as he could into the sea. He knelt down again.

"The Board can't come and rescue us," he said, "and I don't trust them to keep our wives informed of our progress. We'll tell our story in May or June when we get back."

If they were allowed to speak, of course. And if they came back.

Saul just shrugged. This was a very humble Saul Vandam, quite unlike his former self. He might be wondering if he would be left behind when the canoes departed in the morning. Doig could almost feel sorry for him. Almost-almost.

"You ought to volunteer to help with the paddling. If we have any casualties, you'll get conscripted anyway, and volunteering will look good."

"Yes." After a long pause, "Are we going north or south? Which river?"

"South, the one the *Moctezuma* steering committee named the Nile."

"Why?"

"Because more of the points of interest in the starship remote-sensing records are that way, and because Arena went the other way."

"What?"

"The only surviving log of one of the earlier expeditions was written back in 99 by a man named Rupert Arena. They went north, up the Mississippi, but didn't get far, no more than a couple of hundred kilometres. The river was all rapids, so there was constant portaging. The spiders kept picking them off. The Nile can hardly be worse."

"I wish I hadn't asked."

"Don't mope!" Doig snapped. "If we do get back, you'll be a hero, with all the rewards that brings—fame, fortune, and fairly frequent fucking. Isn't that what you want?"

"And what do you want?" Saul asked sourly.

"I want to save the world."

MORNING CAME NONE TOO SOON, for the dawn cold bit like wolf spiders. Long before sunup, the canoes were loaded and launched. Although paddling was hard work, it did thaw out the bloodstream. The wind had dropped, and the sea was much calmer.

After a couple of hours, they reached Touchdown Island and detoured into Freshwater Cove, where they could fill their canteens at the stream that had given the little bay its name. The water came chattering and splashing out of the forest and quickly vanished into the shingle beach. Taking no chances, Doig had one man from each canoe refill the bags, a task that required several trips, while others stood on guard at the waterline with blazers. Still others had to stand in the sea itself, holding the canoes away from the shore, whose shingle might damage them.

No monsters emerged from the trees, but when the task was completed, and the canoes were ready to leave, he scrambled out into shin-deep icy water and held up the second of Saul Vandam's metal boxes.

"This, friends," he said, "was sent along for our safety, a gift from the Board. It seems that wolf spiders can detect radio waves, and this gadget will repel them. Far be it from me to distrust our noble leaders—" pause for jeers—, "but since we know that Touchdown Island is infested with wolf spiders, I now propose to run a test. Please keep a close watch and shout if you see anything suspicious."

Shivering, he waded ashore, laid the repellant down on a dry spot, and clicked the switch. Then he began to walk up and down, flapping his arms to keep warm. He decided he would count up to five hundred. He had reached three hundred forty-eight when the others began to yell warnings. Grabbing up the box, he ran back to Lewis and more or less fell into it as the crew began back-paddling.

Wolf spiders could not swim, but within seconds, a dozen of them were lined up along the strand waving their mandibles, and more were still emerging from the trees. Nobody said anything as the expedition paddled away. The conclusion was too obvious. As Saul had suggested, the repellant was actually an attractor, and the Board wanted all thirteen explorers to die.

Of course, if any of them did manage to return, they would have to be silenced to keep them from reporting this treachery.

BEYOND TOUCHDOWN, even Melchior had only a scant idea of the geography. Indeed, Doig knew more than he did from his long study of *Moctezuma*'s orbital records, but they were centuries old and could not be completely trusted on scenery that could change quickly, such as rivers and coastlines.

The rocky cliffs of Southmain gradually descended until the coast presented a forbidding line of jungle and nothing else. Eventually, Doig began to worry about a campsite, so he led the expedition nearer to shore, keeping a wary eye open for rocks. A closer view showed that the coast was a rocky shelf, roughly a kilometre wide, swept clean by the tides and storms. The jungle beyond it grew atop a low cliff and looked completely impenetrable, but spiders could squirm through almost anything, as Ivan Wong had discovered long ago.

Worried and exhausted, they came at last to a rocky islet ringed by breaking waves. Doig called for *Clark* to close in on *Lewis* for a general conference. The danger of wrecking one or both canoes was obvious, but this was the only possible refuge they had seen. The alternative would be to carry everything over the rocky shore until they were above the present high-tide mark. The sides of the islet were steeper, so the journey would be much shorter. Some men were going to get very wet and perhaps battered by the waves, but no one had ever said this journey would be easy, and they all agreed the attempt should be made

When the ordeal was over, they settled down to sleep on cold rock. Doig made a brief note in his log. They had survived Day Two.

HE HAD great hopes for Day Three, Saturday, because he expected to reach the delta of the Nile. They started late, having had to wait for the tide to bring them enough water, but no one complained about the delay, for the wind had fallen, and the air was warmer. While loading, they had their first accident: Tonis Horsfall slipped and banged his ribs. He insisted they were only bruised, not broken, but was obviously in pain.

To the astonishment of everyone except Doig, Saul Vandam then offered to paddle for him. Remembering how skinny the crewman had looked back in the shirtless days of summer and doubting that he would be able to stand the pace for long, Doig put him right behind himself on the number-two bench in *Lewis*. From there, his appeals for mercy, if any, would be audible.

Around noon, the shore changed character. The jungle grew higher, sunshine shone on golden sand, and even the smell of the sea changed. They veered in closer and located the mouth of a river that must be the source of the sand. It was a much narrower stream than Doig had expected and, therefore, not one of the main distributaries, for the Nile was a mighty river, comparable to its namesake back on Earth. Of course, the *Moctezuma* records were five hundred years old, and the river could well have changed its course in that time.

They beached the canoes and disembarked. Doig's first action was to check on Saul, who had not spoken a word all morning. His hands were covered in blood.

"Hear-this!" Doig shouted. "All come and see." He made Saul display his burst blisters, which were greeted with cheers and enough thumps on the back to make the crewman stagger. For the moment, at least, he was one of the boys, but now they had two men in bandages.

Taking that as a warning that too much haste could mean too little speed, Doig declared a half-day break. The water was much too cold for voluntary bathing—the river was bringing down slabs of ice—but the surroundings were more pleasant than any they had seen so far. They set up the spider-proof copper fence around their camp and ate a leisurely dinner in quite comfortable sunshine.

Their leader's mistake became evident soon after: he had made camp at high tide, and the sea was not going to come back for them until noon the next day.

WHEN THEY DID SET off on Day Four, though, they discovered that the ebbing tide was running in their favour, which meant that they had passed the narrowest part of the Gut and were now in the domain of the Western Ocean. By sunset, they were pitching camp on a sandbar at the mouth of a much larger river.

The next day, Monday, was exciting in that they were paddling upstream, heading inland at last. The banks were lined with dense jungle, which soon became monotonous, and the approach of spring was bringing out bugs, which buzzed and bit. The fragments of ice that floated by were too small to damage the canoes and could be fished out and used as a source of drinking water, for the estuary was still salty. They made no effort to pitch camp in the sinister undergrowth ashore, keeping instead to the many sandbars that offered safer landings. Those were a blessing that would not be available on their return journey, when the perihelion tides rose higher.

On Tuesday, they came to a divide where the river had split, so beyond that, they were paddling up a much larger stream. Although the current was gentle, it carried tree trunks, some of which were far larger than any Doig had ever seen. Even a small one could have stoved in a canoe, and it was his job, as front man, to keep an eye out for them.

They no longer had to worry about drinking water, but Doig was starting to worry about food. Monotonous as their diet was, the amount of it they consumed after hours of hard exercise was far beyond what he had estimated, and their supplies were running low. Most spiders were edible, although the carnivorous varieties, such as wolves, usually had a rank taste. But they had not seen a single spider other than the infuriating biting bugs.

"Hear-this!" he announced one afternoon as they were taking a break in a patch of calm water downstream from a sand spit. "According to Rupert Arena's log, the Mississippi contains edible fish, quite unlike the saltwater octopussies. He described them as delicious, so I brought along some nets. Let's see if the Nile will be as obliging."

The nets were based on records he had seen of fishing gear back on Old Earth, looking like tennis rackets with long handles and very loose strings. He issued two nets per boat, and it wasn't long before Enock Scrivener in Clark let out a howl of triumph and held up the net to show something silvery thrashing around in the mesh. By nightfall, they had a dozen of them, so they built a fire and roasted them. The taste was strange but not unpleasant. If they turned out to be poisonous, that would explain what had happened to all the previous explorers, but the alternative was going to be starvation, for they no longer had enough rations to see them home again.

Fish were not the Nile's only inhabitants, though. When they left the tidal stretch and reached fresh water, they encountered enormous amphibious spiders, leathery instead of furry and equipped with mandibles that looked as if they could bite a canoe in half. They lurked underwater in herds with their antennae floating on the surface and their upper eyes just above it. Once in a while, one would rear up and thrash the water with its front legs as if warning the strangers away. Following the traditional comparison with Earth fauna, Doig named them hippo spiders. He suspected that they were herbivorous, for they were simply too big and too numerous to be hunters, but they looked extremely dangerous.

By Wednesday evening, they were out of the jungle and had been on the road for a week, so he declared a party. They camped on an island sandbank near the eastern shore. There, they should be safe from any dry-land predators, and there were no footprints to suggest that any river fauna came there. The hippos did go ashore at night, and Doig was sure that neither blazers nor fragile copper fence would stop anything so huge.

The local driftwood burned wonderfully, shooting sparks into the darkening sky. They had roast fish, fresh water, and the last of their smoked meat. After another hard day's paddling, they could make do with that. As they unfortunately lacked the normally essential party ingredient of beer, they sang a few lewd songs instead, and Doig gave them a pep talk.

Having congratulated them all on coming so far without any serious mishaps, he got down to business. "According to the old orbital pictures, now that we are out of the delta, we should see no more jungle. From here on up, we shall be passing through much more open country. Admire the view, please," he said, pointing to the northeast, "because there isn't any. We can't even see Mount Moctezuma!"

He turned to the west. The river was several kilometres wide, so the far bank was a fuzzy dark line; beyond it stood the Faraway Hills, silhouetted against the sunset's pink glow. "They look a lot more like mountains than they did from the Pale, which gives you an idea of how far we have come. The river will take us closer to them in a few more days.

"The foothills are interesting because the *Moctezuma* scientists were fairly sure that they contain iron ore. I'd like to set up a camp soon and send a scouting party over there to pick up samples. If we're really lucky, we'll find a navigable—"

"Why?"

The voice was that of Saul Vandam, who had been speaking about two words a day. A permanent cloak of misery wrapped him like a black fog, so much so that Doig had wondered whether—and almost hoped—he would jump overboard or wander away to be eaten by something. Now, suddenly, Saul looked ready for an argument. Doig had always known he would cause trouble eventually. Perhaps the time had come.

"Why what?"

"Why bother? How far is it?"

Doig shrugged one shoulder. "Fifty K or so."

"So two days' hard walking? And two days back? How many kilos of iron ore can you hump on your back for two days, Captain Gray? How many tons can you load into a canoe? Why bother? Just to score points off the Board because it didn't know there was an inaccessible mineral deposit a week's journey away?"

"Because we came here to explore this world, which our forefathers should have done four hundred years ago. Because you cannot know what you will find before you find it." *Not good enough!* "Because I want our children to grow up."

"Hear, hear!" Buster shouted, and many voices joined in. But Doig knew that the issue had not been resolved. Saul's question had not gone away, and his own answer had hardly been convincing. Then he saw a hand raised. "Tengiz?"

When choosing his team, Doig had consulted some of the instructors at Only U, and several had recommended Tengiz Silva. He was bright, they agreed, and he was majoring in planetary science, so he might be valuable. He was also keen and had lied about his age to get on board. He was the only man present not sporting a beard.

"We might be better to save that side trip for our return journey," he suggested. "Right now, I think we should make all the progress we can upstream before the flood comes."

About ten voices shouted, "What flood?"

He grinned at the reaction, scanning all the firelit faces. "Haven't you seen all these sandbars and the height of the banks? This mighty river isn't anywhere near its annual maximum flow. I don't know when that will be—just after perihelion, I expect, when the snow on the mountains melts, so we may be safely home before it happens, but I still think we're at low water now. Or we were. Last night, I stuck a twig in the sand when we arrived, and there was a centimetre of water around it when we left in the morning."

"Somebody give that man another beer," Buster shouted.

Tengiz's advice seemed good, so the team all agreed to continue upstream as far as possible, with only Saul Vandam abstaining. He could never agree with anything.

THE NEXT DAY, they saw their first elephants, a herd of a dozen or so in the distance. *Moctezuma* had detected them from orbit but had made no detailed images. Binoculars showed them to have the usual spider body plan, but they walked on six legs, the front pair having evolved into prehensile arms used to gather vegetation and stuff it into their mouths.

On subsequent days, they saw much more wildlife. On old Earth, the many ecological niches had been shared among numerous different phyla, but on Neweden, the spider plan had taken over everywhere. The same ecological adaptions could almost be matched one-on-one: hippo spiders, elephant spiders, antelope spiders, eagle spiders, vulture spiders, gerbil spiders. The *Clark* crew thought they saw a tiger once, back in the delta jungle.

Those town-born men had lived underground or partly underground all their lives, and some of them found the huge openness of the Southmain plains almost frightening, yet others loved the endless vistas and the sense of freedom. Each night, someone was sure to remark how fertile this land looked. And inevitably, somebody else would point out that it wasn't habitable for humans. They would freeze solid at aphelion and mummify or incinerate in summer.

The Nile was curving to the west as they continued upstream, bringing them closer to the Faraway Hills. Doig had known this would happen and had marked several anomalies that he wanted to explore in the foothills, where *Moctezuma*'s remote sensing had detected a great variety of both rocks and vegetation. On February 20, two weeks after they set out, they camped on the bank where a tributary joined the main stream. It was a much smaller river, only six or seven metres wide, but it provoked that evening's discussion in that it was the first thing they had encountered that seemed to deserve a name. After a while, they agreed that they should take turns issuing names, and Doig should begin. And so, the Babette River was named.

Doig had marked it on his photographs, and he eyed it longingly as a potential path to the prospective iron ore outcrops. He did not suggest a side excursion, though—not then. A new day brought new data.

Mornings were still cold, and the rising sun clearly showed a line of white smoke rising from a cut in the foothills that lined up well with the Babette's apparent course and was almost certainly its channel. After some discussion, the expedition agreed that whether they were seeing smoke or steam, it should be investigated. Doig suggested that *Lewis* explore up the tributary and *Clark* wait for its return. He left Saul Vandam behind, too, and some other unnecessary baggage.

The Babette was a much trickier canoe road than the Nile because it was narrower, shallower, and faster, running over gravel and cobbles. By noon, the paddlers were flagging, and they came to a stretch of rapids that would require a long portage. Sensing mutiny brewing, Doig called a lunch break.

After chewing over and around the problem, they all agreed that they would leave *Lewis* where they had beached it and proceed on foot for a change. The landscape was more rolling than it had been down on the Nile floodplain and covered with scrubby vegetation, rarely more than knee-high. Nothing of any great size could hide in that, but small things could be dangerous, too, so they proceeded single-file, blazers in hand.

They walked for an hour or so without seeing many stretches of navigable water. Doig's right shoe began to pinch, making him worry about the condition of everybody else's footwear, too. He should have ordered everyone to bring spares, but he had failed to foresee how much of their exploration would have to be done on foot. More and more, this expedition was feeling like a mere practice run for a generation of similar trips.

Then a longer shadow joined his, and Tengiz Silva was strolling along at his side. "Present for you, honoured boss." He handed Doig a reddish rock.

"What is it?"

"It's a rock. There's a lot of them just lying—"

"What sort of a rock?"

"A rock rich in iron." Tengiz's youthful face split in a triumphant grin. "Hematite, mostly, with some magnetite, maybe. It precipitates out of water, especially near springs. You noticed our steam beacon disappeared as the day grew warmer? So, there must be a warmish spring contributing to the Babette River, and it's bringing down pieces of iron ore to save us having to go all the way up to their source, yes?"

"Certainly. And you can have the first beer tonight as a reward." Doig looked around at the circle of beards. "Anyone want to carry on, or shall we take Dr. Silva's word for it?"

The motion to return having passed unanimously, the expedition turned and headed back downstream. Doig, who had omitted to bring a bag of any sort to collect samples, found himself carrying the hematite, which grew steadily heavier as the afternoon wore on. Going down was faster than going up had been, and that would certainly still be true when they were back in the *Lewis*. They should have no trouble in reuniting with the other half of the expedition before nightfall.

Or so he thought until they arrived back to the place where they had beached the canoe. Huge footprints by the river confirmed that a herd of elephants had come to drink there. They had evidently taken a dislike to *Lewis* because they had trampled it flat.

Six weary, hungry, frightened men sat down in a circle, and five of them looked at Doig. All five were trying not to seem reproachful, but he knew they must be blaming him and were right to do so.

"My fault," he said. "I should have left some of us behind to guard the canoe. If you want to depose me and appoint a new leader, I shan't argue."

After a moment, Buster said, "You got us into this, boss. You can get us out. All in favour?" He raised a hand, and the other four followed his lead.

Doig wished they hadn't, but to refuse their forgiveness would be a second betrayal. "Then we camp here tonight. There are fish in the river, so we can eat. Tomorrow, we walk downstream to join the others. After that, we decide what we want to do. Any discussion?"

After a respectful moment, the youngest tentatively raised a hand.

"Yes, Tengiz?"

"We've explored twenty kilometres of Babette River. Why did the herd decide to do its dance just here, right on top of our boat?"

Doig had been wondering the same. "I expect they thought it smelled bad."

"No other suggestions?" He was a very smart young man.

"I just suggest that while there's life, there's always hope." Doig's own notion was too farfetched to mention, but he wondered if the kid was thinking along the same crazy lines as he was.

Buster Bruknar, although not the most perceptive of men, knew Doig better than any of the others did and was regarding him now with deep suspicion. "Whatcha holding back, bossman?"

"Nothing."

"Yes, you are."

Doig spread his hands as if to show that they were empty. "Look, we're in very deep doo-doo, and I don't deny it. But there is one teeny-weeny ray of light in this tunnel. It's because of something my father said. I don't remember it, but my mother told me. It was always a one-in-a-billion chance, and now it's perhaps one in nine hundred million. And that's all I'm going to say because I don't want to raise false hopes. We'll talk again tomorrow."

They rescued what they could from the supplies that had been left with the canoe and netted some fish for a meal. Lacking their copper fence, they posted double guards, and Doig assigned the first shift to himself and Dell Firmin. Sunset and darkness followed.

They had brought bedrolls, but some of them had ended up in the river when the canoe was destroyed, so sleeping arrangements had to be improvised. As the first snores were starting, Doig was sitting on the ground, brooding, when Dell tapped him on the shoulder and gestured for him to rise.

Far away across the plain, a light twinkled under the stars. Fire meant people, and a fire visible all the way from the Nile would be no ordinary campfire. The two men watched it in silence for a while, wondering. If the *Clark* crew had sent out a search party for them, the fire should be much closer . . . if they had been attacked by some sort of spiders, they might have started a brush fire for defence . . . they were sending a warning . . . appealing for help . . .

Finally, Dell said, "Well, boss?"

The fire could mean utter disaster and certain death, but to say so would be cruel, and there was a wisp of a hint of a chance that it might even be good news.

Doig said, "Make that a one-in-eight-hundred-million," and sat down to brood some more.

THE MOOD in the morning was grim. Some of the *Lewis* wreckage could still be of value, but not when it had to be carried for hours. Doig decreed that everything be left behind. If necessary, *Clark* could come and get it.

So, the long walk down the Babette River began. Probably none of them had realized how fast they had been travelling the previous day or how slow walking would seem in comparison. After an hour or so, Doig realized that his duty as leader was to do something to raise morale. He was trudging along beside Idriss Devine, who had been married very little longer than Doig himself and whose wife had given birth to a baby boy just a week before the expedition set out. Their decision to name the boy Doig Devine must seem very ironic now that the eponymous Doig had screwed up so badly.

He got his cue when Idriss said, "What did you mean by what you said about the elephants last night?"

"I was clutching at a straw. You know we're here because the colony is heading for disaster, right? And we're hoping to find something that will help, right?"

"And we all knew it was a fogging long shot. So, what's the straw?"

"I'll tell you. Think it over and see if you can come to the same conclusion I did. I warn you—it's very farfetched!"

Idriss shrugged. "What's the prize?"

"Hope. Faint, faint, hope, but better than despair."

"Shoot."

"I met my mother very briefly last year, and I cross-examined her on what my father had believed the Board ought to be doing—apart from dropping dead, that is. For her own protection, he had never told her much, but she mentioned a couple of things he let slip that might be relevant. One was the word

'Sabine,' and the other was a man's name, Halapeno Guzman. The first is too farfetched even for me. Perhaps he was really just dreaming. But Halapeno is interesting."

"Never heard of him."

"Nobody has. I found only one mention of that name in the archives—but remember that the archives have been laundered more than once, so there could have been others by the same name. The Jalapeno Guzman I found was born in 132 and thrown to the spiders for murder and attempted kidnapping in 154, three hundred fifty-five years ago."

Idriss looked at Doig with rank disbelief. "And that's good news?"

"I warned you it was farfetched. Keep it to yourself, think it over, and send someone else forward."

Over the next hour or so, he told each of the others in very much the same words, and the first relevant comment came, surprisingly, from Buster, who did have a knack for separating wheat from chaff.

"Never heard of anyone being found guilty of kidnapping before."

Doig said, "Quite."

The last man to be told was the youngest, Tengiz Silva, who, in some ways, was certainly the smartest. He stalked along in silence for several minutes before saying, "You think the date's significant, then?"

Happy at this reaction, Doig said, "Very."

The strange fate of Jalapeno Guzman did provide a topic of conversation during that long day, but Doig knew that none of the others could put even as little hope in it as he did. He knew he was deluding himself, but it made him feel better.

BY THE TIME the exhausted hikers returned to the place where the Babette joined the Nile, the sun was setting behind the Faraway Hills. No one shouted a greeting; no one ran to meet them. The fire that Idriss and Doig had seen the previous evening had been a scrub fire that had started near the river and spread uphill, driven by an easterly breeze, before dying out of its own accord.

The source of it had been the *Clark* and all its supplies. From what the *Lewis* crew could make out, studying the ashes in the fading light, the canoe itself had been cut into three pieces and heaped up with its contents before being set alight. Nothing was left except charred spider bones and a few metal implements—the kettle, a shovel blade, crumpled solar panels, and so on.

This was utter disaster. There was no way home except by boat, and now they had no boat and no way to build one.

It was Idriss who found the reason for the fire. Poking through the ashes with a stick, he found a blackened human skull and then a pelvis. The blaze had been a funeral pyre. Six unhappy men studied the skull.

"Logan Foley," Buster said. "That gap between his front teeth? He used to whistle through it when he was concentrating on something."

Other voices muttered in agreement. Logan had left a widow and two orphans back in the Pale.

"Well, boss?" Idriss shouted. "What happened to the rest of them? Who did this? Your precious Jalapeno Guzman?"

Five pairs of eyes stared accusingly at Doig. They were seeing certain death. He saw triumph.

"Spiders do not light fires," he said. "Only people do. Jalapeno died back in 154 and almost certainly left no survivors. Before you lynch me, tell me this. If we find a good place to live in these parts—somewhere to shelter from perihelion and aphelion both, somewhere we could live a decent life in freedom—what would be the first thing you would want?"

Buster spoke first. "Shadiya!"

"Right. We'd want our women and children to come and share it. And what's the last thing Chairman Precious Ruckles and his Board of toads want?"

"Another colony!" said several voices.

"Right. Another colony would strike at the root of their power. Starting in Year 25, at least nine exploratory missions were sent out to look for exploitable resources. I don't know which one struck gold, but I think that one of the early ones did; it found somewhere habitable—much more habitable than Touchdown and the Pale. And I think those successful pioneers began sneaking back to the colony to rescue their wives and children. The Board didn't notice at first. I believe, although I cannot prove, that Jalapeno Guzman was a member of the mission that sailed in 152. He would have been the right age. But when they went back for their wives and girlfriends, he got caught, and, of course, in the Board's eyes, what he and the others were doing was kidnapping. They very likely tortured him, but they certainly gave him to the spiders and blocked any further exploration. The 152 mission was the last."

Amid the shouts, Buster was loudest. "So, where are these homicidal settlers?"

Doig flopped down on the ground cover. "I don't know where they are, but they know where we are. I hope they'll drop by in the morning and bring us breakfast in bed. I don't know this, but I'm willing to bet that their home base is in the Faraway Hills."

"That makes no sense!" Buster said. "In winter, hills are colder; in summer, the radiation is worse." Then he cautiously added, "Why?"

"Because last spring, I started studying remote sensing.

Moctezuma scanned the entire planet in dozens of ways: gravity, magnetic, radio. All the records are still there, in the databanks, although they're getting badly degraded now. The one exception is the Faraway Hills. Those are gone, wiped, blanked. I did find some small-scale visual images, and when our geological expert joined our party, I showed him. Tengiz?"

"Karst!" Tengiz proclaimed. "Absolutely, certainly, karst."

Buster growled menacingly.

Tengiz grinned. "Karst topography is what you get when limestone is eroded. Sinkholes, underground rivers—and caves! Huge caverns dozens of kilometres long, sometimes."

"That's where the first explorers would have headed first," Doig said. "Why go back to the colony to spend your life hacking tunnels in pumice when nature had already provided them for you? Warm in winter, cool in summer, likely with loads of fresh water. Yes, I suggested this expedition in the very faint hope that there was another colony, and that it has survived. Now I'm sure of it."

After a moment, Buster called for three cheers and got them. Doig recalled Dad telling him that men live on hope.

WEARY, cold, and hungry, they spent a doleful night. Before dawn, Dell Firmin, their best shot, took a rifle and went off to hunt. He returned an hour or so later with a small antelope, which was a delicious treat. As they ate, the sun rose higher, shining hotter now, in the middle of February. Fed and warmed, the castaways had nothing to do but lie on the mossy ground cover and talk. Why did the settlers, if there were any, hate canoes so much? Why had Logan died? What had happened to the rest of the men they had left behind? Could there be such things as intelligent spiders? What were the *Lewis* men to do if the unknowns did not return?

Waiting was not something Buster did well or often. Toward mid-morning, he roared, "You're the leader, Doig, so lead us! Give us something to do!"

"Hear-this," Doig announced. "All hands: observe the eagles. Leader out."

All eyes looked upward at tiny specks floating in the blue. It was hard to believe that flying things of any size had evolved from spider-shaped creatures, but so the biologists had long since convinced themselves and everyone else.

"What about them?" Elijah growled. "They're always there."

"Only when the sun gives them thermals to soar on," Tengiz said. "And those could be vulture types, waiting for carrion. Meat like us, maybe."

"Yes to all that," Doig said, "but those two above us are working as a pair. And they were doing that above us yesterday, but I never saw any pairing before that. Could be a mating ritual, but who knows?"

Tengiz laughed. "So, now we have intelligent flying spiders?"

Nobody answered. Doig was feeling a lot less worried than he would have done had the unknowns killed all of the *Clark* team. That Logan had been the only one to die suggested that he had tried to resist, although he might have been shot or blazed out of hand as an example to cow the rest. But why had the others been led away, and where to? It was hard to dream without imagining horrors like slave mines or fattening pens.

Buster said, "Hey! Where'd the other one go?" He was still staring straight up.

"Southwest." That was Tengiz, who had very sharp eyes.

The remaining eagle, or vulture, continued to circle directly overhead.

Doig scrambled to his feet and stared southwestward. If the spy had gone that way, it must be reporting, or summoning . . . or something. There was a low knoll in that direction, its scrub cover burned to the roots by the previous evening's fire.

"Going to take a look." He set off in that direction, and at once, Buster was walking at his side.

"Looking for what?"

"Anything," Doig said. "Horse spiders or, more likely, elephants."

"Intelligent, sharpshooting, talking elephants?"

"Domesticated elephants. The elephant mammals back on earth had big brains; they were pretty smart. People rode on their backs in cabins called howdahs."

"Sometimes I think you're wired straight into the archives."

Doug often wished he was, but his all-protoplasmic guess was right this time. In the distance, a troop of five elephants was plodding in his direction. They were certainly carrying burdens. Buster thumped his shoulder.

Doig handed him his blazer. "I'm going to stay here. You go and warn the others to wait where they are, and on no account let them wave any weapons around. We don't want more Logan Foleys."

Buster obediently strode off, and Doig remained to await his fate, studying the great beasts as they drew nearer. Evolution had done a fine job adapting the basic spider mould. Their sickle-shaped mandibles were at least two metres long. The front limbs served as arms and ended in finger-and-thumb digits, all presently folded in front of them; they used the other six legs as twin tripods—front and back on one side paired with the middle on the other—striding along with a rolling motion. Their wide-set upper eyes would give them panoramic vision, while the lower pair were close together to focus on footing and potential food. Most amazing of all, though, was the sheer size of them.

Long before they arrived, he heard their breathing, about the lowest note on a tuba played by a man who never needed to draw breath. As they drew nearer, he sensed that he might be hearing only the upper harmonics, and the primary tone was below his hearing, subsonic. There were subtle vibratos, too, so perhaps the great beasts were talking among themselves.

Doig stood his ground while the leading elephant headed straight for him as if intending to walk right over him or chop him in half with its mandibles. At the last minute, its rider barked a command, and it halted, as did all its followers. Its lower eyes regarded Doig with an angry, hungry look, although a monster so enormous would have to be herbivorous.

"Are you Doig Gray?" The voice came from a man seated in an open box on its back, about four metres up in the air.

"I am. Who are you?"

"Never mind. Throw down your weapons."

"I have no weapon except this knife."

"Throw it away. Gracie, rest!"

The elephant bent its legs until its torso rested on the ground. The driver scrambled out of his howdah box and slid down between the first and second legs. He came around to Doig.

He was short, brown-skinned, and barefoot. He was probably in his thirties, wiry and tough-looking, armed with a primed blazer and wearing only shorts and a headband to control shoulder-length hair. His clean-shaven face made Doig conscious of his own bewhiskered state. Doig offered a hand to shake, but it was ignored.

"Strip!"

"Why? One of my companions was murdered here yester—"

"You people do not belong here, and he resisted arrest. Strip or die."

He was probably bluffing, since he was close enough to be burned by the backwash from a blazer shot, but Doig shrugged and obeyed, discarding everything except his shorts. Meanwhile, the other elephants' mahouts had arrived, two men and two women. One of the men took up each of the garments in turn, examined it for weapons, and then handed it back. They kept his shoes. Doig dressed again, getting himself thoroughly smeared by the dark ash that covered the ground.

"Now go to your men and tell them to—"

"I will do nothing more until you tell me who you are and by what right you give me orders."

"I am Senior Mahout Findlay, and if you do not obey me, we will go away and leave you to starve. Your position here is hopeless."

"And if I do obey you?"

"As long as you continue to do so, you will be fed and not harmed. You will be taken to be judged by the Mothers, who rule this land."

There wasn't much wriggle room in his terms, but Doig had come to this land because he detested tyranny. Again, he offered a hand. "I give you my word that my men and I will obey in return for your personal guarantee of our safety."

Findlay scowled. "I am not negotiating; I am enforcing the law. Now, you will kneel to me as a sign of obedience, or on my count of three, you will die. One . . ."

Doig waited until about two-and-a-half before he knelt. He knew that his companions were watching, and he would wear black ash on his knees as badges of shame, but he had forbidden more Logan Foley martyrdoms.

"Now, go and send your men over here, one by one, to be searched for weapons. They may bring their bedrolls but nothing else. Dakarai, go with him and see that he does not cheat."

Dakarai was a larger, somewhat older man with white fuzz on his chest. He had lost most of his head hair, and the greying remainder was tied back in a ponytail. He was armed with a large blazer. He said, "Move, slave."

IT DID NOT TAKE LONG to disarm the visitors and line them up in front of the elephants. Findlay's squad collected weapons in one sack and footwear in another. While this was going on, a huge flying spider swooped down, circled twice, and finally perched on the back rail of one of the howdahs. One of the two women was there to free its rider, a boy of around seven or eight, who had been securely strapped in place. She hugged him and praised him. A few minutes later, the second bird arrived, that one being ridden by a girl of around the same age. The children rewarded their aerial steeds by tossing them scraps of food, keeping out of range of the deadly mandibles.

Doig's studies in the history of old Earth had taught him to be unsurprised by domesticated elephants, but flying cavalry was a novelty.

"Slave Gray, come with me," Findlay said.

Carrying his bedroll, which Buster had brought, Doig followed his captor over to the leading elephant, still patiently resting.

"This is where you set an example for your squad. Stand there." Findlay pointed to a spot directly between the points of the gigantic mandibles.

Doig obeyed as nonchalantly as he could.

"Raise your bedroll up high." Findlay gestured. "Gracie, load!"

The spider unfolded its arms, gripped Doig gently under his arms with its two pairs of opposable fingers, and hoisted him up over its head, laying him in the howdah on its back. The howdah was an open box fitted with three two-seater benches. There was some storage space behind the rear one and a perching rail at the very back.

Doig turned to face the front and grinned to reassure the watchers. There was something dreamlike about all this. A moment later, Tengiz was lifted up to join him, and the others were safely loaded on other elephants. Then, their respective mahouts were hoisted aboard, and the procession wheeled around and set off in the direction from which it had come.

Travel without effort was a pleasant change. The seats were padded, and the spider's rolling gait was not uncomfortable. Doig decided he was enjoying himself, and Tengiz was grinning like a schoolboy.

"Where are we going, boss?"

"I haven't inquired." Doig leaned forward to Findlay on the front bench. "Where are we going, Senior Mahout?"

"To Sabine."

Yay! How had Dad known that name? "Who or what is that?"

"Wait and see." Findlay was not a polished conversationalist.

"How long will it take us?"

"Weeks."

Doig leaned back. "Enjoy the ride," he told Tengiz. "Seems you have time to work on that moustache."

THE ELEPHANTS SWUNG ALONG TIRELESSLY, and their rocking motion was almost soporific. They had an animal odour that Doig found unobjectionable, and their posterior exhaling orifices rumbled constantly as if speaking to one another. Gracie, as the dominant female, led the way and set the pace. About once an hour, she would turn her head sideways and vomit out her castings in a barrage of orange-coloured missiles. After that, she would feed as she went, gathering shrubbery together with her long arms and either hauling it out by the roots or chopping it loose with her mandibles. Either way, it was all stuffed into her mouth until she had a bellyful to digest.

Tengiz was bursting with questions, which Doig discouraged when they were directed to him and went unanswered when addressed to Mahout Findlay, surely the least chattery person on the planet. The youngster's own comments were interesting, though, for he was a sharp observer. He pointed out how the vegetation varied, signalling changes in the underlying bedrock, and how the hills ahead had been shaped by the extreme climate. Several times, he spotted traces of the passing of other elephants.

"Seems like we're following the *Clark* crew!"

"Or just retracing this herd's path?"

Doig saw at once that he'd blundered.

"No, boss. They always puke to the left and graze to the right, see?"

Doig hadn't seen.

NO LUNCH WAS SERVED, but Findlay did pass a water bottle around. About two hours before sunset, he stood up briefly and shouted something to the next elephant, one of those with a female mahout, an eagle, and an aviator child. The boy clambered onto the bird's back, and the woman fastened him there and untethered it. It leaped upward, beating its huge wings as it fought for altitude.

"That is one brave kid!" Doig remarked.

Surprisingly, Findlay responded. "He has faith in the Holy Stars."

Oh! Like that, was it?

Tengiz looked to Doig in surprise, but Doig was hastily trying to recall everything he had read about religions on Old Earth. There had been a lot of them, and they tended to generate massive trouble whenever they met. The *Moctezuma* charter had forbidden religious discussion except within families and discouraged it even there. The Neweden colony had grown up with no religious buildings or associations.

"Tell me what you know about the Holy Stars, Senior Mahout."

Findlay was watching the climbing eagle. "It was they who led Roman Rietveld to Sabine and blessed it."

Rietveld was not a crew name, nor was it a cargo name that Doig had ever encountered. "And what year was that?"

"Forty-eight."

"And how many people live there now?"

Intent on the eagle, Findlay did not reply.

Doig and Tengiz exchanged thoughtful looks. If Earth had ever managed to fund and dispatch a second stellar colonization, it would not have been aimed at the same planets as *Moctezuma* had been. Findlay and his band were human, not spiders. So, Sabine could only be an offshoot of the main *Moctezuma* colony, almost certainly seeded by one of the exploratory expeditions sent out from the Town. Doig was not satisfied that he had ever found a complete list of those projects, let alone of their personnel, but he was convinced that no

Board would ever have allowed women to participate. So, Sabine could only have flourished by "kidnapping" women from the main colony, as he had suggested.

"The name Sabine is curious," he told Tengiz. "Old Earth had a legend about a man called Romulus, who founded the once-great city of Rome. He began as leader of a gang—probably a war band of some sort. Having no wives, they kidnapped women from a tribe that lived in the nearby Sabine Hills and thus became the ancestors of all Romans."

Findlay could certainly hear, but he continued to watch the bird and its child burden, showing no sign of listening.

"What did the Sabine men think about that?" Tengiz inquired, eyes twinkling.

"Quite a lot, and in no kindly way, but when they went to take their daughters and sisters back, the women begged to be allowed to remain with their lovers."

"That was the Romans' side of the story?"

"Correct. The Sabine version has not survived."

And the Neweden version was somewhat distorted if that legend was the origin of the name. A man named Roman might certainly have made himself familiar with the ancient empire and known the legend. It was certainly a hint that Roman Rietveld and his friends, having gone exploring for resources but finding a more habitable place instead, had gone back incognito to retrieve their wives and sweethearts. Assuming, also, that the Board of the day had not discovered what was happening, then it would not be impossible that successive expeditions had followed the Rietveld example—until 154, when Jalapeno Guzman had been caught while mate-retrieving. There had been no more expeditions after that. Guesswork, but it made sense.

The child on the eagle had seen what he had been sent to

locate, and Findlay changed Gracie's direction slightly toward where he was circling. The rest of the pack followed in line.

Their destination turned out to be a watering hole, a small lake where an earthfall had dammed a stream. Two women, one man, and three children were already there to meet the arrivals. Signs of frequent occupancy were clearly visible—close-grazed shrubbery, heaps of elephant castings, and old fire pits. Doig asked Findlay if the *Clark* team had come that way the previous day but received no answer.

Findlay himself was now wearing shoes, but the prisoners were refused theirs, which effectively hobbled them, for the footing was made treacherous by spiky plants and bitten-off stumps.

"I'm quite willing to promise that we won't run away," Doig protested, but the surly mahout ignored him while continuing to attend to Gracie. As soon as he unfastened the straps holding her howdah, she lifted it off her back and set it on the ground. Then, she rose and seemed to stretch her legs as if happy to be rid of that burden before stalking off to the pond to bathe. The elephants were marvellous beasts, but they weren't the answer to the colony's problems. Even ten thousand elephants would not save the world for humans.

The missing eagle had returned, and its rider had been released. He looked no more than eight or nine, skinny and blond, and he chattered happily as he trotted along beside the woman who was presumably his mother.

Doig intercepted them. "That is one truly heroic son you have there, ma'am."

The boy backed away from the stranger, reaching for her hand. Doig was not flattered to be seen as more alarming than a trip thousands of metres into the sky. He dropped to one knee.

"Hi. I'm Doig. What's your name?"

"My name is Hector. You're a slave." The aviator tugged his mother away, and they continued their journey. She had been amused by that exchange, but her smile had been for her son, not Doig. She, too, was blonde and had blue eyes. Several of the other Sabines also had fair hair, which was almost unknown in the Pale.

The rest of Doig's team came limping over to him, and he braced himself for a difficult meeting. They made themselves as comfortable as possible on the rough ground.

"Tengiz and I have learned," he said, "that we are being taken to a place called Sabine, which is apparently some distance away. What else have any of you heard about it?" Surely, not all mahouts were as taciturn as Findlay.

Elijah said, "We heard it's up in the mountains."

Buster added, "I heard hints that it's on the coast."

"Vandam!" Doig said. "That's a thousand kilometres away." He had never studied data on lands west of the Faraways because he had expected to explore the drainage basin of the Nile.

"Sounds like we won't be going home too soon," said Idriss.

True. *Oh, Babette!* The Hector child had called Doig a slave. So had Mahout Dakarai. The word brought back dark memories of Copper Island.

"Problem Number One, then. Ours is the first expedition to leave the Pale in three and a half centuries. Even if Findlay and his army are based on this side of the hills, how did they know we were coming? The continent is far too huge to be scouted by a few children riding birds, and nobody stands guard for three hundred and fifty years. And if they started out from Sabine, that question gets a thousand times tougher because they must have set out last year, before winter set in."

No one offered answers. He was the leader, the universal expert, Mr. Know-It-All.

"Problem Number Two," Buster said. "What do they want

with us? Why did they smash our canoes and kill Logan? Why carry us off as prisoners for a thousand kilometres?"

"Good one," Doig agreed. "Problem Number Three is that Mahout Findlay mentioned the Holy Stars, as if they are benevolent gods."

Buster nodded. "So did our mahout, Dakarai. He said that the Holy Stars had given all these lands to 'their' people. Meaning them, but not us."

What Doig knew about religions was very little, but certainly more than any of the others did. "Listen, then. Everyone has beliefs; everyone thinks their beliefs are correct, and all others are therefore wrong. If some guy tells you that breaking a mirror will bring you seven years' bad luck, there is no point in arguing with him or asking for evidence. Yes, there have been people who believed that, and even worse nonsense. But if you meet one, just thank him for the warning and leave it at that, okay? If he asks you to which god you sacrifice your firstborn, find some polite way to say you are not allowed to discuss it—which, going strictly by the *Moctezuma* charter, you are not.

"And never forget," he added, "that Findlay believes his Holy Stars allow him to blaze us if we disobey his orders."

There was nothing more to discuss until they gathered more information on their thousand-kilometre trek to the mysterious west, but their captors had a fire burning and sending out delicious odours of roast meat. Someone had been hunting and gathering.

Before anyone began to eat, though, Senior Mahout Findlay had to address a long prayer of thanks to his Holy Stars, some of whom were already appearing overhead. Then the Sabiners said, "Amen." The prisoners remained silent. Slaves or not, they were given generous helpings of meat and baked tubers. Doig reluctantly decided that it was the best meal he had eaten since leaving the colony—even better than most of Babette's cooking, a cargo skill she had yet to acquire.

THAT DAY SET the pattern for the next four. Yielding to Doig's pleas, Findlay returned the explorers' shoes so they were able to move around and exercise, but they continued to be addressed as "slaves" and treated as prisoners.

The caravan continued southwestward toward the mountains, although the massive elephants were clearly unhappy when required to climb any but the gentlest of inclines. The landmark that seemed to represent their destination was a group of three peaks close together. The Sabiners called them "the Triplets."

Spring was progressing toward summer, and the killer heat of perihelion. The mahouts began erecting awnings on the howdahs to give shade during the worst part of the day, but even the low sunlight of the mornings and evenings was becoming fierce. The diet was monotonous, rarely enlivened by fresh meat. Those were merely physical discomforts, which could be endured. Far worse was the mental torment of knowing that there was now no possibility of returning to the colony before perihelion. Chi Brigham had promised the explorers that their wives and children would be supported until they returned, but he had said nothing about what would happen after they were given up for dead. Babette would be a mother by now, but she knew no trade. Family and friends had rejected her. How would she feed herself and her child?

Doig found it hard not to brood on Babette and their child, two people dependant on him whom he had failed utterly. As Saul Vandam had said, he had probably walked right into the Board's trap by agreeing to lead this expedition. He had already lost half the men who had trusted him enough to join it and seemed certain to lose the rest. No matter how he tried, he could not foresee a happy ending to this disaster. Early death in a salt mine was about the best fate he could imagine. Until then, all he could do was keep up a brave front and hide his despair from the others.

HE WAS WAKENED by a light being shone on his face.

"That him?" said a voice. "Petrovich? Is this him?"

Doig grunted angrily and put a forearm over his eyes.

"He's grown a beard," said another, deeper voice.

"Idiot! So have you. Is this Doig Gray?" The first speaker was a woman.

A boot prodded his ribs, not gently. *What? Why?*

It was the middle of the night. In the distance, elephants were snoring.

The man laughed. "Yes. That's Best Boy."

"Gray!" the woman said. She nudged him again, harder. "Wake up. You're leaving."

"Huh?" Doig sat up, still shielding his eyes from the light. The other explorers, lying nearby, stirred and growled at having their sleep interrupted. "Who the shit are you?" And why should he do whatever she said?

"I am Captain Lee Idonea of Sabine Security, and I was sent to fetch you on a matter of great personal importance. Get up."

He pulled his knees close, keeping his buttocks on the ground. She turned off her flashlight. As his eyes adjusted to the starlight, he made her out, a seemingly short, trim woman. Or else she was of average height, and the man at her side was enormous. Some metres away stood three or four other men in mahout costume, watching warily.

Idonea raised her voice as if addressing them. "You! Mahouts! Bring me some rope, and we'll tie him up."

"Hold it!" Doig barked. "My companions and I have already been kidnapped once. If you represent the law around here, then I charge—"

"Shut up. Kam can explain on the road. Just understand this, Gray. The matter is hugely urgent. If you don't get to Sabine in time, you will regret it all your life. If you do, then whatever it may have cost you will seem worthwhile."

"But my companions—"

"No. This concerns you only, strictly just you. They will follow."

"Let me help you, Best Boy," said the giant. A huge hand clamped around Doig's upper arm, hauled him more or less upright, then released him, hopelessly off-balance. Before he collapsed, he was scooped up in two mighty arms and lifted like a baby.

Sudden memory broke through the bonds of sleep. *Petrovich?* "Are you Kam Petrovich? Allbrawn? Is it you?"

Clutched hard against that massive chest, Doig felt a couple of earth tremors to indicate laughter. "In the flesh, and lots of it. Now, be careful. This is a night mare, and you must never get in front of it, or it will eat you."

This must all be a nightmare, for how could Kam "Allbrawn" Petrovich have ever found his way from Ms. Wills's classroom on Copper Island to the interior of Southmain? But what Kam meant by a night mare was yet another type of spider, not as huge as an elephant but not far from it. He proceeded to hoist Doig up, head high, pushing him against the rank-smelling whitish fur until he found straps and handholds leading up to a sort of roofed howdah, much like a doll-sized version of the cabin on the sled that had carried the young Doig to the Pale from Copper Island so long ago. Having no choice, he scrambled inside. There were two seats there, and in a moment, Kam scrambled into the other.

"Strap yourself in!" he commanded.

"No. Wait! What—"

"No time."

"Here!" Idonea shouted, thrusting a waterskin up at Doig, even as the night mare was rising from its crouched position.

Doig grabbed the heavy bag and hauled it inside with him, tucking it between his legs. Angry voices raised in the background sounded like Buster and Idriss. And then, the night mare was up and rushing through the night at what would have seemed an impossible speed in broad daylight because the ground was rough, littered with boulders, and cluttered with thorny bushes. None of those factors seemed to matter. The violent rocking was enough to make a fish seasick.

"Don't worry," Kam said brightly. "Night mares are cave dwellers. They see fine in total darkness because their upper eyes emit in the infrared. Think I got that right. Or was it ultraviolet? I'll show you how to put on its day filters when we get closer to dawn."

"Um, er . . . me?"

"We have a very long way to go, Best Boy. It will take us at least three days to get you to Sabine. We'll have to take turns with the driving. Try these."

Kam handed him a weighty handful that he discovered—mostly by touch—to be a cumbersome set of goggles. When he put them on, he could see a faint glow on the ground ahead and the mare's front legs dancing over it, rushing between boulders and thorny bushes.

After a moment, Kam said, "I need those back, please. There's no chance of meeting people in this desert at this time of night, but there could be wildlife, and even that would distract the mare. It would attack at once, and after feeding, it'd want to sleep for weeks. Wild mares feed only once or twice a year when the surface livestock take shelter in the caves from aphelion or perihelion. Also, once in a while, a mare will try to scrape against a low branch to get rid of its load, and that means us."

Doig hastily returned the goggles. Kam put them on and then produced something that Doig thought was a fruit he was about to eat, but he spoke into it. "Heritage Two calling Heritage One."

The thing made noises.

"Pick up complete," Kam replied. "Yup, he's in good shape. All well your end? Have a nice day. Out."

Obviously, the gadget was a radio and one far smaller than Doig had ever seen. In his dreams about a second, secret colony, he had always assumed that it would be smaller than the Pale and technically more primitive. Domesticated elephants and children strapped aboard eagles, astounding as that was, had tended to support these prejudices. Pocket-sized radios and seeing in the dark did not.

He had much to learn.

"Kam Petrovich, you great rogue, how did you ever get here?"

The big man laughed. He was leaning back at ease now, holding the reins lightly, apparently letting the night mare choose the route but keeping an eye on a compass that glowed softly in the darkness. "How did I get to be a mare driver? Three days' seconding the captain as we came to get you. Most of the time, I'm a ladies' hairdresser. They sent me along to be sure we got the right man."

The worst thing was that Kam Petrovich had never been known for joking or making up stories. He had not been called

Allbrawn for nothing. What Kam said was whatever he thought was true, always.

From what Doig could see in the starlight, Kam was even more enormous than he had been at fourteen, when he had often been hauled out of school to work in the mine, pushing ore carts around. Some boys had called him "Nobrain," although Doig never had. Doig had done all his assignments for him. Kam had named him "Best Boy" and been his bodyguard when the hazing started.

"It's a long story, but we have all night. Ask."

"Why we were ambushed and kidnapped, and why was one of us murdered? What do your people want with us?"

"Mm. Your man's death was not planned. I heard that Senior Mother Usha was absolutely furious when she was told of it. There will be an investigation, and whoever was at fault will be punished. What exactly the Mothers want with the rest of you all I don't know. Told you, I'm just a hairdresser in Freeport."

Patience was vital when talking with Petrovich. "Well, start by telling me how you got from Copper Island to the Faraway Hills."

"Ah. You remember my dad? Big man, unless he stood near me? Died a couple years ago of lung fever."

"Sorry to hear that. Morris, right?"

"Right. Morris Petrovich. He worked the secret radio in abandoned Cross Cut Twelve for your dad. He was what the Board would call an accomplice."

Normally, Doig hated to talk about his father's martyrdom because it always ended with either, "Count me in when you start your revolution" or, "What are you going to do about it?" But this was going to be different.

"My father was sentenced to ten years on Copper Island, which was expected to kill him but didn't, and he was almost due for release. So the Board sent its chief assassin, Dhaval Guldberg—"

"Don't know his name. But they were both betrayed, probably by a man called Desjardins, my dad thought."

"I know all this."

"No, you don't! There's more, but I warn you now that it has no fairytale happy ending. Our dads must have been betrayed because the killers knew about the hidden radio. They seized both our dads and chained them in there with another man. Dunno his name. The roof in Twelve was known to be unsafe, and they planted explosives to bring it down. What you can't ever have heard is that, as soon as the killers left, a gang of miners came to rescue the prisoners."

Now, he had Doig's complete attention. He barely registered that he was on his back with his legs in the air as the night mare scrambled up a near-vertical cliff.

"The rescuers moved the explosives along the tunnel to what they hoped was a safe distance from the prisoners and set to work to release them. They freed my dad, but while they were working to free the other two, the bomb went off, and the roof came down. My dad had already left, so he went back to see what had happened and found them all dead except your dad, who was badly hurt.

"He fetched other men to help him move your dad to a safe place. Then, they both had to stay out of sight because the crewmen in charge of the mine thought that the missing bodies were all buried under the rockfall. They would have finished the executions had they learned otherwise, but my dad and his friends managed to keep your father alive. He was his own doctor, telling them how to sew back him together."

Doig closed his eyes in pain. If this was the truth, it was even worse than the lies he had always believed. "But they didn't tell us! Not me, not even my mother?"

"How could they? Could you have kept the secret at that age?"

Yes, he could, but how would Mom have endured Hassan Finn had she known her husband was alive and in need of her care? Doig needed to scream.

"So how does it end? When did my father really die? Or are you going to tell me that he's still alive somewhere?"

The night mare was scrambling down a very steep hillside, sending a blizzard of rocks rattling ahead. Its passengers were hanging in their straps. Then, it *did* occur to Doig that he was fastened on the back of a ferocious carnivore racing over rough terrain in a pitch-black night, being guided by the hands of a man who had not earned the name of Allbrawn Nobrain for nothing. But none of that mattered.

"He's still alive, but only just. He's dying, Doig. Sorry. That's what all the hurry is about. The Mothers want us to get you to Sabine in time for the two of you to say goodbye."

Doig said nothing. He couldn't.

"In April," Kam continued, "the men from Freeport arrived, and I was told for the first time that my dad was still alive, and would I help him carry your dad out to the boat? So, of course, I agreed. I was the biggest man on the island back then, remember? Dad and I had to wade carrying the stretcher. Man, that water was cold! But the crewmen would have noticed anybody else missing, except me and my dad, because they thought he was dead and they did not pay attention to kids. Only Miss Wills did, and Dad said that she knew what was going on."

Incredible or not, this had to be true! Kam had not been reciting a lesson. "Thank you, Kam. For rescuing my dad, I mean."

"Oh, I would've done it for anybody, but it was an honour in his case. And my dad said I had earned my freedom too, and so did I want to go away with him. Of course, I said yes, and so I sailed away in *Sunbird—*"

"In what?"

"*Sunbird.* It's a ship. Has solar panels on three masts, ever so high, and at first, I was scared to climb to the top, but in a week or so, I managed it, one very calm day. The captain didn't want to go through the Gut, even on the midnight bore, because the Ruckles gang mustn't know about Sabine, so we sailed all the way around Southmain, but I thought we were going to be cooked at perihelion. We got rainstorms and had to use the panels as wind sails when we got near Freeport. Dad stayed there because he was too weak then to manage the journey inland to Sabine. But he managed it later. What else do you want to know?"

THE REST of that night and the days and nights that followed were blurred by lack of sleep, constant bouncing and rocking, and periods of sheer terror. Kam was not the best storyteller in Neweden, but Doig learned a lot. The name "Sabine" had originally meant the vast system of caves in the Faraway Hills that Roman Rietveld's expedition had discovered and colonized. But now, that was called Cave City, and Sabine meant the whole colony that had resulted, as opposed to the original one, which was referred to as the Pale. Most of the Sabiners now lived in a city, Freeport, on the western coast of Southmain.

Sabine colony was ruled by a council of five women known as the Mothers. Each year, the most senior retired, and a replacement was elected. Kam's knowledge of politics ended there, but that was enough to warm the cockles of Doig's heart.

Time stopped having any meaning, but it was probably the third morning when Doig heard Kam talking and realized that he was speaking to his radio. It was mumbling back to him. The night mare was progressing up a long slope of farmland—fields, fences, and vineyards. On the crest of the hill ahead, a thin vertical line standing against the sky could only be a radio mast. In a flash, Doig recalled his meeting with the Board and their complaints about hackers breaking into the archives. If those hackers were the Sabiners, then that explained umpteen things, especially how they had known to expect the expedition's coming.

Why had he not worked that out weeks ago? Because he had always assumed that the second colony would necessarily be small and primitive. That might be far from the truth. In three hundred fifty years, a population could grow a thousand-fold, and if the Sabiners could hack into the Pale's archives, their technology might be just as advanced, or even more so. Without the Board's incompetence and selfish tyranny, Sabine might have progressed much further and faster than the Pale.

How much had Dad known about Sabine?

"How much of that did you hear?" Kam asked.

"None."

"Afraid we're too late. Your Dad passed away two days ago. They say he heard about the baby, though. I'm taking you right there."

Doig could only mumble his heartfelt thanks for a brave try. He was sleep-starved, famished from lack of adequate food, and one all-over bruise, but Kam must be in even worse shape, for he had made the trip both ways, and it wasn't his father who—

"Baby? What baby?"

"Yours. Born last week. Both well. Named Pablo."

Oh, no! Did Babette really believe the Board would tolerate another Pablo Gray?

THE NIGHT MARE had slowed down a lot now, which was hardly surprising after five or six days' steady running without food or water. Kam was directing it toward a stout masonry building abutting a rocky cliff whose arched opening looked as if it might lead through into a cave, for the interior was black as night. It was flanked on either side by raised platforms like docks, and several people were waiting there as a reception committee. A large spider of some sort was tethered below them.

"That's its supper," Kam said. "Be ready to leap out fast because it likes to eat in the dark."

He had hardly spoken when the mare saw its reward and speeded up to a gallop again. It finished the journey with a predatory leap, taking Doig and Kam with it. Its landing was a trifle unsteady, possibly because Kam's greater weight threw it off-balance. It did manage to sink its mandibles into its prey, though, and the victim died with a single squeal.

Doors flew open, and the passengers were dragged out onto the platforms. Spidermen with long poles expertly hooked away the mare's harness and goggles. The cabin was left on its back. The mare lifted its meal and vanished with it into the darkness ahead.

A voice said, "Welcome to Sabine, Citizen Gray."

DOIG SPUN AROUND. The speaker was a striking young woman clad in an elegant floor-length robe of rose colour. Her hair was golden, drawn back and trailing down her back out of sight; her eyes shone a brilliant blue at exactly the same height as his own, and her features were so flawless that they could have been cast in bronze. Most remarkable of all were her jewels—necklace, finger rings, and pendants dangling from her ears. Doig realized how long he had been deprived of female company, for the mahouts had kept their prisoners well apart from their own womenfolk, and none of them had come close to matching this vision.

"You are Doig Gray?"

"I am." He realized that he must be gawking. He must also look an appalling mess and probably stank.

"Come with me, Gray. Doer Guzman wishes to meet you." Her voice and manner conveyed authority like whipcracks.

She began to move, but he did not. He wasn't sure he could. The world was still swaying and bouncing.

"I am told that my father has died."

She turned, a frown spoiling the perfection of her forehead. "Yes, two nights ago. I offer my deepest sympathy, and of course, the Mothers and the Doer—"

"I wish to pay my respects to my father before I do anything else. Has he been buried yet?"

"No. The Mothers ordered that we wait for you. I will take you there."

This time, he followed, albeit in a very unsteady stagger. She led him through a human-sized door and then downstairs into the hill. The temperature was lower there. The tunnel had once been a natural cave but had been civilized—the floor levelled and narrow parts widened. It was lit by frequent panels attached to the roof. The walls bore a sheen of green algae near those, but the air was fresh and deliciously cool.

"So who is Doer Guzman?"

"He is the chief of the executive branch of government."

"I will be very honoured to meet with him. And your name, ma'am?"

"We don't use honorifics like 'ma'am' here. Just 'citizen' and usually only given names. I am Sandra Amets, Doer Guzman's chief of staff."

"And what does a Doer actually do?"

"Whatever the Mothers decide must be done. The Doer carries out their instructions."

"Sounds like a sensible arrangement. I've never had much success giving orders to women."

Amets's mouth did not even twitch. She continued her march, stiff-backed and deadpan.

The Sabine labyrinth was far larger than the Town and comprised more levels. Being based on natural caverns, it was also much less regular. Frequent arrows painted on the walls must represent guides for anyone who understood their respective meanings. Amets's route led along corridors and across much larger caverns, sometimes on high bridges.

They passed other people, all neatly dressed, well-groomed, and apparently healthy. Woman wore long dresses, men long-sleeved shirts and full-length slacks—the temperature in the caves was on the cool side for skimpier garb. Doig had been wearing the same clothes for a month, and they were almost falling apart. Both sexes seemed more amused than shocked on seeing the shaggy, unwashed stranger.

More stairs, going up this time. The exercise was starting to loosen his knots.

At long last, Amets halted at a door. "I know you must be chagrined that you did not arrive in time to speak with your father, but he knew you were on your way, and he recorded a message for you. The Doer will tell you how to view that. He went down very quickly these last few days."

"So, what did he die of?"

"It is not pleasant. You really want to know?"

"I really want to know."

"His wounds. He truly was murdered by Dhaval Guldberg and the Accident Squad. Without the injuries from their assault, he would still be alive today. The blast broke several bones and dislocated his left arm, but those eventually healed. He was also sprayed by tiny rock fragments. They destroyed his left eye and the left side of his face. Here, he wore a sort of mask to hide the scar tissue. What could never be treated were the dozens of splinters that were left inside of him. Some of them festered. Some damaged internal organs. Some made their way into major blood vessels and did further damage. In the end, though, he died peacefully. One of the embolisms caused a massive cerebral hemorrhage. He suffered a stroke in his sleep. He never woke up and died two days later. You still want to see him?"

Doig swallowed hard and nodded. Amets opened the door and stepped back to let him enter, then closed it. The cave beyond was three steps down and just large enough to hold three bed-sized tables. Two were bare. One bore an obvious body covered by a sheet. The light was dim, and the air much colder than the caverns and tunnels he had passed through to get there, so much so that he remembered the air conditioning in the Vandam Palace last summer.

He went over to the solitary occupant and cautiously drew back the sheet with a trembling hand.

Shock.

At first, he thought there had been a mistake. The cadaver had a white beard, and the left side of its face was hidden by a mask. The right eye was closed, the pale, sunken flesh disfigured by random scars. Yet it was—had been—Dad. The woman had stayed out in the corridor, so it was safe to speak.

"I'm sorry we didn't get a chance to say goodbye, Dad. That saved us both a lot of tears. You took a lot of killing. I swore then that I would be avenged on the killers, and that still holds. Dhaval Guldberg was the leader, and he will die for this." Pause. "I'm glad you got to Sabine, Dad, and saw that there was still hope for mankind on Neweden. I didn't ask to be your successor. It just sort of happened." Longer pause. "Goodbye, Dad."

He covered up that horribly immobile face again.

Then he wiped away his tears and went out to the corridor, where Sandra Amets waited.

He said, "Thank you."

She just nodded and led him back the way they had come.

THROUGHOUT THE ENSUING WALK, Doig's thoughts were far away and long ago. He struggled to collect them when Amets opened a door and gestured him into a large, roughly circular room, obviously an office. It was brightly lit by a magnificent chandelier hanging from a soaring roof. The floor was covered with carpet, and the furniture grandiose. It wasn't the Vandam Palace, but it had ambitions in that direction.

Doig especially disliked the giant viewbox pretending to be a window, currently offering a view of a massive waterfall, which he assumed was back on Earth, umpteen light years away—showing it as it had been several thousand years ago. He was also seriously nettled at being frog-marched into a formal meeting while he was still in the squalid condition that weeks of rough living and days of night mare riding had left him. Such treatment reminded him of Vandam Palace.

The man seated at the great desk on the far side looked up, then bounced to his feet and came marching around with a vast, toothy smile to greet the visitor. "Doig Gray!"

Doig ignored the outstretched hand and kept both his own in his pockets. "That's me."

Guzman stopped as if slapped. He was in his forties but would probably deny it if asked. His hair hung in ringlets, and his shirt was embroidered but sleeveless to show off melon biceps and forearms to scale. Even in his elevator shoes, he was short. He had a noble profile, but he did not convey a fraction of Chairman Ruckles's menace and dominance. In fact, he was not unlike Hassan Finn, who abused Mom.

"You are welcome here, Doig. We want you to consider yourselves as being among friends."

"Friends?" Doig's long-restrained anger burst forth. "I wish we could be. But your lackeys killed my friend and companion, Logan Foley, destroyed our boats so that we are stranded far from home, burned our equipment, and brought us here against our will and without explanation or apology. Those are not the actions of friends."

Sandra Amets stood frozen in place, listening to this unexpected confrontation. Doig wished he could take his eyes off Guzman to see what she was thinking. Waldo Ruckles would have ordered the upstart taken out and flogged unconscious.

Guzman had flushed scarlet, a curious reaction. "Those events are already under investigation. The Mothers were greatly upset when they heard about them. I will personally make sure that the men responsible are severely punished."

Responsibility, like charity, begins at home—that had been one of Dad's sayings.

"Do come and sit down, Doig. You don't mind if I—"

"I will stand. My ass is black and blue after days and nights on that night mare. Tell me about my companions. How do they fare?"

Guzman refused to be baited. He took a step backward, leaned against the table, and folded his arms so that Doig could admire them.

"They fare very well. Your two crews have now been reunited, all eleven safe and sound. As of last night, Senior Mahout Findlay estimated that he would deliver them here in eight or nine days. Our radio communication works better after sunset, for technical reasons I do not understand. You will be able to talk with them tonight if you wish."

"That would be a relief." Doig trusted Guzman about as far as his fingernails had grown since he entered this office.

"Understand, please, Doig, that the land between here and the big river is practically desert. We have a couple of small mines there—also, the mahouts' settlement. They transport the ore. The mahouts are rough people, largely uneducated. They have some strange superstitions about stars."

"So we discovered."

"The Mothers are very anxious to meet you. I realize that you will want to freshen up beforehand . . ."

Doig felt his temper snap. He took a step forward, menacing. "Chairman Ruckles, the tyrant, dragged me in front of his Board when I was half dead from loss of blood and septicemia. I will not be treated like that again, Doer. I need food, at least eight hours' sleep, a bath, and fresh clothes. Probably more food then. After all that, I will be happy to talk with the Mothers or you."

Guzman blandly ignored the tone and posture. "Of course. Come, I will show you to your room."

IN SPITE OF, or perhaps because of, his childhood experiences, Doig disliked the idea of living underground like rabbit spiders. Nevertheless, he was impressed by his personal cave. It was an awkward Y shape but roomy and bright. One corner was curtained off as a bathroom—with a shower, a toilet, and running water. Another led to a sort of balcony that overlooked an enormous cavern at least a hundred metres from the stalactites above to the stalagmites below.

"I will have food brought here right away," the Doer said.

"Press that button if there is anything else you want. Light switch and temperature controls here. You can access your father's farewell message on that viewbox. He said to tell you that the password was your sister's other name."

Doig mumbled thanks and waited until Guzman had left. Fed, clean, or rested—which luxury first? He had never felt grubbier in his life and rarely hungrier. He began by washing his face and hands. By then, a youth had arrived with a laden food trolley. It was all cold stuff, and looked as if it had been waiting for him for an hour or so. He decided to have a quick snack and then a shower but discovered that he could not stop after just a few mouthfuls. He gorged until he couldn't keep his eyes open, at which point he shed his clothes and fell into bed.

HE AWOKE WITH A START, wondering where he was. He had left the lights on but had no clue as to what time it was outside the caves. He sat up and saw the big viewbox. With no keypad in sight, he decided that it must be voice-controlled, like the machines in Vandam Palace. After several tries, he persuaded it to tell him the time, which was twenty-one hundred hours. He had slept the day away.

Helen had been four when her sister was born and had confused Camilla's name with that of her favourite dessert. So Dad's clue about Doig's sisters simply meant, "Vanilla."

A couple of more guesses at the proper commands and the voicebox suspiciously asked for the password.

The screen brightened slowly as if to prepare the viewer for a disagreeable sight, but Doig knew what was coming. Dad was propped up in bed, with the left half of his face covered by the mask and his right arm in a sling. At least this time, his eye was open, but there was little more colour in his cheeks. He looked about a hundred years older than Doig remembered him and was obviously a very sick man.

He spoke in a whisper and in short phrases. "This message is for my son Doig . . . and no one else. If you are some other nosey-parker gatecrasher . . . then go away . . . if only to respect . . . a dying man's last wish." Then, he smiled. It was one-half of the old smile that Doig remembered.

"Some hope! Doig, my son . . . I'm told you are your way . . . and will be here in a few days. I have a strong hunch . . . that I will not be here to greet you. Even if I am, I would never in . . . twenty years . . . be able to tell you . . . how proud—extremely proud—I am of what you have achieved so far. I know that you have steered a very clever course . . . between frightening the Board into . . . disposing of you . . . and disheartening your own followers. I have heard of your crazy courage in rescuing that awful Lizzie . . . Wong woman from the spiders when you were on Touchdown. I have watched the video . . . of your meeting with the Board. I could not have done that . . . had I not been assured in advance . . . that it ended happily. That was magnificent! That was an epochal moment . . . in the history of Neweden."

He paused then, breathing hard as if gathering his strength. Doig was already fighting back tears, and he saw that Dad's one eye was blinking, too.

"And now I know that you successfully . . . led your expedition into the interior and made . . . contact with the Sabiners. I was certain that the Board . . . would somehow sabotage you to make . . . sure that you would never return. If it did, then you detected . . . their efforts. You outwitted them again. They are so venal and so stupid!

"I commend the Mothers to you. Working together, you can bring freedom . . . and a true future . . . to humankind on

Neweden." He tried another smile, but it was a travesty. "Remember the fins, Doig!"

Again, he paused, and then made an effort to say more, but he had run out of strength. He raised his free hand as if in blessing, and the picture faded away.

Doig wiped his eyes with a knuckle. "I am going to try, Dad, and to avenge you, I will strangle Chairman Ruckles with my bare hands." Then he added, "And feed Dhaval Guldberg to leech spiders."

THERE CAME a knock on the door. He had been told he would not be disturbed, so were they spying on him? He called, "Who's there?"

"Kam," said a muffled but recognizable voice.

"Come in."

Enter giant—shaved, well-clad, looking excited. "The Doer is coming to get you. To take you to meet the Mothers! Twenty minutes, he said. I'll run your shower." Kam headed for the bathroom alcove.

A royal reception did sound worth waking up for, although breakfast first would have been better. When Doig emerged, drying himself, he found Kam waiting for him with an open cutthroat razor, something he had only ever seen on ancient Earth videos. The shaving turned out to be both painless and bloodless. It did prevent Doig from asking where the Sabiners had acquired high-quality steel. The colony had almost none of that because *Moctezuma* had been built of much lighter materials.

Then, a hot towel was spread over his face, and that, too, prevented questioning. Clearly, the Sabiners had found Kam employment that was within his limited abilities. A man with a job he can do well will be happy doing it.

Which obviously raised the question of what was expected of Doig Gray. The Sabiners must see some value in him, or they would not be giving him the royal treatment like this. In a few moments, Kam whipped the hot towel off his face and announced that Doig could not possibly appear before the Mothers with his hair like that, and, yes, he certainly could cut a man's hair with a razor. So he did.

Doig's clothes were laid out for him—full-length slacks and long-sleeved shirt, both in a shade to match his name. They were very similar to the outfit he had worn when he visited Vandam Palace. He was letting his valet brush his hair when there came a peremptory knock on the door, and Doer Guzman stuck his head around it and asked if he was ready. Doig paused just long enough to admire himself in the fake viewbox, which was now acting as a mirror, before turning around to answer the question.

"Ready for what, sir?"

"I would say that you are ready for anything," Guzman said with a soapy smile.

"So would I. Kam, old buddy, you are a wonderful valet. I have never been better turned out in my life. Thank you very much."

The big man's childlike blush confirmed that he was truly in his element. Sabine had worked out well for him.

"COME! NO TIME TO WASTE." Guzman disappeared out into the corridor, and Doig ran after him. The Doer was not as speedy as a night mare in a hurry, but obviously, living in Sabine was good exercise.

"Please, would you explain to me what is about to happen?" Doig asked, striding along beside him.

"Just a formality. You are to be presented to the Mothers. You, remember, are the leader of the first expedition from the Pale in centuries. This is a historic occasion! Furthermore, you are the son of the late great Pablo Gray, whom we rescued from Copper Island in a thrilling adventure that attracted the attention of the entire population of Sabine. Everyone will be watching this."

"When you say 'everyone,' just how many people are you talking about?"

"Everyone who lives here in Sabine."

"And how many in all?"

"Tens of thousands. I can't be more exact; we are overdue to hold another census. Turn here. You just need to say some nice words about how happy you are to be here, and so on."

"When you talk about Sabine, do you mean only the people who live in these caves, or do you include the population of Freeport?"

Guzman shot him a surprised look, perhaps wondering how he had heard about Freeport.

"They, too, will be watching you. We go up these stairs now."

Why the big hurry? Doig was certain that he was being frog-marched into something, and he did not know what. "Tell me about Jalapeno."

Again, the Doer showed surprise, but this time, he smiled. "Jalapeno Guzman? How did you hear about him?"

"My father knew of him. He was an ancestor of yours?"

"So my family's tradition insists. The records are scanty back then. You see, Roman Rietveld led the first expedition inland back in 25. We know that because he carved an inscription in the rock. He came specifically here, guided by

Moctezuma's remote sensing, which showed huge gravity anomalies here that could only mean substantial caves."

"I believe you, but there are no such records in the Pale's data files now."

"There are in ours, so yours must have been redacted quite recently. Even then," Guzman continued, "back in the Pale, the crewmen were lording it over the rest, so Roman and his gang decided to keep the Sabine caves a secret from the Board of the day. The caves were far more habitable than Vandam City on Touchdown, which is where the main colony was located then, and the soil hereabouts is a lot more fertile. So, each spring and fall, the pioneers sneaked back to the Pale and enlisted women to join them. I expect they began with their own wives and children if they had any. Amazingly, they managed to keep doing this on and off for more than a hundred years."

"Ah, but then, Jalapeno got caught?"

"He may not have been the first, but he was certainly made an example."

"Fed to the spiders," Doig said with a shiver. "Are you descended from that Guzman?"

"I like to think so," the Doer confessed, with unexpected humility, "but the colony was a century and a half old, so there could have been dozens of men of that name by then."

There were none in the Pale now. Of course, family names could die out naturally from an imbalance of girl babies, but successive Boards might have made sure that this one did not survive.

"That seems to have ended the recruitment," Rex Guzman said. "By then, the Sabine colony was prospering on its own. And here we are."

"Here" was a roughly oval cave, about twenty metres long and half that wide. The roof was so high that it was shrouded in darkness—architects in Sabine clearly had to make do with whatever they were given. But the eye-catching wonder was the hardwood floor, straight-grained and gleaming gold. The Pale had no timber even close to such quality. Near the centre, six chairs were arranged in an arc, facing a seventh. There were no Mothers in sight, nor anyone else, either.

"Better early than late," Guzman remarked happily. Why all the hurry to get there? Was he scared of the Mothers? Was keeping them waiting a capital offence? Or was he just trying to rattle Doig? "We call this the ballroom. Why don't you just stay right here until I call you in to join the picture? Then I will introduce you to each of them, and so on."

"You expect me to make a speech?"

"Oh, a few words. Nothing fancy. Serious matters can wait for another day." He headed for the chairs. His elevator shoes trod silently, but the boards squeaked. The rock underneath might be very uneven, possibly covered with fallen boulders. Get a few hundred people dancing in there, and the floor would drown out the music.

A procession of five women walked in from the far side and met Guzman at the chairs.

None of the Mothers was young, and it seemed that they had deliberately chosen outfits of different colours. Four of them sat down. The fifth, who happened to be the shortest, spoke with Guzman. If they were arguing, she won. He picked up a chair and departed by the way the women had entered while she waved to Doig to join them. Amused, Doig concluded that Doer Guzman was no Chairman Ruckles, but the dumpy lady might be.

She advanced a few steps to meet him and clasped his hand in both of her smaller, plump ones. "Citizen Gray, I am very happy to meet you at last. I am Kate Usha, this year's Senior Mother. I assure you that we are all horrified by the way one of your companions was murdered. Between you and me, Rex

Guzman is in some ways an idiot, so he appoints worse dullards to help him and fails to instruct them properly. Now, come and meet the others."

Ignorance was making Doig's head spin. What in the world was going on here? Why had the Sabiners gone to so much trouble to intercept his little expedition, kidnap the explorers themselves, and drag them all the way back to this underground city? And now, why lionize him like this? He was enough of a cynic to believe that the only possible explanation was that they wanted to use him for some purpose of their own, but he could not imagine what that might be. He was Pablo Gray's son, but so what? Dad was dead, and he had been a person of no importance, either.

Never having had trouble with names, he easily memorized the four others now thrown at him: Tabita Trees, Minna Adah, Greta Keone, and Selena Colette. Their motherly manner might be a pose. They all seemed like solid, practical persons. The oldest of them was probably Minna Adah, who was overdoing the pretense with her embroidery hoop and calico apron. It occurred to him that he might be the first person in the history of the planet to meet both the Pale's Board and Sabine's Mothers. Except, possibly, Dad?

"Our meeting will be shown colony-wide, Citizen Gray. You are very welcome! It is tragic that you arrived too late to meet with your father."

"I have mourned him for six years, and I am most grateful for the way you rescued him and gave him a more dignified ending. I have viewed the message he left for me. It was very touching. I will treasure it always."

"All Sabiners honoured him for his stance against the tyrants. We mourn his end. Now you have arrived in his place, and we want to give them a chance to see you. Would you rather make a speech or answer some questions?" Kate asked.

"Answer questions, please." Any question should give him a clue as to what answer they wanted.

"Then I'll just say a few opening words and hand it over to you."

"Is there anything you don't want me to mention?"

"I think we'd rather keep the death of your man off the agenda tonight. It will be properly investigated, I promise. Keep it happy time. Is there anything you would rather not be asked?"

"I know you have spies in the Pale reporting to you by radio. Is the reverse also true? Will the Ruckles gang learn of what we say tonight?"

"Stars!" Kate said, looking shocked. "How did you know about our friends in the Pale? I'd certainly rather you didn't mention *them* because very few people in Sabine know of them, and I hope no one in the Pale does. I don't think the Ruckles gang has spies here. We usually assume that they do not even know we exist."

Minna glanced up from her embroidery. "Play it safe, mm?"

"Definitely!" Kate said. "Remember that, all of you."

"When was the last time you ate, Mr. Gray?" demanded Tabita Trees, who was tall and austere. Kate wasn't the only smart one.

"This morning," he said. "But I won't fade away."

"We'll keep this a very short meeting!" Kate said decisively. "We can get together again tomorrow and talk business then. Please, all, find a seat." She went to the solitary one, and the others found places in the arc, Doig going to the right-hand end.

Obviously, he had found the brains that ran Sabine. Or, rather, the brains had found him. Guzman was a figurehead and possibly a handy scapegoat, but these mild-mannered ladies with their homespun manners knew what they were doing and where they were going. He wished he did.

Kate glanced them over and then stood up, which was probably a signal to begin the public recording. She was, as promised, brief: it was a great pleasure to greet the worthy son of the late Dr. Pablo Gray . . . first official visitor from the Pale in three and a half centuries . . . welcome . . . all clap.

Doig rose and went forward to shake her hand again. Then, she yielded that chair to him and went to join the other Mothers. He sat down facing them and tried to look ten times more relaxed than he felt. Dad's message had told him that the Ruckles Board had recorded their meeting with him, which he had not known at the time, and the Sabiners had hacked it out of the Board's files, which he was sure the Board had not known. So he was on public view for the second time, but this time, he knew it.

The first questions were predictable. "Do the tyrants on Touchdown know about your expedition to the interior?"

"Of course. They approved it and funded it."

"What did you hope to find?"

"We were prospecting. Neweden is not habitable without technology. The Pale is dying because it is running out of raw materials." *One reason.*

"So, you did not come looking for Sabine?"

"None of us cargo people knew that Sabine even existed, Mother. I doubt very much that the Board knows of it, but I am not sure."

"Then," said Selena Colette, who was visibly the youngest, likely young enough to still have dependent children, "you could not have been counting on finding shelter. So, you must have intended to return to the Pale before perihelion."

"Correct." He wondered what was coming. Should he mention the destruction of the canoes?

"It is March already. What will happen if you fail to return?"

If? Not when?

"Our wives will despair. Older children will weep, of course." He flipped a mental coin and went for it. "The Board will celebrate."

Shock and outrage!—either real or feigned. "The Board members want you to fail?"

"They tried to make certain of it. They supplied us with poisoned rations. They gave us a spider 'repellent' machine that not only would not repel but, in fact, would summon every spider that could reach us."

Tabita Trees said, "You are accusing the government of the Pale of trying to murder you?"

"Why not? They murdered my father. Just by existing, I remind people of their crimes. Therefore, I must die. And so must my companions, but we're only cargo and don't matter in the Board's eyes."

There! He had done it. Saying that was treason. He had crossed a line that he had always skirted in the past.

There was a pause, and he wondered if any of these peaceful-seeming old dears would dare to take the next big step. It turned out that they had all been waiting for Senior Mother Kate, and she had been weighing words very carefully.

"Then, it would appear that we have done you a grave disservice by bringing you to Sabine so that you cannot return to the Pale as planned."

Now what? Governments did not admit to mistakes like that! And suddenly, his tongue ran away with him, and he heard himself say, "One thing I learned from you is that after I left, my wife gave birth to our first child, a boy she has named after my father. I doubt if he will live very long. The Board will see to that. Just by being Pablo Gray's son, I have given them trouble, so they will not let his grandson survive to give them more."

He saw the respectable ladies' disgust and felt a similar reaction hit himself. Why had he gone and said that? It sounded maudlin, whining, until the rest of him caught up with his tongue. But then, he remembered Guzman's strange reluctance to inform him of the size of Sabine's population and the extraordinary pains the Mothers had taken to bring him to the underground city. He must have something they wanted very badly.

For the life of him, he could not imagine what.

Fake it.

"Unless," he added, "the two colonies can cooperate to our mutual advantage. Even the Board must welcome that." It wouldn't, of course.

That was the right answer! That was what Senior Mother Kate had been wanting him to suggest. She stood up, which was probably the signal for whoever or whatever was controlling the hidden cameras to turn them on her.

"On that happy note, I think we should adjourn. Citizen Gray has not eaten all day and is sadly in need of some sustenance, and we all need to think very hard about his interesting comments. Welcome to Sabine, citizen."

Obviously, no one must commit to anything yet.

"THAT WENT WELL, KATE," Minna Adah remarked, packing away her embroidery.

Kate was still in charge. "Indeed it did. Thank you, citizen."

"Doig, please," he said. "And it is I who should thank you for your hospitality and the way you treated my father." *When do I get the bill?*

She gave him a motherly smile. "Tomorrow, we will be returning to Freeport. It is a much more pleasant place to live than Cave City, although the caves do still have some uses. If you will accompany us, we can talk on the way."

On elephants? Night mares? More travel? How far? He didn't ask.

Kate skillfully shepherded him toward the door he had come in through. "I will get someone to show you to the all-night café . . . Oh!"

Out of the shadows stepped Doer Guzman. "No need, Kate. I promised Doig that I would let him radio his men to reassure them that he had arrived safely."

Neatly done! Having left by a door on the far side, he must have circled around by some other path. Evidently, the senior Mother was not the only smart strategist in the upper circles of Sabiner government. Doig had better choose which side he wanted to support.

"That's very kind of you to remember, Doer," he said, "but I fear it's much too late to call them now. The mahouts all go to bed at sundown. Elephant riding is a lot more tiring than it looks. Maybe tomorrow?" he added, just in case Kate missed the point. "And I wouldn't mind some more shut-eye myself. I'm about a night and a half short still."

Kate caught the fly ball like a pro. "But I know how hungry you are. If Rex, here, will just show you to your room, I'll see that the cooks send you a nice hot meal right away."

SAFELY BACK IN HIS ROOM—WHERE his bed had been made for him and his discarded hair cleaned off the floor—Doig passed the time waiting for his "nice hot meal" by replaying

Dad's farewell message. He had a hunch that he had over-looked a clue to something in there.

Yes, he had. *Thanks, Dad!*

The hot meal arrived and was delicious. Doig ate more of it than he had expected, aware that a palatial lifestyle could be dangerously addictive.

There was a limit to how many hours he could sleep in a given twenty-four, but when he found himself alert in the middle of the night, he started up the viewbox. The most inter-esting record he located was that of Doig Gray being hectored by the Ruckles Board last perihelion. The fact that the said Doig looked two steps outside death's door certainly added to the effect, but the way he stood up to the bullying impressed even himself.

Vanity could be dangerously addictive, also.

Then, he tracked down some census data, and those, he found very encouraging.

KAM BROUGHT Doig breakfast in bed. Which was thoughtful of him but not much needed. Of course, Doig thanked him and prepared to eat something as a gesture of gratitude.

Kam was excited. "We're going down to Freeport! It's much better living than these horrid caves."

"How far is it?

"Something over two hundred kilometres. The Mothers want you down at the stables in about half an hour."

That sounded like more night mare riding. Doig suppressed a shudder, but if the old ladies could handle it, he certainly could.

THE STABLES WERE a group of caves lower in the mountain—dimmer, larger, and wetter than the human habitation levels. The constant dripping noises would drive people mad, but the spiders in their stalls paid no attention, and the stalagmites were allowed to grow in peace. There was no sign of the Mothers yet, but a line of six long wagons stood on the roadway. They were all the same: open-topped and entered from the rear. A narrow corridor led to the front between seats arranged on either side, for a total of ten in all.

Kam led Doig to the front wagon, which had a team of three spiders already harnessed. These were of a species that Doig had never seen before—large, but not as large as elephants or night mares; probably not too dangerous because the shape of their mandibles indicated that they were herbivores. Still, the variety of spider species the Sabriners were able to bend to their own purposes was nearly as impressive as their command of technology.

He was astonished to see Sandra Amets sitting in what was obviously the driver's chair, dressed to the nines as before, this time in pale green.

He greeted her, and she responded, looking down at him with the merest trace of a smile.

"Two hundred kilometres to Freeport?" he asked. "How fast do these beasties run?"

She actually laughed. "Nearer three hundred, but this is just local transportation. Today, we will have you to the coast in less than four hours. There is almost no wind."

Sabine was full of interesting surprises. What had wind to do with it?

The Mothers duly arrived, each in a two-seater trap pulled by a hound-sized spider and driven by a youthful flunky. They had very little baggage, and Doig wondered if they had come up from Freeport specifically to greet him. Or to say farewell to Dad, perhaps?

Senior Mother Kate smiled at Doig but frowned at Kam Petrovich. "We did not reserve a seat for you in the car, Kam. I'm sure they'll find room for you on tomorrow's run."

Kam's face fell. He had been enjoying his reflected glory as valet to his hero, Best Boy, and now reality had suddenly been thrown in his face. Doig assumed that the Mothers were setting up a private conference with him and did not need any ladies' hairdressers present.

"Tomorrow?" Doig said, extending a hand to shake. "Thanks for your help here, Allbrawn. I'll see you in Freeport tomorrow, and you can show me around. Stay out of trouble until then, right?"

Kam beamed at the prospect and took Doig's hand in his own as if wrapping a parcel.

The travellers embarked on the wagon. Doig was not at all surprised to find himself across from Kate Usha, with the other Mothers before and behind them. There were no other passengers.

The team began to move. The wagon rocked and squealed.

"This is the worst part," Kate said. "You'll find the car more comfortable."

"It's all incredible to me. This is a world I did not know existed."

"Of course." After a moment, as they entered a narrow tunnel that seemed artificial, Kate asked very innocently, "What is the population of the Pale now?"

"The Board claims about half of yours, but it may be exaggerating."

She gave him a surprised glance and then chuckled. "You inherited your father's smarts, Citizen Gray."

"If I claimed a third of them, I would certainly be exaggerating."

Her face displayed disbelief. "He was a great help to us. The idea that Sabine should cooperate, or even amalgamate, with the Pale has been around for a long time, but there has always been strong resistance, mostly fear that they would swallow us. We are a democracy, Doig, and the people rule. Dr. Gray showed us how to penetrate the Pale's files, and that showed us how absurd our fear was. We are far more likely to swallow them, he maintained."

Doig was not convinced of that yet, but he still had much to see. Freeport, especially.

"Last perihelion there was a big change in public opinion. Do you know what provoked that?"

He shook his head.

"Your lecture to the Pale Board! When you listed the dangers that threaten to wipe out the Pale, you opened our eyes to the fact that the human species must indeed learn to cooperate if it wants to survive on Neweden. That was why we broadcast within Sabine."

"And the Board has to go." That meant revolution and war, of course.

Kate just nodded, noncommittal.

The harnessed spiders did not run much faster than a man would walk, but they pulled the wagons as fast as the passengers would want because the springs were soft and the seats hard. Their way lay through a long series of caves and tunnels, mostly natural but some artificial. Their destination, Kate said, was the other side of the mountain.

"How old is all this?" Doig asked. "It must've taken centuries to construct."

"Yes. It was the cave system that made our colony possible. Only when we had a fair-sized population were we able to build year-round housing down on the coast. Cave City is still useful, though. Some people still prefer to estivate here."

The wagon journey ended abruptly with a short, steep descent into a large natural cave with much brighter light, much warmer air, and a view of mountains through a high-arched opening ahead. Doig was relieved to be leaving the underground city, for it reminded him too much of his child-hood on Copper Island.

Hanging almost directly above them was a cable car, obviously large enough to carry a dozen people or more. By choice, he would have run up the stairs to it, but the Mothers preferred to use the elevator, so he went with them. The car ran on two of four steel cables that stretched out as far as he could see, disappearing into the valley ahead. He could make out more of the supporting towers beyond that. The scale must rival some of those he had encountered in his study of Earth history. Another Sabine marvel! The car itself was coated with solar panels, so it might run slower in rainy weather, and it might not run at all during strong winds. But it certainly looked more appealing than a night mare.

A rapid count told him that there were twenty seats in the car. Each chair was on a pivot so the occupant could look out at the view or hold conversations with neighbours. There were no other passengers, which confirmed that Kate had lied to Kam. Nor was there any sign of a human driver. When all six were seated, Kate said, "Everyone ready? Selena, dear, would you do the honours?"

Selena, the youngest, went back to the rear and shut the door. She pressed a button that made a horn sound, then returned to her seat. In a moment, the sound stopped, and the car slid out into the sunshine and scenery.

They were three on a side, but the corridor was so narrow that they made a passable conversational grouping. Minna brought out her embroidery, and Greta some knitting—baby clothes, apparently.

"Gyroscopes," Kate said, probably to explain the persistent quiet hum or the smoothness of the ride. "Now we can talk seriously and without being overheard. There are too many dark corners and odd acoustics in the caves.

"Understand, please, Doig, that we are not frightened of secret police or illegal violence, as you are in the Pale. We just don't want to start rumours. We may discuss among ourselves lots of things that never happen. We do announce our decisions when we reach them, but not before."

Doig nodded, although he was not entirely convinced. The Mothers certainly did not trust Doer Guzman, so there must be some political opposition. Indeed, Kate had earlier conceded that the Sabiners were divided over the amalgamation issue.

He wished they would put off the political chatter for a while because he wanted to inspect the mountainous scenery, which was unlike anything he had ever seen.

No such luck.

"Last night," Senior Mother continued, "You mentioned mutual advantage. I can see how the Pale would benefit from cooperation. We could send you food by the shipload, for example. We have timber and metals that you lack. But what can you offer us in return?"

Doig had only one arrow in his quiver, so he might as well shoot it now.

"Your birth rate is dropping. As far back as I could trust your records, you enjoyed a population increase of more than three-point-five percent per year. That is very high, but in your last census, it dropped below the long-term average—a small drop, but statistically significant."

Tabitha said, "Your father told you this in that goodbye message he recorded for you?"

"No, but he did drop a hint," Doig admitted. Which had been typical of Dad. "He reminded me about the Finns. A couple of our 'crew' families in the Pale have become so inbred that their children are ugly and moronic. Some of them cannot even reproduce. I went through your records last night. Many things may have caused your drop in births, but one of them is definitely inbreeding."

"Your father was right," Kate sighed. "And so are you. What he is saying, girls, is that we need the Pale's DNA."

When no one else spoke, Doig continued, "Sabine was founded by comparatively few people, and some of those were already related. From the family names in your records, I calculated about three hundred and twenty founders altogether. The Pale started with thirty crew members, but it also had thousands of frozen ova. How many of those were thawed out and reared to adulthood is not recorded, but we have over twelve hundred family names still in use, which suggests more than twice that number of founders. Together we stand, Honoured Mothers; divided, we die out."

Kate said, "But will the Board ever agree to cooperation?"

"Never! They will never share power. And the problem would not be confined to the Board. The rest of the crewmen will not willingly throw away their nametags."

"Something else that we have and the Pale does not is a democratic government," Minna Adah said prissily. "We elect our officials; we do not inherit them."

Then, the solution was obvious, but no one wanted to put it into words.

"I will have to speak to my companions," Doig said. "But if they agree, how willing would you be to support a revolution?"

"Let's take a short break," Kate said. "We're about to cross the Rhine Canyon. It's one of my favourite views."

Everyone swivelled around to admire the roaring water

hundreds of metres below the car. Greta Keone rose and fetched bottled water from a bar at the rear. But even a mountain valley was not infinite, and soon, the car was climbing over forests again.

"We hope to dam one of these rivers soon," Tabitha Trees said. "Then we will have enough power to smelt aluminum and will be able to build some airplanes."

Weep for all the centuries wasted in the Pale!

Kate brought the meeting to order with the question no one had wanted to ask. "Just how would you go about overthrowing the tyrants, citizen?"

Doig had spent hours in the night wrestling with that horror. "My prime concern, honoured Mothers, is that I have a wife in the Town with a son I have never seen. Almost all my companions are married, and we know that our women and children are hostages. It is possible, but perhaps unlikely, that the Board has already rounded them up and imprisoned them somewhere in Vandam Palace. Can your spies tell us that?"

"We can ask. When we reach Freeport, I will introduce you to our intelligence chief, Lindsay Devon. Assume they are still at liberty. What then?"

"When you sent *Sunbird* to Copper Island, it avoided Touchdown and the Town by sailing all the way around Southmain. But to go the other way, through the Gut from the west, would be a shorter and quicker way to the Town, wouldn't it?"

"Probably. Again, you will need to speak to the experts."

This conversation was pointless. "Let me state something I do know, then. I will not declare war on the Board while my wife and child are in its power. I am certain that my fellow explorers will feel the same. So, our first move would have to be a lightning raid to rescue the hostages. If we can pull that off, then the Board will be shaken to its foundations. It may very well fall of its own accord without further action by Sabiners."

The thoughtful silence was broken by the austere Tabitha Trees. "Twelve explorers? How many wives? How many children? How many passengers in all?"

The discussion proceeded from there. Doig did the calculations: some babes in arms, some adolescent sons and daughters bigger than their parents. At least fifty, perhaps sixty.

The questions continued. How big a ship? How many sailors risking their lives also?

With the details established, Kate looked around, waiting for more comments. Receiving none, she said, "That is a deal breaker, citizen? The first act must be to free the hostages?"

"Yes, Mother, unless my companions overrule me. I, too, believe in democracy."

"Then, we have a decision, and that gives us something to start work on when we reach Freeport."

Clever lady.

"Another matter, one I am reluctant to mention, Mothers, is that, while I appreciate these clothes I was given, I have nothing else. My companions, when they arrive, will be in worse shape than I was. Everything we had was destroyed or abandoned by your men. We are due compensation for that, and for the canoes we spent half a year building."

Kate pouted at being panhandled. "We are aware of that. Admiral Devon has been directed to extend you credit. There are many good stores in Freeport."

ABOUT TWO HOURS after they left Sabine, another car passed them, heading in the opposite direction. It seemed to be carrying more cargo than passengers.

Eventually, they left the mountains and descended over green hills. Doig was amazed by the bountiful landscape, like pictures of Old Earth. When a silvery line of ocean appeared in the distance, his companions began pointing out and naming the many offshore islands—Fortunate, Heather, Catalina, Gala, and Drunkard's. They were all inhabited now. This, obviously, was where *Moctezuma* should have landed—if not on the mainland, then on one of those islands.

Freeport turned out to be a town of attractive wooden houses with very steep roofs, almost certainly designed to shed heavy snowfall. They stood well apart, no doubt because wooden buildings were flammable, but the intervening ground was mostly being exploited as vegetable gardens. He wondered how they handled the spider pests.

The cable car terminal was a larger version of the same steep-roofed design, with one end open. The car slid slowly into it and came to a halt.

The mountains had been beautiful. The coastal settlement left Doig seething mad. This was what the Pale should have been. Five hundred years had been utterly wasted.

He was the last of the passengers to disembark and join the others on an otherwise empty platform. The air was much hotter than it had been that morning up in the hills. It was moister, too, and had a familiar tang of the sea that he remembered from his childhood.

"Admiral Devon was supposed to meet us," Kate said, scanning the station with a frosty eye.

Then the elevator door opened, and out limped an admiral. He was very large and bulky and rather top-heavy, and his uniform made Doig bite his tongue to hold back a grin. *Lindsay Devon, intelligence chief?*

Ever since the canoes had been smashed and the Interior Expedition thus trapped in the wilderness, Doig had known that there must be a second colony, and it must be kept informed by spies in the Pale, for how else could the expedition have been intercepted? When he saw the radio mast above Sabine, he had known how the espionage was worked. The extent of the Sabiners' technology had astonished him, but obviously, their spies were hacking into the *Moctezuma* archives.

Here was another example and a ludicrous one. Ignorant of naval matters, someone must have asked the Earth history files what an admiral wore, and the machines must have judged by the amount of data in their records, not by relevance.

Admiral Devon was garbed like some hero from the great age of sail. He wore tight-fitting white breeches and a dark-coloured cutaway coat decorated with masses of gilt braid and epaulettes. His hat was almost as wide as his shoulders. He came limping forward, leaning on a cane, and Doig realized that he had lost a foot and wore a prosthesis. His head was large, his hair white, his face large and puffy, and he was scowling ferociously.

Then, Doig comprehended that Admiral Lindsay Devon was a woman.

An angry woman, of around fifty. She bowed awkwardly to the group, muttered, "Mothers," and then turned her scowl on Doig. "I was told to expect an army of a dozen." Her voice boomed like a canon.

"This is Doig Gray, Admiral," Kate said.

"Know that. Saw you all on the viewbox last night." She thrust a hand at him. "Did a fine job. Damned sorry about your dad. Great man."

Doig thanked her, and they shared a firm handshake. "Can you eat a lunch for twelve, citizen?"

"Given time," Doig said, happy to play along.

Her scowl deepened. "And you think that you can overthrow the government of the Pale?"

"There are twelve of us and only four of them. Cargo

greatly outnumber crew and will rise when given the chance. But," he added more quietly, "we will need some help from you, Admiral."

"Our ships are built of wood, General. Do you know what one shot from a blazer would do to a wooden ship?"

Maybe her age-of-sail outfit was not so inappropriate after all.

"I can guess, ma'am. I believe that our cause is worth dying for, although I do not intend to do so, and I hope that nobody else will either, except some criminals, who will be given fair trials if they can be taken alive."

Admiral Devon raised eyebrows to signal disbelief, then swung around to face the audience, most of whom looked amused, as if this had been a typical performance. "Your dog carts are waiting downstairs, Mothers. I am going to deliver this young man to the lunatic asylum."

She spun around—turning her back on the government— and headed at a rate of several knots for the spiral staircase, which she then descended, cane, pegleg, and all, moving just as fast as Doig could.

Out in the street, the sunlight was fierce, a warning that winter was long gone and perihelion was coming, and yet it was not as brutal as it would have been in the Pale. The difference, Doig decided, was in the sky. Here, it lacked the pure blue emptiness that he was accustomed to. It was cloudless, but it had a faint milky patina that must come from the nearby misty sea.

Six spider-drawn, two-seater traps were waiting at the road-side, five of them containing a human driver. The admiral headed for the sixth with Doig at heel.

"All aboard!" she barked, but when Doig squeezed in beside her bulk, she said in a more reasonable tone, "It isn't far. I'll try not to crush you on the corners."

There were no houses in sight and few people. The buildings all seemed to be warehouses.

"This is the dock area. I was serious about expecting an army, although I know the rest of your expedition is still crawling along at elephant speed. They'll get here in a week or so, so it seemed easiest just to commission *Sunbird* and put you all aboard. Most of our craft are bulk carriers for ore and suchlike. It has plenty of cabins."

"So what is its usual purpose when it isn't rescuing political prisoners?"

Lindsay's glance at him almost seemed to express surprise that anyone would care. "Exploration. Neweden has less dry land than Old Earth, but there are three other small continents and a lot of islands. Tin, phosphorus, sugarcane . . . lots of useful stuff. The tropics are a problem, though. Tropical seas very nearly boil at perihelion, and the hurricanes are murderous. So we can't do much in the southern hemisphere until we have weather satellites."

It made Doig want to weep. So much time and opportunity wasted in the Pale! There, they had used up their total resource of metal—copper—putting flush toilets in Vandam Palace while Sabine was looking ahead to weather satellites.

Despite the Admiral's warning, there were no corners before she reigned in at a gate labelled SABINE NAVY. NO ADMITTANCE. A youth in uniform ran to open it and saluted as the admiral drove through.

SUNBIRD WAS TIED up straight ahead.

Barque? Schooner? It was much larger than Doig had expected. Its masts soared about thirty metres into the sky, supporting the largest solar panels he had ever seen. These were obviously movable, too. They were quite unlike the sails of the ancient European ships that he had seen in his historical studies but reminiscent of ancient Chinese junks, whose sails had been solid wood or bamboo.

The Pale had nothing at all like the great sweep of timber making the hull; he could compare it only with the wooden floor in the Sabine ballroom. Conrad Melchior's Touchdown ferry had been barely an ugly rowboat compared with this beauty. There were ten or a dozen men up aloft, apparently working on the gears and motors that controlled the panels.

Devon pulled up at the bottom of the gangway, rocking the cart mightily as she disembarked. Doig slid out the other side and then just stood there, staring up. The admiral waited for him to finish his appraisal.

"So, this is the ship that rescued my father! Who do I thank first?"

"That depends on whose version of the story you believe. Who told you about it?"

"Kam Petrovich."

Devon snorted. "A great kid. But even his father called him Allbrawn."

"I honestly think he enjoys that name. Doer Guzman filled in some details."

"Ha! Did he imply that he had something to do with it?"

"I think he used the word 'we' several times."

"Back then, Rex Guzman was a carpenter building substandard housing on the misleadingly named Paradise Island. He's a narcissistic clod. The Mothers could dismiss him by unanimous vote, but that would be politically unpopular and might make matters worse. The trouble with democracy, Citizen Gray, is that the stupid are sometimes the majority."

Having relieved herself of that profundity, the admiral marched off up the gangway. Doig followed, grinning. He had decided that his new ally was a true one-of-a-kind character and had undoubtedly designed her own uniform.

They were met on deck by a slim, trim man in his thirties wearing a practical uniform and a thick golden beard: Ian Singh, captain of *Sunbird*.

As they shook hands, Doig said, "So it is you that I must thank for rescuing my father from Copper Island?"

Singh's gaze flickered momentarily to Admiral Devon and back. "I just obeyed orders, citizen, as a first officer should."

Doig bowed to the admiral.

"We all obeyed orders," she said gruffly, "and we were all volunteers. Show him his cabin, Captain, and where he goes to pee. Then, let's the three of us have an overdue lunch."

Doig followed Singh below decks and along a corridor lined with doors. "These are not closets; they're cabins for the scholars. We don't allow cat swinging aboard *Sunbird*. But we put you in this one. It's roomier."

It was still small by landlubber standards, but what caught Doig's eye at once and tightened his throat was a brass panel on the wall inscribed:

In this cabin, Dr. Pablo Gray journeyed from captivity on Copper Island to freedom in Sabine. March, 505.

THE ENSUING lunch for three in the officers' mess should have been a memorable event. The food was tasty and ample, and the conversation fascinating as Captain Singh described *Sunbird*'s recent exploration of a landmass now named Westmain and the storms that had almost torn the ship to pieces on the way home. Yet afterward, Doig could recall very little of the meal except the fine quality of the coffee at the end. He was too aware that his luncheon companions held the power of life and death over his prospective revolution. The Mothers might chatter all they wanted, but if Admiral Devon said whatever plan Doig suggested was too dangerous, then it wouldn't happen.

Eventually, after the third cup of coffee, Singh produced a chart and spread it out on the table, pinning down its corners with dirty dishes. Three heads peered down at it. It was all there—Freeport and its islands, the Gut, Touchdown Island, and the Town.

"So, what did the Mothers decide at your cablecar conference?" Admiral Devon growled.

"Decide? Nothing. They agreed they would consider rescuing the hostages," Doig said. He outlined the hostage problem. No rescue, no revolution. No revolution, no union of colonies.

The air seemed about to freeze. Why risk the ship? And the crew? The other members of the Interior Expedition might be willing to follow Doig's lead, but why should the sailors? It would be like rushing into a burning building to rescue total strangers.

'When?" Singh demanded.

"Unless the Board has already rounded them up, which I think is unlikely, they will not be molested until after perihelion. Perihelion is a public holiday when the crew elite wine and dine in Vandam Palace. After that, they can reasonably write off our expedition personnel as dead. Our wives will then be declared widows and, um, redistributed."

The two Sabiners grimaced. Briefly.

"I assume you expect us to sail *Sunbird* north to the Gut," Singh said, "and then ride the tide eastward to the Town pier? At night, of course? By the light of the summer aurora? Then you and your crew disembark, round up your families, and lead them back to the ship?"

"Exactly," Doig said, feeling put down for being so predictable.

The admiral made her peculiar snorting noise. "Assuming we avoid all the summer hurricanes, of course. And any stray crewmember who happens to notice *Sunbird* in the harbour and chooses to blast it with a blazer. Not to mention the perihelion tides in the Gut."

"June brings maximum tides," Singh muttered.

"Almost everyone stays underground, even at night," Doig said. "The temperature is usually in the low forties. Even that can be deadly in damp air, as you know. But you would need to post a cordon of marines around the docks and let no stranger within blazer range." The obvious lack of enthusiasm made him feel that he was clutching at straws. Small straws. Wisps.

"Last perihelion," Devon said, "I got hold of the Board's recording of its meeting with you, citizen, and the Mothers put it on public viewbox. Your father's story had already created enormous public interest, and overnight, you became a hero, too. But the people in general are still deeply divided. They can see that the Pale needs rescuing, but why us? What's in it for Sabine?"

Doig was fairly sure that the Mothers would decide political matters like that. He would not reveal details of his meeting with them, but he could repeat his own case. "Briefly, Admiral, both colonies are dying. Sabine had too few founders. You have reached the maximum population you can sustain without an infusion of new genes."

"Gr—e—a—t!" she said, dragging the word. "So, we don't just have to rescue them from their own folly; now we have to marry them?"

"In the long term. Out-cross offspring should be healthier." Doig's arguments seemed weaker by the minute, even to him. His hopes were underwater and sinking fast.

It was Singh's turn to throw a punch. "A dozen or so wives and how many children?"

"Don't know," Doig confessed. "Some babes in arms, none as big as Allbrawn Petrovich."

"Between forty and sixty people," the admiral said. "*Sunbird* can't hold that many plus crew. What do you think of his proposal, Captain?"

"Spider shit, sir. We can't risk the ship like that."

Devon nodded agreement.

Doig said, "Then how?" *There must be a way!*

"Scooters?" the captain suggested.

The admiral nodded again and jabbed a chubby finger at the chart. "Right! Here, Gray, is the Mississippi delta on the Northmain shore. It's too far west for the bore to reach it, but the river keeps pouring out sand, and the summer tides rearrange everything, so it won't stay still long enough for us to map it in detail. From there, the Town ought to be within range of the scooters?"

Singh's turn to nod. "Using the tides and the new capacitors, I'd say so, ma'am. Long as they're not overloaded."

The admiral heaved herself upright and reached for her cane. "Good. Let's go and find Vasily."

Bewildered, Doig followed her up the companionway to the deck. There were fewer men overhead, and for the first time, he noticed the harbour. Other ships were moored both fore and aft of *Sunbird*, and a couple rode at anchor in the bay, all of them smaller. Many boats were moving out there, some with sails, some without. Beyond the headlands that enclosed it were islands, obviously inhabited. It was a breathtaking scene, proclaiming the success and prosperity of Sabine.

"There!" Devon pointed. "And there. Those little boats? *Sunbird* carries two of them. We call ours 'scooters.' That probably began as 'scouters.' They're nippy. The power's stored in capacitors, relying on the mother ship for recharging. Range is about three hours, and they carry up to six adults. If we anchor *Sunbird* at the Nile Delta, the Board has no way of getting at us. Then, you and your lads go in at night and fetch your families."

Now, it was Doig who was nodding like a drinking chicken. "Brilliant! And if we start to overload *Sunbird*, you could have another ship shuttle them back to Freeport?"

"Yes, yes. You'll need a supply backup anyway. Ah, here he comes."

Captain Singh had briefly left them and was returning with a young man in workers' coveralls who sported a crest of the reddest hair Doig had ever seen outside historical movies. That gene had died out in the Pale.

"Doig Gray—Florentin Vasily," Devon said. "Florentin's our expert scooter pilot. You know who Gray is, Florentin."

Florentin was as tall as Doig and skinny as a paddle handle, seeming barely adult. His eyes—green eyes—were wide as he grabbed Doig's hand and pumped it. "Am honoured to meet you, citizen. Saw you on the viewbox last night. Sorry about your dad, but—"

"How long," barked the admiral, "will you need to teach Citizen Gray to handle a scooter?"

Florentin blinked. "Half a day, ma'am."

"Good. Start now. The rest of his band is due here in a week. How soon can you be ready to sail, Cap'n?"

Singh did not hesitate. "A week'll be ample, ma'am."

"Then you should be back before the middle of April. Call it Operation Hostage. I'll go and write out your orders. Any questions, citizen?"

"Two things, ma'am," Doig said quickly. "Senior Mother Kate said that you would arrange credit for me. I have nothing but the clothes on my back, and my companions will be in the same state."

"Right. And the second thing?"

"I'd very much like a radio link to my companions. Doer Guzman explained that there are technical reasons why this has to be done in the evening, but—"

"The technical reasons are because nobody wants to listen to Doer Guzman's blabber. The captain here can arrange that. Carry on, Captain." And off she hobbled, *tap, tap, tap* across the deck.

The two sailors watched her go with smiles that seemed almost affectionate.

"Quite a lady," Doig said softly.

"Quite," Singh agreed. "I think she learned how to act tough when she was a cadet in an all-boy class, then the habit stuck, but it's no fake. When we were coming back around the south coast of Southmain in May of 505, and the solar panels started melting, I know I was gibbering like a jelly, but Lindsay Devon never twitched an eyelash. Pilot, go and get dressed. Citizen, come with me."

He led Doig forward again to a glass-fronted superstructure that was obviously the control room. There, he sat down, donned headphones, flipped switched, turned dials, and, in a moment, was speaking to someone far away. After a few more seconds, he rose and handed the phones to Doig.

"This is Doig Gray. Who'm I talking to?"

"Tengiz Silva!" said an excited, recognizably youthful voice. "That really you, boss? We all thought you must have been eaten by spiders."

"No, I'm fine. I'm more than fine; I'm damned nearly flying. I'm in a town called Freeport, on the shores of the Western Ocean, and it's splendid, just like Old Earth! I gather they expect to get you here one week from now. How are things where you are?"

"We're all going mad with boredom, our clothes are rotting off us, and some of us are starting to talk to the elephants."

"Well, look out if the elephants start talking back. Tell everyone the good news. See you all in a week. Doig out."

The captain accepted the headphones back. "You didn't mention the rescue mission."

"Being ultra-cautious," Doig said. "I have no reason to believe the Board even suspects that Sabine exists, but if it gets a shadow of a hint of what we're planning, then our families will vanish before we get there."

Singh nodded approvingly. "Good thinking."

OUT ON DECK, Florentin was waiting in a sailor uniform, looking younger than ever but eager to begin teaching the great Doig Gray.

Jabbering jargon, he led his apprentice back amidships to where a smartly painted scooter hung from two giant davits. It was no more than ten metres long, comprising a six-seater cabin with a pointed bow and a squared-off stern equipped with a rudder and two small propellers. One began, Florentin explained, by punching the code into the pad nearby—thus. The current code was 378, the number of days in a year. Then, the davits would hoist the scooter over the bulwark, and the gangway would open so they could step aboard *thus* through the scooter's hatch. Doig joined him on the fore bench and stared aghast at the array of knobs and switches.

Then, one closed the hatch *thus* and ran through the check-list . . . after that, one lowered the scooter to the waterline thus and cast off the lines thus and started the motor *this* way.

But the scooter was as nippy as the admiral had promised, and once underway, child's play to operate. Apart from the rush of water going by, it was almost silent, too.

"Why did you think you'd need half a day to teach me this?" Doig asked, exhilarated by the motion.

"You'll see. Head out to sea. That way."

There were waves out there, that was why. Also, there was power consumption to consider, which depended on speed, and so on. There was also returning to *Sunbird* and hoisting the scooter back on board without smashing anything. But when all that had been achieved, Florentin insisted on taking Doig ashore and buying him a beer. Or two.

Having no credit yet, Doig had to rely on promises for further rounds. Again, they made it back to *Sunbird* without smashing anything.

DOIG WENT OUT for another scooter trip the next day, this time with the ship's second pilot, Abdul Ma. Later, now fortified by the unlimited credit of the Sabiner Navy, he met Allbrawn off the incoming cable car and was guided by him on a mammoth shopping expedition.

And later, he bought beer for Kam, plus Florentin and Abdul. It was quite foreseeable that those two might have to risk their lives in Operation Hostage.

Days flew by. He met again with the admiral and twice with the Mothers. He suggested that *Sunbird*'s two scooters be painted black and fitted with more powerful lights, and this was done. He ordered clothing for the other members of the Interior Expedition, guessing at sizes when he couldn't remember them.

And at last, he was able to greet his long-lost companions as they stepped off the cable car. He had previously noted a plinth where he could stand and be seen by all. They cheered him. They had been clothed in Cave City, but they were still bearded and shaggy-haired. He noticed a lingering odour of elephant spider.

"Welcome to Freeport and the Republic of Sabine! I apologize for the weather. It was sunny until this morning. There is a coach waiting for us downstairs, and it will take us to the noble ship *Sunbird*. I will tell you a lot more when we get there."

Still determined to preserve secrecy, Doig had arranged to have Kam Petrovich act as driver, and the only problem with that had been fitting into the driver's seat alongside him. When the coach drew up alongside the ship's gangplank, Doig stood up to make his speech.

All eyes fastened on him. The only sound was the beat of rain on the roof. Kam squirmed loose and took the place Doig had left, where he could at least stretch his legs.

"You all know that my father was sentenced to ten years on Copper Island for stating publicly that the Pale colony was dying. By now, everybody knows that this is true, but nobody is yet allowed to say so or do anything about it. The *Moctezuma* was set down in a very bad place to start with, and the settlement has been grossly mismanaged ever since. It may surprise you to know that the Sabine colony is also in trouble, although their leaders are trying to deal with the problem. Sabine was founded by very few people and has grown much faster than the Pale was ever allowed to. Its gene pool is running dry; it needs fresh blood, or it will start producing Lees and Finns. The two colonies must combine and cooperate! Each can supply what the other lacks so that together they may flourish, but divided, they both are sure to fail."

He paused, expecting questions, but everyone waited for the rest.

"You also all know that the Board tried to kill us with their poisoned rations and fake spider repeller. In my view, those acts freed us from any obligation of loyalty. The gloves are now off. I have always denied that I was a rebel, but when I met with the Mothers, the ladies who are elected to govern Sabine, I proclaimed it, and I do so now. Down with the Board! Long live the Revolution!"

He had been hoping that five or six of them would support him. He had not expected unanimity, yet eleven men waved fists in the air and cheered. Only Saul Vandam did not.

Doig raised both hands in an appeal for silence. "Are there any other candidates for the job of leader?"

All he could see were heads shaking from side to side to indicate negative. This was what he had feared would happen ever since that night he had been cheered in the Trog's Rest. He had never sought fame, but now he had no option but to accept it. From now on, he must wear his father's mantle and write their joint names in history, for better or for worse. To succeed would be a historic triumph. Failure would bring disaster and the end of *Homo sapiens* on Neweden.

"But I also said that I could take no action while the Board held my wife and son hostage. I assumed that you would all feel the same. So, the government of Sabine has organized an expedition for us to go north and rescue all our families. If you want to come, please raise a hand."

Buster's hand shot up, then Conrad's, and more followed. Doig had not expected that much support. The only holdouts were Tengiz Silva, Saul Vandam, and Tonis Horsfall, who were all unmarried. For the first time, he dared hope that it was going to work!

As the hands were lowered, young Tengiz Silva raised his.

"I didn't know this kid was so precocious," muttered Dell Firmin, who was seated beside him.

When the laughter faded, a pink-faced Tengiz said, "Only

in my dreams! Boss, you seem to be planning a midnight raid on the Town to rescue wives and children, right? Logan Foley already gave his life for our cause. I happen to know where he lived, and his family knows me. I would like to go to them and try to persuade them to join us. Sir?"

Buster shouted, "Yeah!" Other voices agreed.

"It seems that your offer is accepted," Doig said, "and I thank you for it."

"Boss?" Now Tonis had his hand raised. "I have no wife and kids to rescue, but I do have a widowed sister-in-law with two young children. Her husband, my brother, was eaten by spiders while working on the Frontier Squad, so I count him among the Board's victims. I would love to come along and rescue his kids, if I may. I am a fair shot with a blazer."

"I'm hoping we won't need blazers yet. I'd love to accept, but Captain Singh is concerned about numbers. When we have counted the number of children already committed, I will ask him."

All eyes turned to Saul Vandam, who was seated at the back. He smiled bitterly. "I would offer to come, but I know you can't trust me enough."

"I will trust you," Doig said. "They murdered your father, too, and tried to feed you to the spiders with the rest of us. Anyone here have problems trusting Saul?"

Heads shook, and a few men grunted negatives.

"I would really like to have you join the Freedom Fighters, friend, because this will be only the start of our adventures, not the end. I'm sure that the Town will rally to our cause, but the Board may try to make a last stand on Touchdown Island. You and I and Conrad are the only ones here who have seen the inside of Vandam Palace, and he only knows the underground parts. So I will trust you—if you will say the words."

Saul smiled cynically and said, "Long live the revolution,"

with no sign of enthusiasm.

Doig was much relieved. He had arranged with the Mothers that Saul would be detained if he chose to remain in Freeport. Give him ten minutes near a radio, and he might be able to sabotage Operation Hostage.

"Also, friends, you may have noticed that the overall mass of the team has increased since we were last together. I am happy to introduce to you Kam Petrovich, who was a school-mate of mine on Copper Island. Stand up, Kam. As far as you can. Kam also answers quite peaceably to the name of Allbrawn. He is Pale-born, as we are, and his father was one of my father's collaborators. Kam himself played a role in the famous Sunburn rescue mission. In fact, he can claim to have been a Freedom Fighter longer than any of us. It was he who hauled me away from the mahouts' camp and took me to Cave City. He is eager to join our army, and he does meet the height requirement . . ."

Allbrawn was accepted by acclamation.

Buster was next. "When do we start?"

"Do you have other plans for this afternoon?" Smiling, Doig waited for the laughter to end, then pointed out the window. "No? Then there's the gangplank. Freedom Fighters board now. We have clothes for all of you aboard, plus food and so on. Even soap. You remember soap?"

AN HOUR LATER, without fanfares or announcements, *Sunbird* slipped quietly out of the bay and set course north-ward. The date was February 42, so the sun was growing warmer day by day and the winds stronger. The ship drew power from both, but at times, they conflicted. If the wind blew from the north while the sun was to the south, for example, the officer on duty had to decide how to aim the solar panels, for they also served as sails. Sometimes, the topmost panels were set at a different angle from those below them, giving each mast a helical twist.

Every day, and sometimes at night, the Freedom Fighters spent hours in the scooters, having "dry" lessons aboard. The fastest learners were former ferryman Melchior and sharp-witted Tengiz Silva. Of course, boats hanging from davits were very different from boats afloat. What was rarely mentioned was that the botanists and geologists who had perfected these craft to aid them in exploring the coasts of Westmain had never done so in the dark. The only trip a scooter had ever made at night had been a cautious circuit of Freeport harbour, carrying Doig and Florentin.

On March 3, they sighted land, and the following day, at about the noonday high tide, they reached the Mississippi delta. The ship anchored in deep water, and the scooters were swung out and sent to map the shallows.

It was two days before they found an anchorage to Singh's satisfaction. The tides there had a range of around two metres, but this would increase minutely every day. Eventually, the shallows and deeps would become islands and channels. The currents were swift and treacherous. The sooner Operation Hostage began and finished, the better.

It was a sunny day, not too windy. Doig called a meeting on deck.

MOST OF HIS team sat cross-legged, but a couple found room on a hatch lid to sit upright. He stood on the windward side, with Florentin and Captain Singh beside him.

"Here is the plan," he said. "If there are objections, it can still be changed. Tonight, we will send in both scooters on reconnaissance only. We need to know whether rescue missions are even possible. For example, the capacitors may not have the range we hope for, or the currents may be too strong. The pilots will be Florentin and Abdul; the passengers, Conrad and me.

"If all goes well tonight, on Night Two we will begin the rescues, normally just two families per night, but there are some who live very close to the pier, so we may have time to double them up. The first night will be dangerous if we have overlooked something. For example, we had keys to the pier area when we were building the canoes, and some of us brought them, but what if the locks have been changed?

"Even that first rescue will be risky. Our families may be under surveillance, although I honestly don't expect that—it is just as dangerous to overestimate your enemies as to underestimate them. Subsequent visits will become steadily more dangerous because neighbours will notice the absences and the word will spread. We therefore divided the families into school-age and preschool. Those with only preschoolers will be Group A and those with any older children Group B. I will call for a vote to confirm that procedure in a moment.

"I have long been convinced that Ivan Wong's fatal first-man-on-the-planet excursion was a sucker punch, so I gave Captain Singh a list of our names in the two groups and asked him to put each group in random order. Questions or comments, please?"

Heads shook. Incredibly, most of the weather-beaten faces were smiling. Buster's was the hand that rose first. "I move the plan be accepted."

Shouts of "Seconded!"

"Against? I see none. Motion carried. Thank you all."

He wondered how many of them were going to die.

AT ABOUT TEN O'CLOCK, the reconnaissance mission set out, Doig with Florentin and Conrad with Abdul. Granted that the stars were glorious, Neweden sadly lacked a big, bright moon. *Aurora borealis* would not appear until later in the spring.

Florentin was the pilot. He drove *Liberty Two* after Conrad's *Liberty One* into the centre of the Gut to catch the easterly flow of the rising tide. The current from the east was always stronger, although there would be no bore yet, so they must hope to time their arrival at the Town for slack water at high tide. Doig held a recorder and kept reporting time, capacitor readings, and so on.

At eleven-fifteen, the radio beeped.

"*Liberty Two*," Doig said.

"Island to port. Suggest increase speed."

Those lights must be from Vandam Palace on Touchdown. "Agree. *Liberty Two* out."

If the Board had caught that brief exchange, either they were infinitely smarter than Doig believed, or Fate was playing with marked cards.

At eleven-fifty, they saw the glow of the Town to port and changed direction. So far, everything was going amazingly close to plan.

Doig's original idea had been to time the rescue missions months later, very close to perihelion, when the streets would be deserted. That would not be the case now, although he expected few people to be about at midnight. Instead of wearing dark clothing and scurrying through the shadows, as he had expected, the trick now would be to stalk around boldly, playing innocent.

They had used only twenty-eight percent of their power.

That was excellent!

Conrad's *Liberty One* led the way in to the pier. About half of the long ramp was still visible, but the tide was about to turn, and they must not leave either scooter unattended.

Florentin expertly closed in on a bollard just aft of *Liberty Two*; Doig opened the hatch and looped a line around it, then scrambled out. Up ahead, he saw Conrad hastening toward the gate. *Too fast!* Standing orders appropriately stated, *Don't run!* Doig strolled after him, and in a moment, Conrad remembered and slowed to a walk.

When Doig joined him at the gate, he already had it unlocked. All foreseen obstacles were falling like raindrops. Outside lay the deserted street, dimly lit by the low lamps.

"Go for it!" Conrad said.

"What?"

"Everything's working out perfectly! Go and get Babette and the boy. If the Board ever catches on, she'll be the first one they'll grab. You can be back here in twenty minutes; if not, we'll look for you here tomorrow." He underlined his remarks with a powerful shove.

It was wrong! The leader should not break his own rules to his own advantage. The others would see it as cheating—but 147 Suleyman Street was the second-closest of the target addresses.

"No. I said I would take my turn like everyone else and—"

"You got your house key?"

"What? Well, yes, but . . ."

"Go and lead, Leader!" This time, Conrad pushed him through the gate and closed it.

The temptation became irresistible. Doig turned and walked away. Properly, his turn to fetch his wife wouldn't come up until Night Four, and this was only Night One. *Cheater!*

Keeping to a walking pace was torment. Almost immediately, he saw two men heading toward him. They were arguing, one of them waving his hands to emphasize his point.

Then, Doig realized that he wasn't wearing a nametag. Nobody had remembered nametags! If these were crewmen and they noticed that, they would stop him and question him. They would recognize him! He slowed down so he would pass them in a darkish area midway between two street lamps.

They didn't even glance at him. He heard, ". . . vitamin C, they're developing scurvy, so all their teeth . . ." and he was past them, and the stairway down to Suleyman Road was right there.

He couldn't help running down. There being no one in sight in the tunnel, he ran all the way to his door. He stumbled up the steps, fumbled for his keys. His hands shook as he unlocked the door. *Quiet! Mustn't wake the baby.* He turned on his flashlight at the lowest setting.

Nothing. No furniture. No dishes by the sink, no food. He drew his blazer with his left hand. Two quick steps to the bedroom . . . nothing in there, either, not even a killer posse waiting for him.

The expedition had been betrayed! In a sudden panic for the safety of the scooters, he dashed out of the house, down the steps, and along the tunnel. He tried to walk calmly, then realized that there was no need now and broke into a run.

The pier gate was locked. Again, he had to use his flashlight and fumble with keys. The pier itself was unlighted. He could not see if the scooters were still there or not. But his use of the flashlight had been seen, and another gave an answering flash. Then, he managed to slow to a walk. Slipping on algae or tripping over seaweed would only add to his problems, and he had more than enough of those now. Failure rode on his shoulder like a ton of gravel.

He reached the scooter, splashed through freezing, ankle-deep water, and tumbled in through the hatch. Florentin shut it and backed the boat away from the pier.

"Trouble?"

"Not there. Gone. They knew we were coming."

Neither spoke again for a long time. Florentin concentrated on piloting the scooter. Doig sat and let his tears flow.

SUNBIRD WAS ABLAZE with lights to guide the heroes back. Everyone was on deck. The cheering began as the davits lifted the scooter over the bulwark. Doig opened the hatch and stood up so they could see him. He raised his hands for silence.

"Bad, bad news! Everything went fine until I broke my own rules and ran home to collect my family. They weren't there. The Board must have known we were coming."

In the terrible silence, Buster stepped forward and helped him out of the scooter.

THE NEXT MORNING brought gale-force winds and torrential rain. The Freedom Fighters met in the officers' mess, where there was barely even standing room. Captain Singh and Pilot Florentin were there, too.

Doig reported on the events of Night One and how well everything had gone until he disobeyed his own orders. At that point, Conrad intervened to take the blame for bullying him into doing so, which was no excuse.

"The only good that came out of it," Doig said, "is that we have escaped without losses. Operation Hostage has failed. We can go back to Freeport and plan something else. I hereby resign as leader of the Freedom Fighters."

"Not so fast!" Whenever Captain Singh spoke, people listened. "Last night, I reported to Admiral Devon. This morning, I received his reply. He is Sabine's intelligence master, as many of you know, and he has agents in the Pale. He ran a search of all their reports for mention of Barbette Gray ever since her marriage to Doig. On February 7—that was a week after you left—there was an announcement that the Board had voted to honour Doig Gray by raising him to crew rank without name change. Babette was restored to the crew rank she held when she was Babette Dattu."

Singh looked around the faces as if watching the minds behind them working. "I doubt that 'Crewman' Gray cares a splash of spit about that 'honour,' but it does change the situation. Do any crew live in your neighbourhood, Doig?"

Buoyed by a surge of hope, Doig said, "No! No, of course not."

"Then your wife was very likely moved to a newer, grander home more befitting her restored class?"

Doig just nodded. Possibly a small suite in Vandam Palace? With barred windows? But the spurious honour granted him in his absence was more evidence that the Board did not expect him to return alive. It had cost the Board nothing, and the masses might believe that it was a genuine award. Doubtless, Babette's family and friends had pleaded her case.

Mutters of excitement . . .

"I suggest," the captain said, in a tone that strongly discouraged disagreement, "that we proceed with Operation Hostage as originally planned, in the hope that the other families have not been moved. The current storm may rule out tonight, although it seems to be waning already. Doig, the admiral will ask his agents to discover your wife's present address."

On the way out, Doig was the victim of a cynical smile from Saul Vandam. "Legal crew, huh?"

"Life is full of wonderful surprises," Doig said.

BY NIGHTFALL, the weather had improved enough that Singh ordered Night Two to proceed. The scooters returned with two rapturous wives and four sleepy toddlers.

After that, the abductions seemed almost routine. Nights Four and Five brought the first children of school age. Night Six was delayed for two tormented days by bad weather. A support ship, *Rietveld*, arrived with provisions and took away some of the reunited families.

On Night Six, Tonis Horsfall rescued his sister-in-law and her sons. The other scooter took Tengiz Silva on his mercy mission to free Logan Foley's widow and children. Their door was answered by a man Tengiz had never seen before, who told him to get lost or eat his own teeth. The sailors found that story funny, but the men who had known Logan did not.

The original program for Operation Hostage, assuming that all the hostages would have been liberated by this time, required Doig to hack into the Pale's public announcement system and proclaim the Revolution, with a demand for the Board to hold free elections. But by then, Admiral Devon's spies had reported that Babette Gray and her son were now living in Vandam Palace on Touchdown Island.

Doig, therefore, refused to proceed with his Hear-This, as in the original plan, although he said he could not object if someone else read the speech. He admitted that living hostages were valuable while dead ones were not, but he would not deliberately expose his wife and child to any more spite and malice from the men who had murdered his father.

Back in Freeport, the Mothers met in emergency session. They supported his stance and ordered *Sunbird* home. After five hundred years, freedom would have to wait a few more months.

THE SABINERS TREATED the refugees well, finding them housing and employment. Doig accepted a post at Freeport University, lecturing on Old Earth history. His furnished rooms on campus were better accommodation than anywhere he had ever known, except during his brief stay in Vandam Palace.

He was lonely, worried, and depressed by a sense of failure. It seemed that the world did not want to be saved, at least not by him.

On the fourth evening, as he was wrestling to put together a program for his lectures, he was startled by a thunderous knocking on his door. When he opened it, in limped Admiral Devon, cane in one hand, bottle in the other.

"Time we talked," she proclaimed, heading for the comfortable chair. "You like rum?"

"Never tried it."

"There's always a first time. It's often the last." She lowered her bulk into the chair.

Doig fetched two tumblers. "What do you take in it?"

"Doesn't matter, you still just taste rum—but I find a little water helps the scars heal."

He fetched some water in his other tumbler. By that time, the first two were both three-quarters full of an ominously dark liquid. He brought the other chair over and sat down. Whatever this was about would be more interesting than lecture planning.

Devon raised a tumbler, then paused. "Before I forget, Seven Hundred reports that your wife is being well treated.

Her family has taken her back, and her brother is also living in the palace."

Relief broke over Doig like a great wave. "Seven Hundred?"

"One of my sources. Who he or she is, I have no idea, but they know the codes."

"Then, thank them for the good news." It was wonderful news, if true.

Devon raised her tumbler again. "To Operation Liberation!"

"Here's to it, whatever it is!" Doig tried a sip of rum. He felt inebriated before he even stopped coughing.

The admiral swallowed half of hers and smacked her lips. "Other good news. Operation Hostage threw the Board into a screaming panic. The disappearances were known all over the Town before Waldo Ruckles could even call a meeting. He had to issue a Hear-This denying that he had murdered all your women and children."

Doig smiled for the first time in two weeks. "How did he explain the disappearances?"

"He didn't even try. He announced another cut in the bread ration to give the people something else to think about."

"That could help us. What's Operation Liberation?" He managed a third mouthful of rum without choking. "Tell me about it."

"I came here so you could tell *me* about it. Don't pretend you haven't been thinking about it." The admiral drained her tumbler and reached for the bottle. "Stop me if you know this. About twenty years ago, your father was the best surgeon in the colony, so he was posted to Touchdown to attend to 'important' patients— much against his will, of course, but he had no choice in the matter. While he was there, he worked out how to hack into the ancient records. That was when he discovered that the

Board had been telling lies for centuries. He even found notes on Jalapeno Guzman's trial, which mentioned another colony located in the Faraway Hills.

"The Board back in Jalapeno's day had suppressed that information and ended all further exploration of Southmain. They suppressed it so well that even their own successors forgot about Sabine, or just smugly assumed that it had died out. Guzman probably lied a lot about it.

"Of course, your father also learned that incompetent and corrupt government was leading the Pale itself into disaster. He tried to spread the warning, was ordered to stop, and was eventually handed a death sentence, commuted to ten years' penal servitude. But by then, he was in contact with Sabine."

"How?"

"By radio. The Pale used radio between the Town, Touchdown, and Copper Island. Sabine was using it between the caves and Freeport and also to keep in touch with boats, islands, and outlying mines. Your father was a clever man with clever friends. They built a set and scanned the spectrum until they found an outside signal. He helped Sabine hack into the Touchdown records and we eventually uploaded everything in the *Moctezuma* files. He stayed in touch with Sabine and his friends in the Pale, even from Copper Island."

Blinking back tears, Doig just nodded.

"When 'Cargomaster' Guldberg was setting the bombs to kill your father, he stole the radio," Devon said. "Then, the Board discovered that your father had been corresponding with someone outside the Pale. He'd never told you this?"

"No." Doig had lost the chess set that had been meant to tell him. The Board had probably learned a lot more from that than they had from the radio.

"They had made your father a martyr. They did not dare make you another, and they certainly weren't going to tell anyone about the second colony. So, you grew up, made yourself a hero by rescuing that woman from the spiders—and volunteered to go exploring!"

"Which the Board saw as a good way to get rid of me."

"Also, to discourage any other would-be explorers. But you are still leader of the opposition, whether you like it or not. How do you think Operation Liberation should proceed?"

"My last plan didn't work very well."

Admiral Devon's scowl would have terrified Nelson or Blackbeard. "It worked perfectly. You couldn't know that your own wife wasn't there. It's your homeland, lad. We'll help within reason, but you have to tell us how."

Doig emptied his glass. He was two glasses behind the admiral, and she seemed a lot more sober than he felt.

He heard himself say, "You hack me in on a general Hear-This. I identify myself, say I'm speaking from Freeport, and it's a far richer and more successful colony, and so on. It's also a republic, and it is willing to help the Pale—with food and in other ways. The next voice they will hear is that of Kate Usha . . ."

Devon was nodding. "Saying what?"

"That nametags must be outlawed immediately. That Sabine's help is conditional on the Touchdown gang calling free and honest elections to replace themselves. That Kate's own term as Chief Magistrate ends at the end of the year, so the change of government must be in effect before then, or the offer of help is withdrawn."

"Excellent! I'll put that before the Mothers tomorrow. Will it work?"

"Not a hope. Not even if she throws in a shipload of wheat and pardon for all previous crimes."

"So what happens next?"

"I rally the Freedom Fighters, and we go in there and

massacre the bastards."

"When?"

"Right at aphelion, when they're least expecting us."

Rum did not promote rational thinking, but it did encourage braggadocio.

THE NEXT DAY, Doig Gray left the university and moved into an apartment near the docks and an office next to the admiral's, listed on the payroll as a clerk in the Planning Department. In private, they called it the Plotting Department.

THE MILLS of governments grind slow.

In May, the Mothers voted to hold a referendum that would give them authority to negotiate terms of union with the original colony.

IN JUNE, the Sabiners voted Yes by a 60-40 majority. The Doig and Kate Hear-This was duly hacked into the Town's voicebox system. For several nights after that, Doig had nightmares in which he murdered his wife and son. By day, he could only trust that living hostages were still more valuable than dead ones.

IN JULY, the Board—awakening at last to its peril—reacted by tracking down illicit radio transmitters, arresting Devon's spies, and warning that all traitors would be fed to the spiders. The only Sabine agent to survive the purge was Seven Hundred, or so that source claimed. It was still giving the correct codes, so the Plotting Department had to assume that Seven Hundred, whoever that might be, had not been turned.

Perihelion in Freeport was miserably hot and humid, but heavy cloud cover blocked the sun's murderous ultraviolet, while the prevailing wind off the ocean kept the temperature within endurable limits. The rain was warm enough for a shower.

IN AUGUST, Doig called a meeting of the Freedom Fighters in the Admiralty gym, which he could claim was air-conditioned. Which it was, sort of. He had counted out the chairs carefully and was astonished to see that there wasn't an empty one in sight. Every man invited had turned up.

He began by noting that they had all volunteered for the Interior Exploration team except Saul Vandam, who had been drafted against his will.

"He has assured me that he supports our revolution and wishes to continue as a Freedom Fighter. I believe that he has personal knowledge that will be extremely valuable to our cause. Does anyone object to Saul's inclusion?"

No one did, which was a relief.

Doig then asked them all to honour their guests, Mother Tabitha Trees and Admiral Lindsay Devon. He yielded the lectern to Tabitha, and she strode forward to accept the applause, poised and austere as always.

She assured them that the government of Sabine would provide material support and would care for the widows and orphans of any casualties, but native-born Sabiners would not act as combat troops. The Pale must free itself. She wished them good fortune.

Devon followed and spouted some nonsense about Doig being a natural-born leader. "His best quality of all," she concluded, "is that he truly doesn't want the job. You will not be installing a hereditary monarch!"

The guests departed, and the meeting could now get down to work.

"You all know," Doig began, "that Sabine's offer to negotiate union does not expire until the end of the year. It is possible that the cargo will rise and overthrow the crew before we even finish training. In that case, we should be met with bands, banners, and fireworks. Personally, I am not hopeful. Those of us gathered here must plan to overthrow the Board by force. There are four of them and thirteen of us—fourteen if you count Kam realistically. But we can't hope to begin until spring, right?"

Heads nodded.

"Wrong. We attack Vandam Palace as early in January as we can, right after aphelion. They will not be expecting us then."

And then, he led them through the plans that he and Lindsay Devon had worked on for the last eight weeks.

In the end, he called for volunteers. He was hoping for six or eight and was amazed when all twelve raised a hand. How many would die on his crazy venture? Lindsay Devon was right —he truly did not want this job. He just wanted his wife and child and a peaceful life.

The next day, he put Saul Vandam to work drawing maps of Touchdown Island and Vandam Palace from memory. Doig himself began working out training schedules for everyone. Much of what he needed, he had to guess at. Neweden had no experience of, or precedents for, midwinter warfare.

4: FIVE-TWELVE

IT WAS a measure of Sabine's support for the Freedom Fighters that the Mothers were willing to risk even *Sunbird*, the only ocean-going ship in a fleet otherwise made up of coasters. By late December, when it put to sea with the Freedom Fighters, the sun had shrunk to little more than a very brilliant star, giving no perceptible heat but still dangerous to look at. The planet was rapidly chilling out, not down to the temperature of interstellar space, but well below human tolerance. Tides were mere dwarfs compared to the roaring giants of summer, and the winds had faded to zephyrs.

On the east side of the continents, seasonal ice around Copper Island would already be half a metre thick, an immovable, impenetrable pavement. Along the western coast, prevailing onshore breezes, weak as they were, caused both land and sea to cool more slowly.

Sunbird, alas, depended on both wind and sunlight to power it, and both were now reduced to feeble mockeries of their former selves. Its bows had been strengthened with steel to cut through the thin seasonal ice, but if it ever became trapped, then it would be crushed before spring, and everyone aboard would die. Captain Singh barely slept, and every day, the ice was a little thicker.

Hour by hour, Doig lived in dread that Singh would make the fateful decision to turn back. If that happened, he foresaw no second chance to overthrow the Board. No attack by land was feasible, and the only places vulnerable to assault from the sea were the Town pier and Freshwater Cove. By spring, the tyrants would surely have fortified both sites with batteries of giant blazers, ready to repel any attack. They might have done so already, but it was highly unlikely that they would have their defences manned in midwinter.

DOIG WAS AWAKENED BY SILENCE. It was morning, for a faint light was drifting in through the ice-caked porthole. He should be hearing the steady hum of the ship's engines, the rush of water past the hull, the rumble of solar panels being turned, and the constant miscellaneous creaks of a wooden vessel. But nothing?

In sudden panic that *Sunbird* might have become trapped in the ice, he threw back the covers. He was already wearing most of the clothes he had brought, and the rest were spread on the bed for extra warmth. He squeezed his feet into shoes, grabbed up a cloak, and dashed out the door. The corridor was deserted. He ran to the companionway that led up to the control room, his breath smoking.

There were four men there, but the first person he registered was Singh himself, looking like a standing corpse and managing only the wraith of a smile. He said, "Morning, citizen. Can't call it a good morning. Minus eighty-three out there and just enough wind to be nasty."

The ship had to spend power keeping these windows free of ice. Doig scanned the view ahead and saw land—white and rocky, but obviously not just ice. "We've arrived?"

"Freshwater Cove, according to our pilot." He nodded toward ex-ferryman Conrad Melchior, who wasn't smiling under his beard. Every man aboard had grown a beard. Beside him, First Officer Abdul Ma looked equally gloomy.

Now Doig recognized the little bay, with its cliffs and the long ramp on the north side. The snow made everything seem very different. *Sunbird* had arrived, so what was the problem?

"January 3? Two days ahead of schedule! That's very good, Captain. You can't go in closer?"

"No. The bottom's shallower than we had hoped, and the ice is a lot thicker in here. But the really bad news is that our channel is freezing up behind us. We can't stay as long as planned. I want to pull out of here by noon."

"But we agreed on twenty-four hours!"

Singh shook his head like a man imparting a death sentence. "I cannot risk my crew and my ship any more than I have already. We'll have to back out, see? And if the breaking ice manages to wreck even one of our two propellers, that may very well end our game. We'll be trapped here in the winter doldrums. I may have to face a court-martial for deserting you when I get home, but I feel I have no choice. I'm sorry."

So he probably was pronouncing a death sentence—on Doig for certain, and on either Melchior or—if he chickened out—on whoever volunteered to take his place in the first wave, the spider squad.

Doig glanced at the clock. "Five hours, you're giving us? Make it seven, and we'll still have a chance."

Melchior and Ma were watching and listening.

Melchior said. "We can't count on making it there and back in seven hours, Doig."

"No, but we must be able to get there by then, and the other guys will have had time to unload their gear. If we've succeeded, we'll radio the all-clear, and they can follow us. If we don't, they'll know we've failed, and they can leave with *Sunbird*. I will make that a command. But joining me in the first wave is still voluntary." He held his breath, waiting for the ferryman's response.

This could be a death sentence for both of them. At night, the temperature would plumb to some abysmal low that would defeat even their specially designed suits. As always, the sun would set at six. The war must be over by then.

Melchior shrugged. "Then let's grab a quick breakfast."

Good man!

"You're both crazy," said the captain. "Seven hours it is. But not a minute longer."

Doig glanced around and saw that some other Freedom Fighters had arrived and were packed tight in the companion-way, listening to what was being decided over their heads.

"Dell," he said, "and Buster, dress up right away and move our sleds over to the dock ramp for us, please. That should save us a little time. Conrad and I have to grab some breakfast and then go like hell."

FOR THE LAST FIVE MONTHS, the Freedom Fighters had been training for their revolution. They had studied guns, locks, radios, first aid, even unarmed combat. Toward the end, they had spent most of December in the hills above Freeport, learning how to snowshoe. Somehow, they must travel from Freshwater Cove to Vandam Palace, and *Sunbird* would not be able to spare them the power to use its scooters or any other vehicle. The distance was not great—the three Fighters who had previously made the journey agreed that it was less than ten kilometres—but the terrain would be rough even on the official roadway, and the temperature murderous. They would have to carry battery-powered air heaters in addition to their weapons and other essentials.

Spider fur made good winter garments, as Doig had learned on his childhood journey from Copper Island, but it was flammable, which was why blazers were the best weapons against predatory spiders. To stop a wolf spider with bullets required shooting it to pieces; Aberash Whitehead had discovered that while trying to save Ivan Wong.

Saul Vandam, who had spent his childhood in the palace, insisted that the Board's first line of defence was Queen Tina and her many wolf sons, and he knew of no others, other than stout locks on the doors. The spiders estivated during perihelion and hibernated at aphelion, but Doig's nasty experience of a year and a half ago had shown that they would wake up whenever food became available. If the Board cabal didn't have some way of rousing their guard dogs when necessary, then they were even stupider than he thought they were.

After destroying the wolves, they must fight their way into the palace. No one except the twenty or so men of the guard carried arms there, or so Saul insisted, and Agent Seven Hundred confirmed. So, the first item on the Freedom Fighters' battle plan must be to take out Tina.

As Doig knew from his studies of Old Earth history, battle plans rarely survived first contact with the enemy.

Only Doig had ever seen Tina's nest. He had made the round trip from the cove to the palace and back once and Conrad several times in his years as ferry pilot, while Saul Vandam knew the country well. But Saul had flatly refused to have anything to do with the spiders. Hence, the first wave must comprise Doig and Conrad.

According to that already-wounded plan, the rest of the Fighters would unload their equipment at the cove. The first wave would return before sunset. Then, the entire expedition would overnight on board, ready for a start at dawn. Captain Singh had now vetoed that idea.

Nature, too, was being less cooperative than Doig had hoped. He had expected the cove to be a flattish plain of snow on a flat base of fresh ice, but Conrad had doubted that. He had seen the melting remains of small icebergs there in early spring, and obviously, he had been right. The spring-fed stream might be at fault, continuing to pour in fresh water as the air temperature dropped below zero. Fresh water being lighter than salt, it would have puddled out over the ice when the sea began to freeze, melting it in parts and thickening it in others. Or, early December's wind and tides might be the villains. Whatever the reason, the cove was a hillocky nightmare of ice boulders and snowdrifts.

The Freedom Fighters would certainly need snowshoes in the forest, so Admiral Devon's miracle workers had fitted them all with footwear wide enough to be snowshoes but with enough spikes to be called crampons. Captain Singh refused to allow crampons on his precious deck, so the first wave, Doig and Conrad, had a very undignified departure from *Sunbird*, sitting at the top of the gangplank while other men put on their boots for them and tied their laces.

About an hour after his bargaining with the captain, now fed, dressed, and equipped, Doig waddled awkwardly down the plank onto the ice with Conrad close behind him. They wore body suits that had also been specially designed by the artisans and scientists of Freeport. These were made of a composite both lighter and more insulating than spider fur and also able to provide a small amount of protection from blazers. If the assault came down to an outdoor blazer battle, the

Freedom Fighters would have a huge advantage over the Board's fur-wrapped guards.

Each man was loaded with almost half his own weight in equipment: blazers, automatic projectile weapon, inhalation heater, flashlight, ice pick, ration bag, grenades, and a personal radio that he would not dare use while there was any chance that there might be spider wolves around.

Following a trail left by Buster and Dell, they clambered over a truly horrible terrain, like some great rockery of ice: head-high boulders with deep snow in the hollows. Doig estimated that they were still about thirty metres from the ramp when Conrad cried out behind him. He had fallen and was crumpled in a snow-filled hollow, cursing luridly.

"Damage?"

"Twisted my ankle." Conrad tried to stand and uttered a yell of agony. "Broke it, maybe."

So soon? Barely out of the ship's shadow, the assault had already failed? Doig felt a surge of what felt shamefully like relief. He suppressed it instantly. Not daring to use his radio, he waved his arms and yelled for a stretcher party. The watchers waved back.

"Thanks for trying, buddy," he told Conrad. Then he turned and resumed his trek to show that the game was still on. Someone would volunteer to accompany him, almost certainly Buster, for he had argued strongly that the first wave should be three people, not two, with him as the third. Ever since that long-ago day when they had first met in Chancellor Finn's office, Buster Bruknar had tended to mother Doig Gray.

Doig safely reached the ramp, where Buster and Dell had left the two sleds. Taking up the cord on his, he began the long climb—a lot longer than when he had seen it at high tide in summer. The snow was patchy, and hauling a heavy sled over the bare bits required more effort than he had hoped to expend so early in what would be a long, hard day.

When he paused and looked back, he saw a crowd where Conrad had fallen. It would not be easy loading a heavy man onto a stretcher on that terrain. It would take time to relieve Conrad of all the equipment hung on him and load Buster. *Almost nine o'clock already!* In about five hours now, *Sunbird* would depart. If the first wave had not radioed in that it had destroyed the spiders' nest by then, the remaining Freedom Fighters would sail with it. That would almost certainly be game over for Doig Gray and probably his companion.

When Doig reached the top of the ramp, he saw that Buster was now on his way, and the others had returned to the ship. Doig went slithering back down again to bring up the other sled. That ought to save a few minutes. What had been Conrad's sled was heavier than his own. He hadn't known that.

He was almost at the top of the ramp again when Buster caught up with him, a huge, white, bundled monster with black goggle eyes and a proboscoid nose that looped over his shoulder to the air-warmer on his back. As Conrad had been, he was cluttered like a busy kitchen.

But the initials on his helmet were not BB; they were SV.

"Saul!? I thought you couldn't bear the thought of spiders."

"I can't. But you will never find the track to the nest. Besides, why should you hog all the glory? Let me take that." He reached a hand for the sled cord.

Doig was shocked. Saul never seemed like the hero type. He lacked the physical strength that Conrad and Buster had. He had been pressganged onto the interior expedition. He was always the odd man out, just "legally" crew, meaning neither crew nor cargo. Somehow, there was still a faint odour of traitor about him, as if his life's ambition might be to earn his place among the nobility. If he knocked on the palace door and handed in Doig's head, then he would undoubtedly succeed.

"Well?" he said, and Doig could easily imagine the cynical simper behind the mask. "You going to stand here all day wondering if you trust me?"

Doig gave him the rope. "Glad to have you, Saul. Let's get going. We have a tough day ahead of us."

At the top of the ramp, they came to the wire cage that served as a garage for small carts. All it held at the moment was a shoulder-high snowdrift. The fungoid undergrowth that had filled the forest on Doig's perihelion visit had vanished. The trees tended to have low branches, and there were no leaves now, so the sun—high now but distant and weak—cast striped shadows everywhere. Shrubs growing between them were tough and wiry, so getting the sleds around the cage was a long and maddening struggle.

Once they had reached the road on the far side, Saul said, "Ah! Now we can run." That was a surprisingly Busterish remark from him.

"Go ahead. You won't mind if I sit on your sled?"

With Doig in the lead, they set off along the road, hauling the sleds, which together carried the mortar and shells, spare batteries, a warmed water supply, and a tiny inflatable tent. Doig felt as if everything in his life to date had suddenly faded into insignificance. In just a few hours, he might be butchered alive by angry spiders. Already, the odds were lengthening against him. Buster was as reliable as tempered steel, a crack shot, and an all-around tougher campaigner. Saul had not trained in mortar firing and could not hit a small mountain with that handgun he carried.

But he did know the geography of the island, and that might be vital.

The road was even rougher than Doig remembered, and

the lack of foliage had allowed the winds of early December to swirl through the forest almost unhampered, building drifts everywhere. Life became an endless series of hauling the sleds up and then letting them carefully down. There was often black ice in the hollows, and one more fall could bring total disaster.

Worst of all were fallen trees blocking the narrow track. This meant unloading each sled and reloading it again on the other side. Doig had not counted those delays in his plan. Their progress was fearfully slow. Only rarely was there a chance for conversation.

"Explain these mortar things to me," Saul said.

"They're like primitive rockets. You lie down and steady the gun so that it points up but tilts toward the spider's nest. I drop the shell in. The pin at the bottom of the gun sets off the basal charge. The shell goes up about twenty metres, then falls. When it lands, it explodes, but these are incendiaries. Fireball hits spiders; spiders go whoosh!"

"You're sure of that last bit? The spiders don't cushion the landing?"

"No. It's a hair-trigger detonator, armed by the take-off. We tested it on an air mattress." It had taken ten tries to hit the mattress, but the spider hollow was a much bigger target. And spiders were flammable.

"Why does Sabine have all these clever gadgets and the Pale doesn't?" Saul demanded in an aggrieved tone.

"Because Sabine's leaders are keen on progress. Our Board doesn't want any change. All they need to do is refer to the *Moctezuma* records. Back on Old Earth, people could sit in their own offices and blow up anything in the entire world."

After a moment, Saul said, "That doesn't sound like a good idea."

"No. It isn't."

ONCE IN A WHILE, they would stop for a drink of water and an energy bar, but even uncovering their mouths for a few seconds risked frozen lips.

So slow! Less than ten kilometres? Doig had estimated two hours to the spiders' nest, even allowing for the weight he would be carrying. He and Conrad had made a dry run during their stay in the mountains and had managed twice that distance in a little over five. He had not expected the great snowdrifts or the fallen trees.

HE TRIED to ignore the timepiece on his left wrist, but the sun was already close to noon.

"How far have we come?" he asked at the next tree-trunk blockage.

"We're about halfway to the nest. Roughly." Saul pointed to an open strip in the trees. "That's where *Moctezuma* landed, remember?"

Doig glanced at his wrist. 11:28.

"Then listen. We've used up half our time getting here. If we leave the sled, cast off all the paraphernalia, and go like hell, we can make it back to *Sunbird* before it sails. If we don't, then we're stuck here alone. Two of us against the colony."

"So? I swore an oath to follow you when I joined the Freedom Fighters. You can't ask me. You have to give me orders!" Saul sounded amused.

"I am asking you. You choose."

"No." He *was* amused.

"Then we can both be martyrs. We carry on." Doig began to unload his sled. He thought there might be enough then to slide it under the tree instead of lifting it over. If he gave up now, he would probably kill himself eventually.

Saul chuckled. "Just testing. I knew you wouldn't give up."

A LONG TIME LATER, Saul said loudly, "That's the cut."

Doig had almost plodded right on by. He was very weary. "Thanks. I did miss it. If we win, you can claim the credit."

They started along the road cut, and the going became even worse, snow masking deep holes and heaps of rubble. He remembered crazy Lizzie Wong babbling in the bus about the ruins of Vandam City.

How far did they have to go through this endless snow-bound hell? The only other landmark he could hope to find was the trellis passage to the nest, but that had been virtually destroyed when Ernie Venugopalan fell through it. Now the colony had run out of copper, the Board would likely not have replaced or repaired it. It might have been removed and recycled.

But the trellis must have been built over a century ago before the wolf spiders were reintroduced to Touchdown. Would even the Board tyrants order such a project now, so close to the spiders' nest? He must gamble that it was still there and not hidden in the snow.

IT WAS THERE. The road end of the walkway had not been wrecked, and the upper half was still menacingly visible at the roadside.

Saul said, "Now what?"

"Either we try to get closer, or we start shooting from right here."

"We got five shells, right? What do the wolfies do if we shoot off two and miss twice?"

"Tina may wake them up and send them out to find out who's shooting at her."

"You believe that?" Saul asked rather shrilly.

"No. I think they'll react as they would do to thunder and just sleep on."

"I'm always in favour of doing things the easy way."

Doig eyed the overhead branches and tried not to image a hair-trigger incendiary shell exploding right overhead. The trellised walkway had been straight, he remembered, but had climbed quite steeply. He was going to be shooting almost blind, but they probably couldn't get the sleds any closer over that terrain anyway. He picked a solid-looking exposure of pumice on the far side of the road and set the mortar on top of it. He tilted it in the general direction of the spiders' nest, or so he hoped.

"You hold it there," he told Saul. "But stay below it because there's a flash when it launches."

"And you?"

"I do it kneeling and at arm's length." Doig had done it a hundred times.

This was Saul's first time, yet the gun did not quiver as he lay there, steadying it with both gloved hands.

"Ready. On three. One, two, three."

The shell broke the aphelion silence with a roar like thunder. A moment later, there was a distant flash and a smaller bang, nothing more.

Doig raised the angle of the mortar and tried again.

Same result.

"You want to try getting closer?" Saul asked from the snow.

"No." Doig went back to the sleds and returned with two more shells. "Do or die!" He tilted the gun even closer to the vertical but turned it slightly to his right. *Boom!* again, but this time, the impact was followed by a huge roar and a volcano of fire in the forest. He felt the heat on his eyes through his goggles and watched, fascinated, until it burned itself out.

The Freedom Fighters scrambled to their feet and indulged in a victory hug.

"That fixed the little monsters!" Saul said.

Doig had not expected that much success. If the palace had noticed, there could be no surprise attack

He reached for his radio and glanced at his timepiece. "The ship may still be in range. Might as well send the good news home to Sabine."

"Don't! If there are any spider survivors, you'll summon them. And *Sunbird* sailed ages ago."

"What!?"

Saul laughed. "Oh, Doig, Doig! Orders or not, did you really think the gang would leave without you? I'll bet you all the beer you can drink that they've been an hour behind us all the way, and now they're waiting for us back at the road turnoff."

The light on Doig's radio flashed. He pressed the receive button. Tengiz Silva's voice: "Well done, boss!"

"Where are you?"

"We're coming, but your fireworks were a long way ahead of us."

"All of you?"

"All except Conrad. Oh, the language that bad man uses!"

"Thanks, friends. Saul and I will see you at the palace gates."

WITHOUT THE MORTAR AND SHELLS, they could get by with one sled and take turns pulling it. Even fallen trees were less onerous, and they had less need for haste. They could talk about the coming attack on the palace, and Doig brought Saul up to date on the more confidential data.

"Here's the latest. Lindsay Devon still has one agent in the palace—we think. He or she may have been turned. His or her code name is Seven Hundred. Mine is Ninety-nine. The identifier is a list of random words, none of which is a noun. Reply is a shorter or longer list, still no nouns. When we get within sight of the palace, I'll try calling him. If he doesn't reply, then we'll wait for the others before we go in shooting according to plan Dragon."

As Doig remembered his nightmare visit to the spiders' nest, the bus trip from the palace to the turnoff had been quite short. Now, it seemed to have tripled or quadrupled in length. It was three o'clock before they came in sight of that great roof above the trees, shining in the pale sunlight. The tiny two-man army had been working all-out since early morning. Doig was hungry, exhausted, and now could feel the cold starting to bite.

He was amazed again by the size of the palace, the scores of windows glowing warmly in the gloomy winter afternoon. They signalled warmth and food and comfortable beds.

"I hope," he said, "that the Board doesn't offer us hospitality because if it does, I shall be sorely tempted to throw down my weapons and go in with my hands up."

"You do talk a lot of spider shit," Saul said.

Reaching the edge of the trees, they saw the wired enclosure that kept spider wolves away from the garage doors. Between them and the fence was the open area, now covered in elongated snowdrifts like gigantic ripple marks, a metre or more high.

"You said that there are five doors, yes?"

Saul said, "Yes."

"If we blasted open one that leads into the servant quarters, then dashed in and hid there . . ."

"No! There are hundreds of cargo servants, but it would only take one to lead the guard to you. Besides, you can't dash anywhere in that suit, and if you take it off first, you freeze solid."

Sunset was still an hour or two away, but the sun had sunk behind the trees, and the temperature was falling.

"You are too vandam logical," Doig said. "I'm going to hail on Channel One. Listen in because Seven Hundred may be a turncoat, and we'll need to decide what to do next." *Click.* "Ninety-nine calling Seven Hundred. Ninety-nine calling Seven Hundred."

Silence—not even a crackle.

Of course, Seven Hundred might be asleep, or dead, or eating supper, or chained in a dungeon. Going in with guns blazing might be much safer than any sort of negotiating, but that meant waiting for the others. Why were they taking so long?

Then it came: "Windy where what why who when."

Doig's throat was suddenly so dry that he could barely speak. "Terrible to try to taste."

"Welcome, Ninety-nine! Seven Hundred here. You knew me as Louis Louis."

Did he? He struggled to remember the diffident young valet of eighteen months ago. "Is it safe for you to speak so openly to me?"

"Quite safe and the greatest joy of my life, sir. I have your wife here to reassure you, and also Marshal Darren Zelenitsky, head of Palace Security. I will put your wife on now."

Then came a familiar voice, slightly distorted by the radio

but certainly Babette's. "Doig! Darling! Really you? Are you safe? Was it you who set off that firebomb?"

This was the worst agony yet. If Waldo Ruckles was standing beside her, holding baby Pablo in the crook of his left arm and a knife in his right hand, then Babette would have to say whatever she was told to say.

"How's your mother?" Doig barked.

And Babette laughed! "Can't you guess? Until the forest blew up about an hour ago, I was married to the worst, meanest, most despicable traitor in the galaxy, and I was insane not to divorce you immediately. Now she's bragging to everyone she sees that, of course, the Liberator is her son-in-law."

Then came a new voice, a male voice. "Zelenitsky here, sir. You have my solemn oath that you and your companions may enter in safety. I have the members of the Board confined incommunicado at present. Whatever instructions you have concerning their treatment, I will carry out your orders."

Zelenitsky was a crew name, and he was calling Doig "sir"? Offering to take his orders? This had to be delirium, except that Saul was laughing hysterically, practically rolling in the snow.

But Babette's laugh was the key. It had certainly been her laugh, and only skilled professional actors could fake laughter convincingly.

"Just stand by, please, Marshal. Open a door, and we will come in, but I caution you that we have guns and other weapons at the ready."

He switched to the Freedom Fighters' channel. "Guys, we're at the palace, and both Louis Louis and Marshal Zelenitsky have invited us in. If we don't come out, you know who to start with."

"We read that, boss," said Buster's voice. "Well done, both of you!"

A light started flashing above the nondescript pedestrian door beside the large vehicle entrance.

Doig led the way, half expecting to be ripped apart by projectile gunfire at any moment. The gate in the wire spider fence was unlocked and swung open at his push. When he was about ten metres from the pedestrian door, it opened of its own accord, and torrents of fog rushed out, swirling clouds almost masking the brilliant lighting behind them.

Entering blind, he felt the hundred-degree temperature rush even through his insulated suit. He could see nothing except the glow of lamps overhead, which told him that he was in a large hall. Fog swirled everywhere. He could hear Saul muttering angrily. Any moment now, it would clear, and he would find that they were surrounded by armed men, with Waldo Ruckles leering triumphantly in the background.

Then, he heard the door close behind him. The air soup faded to mist. There were only three people. The tall, trim man of around fifty, wearing a blue uniform with gold braid on it and an empty holster at his belt, must be Marshal Zelenitsky. He saluted.

"Doig Gray? The palace guard awaits your orders, sir."

The slim young man in brown was certainly Louis Louis, and his ear-to-ear smile looked one-hundred-percent genuine.

Babette in a sparkling blue gown, lovelier even than his dreams—he tore off his mask.

She recoiled in horror. "That beard has got to go!"

"It will. I brought my own barber. Darlindarlingdarling . . ." Hugging her when wearing what he was wearing was horrible. Yet, even so, holding Babette again was heaven. It had been eleven months.

But Babette, alas, and also Pablo, would have to wait. Business must come first.

"Citizen Louis, it's great to see you again and to meet the

mysterious Seven Hundred. My men will be arriving shortly. Can you direct them to where I'll be when they get here? Which is . . . where are the former directors, Marshal?"

"They are detained in the council chamber, sir, awaiting your instructions."

"I wish to see them." *Unless I do so with my own eyes, I cannot believe that this is happening.* "Saul, you want to come along and view the Epochal Moment? You too, Babette? Lead on, Marshal."

As he spoke, Doig—and Saul, also—had been shedding equipment like trees dropping leaves before aphelion. Doig did retain his handgun. He held Babette's hand and tried to concentrate on lesser things, like making history.

Zelenitsky led them out of the garage into the palatial part of the palace. The elevator brought them up to the little antechamber that Doig remembered. Two blue-clad guards were on duty there, and another four beyond the door marked Private. All saluted Zelenitsky.

Doig had to ignore them as he followed the marshal through the final door into the council chamber, but doing so made the back of his neck itch, for he was still half-convinced that this absolute, unconditional surrender was a murderous hoax. Not all the inhabitants of Vandam Palace were going to be as tolerant of the new era as Zelenitsky appeared to be. Even the palace cargo serfs could not be completely trusted, because they currently lived better than their equals in the Town.

But there were the tyrant directors in the flesh gathered around their great horseshoe table. They were even sitting in the same places as they had before. No one spoke, and only their eyes moved as they scanned the two disreputable ruffians and the turncoat marshal who had brought them. They probably did not even notice Babette. Their combined hatred was so intense that, for the first time, Doig could truly believe that he had won.

Looking at that huge and exquisite table, he suddenly saw it, not as he had on his last visit, as a horseshoe, but as the mandibles of an enormous spider. He stopped outside the gap where he had sat before.

He started on the left with a nod. "Citizen Heiser."

The old man glared in silence, but his jaw moved as if he were chewing something, probably Doig's heart.

Nod. "Citizen Ruckles."

The former chairman had shrunk. His flab was even more shapeless than before, and his jowls had sagged. Silence.

Nod again. "Citizen Zelenitsky." Related to the marshal? They did not look at all alike. The now-deposed director seemed just as lardy as before, his eyes as beady, whereas the marshal was all bone and muscle.

And lastly, a nod to the youngest, Virgilio Vandam. "Citizen Vandam."

That one had some grace. His response was a smile of bored amusement as if this were all a game of no importance whatsoever. "I do wish I'd voted to have them move you over to the cargo clinic to be left to die there."

"But you didn't, they didn't, and I didn't. History is built of mistakes."

Ruckles bellowed, "So what happens now?" He had never been good at silence. "You line us up and shoot us? You managed to get in here, Gray. Do you honestly believe that you can escape alive?"

"I'm sure my chances are better than yours."

"You think you can run this colony, boy? You fancy yourself here, in my chair?"

Doig was too weary for stupid arguments. "It looks like I'm going to have to try. I don't want the job, but I am certain of one thing, old man, and that is that I can't possibly screw it up any worse than you have."

He turned to his ally Zelenitsky. "Marshal, I want these four men confined in secure, separate cells. They are to be treated humanely but closely guarded because I want no lynch violence. They are to await trial on charges of murder and attempted murder, possibly other crimes. You accept these orders?"

The marshal saluted. "Yes, sir!"

"Fair trial?" Ruckles shouted. "And then the firing squad, of course?"

Doig could not hold back a smile. "Would you rather I pardoned you and set you loose in the Town? You would not last fifteen minutes."

Judging by the ex-chairman's obvious outrage, he still did not realize how he was hated.

Then, a loud yell from Saul, who threw himself at Doig, who staggered against Babette, almost toppling them both to the floor. *Bang!* A scream from Babette. Shouts and a drumroll of boots as the outer-room guards came rushing in.

Doig steadied himself and Babette and tried to comprehend a stream of nonsensical images. Saul was clutching an automatic and grinning wildly. Three former directors were still in place, all three of them white as chalk. Virgilio Vandam had disappeared but was quickly located still in his chair but flat on his back on the floor, with a bullet hole in his forehead and a gun beside his right hand.

Marshal Zelenitsky bellowed, "Keep your hands on the table!" obviously addressing Ruckles and company.

Then, it all fell into place. Virgilio Vandam had pulled a gun from somewhere and aimed it at Doig. Saul Vandam had yelled a warning, pushed Doig aside, and shot his namesake before he could fire.

Doig confirmed that Babette was unharmed, although understandably shaking in the crook of his arm. Then he eyed Zelenitsky. "Explain this, Marshal."

"I cannot. I am deeply ashamed of it, sir. You have my resignation, of course. I am happy that your man was able to save you."

"So am I," Doig said with feeling. "Thank you, Saul. Your resignation is refused, Marshal." Zelenitsky might be playing for both teams, but he must be kept on Doig's team, at least for the time being. "Remove the rest of the accused, please."

The Marshal passed on the orders that Doig had given him earlier. His men handcuffed Ruckles, Heiser, and Qung Zelenitsky and led them out. Doig wished he could follow and make quite sure that they were going to the cells and not to hearty meals, beds, and concubines.

He released his wife and bent to peer under the table. There were about a dozen holsters fastened underneath it, spaced evenly all the way around. Three of them still held guns.

"Saul? You knew of this?"

"Yes, boss. My mother told me years ago. When I saw him reach for one, I remembered."

"Your mother?" His mother had been a moronic Lee, seduced by a stupid cargo flunky.

Saul showed his wry, cynical smile. "After I was born and the scandal died down, they degraded her to cargo and made her a cleaner. She used to polish the floor in here."

"Is she still a cleaner?" Babette asked.

"I expect so," Saul said.

Doig said, "Go find her and tell her that there are no castes anymore, and she doesn't have to clean anything more than her teeth from now on."

"She won't understand. You owe me something, Liberator."

Doig agreed cautiously. "Yes, I do. What?"

"Dhaval Guldberg."

Ah! Doig wanted the rule of law, which many nations of Old Earth had achieved, although not all, and the rule of law did not countenance private vendettas. But then came a memory of a desolate, bereft fifteen-year-old boy swearing revenge. For a moment, Doig could almost see that younger self fighting back tears, his fists and teeth clenched. And that wrecked and dying man in Cave City.

"What would you do to him?"

"I want him stripped naked and thrown outside. And I want it recorded and publicly broadcast so that the world will see."

That was a much faster death than the brute deserved, so Doig's conscience remained silent.

"Marshall, there is one man who does not deserve justice. His name is Dhaval Guldberg. He has a cast in one eye. He murdered my father—I have heard testimony on that, and I have heard him brag how horribly he murdered Saul Vandam's father. There have been others. Do you know him? Is he here?"

"Yes, sir. And yes, sir. You want him to die while trying to run away?"

"That would be a fitting description. Advise Citizen Saul Vandam when the breakout is about to happen. Allow him a few words with the suspect."

Zelenitsky actually smiled. "It shall be done, sir." He saluted again.

"Then carry on. Thanks again, Saul—for everything."

Doig and Babette went back to the elevator and down to the garage to see if the rest of the Freedom Fighters had arrived yet.

THEY WERE JUST COMING IN, too late for all the excitement. The efficient Louis had food waiting for them. Doig gave them a brief account of recent events and broadcast an even briefer statement to the inhabitants of the palace.

Then, at last, came a peek at Pablo, who was asleep and not at all interested in entertaining a father he had never seen.

"He's beautiful!" said his father in wonder. "Just perfect. Big for his age, isn't he?"

"He's very greedy."

"Nonsense. I will shortly demonstrate what greedy really means."

And so came a shower, food, a clean, soft bed, and a proper hero's welcome, after Babette had agreed to overlook the beard until tomorrow.

AND YET, even that rapturous reunion did not bring sleep after such a day. The puzzles buzzed like spider bugs.

When exactly had Marshal Zelenitsky made his decision to turn his coat? Had he really not known about those holsters under the table? As head of security, he should have, so had he taken Doig to the Board so that they could do their own blood work? Ruckles had told Doig he wouldn't get away alive.

Had Saul truly not remembered the holsters sooner?

And how had Saul, the lummox gunman, suddenly become such a crack shot?

"Why aren't you asleep?" murmured Babette, a lovesome, warm joy in the bed beside him.

"I never thought it would be this easy. How many people really support my revolution?"

"Almost everyone, darling. Ever since you and that Sabine

woman did your Hear-This. The Board tried to block it but didn't succeed."

Doig thought of all the months of training, the endless work, and that ghastly trek from Freshwater Cove. "Then why didn't the ninnies all just rise up and throw the bastards out?"

"Because they needed a leader. They were all waiting on you."

He didn't want to frighten her, but one other thing he had to know.

"Can I really trust Marshal Zelenitsky? Even now?"

"Of course you can! Like everyone else, he could see that you would be a far, far better ruler than old Ruckles. He's my Uncle Darren. I warned him you would be coming, and today, when you blew up Tina and her army, I went and told him that now was the time. I did promise that you would appoint him a director."

"Oh, you did?" Had that saved the revolution?

"Why are you laughing? Stop it! Doig! What's the matter with you?"

Eventually, Doig got his hysterics sufficiently under control that he could breathe again. "I was just thinking that women are much more dangerous than men. Or spiders. And now I am feeling greedy again, beard or no beard . . ."

HEAR THIS. *I am Doig Gray, Chair of the Provisional Board of Directors. Waldo Ruckles and other members of the previous Board are under arrest, awaiting trial.*

I am proud to report that the revolution was almost bloodless in that the only casualties were two members of the old, corrupt regime who tried to resist arrest: Virgilio Vandam and Dhaval Guldberg

The other members of the Provisional Board are:

Babette Dattu Gray, my wife, who will liaise with the ruling Mothers in Sabine Colony;

Darren Zelenitsky, Security Director;

Sophocles Bruknar, commonly known as Buster, Food and Agriculture Director;

Louis Louis, Director for Internal Affairs,

and Aliyah Suleyman, Director for Education and Research;

As well as chairing meetings, I will concentrate on obtaining an accurate census of the population and then setting up free elections, as required in the original Moctezuma *Charter.*

Note that all distinctions between crew and cargo ancestry are now abolished. Wearing nametags is forbidden. If you see anyone wearing a nametag, remove it, using the least amount of force required, and destroy it.

The recent cut in the bread ration is cancelled because Sabine promises to send us grain in the spring.

Congratulations, Neweden! The long night is over.

Doig Gray out.

APPENDIX

THE CALENDAR

January - 7 weeks
February - 6 weeks
March - 5 weeks
April - 4 weeks
May - 3 weeks
June - 2 weeks
July - 2 weeks
August - 3 weeks
September - 4 weeks
October - 5 weeks
November - 6 weeks
December - 7 weeks

Total: 54 weeks, 377. 86 days

DAVE DUNCAN'S LEGACY

BY ROBERT RUNTÉ, PHD

When I sat down to write what Dave Duncan meant to me, and to other fans and writers of Canadian speculative fiction, I found myself staring at the blank page. As a writer, I'm not usually at a loss for words, but when an author of Dave Duncan's stature leaves us, it can feel as if he took all the words with him.

In fact, Dave has left us a massive legacy of words: sixty-five published books and up to another eleven manuscripts awaiting editing. If one were to (re)-read one Dave Duncan novel a month, it would take over five years to get through them all. By the time you're done, I'm hoping some of those remaining eleven manuscripts will be published.

Dave Duncan's lasting contribution to science fiction and fantasy is characterized by five distinctive features.

First, as a Canadian speculative fiction writer, he often created protagonists who went against the mould of the usual American, mass-market, alpha-male hero. Indeed, in his novel *Hero!*, Duncan satirizes that sort of protagonist—to the frequent confusion of American readers who bought the book (Dave told me once) based on its heroic cover and the book's placement next to David Drake on bookstore shelves. Instead, Duncan's heroes were often ordinary people who got caught up in events outside their control: Wallie Smith, who suddenly finds himself transported into the body of a swordsman on another world in the *Reluctant Swordsman* (still Duncan's most popular series); the humble stable boy in the *Man of His Word* series (still my favourite series); Ivor, the beardless boy-hero of *The Adventures of Ivor*; the randomly chosen female lead of *Irona 700*; the devious conman of the Omar books; and so on. Which is not to say he didn't also create lots of alpha-male heroes when he needed to for the American mass market, but there was usually some moral ambiguity about the character and their actions, some undercurrent of Duncan's patented, dark, self-deprecating humour, that gave Duncan's books a kind of subversive undertone.

Second, his novels were thoroughly researched. Whereas many other fantasy writers seem to think writing fantasy means anything goes, Duncan worked hard to fill in those little details that not only make the scene come alive but teach us a bit about history. Editing the *Ivor* books, for example, I learned that "small beer" means beer mixed with water, so you could drink the water safely, not a tiny glass. And Duncan's vocabulary! I have a PhD, and I still have to look up words every chapter or so, as Duncan somehow knew the exact technical term for any particular device or job description from Carthage to twelfth-century Ireland to the extrapolated technology of his science fiction. His novels are immersive because they are rich in detail and historically and scientifically accurate within the premise of the story.

Third, Duncan built his fantasy worlds from the ground up to create magical systems that were internally consistent and completely original. Unlike others who build endlessly on

Celtic and European mythologies, Duncan was never just rewriting Tolkien. Indeed, the *Man of His Word* series can be interpreted as a critique of Tolkien, as Duncan's protagonist slowly comes to understand that what he thinks he knows about elves and goblins and the rest is actually pretty racist and that those individuals look very different when he comes to understand their cultures. The magical system in *A Man of His Word,* however, is pure Duncan: ingenious, logically consistent, with all its many implications fully developed. Similarly, the action in *The King's Blades* arises organically out of the interaction between the logic of the magical system and the failings of human machinations. Duncan's worldbuilding, in both his fantasy and science fiction, was unsurpassed.

Fourth, Duncan's books always had something to say. A lot of fantasy and science fiction that comes across my desk suffers from *random ramble syndrome*: the characters move around having adventures, good wizard against bad, but the book isn't actually *about* anything. There is nothing to learn from them; nothing to think about while reading or to remember five minutes after the book is set down. Duncan's books always have an additional layer or two: *The Great Game's* allusions to literature and history; *West of January's* examination of sociobiology as Duncan worked out the implications of planetary motion; the inherent corruptibility of state, fundamentalism, and celebrity in *Eocene Station*; and so on. Duncan is never preachy; he never forces his opinions on anyone, and you're free not even to notice anything beyond the surface action if that's not your thing. *Hero!*, for example, has plenty of derringdo, but the book is *about* how heroes are manufactured by political elites to serve questionable goals; aren't necessarily who they seem to be, or necessarily on the side of the angels; and that you can't count on them to save you. The adventure novel is there—one can read the novel without recognizing any of the irony if your mind or politics don't work that way—but the thoughtful reader is left with something to think about. Similarly, *The Traitor's Son* never mentions climate change or anything to do with contemporary politics, but this novel of morally bankrupt leadership on a world rapidly facing extinction might raise a flag or two for those watching the nightly news.

Finally, I loved that Duncan always pushed himself. He was never satisfied to keep repeating the same formula endlessly, as one sometimes sees with other fantasy or science fiction writers. True, he did write more books as series than as standalones, but each series is completely different, not just in worldbuilding, but in style. *The Great Game* trilogy, for example, was among his most ambitious work artistically—perhaps even a step too far for those fans who couldn't connect with the literary style or allusions, but a series I and other critics much admire. Even within a given series, he would often stretch himself and his readers. With the *Chronicles of the King's Blades*, for example, even though the novels are all set in the same world, often with overlapping characters, Duncan pushed how dark he could go as the series progressed and then came back all the way back to a much lighter touch in *One Velvet Glove* and *The Ethical Swordsman*. He even reimagined the series as YA with the *King's Daggers* novels. *Pandemia*, at eight books, is Duncan's other long series, but as Dave explained to me, he only *intended* to write four. When he turned in the last book of the *Man of His Word* series, his then-editor pointed out a logical flaw in the ending, so Duncan had to write the *Handful of Men* series to close that loophole. The editor may have been the one to raise it, but it was Duncan who stretched himself to keep going . . . and you've got to love that world!

Above and beyond all of that, Duncan has been a role model to a generation of other writers, not just because he wrote well and modelled what that took, but because writing was his second career after taking early retirement as a geologist. So much of the mythos of publishing revolves around discovering new young talent—the young Turk who just graduated with a creative writing degree or the artist living in their garret hammering away on keys of the great American novel—that it sometimes feels like if you haven't made it by age thirty, it isn't happening for you. For all of us who were older, who were holding down a career or raising a family while grinding away on our first novel, seeing Dave Duncan writing sixty-five-plus books *after* age fifty-five has been an inspiration.

Duncan tried to retire several times but couldn't do it. He was writing right up to the end—he submitted *The Traitor's Son* mere hours before he fell, and his plan had been to return to working on *Angry Lands*, Book 2 of the *White Fire Chronicles*, the next morning. He loved writing, and that love was obvious in every conversation, in every interview and conference panel—and on every page.

"Dave Duncan's Legacy" originally appeared in *On Spec Magazine*, Vol 30. No 1, issue #111, Summer 2019.

ABOUT DAVE DUNCAN

Born and raised in Scotland, Dave Duncan moved to Calgary, Alberta, after graduating from university to take up his thirty-year career as a geologist. As the oil boom faltered in the 1980s, he sold his first novel and switched careers to become one of the most prolific and popular Canadian authors of science fiction and fantasy, with more than sixty-five traditionally published novels. Early in his career, he was producing books so fast his publisher could not keep up, so he wrote a fantasy trilogy under the name Ken Hood for a different house and a historical novel about the fall of Troy as Sarah B. Franklin.

Duncan won the Aurora Award for Best Novel in 1990 and again in 2007, and was inducted into the Canadian Science Fiction and Fantasy Hall of Fame for lifetime achievement in 2015.

Duncan was awaiting final edits on *The Traitor's Son* when he died on October 29, 2018.

ABOUT SHADOWPAW PRESS

Shadowpaw Press is a traditional publishing company, located in Regina, Saskatchewan, Canada and founded in 2018 by Edward Willett, an award-winning author of science fiction, fantasy, and non-fiction for readers of all ages. A member of Literary Press Group (Canada) and the Association of Canadian Publishers, Shadowpaw Press publishes an eclectic selection of books by both new and established authors, including adult fiction, young adult fiction, children's books, non-fiction, and anthologies, plus new editions of notable, previously published books in any genre under the Shadowpaw Press Reprise imprint.

Email: publisher@shadowpawpress.com.

 facebook.com/shadowpawpress

x.com/shadowpawpress

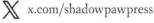 instagram.com/shadowpawpress

MORE SCIENCE FICTION AND FANTASY

SHADOWPAW
PRESS

Adult Science Fiction and Fantasy

The Downloaded by Robert J. Sawyer

The Good Soldier by Nir Yaniv

Corridor to Nightmare by Dave Duncan

Duatero by Brad C. Anderson

Ashme's Song by Brad C. Anderson

The Empire of Kaz trilogy by Leslie Gadallah:

Cat's Pawn

Cat's Gambit

Cat's Game

The Legend of Sarah by Leslie Gadallah

Shapers of Worlds Volumes I-IV, edited by Edward Willett

Paths to the Stars by Edward Willett

The Peregrine Rising Duology by Edward Willett

Right to Know

Falcon's Egg

Young Adult Science Fiction and Fantasy

The Headmasters by Mark Morton

I, Bax by Arthur Slade

The Sun Runners by James Bow

Blue Fire by E. C. Blake

Star Song by Edward Willett

The Canadian Chills Series by Arthur Slade:

Return of the Grudstone Ghosts

Ghost Hotel

Invasion of the IQ Snatchers

The Ghosts of Spiritwood by Martine Noël-Maw

The Shards of Excalibur Series by Edward Willett

Song of the Sword

Twist of the Blade,

Lake in the Clouds

Cave Beneath the Sea

Door into Faerie

Spirit Singer, From the Street to the Stars, and *Soulworm*

by Edward Willett

For details about these and many other great titles, visit
shadowpawpress.com

Printed in the USA
CPSIA information can be obtained
at www.ICGtesting.com
LVHW091914041124
795688LV00034B/937